AF589167

The Last Time I Saw Her Alive

By the same author

Summer Fever

The Heatwave

The Stranger

The Shadow Hour

The Red Letter

The Girl in the Photograph

As Katherine Fleet

The Liars

The Last Time I Saw Her Alive

KATE RIORDAN

PENGUIN MICHAEL JOSEPH

UK | USA | Canada | Ireland | Australia
India | New Zealand | South Africa

Penguin Michael Joseph is part of the Penguin Random House group of companies whose addresses can be found at global.penguinrandomhouse.com

Penguin Random House UK,
One Embassy Gardens, 8 Viaduct Gardens, London SW11 7BW

penguin.co.uk

First published 2026
001

Set in 14.5/17pt Garamond MT
Typeset by Falcon Oast Graphic Art Ltd
Printed and bound in Great Britain by Clays Ltd, Elcograf S.p.A.

The authorized representative in the EEA is Penguin Random House Ireland, Morrison Chambers, 32 Nassau Street, Dublin D02 YH68

A CIP catalogue record for this book is available from the British Library

ISBN: 978–0–241–82738–3

Penguin Random House is committed to a sustainable future for our business, our readers and our planet. This book is made from Forest Stewardship Council® certified paper

For MC, with love and gratitude
for the last decade

There she weaves by night and day
A magic web with colours gay.
She has heard a whisper say,
A curse is on her if she stay

'The Lady of Shalott'
Alfred, Lord Tennyson

1970

She didn't think she would be so calm at the end. Time has slowed, or speeded up, she's not sure. She's watched the waxing moon wheel right over her, the night clear enough to see the slender paring still in shadow. The sky behind it is dark cobalt silk, pulled taut like a tablecloth without wrinkles. The stars are spilt sugar.

She flexes her fingers, feeling for small warm limbs heavy with sleep, but there's no one. She's alone. Unless you count the beetles and spiders and woodlice that make the grass shiver around her. Something crawls over her left foot from little toe to arch, light as breath, but she can't sit up to brush it off. She can barely twitch her leg. Moving her fingers has used up the last of her will. Only her mind spins on, like the planet she's pinned flat against.

A memory then: her father beside her in their narrow strip of back garden, his telescope set up on the lawn and her mother just visible inside, stiff-backed and resentful in her usual chair.

'A thousand miles an hour,' he said softly into her ear, as she peered through the telescope, hand up to keep her other eye closed.

'What is?' she said.

'That's how fast the earth is turning. How fast we're going right now.' She could feel his smile in the dark. Her knees shook with the improbability of it.

She thinks she can feel the spin of it now, even as she lies there so still. She thinks she can hear the old earth's slow heartbeat deep in the ground under her. But maybe that's just the drugs, or whatever it is she's been given. The soft and gentle poison she can feel inching through her blood, slowly, slowly shutting her down.

If only she could see her one last time. Just a moment would do. Tears soak into the hair at her temples.

She doesn't see who adjusts the flower crown on her head so that the thorns prick her skin. She's already unconscious. She doesn't feel the tiny beads of blood drying on her cheeks, like tears, either. The land holds her until she slips away in the dim pearled hours before dawn.

Chapter One

Monday
26 June 2000

My mother named me Rainbird, which should tell you plenty about her and the way I grew up. I don't go home if I can avoid it, and the people I spend my time with now haven't been allowed close enough to know exactly where or what home is. Which is just how I like it.

Occasionally, the place comes up in conversation – mainly the legendary Gatherings and the aborted documentary – but I never say anything because I know exactly how it would go if I did. They would turn to me in astonishment, me with my conventional clothes and neat hair, my knack for assimilation, and say, 'Hold on, *what*? You grew up on the Tanglewood estate? You?'

If you know it at all, and people of a certain age and cultural leaning generally do, then the name Tanglewood is shorthand for a particular scene at a particular time. It's the boutique, English-countryside version of Woodstock, only there's way less photographic evidence and way more mystery, which has only added to its considerable allure.

What did survive is tantalizing. Every colour-soaked picture seems to have been caught during that golden hour before dusk sets in. Honeyed light filtering through white dresses with grubby hems. Shadows stretched to breaking point. Entangled limbs and faraway eyes. You get the idea.

I've worked hard to create a version of myself that's quite separate from all that, and the connotations that come with it for free. I'm not going to ruin it when the reaction wouldn't be much better than admitting I'd escaped the Moonies.

So when my boss Dan rings me on the office landline from Florida, where he's wrapping up a documentary about Death Row, he has no real idea what he's asking me. And that, even though we've worked closely together for the last three years and had an ill-advised drunken kiss a few months back, the scant details he does know about my past are basically invented.

'Why aren't you answering your mobile?' He never greets anyone on the phone. It's part of his cultivated busyness. 'I didn't buy it so you could ignore it.'

'Sorry,' I say automatically.

I turned it off when Angie rang for the third time, wondering what had possessed me to give her the number. I stopped calling her 'Mum' after I left for university. The campus medical centre's therapist thought the distinction would be helpful.

'Well, have you seen the papers?' He sighs before I have a chance to say no. 'Just have a look at the *Mail*, page five. Sarah texted me about it at the crack of dawn. Couldn't get back to sleep.'

I go over to the stack of newspapers we get delivered every day. The *Mail* is second, just beneath the shouty 96-point header of the *Sun*.

There's no real reason why the story Dan wants me to

see should be in a national newspaper, not this near to the front anyway. But beautiful dead women have always been catnip to a particular kind of journalism, especially if they might have got themselves murdered.

'You grew up near there,' Dan bellows into my ear, as I skim-read, loud enough that it feels like an accusation. Some kind of emergency vehicle is approaching him in the street and he waits while it passes, the siren foreign-sounding and deafening. 'Didn't you? I'm sure you said you were born near Stroud.'

'Yeah.' I'm really glad he can't see my face, which I imagine has lost all its colour.

'So you must have heard of the Tanglewood estate.'

I pause. 'Vaguely.'

'Any contacts there?'

'What – in my childhood little black book?'

Dan sighs. 'You know what I mean. Did you ever go there?'

I rub the newsprint-smudged heel of my hand on my jeans. 'Don't think so. Bit before my time.'

'Christ, this is like pulling teeth,' he says. 'It is close to where you grew up, though, isn't it? I haven't made that up. It's near where your mum lives.'

I swallow. Angie doesn't just live on the Tanglewood estate in her own cottage; she's an integral part of it – the only mistress of Karl who lasted the distance, who has been allowed to live there rent-free my whole life. Which I guess makes me an integral part of Tanglewood, too.

'I guess quite near,' I say.

'Right. So, I thought you could take a little trip back.

Catch up with your mum and do a little bit of research at the same time. Fancy it?'

'Now? Not really. It's tricky with my—'

'To be honest, it wasn't really optional. A segment on Tanglewood would be perfect for the counter-culture project now there's a current angle. Did you see the bit about the thirtieth-anniversary event? It's supposed to be *this weekend.* Thirty years since the album came out, thirty years since the last big Tanglewood party. And, according to the bloke in that article, thirty years since some other woman turned up dead. Unfortunate timing, to say the least. Judging by the details, it sounds like some weird pagan thing.'

He's talking too fast. He's always like this when he's scented a new story. He gets bored quickly, Dan. He'd never admit it but he's not a finisher.

Our documentary about the counter-culture of the late sixties – everything from Vietnam to LSD to Dylan going electric – has been in the works for a while. It's basically done. But we both know it's missing something as things stand. There's no obvious hook – no answer to the 'Why now?' question that's bound to be put to us when we pitch it.

'There's too much George Harrison going on about Krishna at the moment,' Dan is saying, as though he's overheard my thoughts. 'It's all just a bit . . . obvious, and too weighted towards America. If there's some hidden corner of England still partying like it's 1970, complete with mysterious drug overdoses of beautiful young hippies, we need to get it in there.'

He waits but I can't formulate a reply. News-printed

words are jumping out at me like tiny bullets. *Gathering. Mortimer-Lund. Lady of the Valley.*

'Rain, you still there? Look, obviously there's not much time so just take the little camcorder and have a dig around. If you play up the local connection, people might be more likely to talk. Borrow a tent and stay on for this Gathering party thing. Get a proper camera in for the day.' He stops, sighs. 'It's bloody annoying I can't be there myself. But there's no way I'm going to be done here by then.'

'I was going to start on those rushes this week, remember?' I manage to interject. 'The bull-fighting guy.'

'That can wait. Tanglewood first, okay? It's the missing piece, I know it is. It's what we need to elevate the whole thing. Make it a bit different. Special.'

And then he's gone, the surprising racket of a Floridian dawn abruptly cut off. I turn on my mobile and see that he'd tried me twice before resorting to the office line. Angie has rung again, too. She hardly ever rings before noon, but I get it now.

I read the story properly. The main picture of the dead woman, still blithely alive in that lost moment, was taken in the grounds I know so well. She's sitting on the top step of the short stone flight that connects the terrace to the flat expanse of grass that's still referred to as the croquet lawn, though no one has pushed a hoop into its grass for half a century. The sun is making her shade her face, and picking out the red strands in her long brown hair. Her skin is lined for her age, though whether from too much sun or too much living isn't clear. Probably both. She looks happy, at least. Her smile reaches her eyes in a way that I've been told doesn't happen very often with mine. Her fingers are crowded with the kind of chunky knuckle-duster rings that Angie favours.

I wonder who took it. If it was Karl. He always had a type.

I also wonder how many other people reading this over their breakfast know how close this photo was taken to where everything would end for her. She had posed there oblivious, a minute's walk from where her body would be discovered at dawn by a gardener who'd only started in the job a few weeks before.

I can't just visualize the place, I can smell it. Cut grass and camomile, the sweet stink of weed drifting over from an open window, my own dirty sun-scorched skin.

It'll take me about two hours to drive there. In all the ways that count, it'll be more like thirty years.

Chapter Two

Tanglewood lurks deep in my bones, and places like that are peculiar to return to. The strangeness lies in their deep, dizzying familiarity. Time contracts: the months and years you've resolutely absented yourself dissolve into nothing.

The soft limestone detailing on the left gatepost is still cracked and shearing off when I pull up. And the gates need oiling more than ever, their iron scream as I push them open silencing the rooks in the fir trees that flank the shadowed back drive no one uses.

Even in the days when the fans and acolytes still travelled here in serious numbers, hardly anyone actually found it, tucked away down narrow lanes that are a shortcut to nowhere. It's always felt as though it's my personal secret, like the trick with the huge padlock that my fingers still remember, making it fall open without the key, which was misplaced some time back in the mid-seventies. Besides, this way I get to arrive on my own terms. On the Dark Ride, which is what the main drive to the manor house is called for mysterious reasons lost sometime in the eighteenth century, anyone can see you coming.

Tanglewood is the sort of place people dream about. You'd think *I* would dream about it, my very own Manderley. That I would sit up, blinking and disoriented in the half-dark of my spartan rental in north London, simultaneously relieved and grief-struck to have left.

But I don't, not least because to dream you need to sleep, and I struggle with that. Still, even on those rare nights when I sink some way into unconsciousness, it never wheedles its way in. I think I'd remember if it did.

Once I've driven through, the gates pulled closed again, I try to phone Dan. I suppose I'm still hoping for a last-minute reprieve but, of course, there's no reception here. Only another couple of missed calls from Angie, which must have come in while I was on the M4. The din from the rookeries above has resumed, that drawn-out *caw-caw* always so wintry and bleak to me, and so different from the summery warble of the wood pigeons that fuss in the trees close to the manor.

I glance at the newspaper on the passenger seat. It's not just the beautiful dead thing that has made national news of what is officially a suspected overdose. It's that a man in his sixties has come forward to say this isn't the first time something like this has happened at Tanglewood, and that's news to me.

And apparently it's not just happened before, but happened in the same way. Both women wearing long white dresses and crowns woven with identical flowers: lilies, peonies and roses with sharp thorns.

'It made me go cold when I heard about it,' the man is quoted as saying. 'I know what that poor bloke must be going through, finding her like that. And the reason I know is because in 1970 it was me.'

There's a picture of him, and I squint at it, searching for a younger version, but I can't see past the jowls and corned-beef complexion. His name, Graham Warner, doesn't ring any bells either, but apparently he was a cameraman on the 1970 documentary team.

In the bottom corner of the page there's a much smaller image from back then, which he must have provided. It's over-exposed and blurry – one of those funny little square photographs that turns everything mustard and brown. He's wearing a shirt with the sleeves rolled up to the elbows and his hair is long enough to tie back. I will myself to remember, for him to coalesce into someone three-dimensional, the estate taking on shape and heft around him – an actual tangible recollection from that summer – but there's nothing. I don't know why I hoped it would be otherwise. I was eight in the summer of 1970 and I can't remember anything before I was nine or ten.

The piece says London-born Warner 'chose to stay on in the idyllic Cotswold-stone village nearest the estate', which is interesting. Maybe I'm overthinking it but it's almost as though he's been waiting thirty years for something like this to happen, and now it has. His eyes in the recent picture are too bright, and that might just be down to how the photographer lit him, but it might also be excitement. Vindication. *At last.*

'I knew something wasn't right back then but I was only a young lad. I didn't listen to my gut. Of course the police weren't interested in a load of hippies and druggies and, well, there were those – I'm not going to name them – who convinced me it wouldn't be good if it got into the papers. That they'd splash her picture everywhere and be . . . disrespectful. I didn't want that for her so I held my tongue. Now it's happened again, to some other poor girl, it seems obvious to me that there might have been foul play then, too.'

Behind him in the photograph, the walls of the room are a blank magnolia. The armchair he's sitting in looks puffy and old, as if it would smell. The fingers of his right hand are stained yellow. The caption below it is another direct quote: 'I suppose you could say I've never got over it.' I dread to think how many hours a day he clocks up reliving the past.

There are internet forums about Tanglewood. I've found them, in the furtive small hours when even London is quiet, at least in the maze of suburban Victorian streets where my tiny flat is. Some are focused on the music: people claiming to have found a bootleg of studio sessions from the first (and last) album, others saying they've got hold of one of the vanishingly rare first presses of that same LP, complete with its original cover art.

This cover, with its mysterious woman shot in black-and-white from behind, her head turned so that her profile is only partly visible, was apparently pulped by the record company before it even left the factory and replaced by an abstract image of green hills. Three, four years ago, when the worldwide web was still barely a thing for most, I can't think where the fans went to trade theories about why the cover changed and who the woman was. Maybe they congregated at obscure record fairs and argued about it there. Either way, none of them seemed to know anything concrete. God only knows how excited they'll be about this new development.

There's another chatroom that's solely dedicated to the groupies, which I shut down without reading on.

Yet another is about the halted documentary, which has become somewhat legendary in esoteric filmmaker circles. I think it was intended to be a fly-on-the-wall for the annual Tanglewood Gathering, but the plug was pulled for reasons no one seems to know. Explanations on the thread I waded through ranged from crop circles to the CIA to a dust-up between the director and Karl – the latter of which seemed by far the most plausible to me. One man was claiming he'd got hold of some footage, but no one on the forum seemed to believe him. All that's really known is that the summer of the documentary also marked the last time the Gathering was held. Until now.

I go over Graham Warner's words again. *Foul play.* Such a strange pairing when you think about it. They fit that time, though: the adults who were more feckless than the kids. Dirty hair and clothes reeking of bonfire smoke. Music that wound through the air like mist until the sun came up again.

It was so beautiful, but I was always vaguely hungry. Angie never seemed to eat anything then so I would forage for my own food in the manor's kitchen or go back to our grace-and-sexual-favours cottage down the valley and wrestle with the tin opener, eat cold baked beans standing up at the sink. In the cracked-edge mirror by the front door, where I would pause before running back to join the rest of them, I looked sharp-chinned and brown. Feral.

Chapter Three

Angie's cottage – mine too, once – is as far west as you can go and still be within the bounds of the estate. It crouches beneath the ramrod beeches that crowd the steep slope behind it, practically part of the landscape. The back wall is built into the limestone so that the ground behind it is level with the ceiling inside. In summer, the interior is as cool as a wine cellar, walls gently oozing damp.

The wisteria has gone over by now, the outlandish purple swags withered and fallen, but the rampant clematis makes up for it, drawing the eye away from the parlous state of the roof and window frames.

I pause on the threshold, breathing in the old smells. Damp stone and the stale onions and garlic of Angie's cooking. Joss-sticks and tobacco smoke, too, faintly. The soft green packet of her Golden Virginia will be on the kitchen table. So will the wonky fruit bowl some admirer threw for her decades ago, full of detritus that is never cleared out: years' worth of dead batteries and protest leaflets and perished elastic bands.

'I've been trying to get hold of you.'

I jump. She's peering down at me from the top of the stairs that go straight up from the front door, impressively quiet on her feet for someone who's heavy now. I have to fight not to do a double-take when I see her, these days, the blade-thin Angie of my childhood still so fixed in my mind.

'You weren't supposed to drive all the way here,' she says. 'A call back would have done.'

The old hurt shimmers through me. *Aren't you glad to see me?* the child inside says pathetically. 'I'll go back to London then, shall I?' is what I say aloud, stabbing my thumb back over my shoulder.

'Oh, don't be daft.' She heaves herself down the stairs and I turn away, so I don't have to witness the effort required. 'I'll make us some tea.'

'I don't drink tea. You know that.'

She tuts. 'You might have changed your mind.'

We sit opposite each other at the table when she's made herself a cup, and I resist the urge to sift through the fruit bowl.

'So, you saw I'd been trying to call, then?' As she reaches for the sugar packet, her hand shakes. It could just be age, and all the years of abusing her health, but then I take in the deep bags under her eyes. Unlike me, Angie never normally has any trouble sleeping.

'My phone's playing up,' I lie. 'But I saw the *Mail*.'

'That idiot Warner. What did he have to go to the sodding papers for?'

'So you know him?' I wasn't expecting that. I thought there was a decent chance he'd made up the whole thing for attention. People, especially lonely ones, do all sorts of strange things.

'They'd have settled for misadventure without him sticking his oar in,' says Angie, as though I haven't spoken. 'Maybe suicide at a push. Either way, we wouldn't have had the police sniffing around like they are now.'

'Did you know her? Willow Green.' Saying her name aloud sends a little shiver down the back of my neck.

She runs her tongue over her teeth. 'Not really. Saw her around a bit. First one he's moved in for years, to be fair.'

'And you always were fair to Karl, whatever he got up to.'

She shoots me a dirty look. 'Still sharp enough to cut yourself, I see.'

'I learnt from the best,' I fire back. We stare each other down for a while, a pair of cats with our tails puffed up and bristling.

'It says in the piece that Graham Warner lives in the village,' I say eventually. 'It's weird he lives so close, don't you think? That he never really left.'

She shrugs. 'It's a nice part of the world. Famously so. Why wouldn't he stay?'

I sigh. 'Have you even read the piece?'

'I wouldn't buy that poisonous rag if my life depended on it.'

'He says she was laid out just like *the one before*, but this is the first I've heard of someone dying in weird circumstances back then.'

'First I've heard, too.' She stirs her tea and lets the tannin-stained spoon clatter to the table.

I shake my head. 'Hang on, I'm confused. You're saying you know who this bloke is, and he *was* here back then, but he's made up the bit about finding a dead woman?'

'Well, it's not something you'd forget, is it?'

'Why would he be telling the truth about most of it and make that up?'

She rubs her thumb and forefinger together. 'Why d'you think anyone makes stuff up for the tabloids? I'd love to know what they pay these days for a story like that. That lot, including Warner, were off their heads the whole time they were here. Supposed to be getting footage, interviewing people, but they were partying as hard as everyone else. He probably had a bad trip and he's embellished it over the years.'

'That's a lot of embellishment.'

'If someone had died, the police would've got wind of it, wouldn't they? They'd have records. Case files and whatnot.' She waves her hand about.

'So, a woman dying wasn't what shut down the documentary, then? Or stopped the Gatherings for good?'

Different emotions pass over her face so quickly I can't read them, like a whole day's weather on time-lapse. 'What do you know about the documentary?'

'There's stuff online about it. Call it professional interest.'

'Online.' She sniffs. 'I don't understand any of that nonsense. People need to be living their lives, not staring at a bloody screen.'

I'm well aware she hasn't straightforwardly answered any of my questions, but this is hardly new territory with my mother. I keep schtum – the old interview technique of letting the other person feel awkward enough to fill the silence.

After a while she shrugs. 'It was all such a long time ago. I can't remember why the documentary didn't get finished. Probably Karl changed his mind – you know what he's like.'

This almost-criticism is so rare that I sit back in my seat.

'Why don't I know any of this stuff myself?' I say eventually.

'Too young. That's why.'

I open my mouth to disagree because that's how Angie and I operate, each as contrary as the other, but she's right. I don't remember.

'Nine is late for someone's first memories, isn't it?' I said to her once.

'I wouldn't say so,' she'd retorted, in her maddeningly implacable way.

It is late, though. I've always known it. But maybe I fell on my head back then and it's as simple as that. It's not as though child safety was a priority in those days. I set my own bedtime when I was ten, out of sheer desperation for some sort of routine, but the damage was already done to my body clock. At least, that's my theory.

'I still don't think it sounds like he's made it all up,' I say, even though I have been wondering. 'He said in the piece that he's never got over it and, if that's true, maybe that's why he stayed nearby all these years. It's actually really sad, when you think about it.'

Angie remains silent as the kitchen abruptly floods with sunlight. It makes the place more charming and shambolic at once. Extravagant cobwebs festoon the corners like ghost bunting, and some of the finger smears on the windows could easily be mine from girlhood. Angie doesn't clean because cleaning is what her repressed bourgeois mother – the grandmother I've never met – filled her days with. I like things neat, but I kind of agree with the principle. Not that I'd ever admit that to my mother.

I try one more time. 'Angie? Are you positive someone didn't die back then? Even accidentally?'

She glares at me. 'I can't stand you calling me that. And, look, what do you want me to say? People like Graham Warner can't tell left from right. Dream from reality. Too much acid will do that to a brain.'

I sigh again. 'How's Ottoline been about it all? She must be devastated.'

'I wondered when you'd get on to her.' Angie is reliably hostile towards any mention of Karl's wife. I watch as she reaches for the teaspoon and pushes her thumb against the bowl until it begins to bend. 'She hasn't taken to her bed, as far as I'm aware, so I assume she's fine. Well, as fine as you can be when you're as mad as a brush.'

'That's a sensitive way of referring to clinical depression.'

She fixes me with a look. 'And you don't know her like I do. I suppose you've only come back for her, to check *she*'s all right.'

I tut and reach for a battered old Zippo lighter to fiddle with. I can't tell how she's going to react when I tell her I'm back for research reasons, especially with the ghost of the old documentary flickering around us. Anyway, now that I'm here, I'm beginning to worry about mission creep. There's always been a mystifying, infuriating part of me that's weak for this place. A part I have to push down when the dark longing for it rises up.

Back in my uni days, the therapist's theory was that I had a subconscious urge to go back in time and plot exactly where my childhood started going wrong. And presumably fix it. I don't know about that. I'm not convinced there was a single thing that did go wrong, just an accretion of toxic shit between me and my mother. I eventually had to put distance between us for my own sanity.

Angie pokes with the wonky spoon at the teabag she always leaves in, then tips in more sugar. Not even in these small ways can she do moderation.

'You always felt so sorry for her, didn't you?' she says, as she stirs. 'And you never could keep away from that mausoleum of a manor house of hers either. Though I suppose anything would have been better than slumming it down here in the serf's quarters with me.'

She lets out one of her mirthless laughs, the kind that has forced me to bite down on the inside of my cheek since I was fourteen. I turn the lighter right up and watch the flame dance four inches high until Angie reaches out and takes it from me, snaps the lid shut.

'What does Karl think about it?' I say casually, but watch for her reaction. And, of course, her dark eyes glitter at his name.

'He came straight down here after she was found,' she says. 'To check I was okay. I wasn't even out of bed. I think it was the first thing he did.'

'Still using his key, is he?'

Her face twitches as she battles to hide her triumph, this tiny victory for the mistress over the wife. And not just the wife, but all the other mistresses who have come and gone while Angie held fast.

I can still remember the exact sounds of Karl's visits, when he would have assumed I was long asleep. His distinctive, sure-footed crunch on the gravel, and the scrape of metal on wood as he failed to find the keyhole on moonless or more inebriated nights.

I understood the noises Angie made when they were in her room together, even though, at the same time, I didn't, at least in the early days. And obviously, Angie being Angie, she always made such a production of it.

In the end, I went up to Karl's studio complex in the old carriage-house and stole a pair of headphones off the mixing desk. Made of cream Bakelite and chrome, they were so heavy on my small head that I could hardly raise it from the pillow to turn over the tape on my cassette player.

If he'd caught me stealing them, I would have got out of it by saying I wanted to listen to his music. Karl is helpless in the face of flattery. He also genuinely needs to make music, be around it at all times. There was always something playing when I grew up, spilling out from propped-open French windows in the manor house, or from Angie's old turntable in our cottage, or amped up and thudding through the walls of the carriage-house.

I never voluntarily listened to music then, just as I rarely do now. I chose story tapes instead – fairy tales about stolen children and dogs with three heads. Girls who couldn't stop dancing and boys with ice chips lodged in their hearts.

'There's a kid,' Angie says now, and I blink back into the present. 'The press don't seem to know that bit.'

'What do you mean, a kid?'

'Willow Green's. Her that died. She had a daughter, didn't she? Nine, I think. Maybe ten. Funny little thing.'

'Oh, God. Is there no father around?'

'What do you think?'

'So she's been taken into care?'

Angie arches an eyebrow. 'No. The sainted Ottoline's taken her in, hasn't she? Even the police don't seem to know she exists. I guess Willow never registered her. When they came, Lady Muck hid her. First time she's bothered leaving her quarters this year.'

'What's her name?'

'Lennie. She's pale as milk, with this long thin plait to her waist. I don't know as I've ever seen her smile. She just creeps around, big eyes drinking everything in. She reminds me of someone else I know, actually.' She lets out another laugh.

I ignore it. 'I think I'll go up to the manor now, see how Ottoline's doing.'

Angie gets effortfully to her feet. 'You know you still haven't said why you're really here. I know you haven't driven all this way just to check your old mum isn't in shock. I'm not convinced you'd do that even for Ottoline.'

'I did want to check on you. All of you.'

She makes a sceptical noise. 'Go on then. Go and pay your respects to the Lady of bloody Shalott. Catch her before she shuts herself up in her turret again.'

'Well, it's not nothing, is it? A dead body on the lawn. Someone claiming it's actually *another* dead body.'

'Oh, but you could see this one coming.' She catches sight of my face. 'I know you think I'm heartless, but Willow was on all sorts. Karl said she mixed things, took risks, didn't know when to call it a night. He wasn't really surprised either. Sad, of course, but not surprised. It's a shame because she was good for his music, he said. You know what he's like. Has to have his muses.'

I have a lot to say about Karl's so-called *muses* but I bite my tongue. It would be nice if Angie and I got past the hour mark before we had our first blazing row.

'I know the papers sensationalize stuff,' I say, 'but the whole thing sounds off, sinister even, and never mind what you think of Graham Warner. Why was she out in the middle of the lawn, all dressed up with flowers round her? Even if the woman in 1970 is made up, this one is suspicious enough on its own, isn't it? People don't arrange themselves prettily when they're overdosing. Someone else must have done that.'

Angie has started rolling a cigarette, but she pauses now, tobacco pinched hard between finger and thumb. She looks me straight in the eye for a long moment, then nods like she's received confirmation from the universe. 'I know why you're here. I'm an idiot for not working it out the minute you stepped in the door. It's research, isn't it? That flash-git boss of yours sent you. You're going to do something on what's happened.'

She goes back to her roll-up, fingers deft, big rings flashing in the dusty sunlight. 'You know, Karl won't be happy when he works it out. Or Lady O.'

'It's not about that, actually,' I say, too quickly. 'That's not the kind of thing we produce. But I did want to ask him about the thirty-year anniversary of the album. About the event on Saturday. Dan and I thought it would be a nice addition for this music documentary we've been putting together for ages about the late sixties, early seventies. To show that the hippie folk-rock scene still lives on. Though I guess Saturday might be up in the air now, after what's happened.'

'The Gathering Y2K, he's calling it,' says Angie, lighting up and pulling smoke deep into her lungs. 'And there's no way he's cancelling it.'

'I just thought . . .'

She narrows her eyes. 'You sure you're not going to go poking around, looking for patterns where there aren't any?'

'Patterns? But you said . . .'

She blows out an expert smoke-ring, which rises to hover above her head like a totally inappropriate halo. 'Remember, there's a line at Tanglewood between what's public and what's private. Always has been. Don't forget that.'

Which only leaves me more intrigued, perplexed and, to be honest, suspicious than I was already.

Chapter Four

It's a relief to get outside. To be away from the smoke and my mother. And myself when I'm with my mother.

The day has turned hot and still while I've been inside the cave-like cool of the cottage. It must be midday by now, the sun high over me, pulsing white and fierce. I pull out my mobile and see it's two minutes past. There's not even a sniff of reception.

My feet have taken me towards the wild sloping meadow I always climbed to get to the house, but I'm beginning to sweat, a tension headache building across my brow. It's much easier to go along the Nuns' Walk but I was always afraid to as a child, and avoiding it slid into habit.

There's been an estate here since medieval times, though it was called Templewood then. Its extent was much larger than what remains today, though that's impressive enough, given what land in these parts is worth. There were a dozen dwellings up on the eastern ridge when the Black Death was still a thing, but they're long gone, nothing left of them but thousand-year-old shadows on a geophys map. It was William the Conqueror who gave these lands to the nuns of Caen, and the long avenue of yews that connects the manor house with the old chapel is named for them.

Karl once told me that the nuns could still be seen

sometimes, on their way to matins or vespers; that this was a place where time could slip its harness. That little tale, no doubt invented for his own amusement, ensured I never dared walk it again. It cemented my chronic insomnia, too. I was always on guard for noises in the small hours, and when they inevitably came – from foxes and badgers and my own deliriously exhausted brain – I would force myself to lift a corner of the bedroom curtain. It didn't matter how many times I did it, I was always fully braced to see a figure emerging from the gloom, grey skirts swaying across time.

Inside it now, the yews are even denser than they look from outside, making it positively chilly. The air smells as old and undisturbed as a bricked-up cellar. It lifts the fine hairs on my arms.

I'm almost at the end and out into the sunlight beyond the yews' sharp shadow-line when my sixth sense prickles. I look up at the west wall of the manor house I've almost reached and stop dead, heart hammering. Behind the wavy old glass of an upstairs casement window is a small pale heart of a face. Its expression doesn't change when we lock eyes.

If Angie hadn't told me that Willow Green had had a daughter, I'd be convinced I was seeing a ghost who wanted to punish me for braving the Nuns' Walk. And not just any old nun ghost, but little lost Caroline. I was too young to remember Karl and Ottoline's daughter who died when she was just four, but I know that was her bedroom. I used to spend quite a lot of time in there.

So, Ottoline has opened up that hallowed room for this poor, motherless girl. For Lennie. A surprise stab of jealousy makes me stop, my hand going to my heart. I can't resist another look before I round the corner, craning to see the little face again. But it's gone, if it was ever there.

It takes me until I get round to the grand porticoed front door to work out what feels wrong. It's the silence. There's no music playing. Karl must be out, or else unconscious after a late-night jamming session. I'll have Ottoline to myself, if she's agreeing to see anyone, if she's really up and about and out of her rooms. The old blend of excitement and trepidation flutters through me at the thought. She has that effect on most people. You want her to approve.

It was after Caroline died that she started periodically retreating from the world, even from Karl, whose nocturnal visits to Angie would consequently grow in frequency. The latter referred to them disparagingly as 'Lady O's spells', though she loved that Karl could sneak down to her almost every night, at least when he hadn't installed some other woman in the eaves of the carriage-house, in the room conveniently above his studio.

Ottoline's most recent spell has stretched into years. She has her own suite of rooms that occupy the south-west corner of the house, affording her not only the best view on the estate, but – according to Pevsner – one of the finest views in all the Cotswolds. On a clear day like today, pushing open one of those heavy old casements and leaning out is akin to being airborne, floating high over the steep-tumbling valley that's almost a ravine. Far below, the river Frome cuts through dense woods that long predate the nuns, a narrow band of mercury twisting brightly away to Stroud and civilization.

Just as always in the summer months, the big front door is propped open with an engraved shell-case full of old walking canes. Ottoline's grandfather brought it back from the trenches, installing it in the hallway that he would inherit, his older brother dead by 1916. The grandfather did the engraving himself apparently, the Rupert Brooke lines so fitting for this place that I didn't realize for years that they were famous, that they weren't about Tanglewood at all.

Her flowers to love, her ways to roam.

I pause on the threshold, hand going out to stroke the smooth cherrywood head of the dog cane I always loved best, not quite ready to announce myself now I'm here. Perhaps Lennie has already done that for me, or maybe she's still up there in that cream- and rose-coloured room. I know it will remain unchanged from when I was ushered in that last time, on the fateful day when Angie got wind of me going there and blew into the manor like a hurricane.

I find Ottoline in the Chinese room, where the light spills in through the enormous Georgian windows, a lattice of lemon and gold. Her signature scent, which always permeates the furthest reaches of the house, is strong in here. I'm no expert but there's lily-of-the-valley and beeswax in it, with base notes of money. It's deeply comforting on a cellular level to me.

Her face transforms gratifyingly when she catches sight of me hovering on the threshold, unsure of my place here after so many months' absence. *Stop tugging your bloody forelock*, I hear Angie saying in my head.

Ottoline rises to her feet with a smile, arms open to receive me. She's still impossibly tall and willowy, though she'll be sixty next year; a vintage *Vogue* illustration from the 1920s come to life.

'Darling Rain, is it really you?' she says, in her breathy alto. What was it Nick Carraway said about Daisy's voice in *Gatsby*? Something about it being low and thrilling. That it promised lovely things ahead. Ottoline's is just the same.

'I heard about what happened,' I begin, when she lets me go. 'I thought I should come.'

'It's typical of you. Always such a considerate girl.'

Pleasure creeps warmly into my cheeks until I remember what mainly prompted my return. Ottoline is much more private than Karl. I can't imagine she's looking forward to the weekend, if it is to go ahead.

I cast around for something to say, afraid I'll blurt the wrong thing, give myself away, as I did with Angie. I never could stand Ottoline's disappointment, which was always in sorrow, and so much worse for it.

But she's turned away from me anyway, her face lighting again. I follow her gaze and, of course, it's *her*, the little wraith from the upstairs window, hovering at the doorway where I just was, plait pulled over one shoulder, fingers worrying the ragged ends of it.

'Ah, here you are with perfect timing, you clever thing,' says Ottoline. 'I've got the most wonderful surprise for you.' She holds out her hand to me and I take it, feeling the cool, dry softness I remember perfectly, even when so much else about my early past is muddled.

'Lennie, this is Rain,' she says, looking between us and

beaming with a lightness I haven't seen in years. 'She's down from London but she grew up here, on the estate. She's always been like a daughter to me, which means she'll be a big sister to you.'

She's still holding out her other hand, but the child doesn't move. She looks like a wild animal that hasn't yet ruled out bolting for the open fields. But then we lock eyes as we did before and I feel something pass between us.

Maybe it's just that she *does* look a bit like I did at her age – knock-kneed and hungry, and not just for food – but it's as if I know her already. And maybe she feels that instant familiarity too, because she comes towards me and puts out her small hand for me to shake, which makes Ottoline clap delightedly. Somewhere in the depths of the house, the phone starts ringing, and her smile fades.

'Why don't you two go out in the sunshine?' she says. 'Darling Rain knows every inch of this place. I'm sure she's got some secret corners she could show you.'

Lennie looks up at me, waiting, but I hesitate. Part of me wants to stay with Ottoline, and not just to see whether it's the police ringing. Not to discuss Willow Green either, necessarily, which would be impossible in front of Lennie anyway. Just to be in Ottoline's presence. It was the one thing I pictured on the drive up, the two of us together, her questioning me gently about London and about my love life, what there is of it, and really listening to my answers. Not a dynamic I've ever managed to achieve with my mother.

Back in the day, when Ottoline was in the clutches of one of her depressions, and when I was sure Angie wouldn't cotton on, I would creep up to her rooms and she would let me sit at the end of her bed and read aloud to her. No one else was allowed in, not even Karl. Only me.

Even more strongly than her own scent, the air in her bedroom always smelt cleanly of fresh-cut roses, even when the vases were empty, and the windows were fastened against the cold fingers of the east wind during winter. I asked about it one day and she said it was her grandmother Adaline's scent. That it had been her bedroom once and she had never quite left it.

I don't remember being scared, not like with the nuns. I liked to pretend that I belonged there too, that I was part of the same line as Adaline and Ottoline. As poor little Caroline. That the ghost was my ancestor, too. Sometimes, when she was very sad – so tired and heartsick she couldn't even raise herself off her pillows – Ottoline called me Caroline. I never corrected her. On the way back to Angie's cottage, I would whisper it to myself: 'Caroline. My name is Caroline. Caroline Mortimer-Lund.'

Once Lennie and I are outside, Ottoline's suggestions always impossible to resist, the little girl turns up her face expectantly to me, grey eyes squinting in the sun.

'So, what's Lennie short for?' I say.

That makes her look down at her feet, which are clad in a pair of ugly trainers that look too big for her. 'Magdalena,' she says, so quietly I almost miss it.

'Blimey,' I say. 'Still, better than Rainbird.'

She almost smiles and, when she meets my eye again, her face looks a little less pinched.

'How old are you?'

'Ten.' She raises her chin. 'I know I'm small.'

'I was small too, at your age. I'm still pretty small, really.'

She regards me, head on one side. 'Shall we go and explore the woods now?'

I can't think of a reason why not so we set off across the long strip of lawn where drinks were served to the VIPs during the party years, giving proceedings an air of control and convention, at least at the start. It's only when we get halfway across the Great Meadow that I remember. In the same instant, I see a flash of blue and white. A length of police tape has caught on a fence post.

I reach for Lennie's thin shoulders, to turn her away from the sight of it, but she resists me, surprisingly strong.

'It's okay,' she says. 'I've seen it already. And it's the quickest way to the woods.'

I keep glancing at her as we pass the spot where her mother must have been found dead just three days ago, but the only sign of any distress is in her slightly clenched fists.

'I'm very sorry about what happened to your mum,' I say, as the ground tips downward, because it's feeling increasingly disrespectful not to, even if she is a child.

'Thank you.' She says it with a dignity that makes my eyes prickle.

'How long have you been at Tanglewood?' I say, after a pause.

'We came just after Ostara.'

Even as the *we* shimmers in the air around us, I can't help thinking that even Angie calls it Easter.

'Ottoline gave me a Cadbury's Crunchie egg,' she goes on, smiling properly for the first time. 'It was a big one. There were two full-sized bars and the egg was in a yellow mug with a chick on it. The handle got broken off but Karl glued it.'

'He's good like that sometimes. When he's not . . . distracted.'

'Is he your dad?'

I laugh, the sound shocked and abrupt. Not because it's a ridiculous notion, far from it. Because I've always suspected it might be the case, and I don't know how this little girl can have come to the same conclusion in the ten minutes she's known me. 'Did someone say that to you?'

'No, but I know your mum is Angie and that she and Karl were lovers in the old days.'

'Oh.' I pause, swallowing another urge to laugh, this time because it's such an inappropriately grown-up thing for her to say. I have the strong sense Lennie hasn't mixed much with kids her own age. 'Do you have a da— . . . any other relatives? Your mum's parents can't be that old.'

'Mum's stranged from them.' Again, she doesn't stumble on the present tense and I'm not about to correct it. 'She left when she was fifteen, though they were never on the same wavelength. She had another baby before me, but she didn't keep that one. She was too young, so she gave it to some people who had a house and stuff. They gave her money and that's how she bought our double-decker bus. That's where we live. It's parked behind the manor.' She bends to pick a long strand of grass. 'When she got pregnant with me, she knew I was a gift and that she was meant to keep me.' She glances up. 'You didn't answer my question.'

She sounds like me twenty minutes ago, trying to get a straight answer out of Angie.

'No, I didn't. But that's because I don't know who my dad is. Sometimes I've thought Karl might be.' I don't know why I'm being so honest except that it feels like the least I can do for this child who is now, to all intents and purposes, an orphan.

The lush grass of the Great Meadow has given way to a winding path through wildflowers as tall as Lennie, lady's bedstraw sticking to our clothes. The way was broader when I was a girl, when there were whole packs of children running wild with trampling feet each summer, seeking out the cool of the woods, and the springs that run through it like silver veins.

'Let's go and see the big ash tree,' Lennie announces. 'Do you know it? Ottoline said it's magical and very, very old. Older than the manor house. She said that the . . .' – she frowns – '. . . I can't remember now whether it was the druids or the ancient Norses. Anyway, some people call it the Venus of the Woods.' She pauses again. 'I think I'm getting things a bit mixed up but, either way, it's a special tree.'

As we enter the hush of the beech trees that make up most of the woods here, bells are starting to ring dimly in my head. An old tale that's maybe merged with my old story tapes but might well have come from Ottoline's strange store. I can't quite grasp it, another hole in the rotted lace of my useless memory.

I haven't been to the clearing where the ash tree stands for years. It's a large, almost perfect circle, which doesn't look natural but is. After the cool of the beeches, the sun feels too much, as though it's a concentrated beam from above. Out in the middle of the clearing, the grass is already parched and yellow. We go over to the ash, which stands resplendent at one end, bigger and broader than

I remember. Beneath it, in semi-shade thanks to the leaf canopy, the last of the season's May bells, or lily-of-the-valley, are hanging on, pretty white mob caps among the green. It comes back to me then, in a rush: the carpet of white here in late spring, mixed with wild garlic. There's a story I once knew about them, too.

'Are you okay, Rain?'

I come back to myself to find Lennie looking at me quizzically. 'Yes,' I say. 'I just had a sudden memory of being here, that's all. When I was a girl. I just . . .' I shake my head, as though water's trapped in my ears.

She nods. 'It threw you.'

'Yes.'

'Did you know that in the olden days people used to have their own ash tree?' She leads me over to it and we rest our hands against the huge trunk. I have the urge to lie down among the roots and go to sleep. It's the heat, of course, and being back at Tanglewood, but I can't shake off the strangeness.

'When you were a baby,' says Lennie, 'you were given a spoonful of the ash sap, and then you were connected to the tree for ever. It was an unbreakable bond. You had to be careful, though. If your ash got sick and died, so did you.'

Chapter Five

I don't feel entirely myself until Lennie and I emerge from the cool embrace of the woods. She sees it first, pointing towards movement in the distance. A huge car is winding down the Dark Ride towards the manor, sunlight glinting off polished chrome, and paintwork the colour of summer skies.

I always loved that car. A 1955 Cadillac Eldorado in Bahama Blue. Karl let me steer it once, sitting on his lap so I could see over the dashboard while he worked the pedals. It's one of my earliest memories and it was midsummer. Every hour of every day seemed to last for ever.

'Karl's back,' says Lennie. She takes off at speed through the long grass, then halts and turns. 'I need to go and do something, but I can take you to him first, if you want. If you're shy.'

I laugh. 'Why would I be shy?'

'People get shy with famous people, even if they know them. Mum says he's a genius. That none of the other bands in that scene would have come to anything if he hadn't done it first. That he influenced everything.'

This time, I can't help wincing at the reference to her mum in the present tense. As for Karl, it's hard to gauge how famous someone is when you know them, when they've always just been there. I definitely don't think he invented the folk-rock scene singlehanded. But I guess he's pretty famous, or perhaps slightly notorious, just like Tanglewood.

Dan put on the album the one and only time I went back to his flat. *The* album.

'Do you know this?' he had said, and when I nodded he looked sceptical. 'Karl Lund was kind of a musician's musician, you know? Never got the recognition he deserved, not on a global scale. It was because he was so uncompromising.'

'He's not dead, is he?'

'Huh?' Dan looked up from his seven-hundred-quid turntable, silhouetted in the light from a vintage Anglepoise. I wondered if I should just go home.

'Well, you said "was",' I said, 'but I'm pretty sure he's still around.' *I could tell you what he's doing right now*, is what I didn't say.

It was a Friday night, half past nine, so Karl would have been messing around in the carriage-house studio with the small band of session musicians who have lasted because they never challenge him. He'd have been drinking expensive bourbon and smoking very good weed. *Hey, guys, listen. I think I've got something special here.* I could hear him as if I was there: the accent he'd chosen never to lose, sugared and summer-day-lazy even when he wasn't especially high.

'Wouldn't have had you down as a folk-rock aficionado,' said Dan, amused and slightly disconcerted.

'There's a lot you don't know about me,' I replied, an answer cribbed straight from the Angie seduction playbook. He came towards me then, as I knew he would, and before he kissed me I watched his pupils dilate until his eyes looked entirely black in the low light.

Disorientingly, and vaguely incestuously, 'Lady of the Valley' wound on in the background, and when I closed my eyes to kiss Dan back, it was like falling through time to meet my childhood. I was pretty drunk already, but it made me spin.

I find Karl in the enormous kitchen, standing at the open double doors of a huge new American-style fridge. He's ageing in the way all male musicians of his era seem to. Instead of getting fat and losing their hair, they shrink and wizen, skin darkening and leathering. They make me think of those ancient bog-men preserved for millennia under layers of peat.

He must be dyeing his hair. Its wet-sand colour is too one-dimensional, too matte. His eyes haven't faded, though. They're still the true blue that speaks of his forebears' Scandinavian heritage and the Pacific of his native West Coast. Or, as Angie would have it, Judy Collins Blue.

He turns when I clear my throat, and there's a beat when he simply stares me down. I begin to panic that he's going to blank me, shut me out because I've exiled myself for too long this time. He's quite capable of that. I've borne witness to it more than a few times.

But then he smiles, the old slow one that looks a little bit wistful, and I exhale. As a grown woman, I can see that if you're already in quite deep with him, and many have been over the years, a smile like that could make you fall completely.

'Hey, sweetheart,' he says. 'Look at you. Just like your mother standing there. Threw me for a second.'

He's never said this before, nothing like it, and it empties my brain.

'I had these missed calls from her,' I manage to dredge up. 'And then I heard about what's been going on . . . So I came.'

'And five days early, too. Couldn't wait to see the place come back to life, eh? I appreciate the support, man.' He puts his hands together in a thank-you, and I realize a beat late that he's talking about his party: the Gathering Y2K. Of course he is. It shows how little I've been at Tanglewood in recent years, how rusty I've got. Karl was never going to cancel because of Willow Green. He's always been the single, blazing sun in his own universe.

I cast about for something to say but he's already turned back to the fridge. It has nothing in it but drink.

'So it's definitely going ahead?' I say, in the end.

But he doesn't seem to hear me. Glass clinks as he inspects labels.

'I bet Angie's happy about you being back,' he says, looking briefly over his shoulder. He's still smiling.

I pull a face as he chooses a bottle of beer. 'I dunno. She seems pretty spiky, even for Angie.'

I used to do this as a child – hint needily to Karl that she had hurt my feelings. Though he made the right soothing noises, I understood eventually that it kind of rolled off him. Most things did if they weren't about him, until they really didn't.

Anyway, he never pressed me on anything, and in a way

that made it easy for both of us. He'd have been a great priest, Karl. It wasn't like that with Ottoline. She would have wanted to know more, and been saddened on my behalf, maybe even suggested she went down to the cottage to have a word. Despite everything, I would never have done that to Angie.

Now Karl starts humming as he reaches into a cupboard and brings out a big packet of crisps. *Chips*. Again, I wonder if he's heard me. He's bad at using his hearing aids. Hates admitting he even has them. But then he seems to click back into focus.

'Come on,' he says, 'this is Angie we're talking about. She doesn't function without conflict. It's her fuel. She runs on it like a car runs on gas.'

I smile back this time. 'I see you've still got the Cadillac.'

'Running sweeter than ever, though O still thinks it's . . . What's that word she always uses?'

'Ostentatious.'

'That's it.' He laughs and reaches round to pull another bottle of beer out of the fridge, holding it up with a raised eyebrow. When I nod, he does his old trick: getting the caps off by jamming the bottles up against the counter and slamming his hand down on them hard. He hands mine over.

I gulp some. It's cold enough almost to close my throat. Then I try a different tack. 'How's Lennie doing?'

'Nice kid. You've met her?'

'Ottoline introduced us. She seems . . .'

He drinks, swallows a small belch. 'Seems?'

'Well, fine. But . . .' I take a quick breath. 'Well, she can't be. I mean, her . . .' I swallow, curse myself for being so timid. 'Well, you know, obviously her mother just died and . . .' I tail off.

I watch Karl's face morph and smooth into blankness. I sip my beer to stop myself changing the subject and letting him off the hook. But, unlike me, he seems comfortable in the silence, tipping his bottle back until it's empty. I watch the Adam's apple bob in his sinewy neck.

Karl has never been anything but benign with me, but I've had years to witness the ups and downs of his and Angie's peculiar on-off relationship. A dormant ferocity is coiled inside him like a snake.

'Thirty years since *Lady of the Valley* was released,' he says eventually, shaking his head in wonderment. He puts the bottle on the side with a chink. The slow smile is back. 'I can't get my mind around it. It feels like last week.'

So that's it, then. Subject closed.

'I actually wondered how you'd feel about me being here partly in a professional capacity,' I say, before I can change my mind. It feels callous, but I'm going to have to say something eventually.

His interest sharpens immediately. 'What do you mean? You want to film here?'

'If you were comfortable with that. We've been working for a long time on this folk-rock documentary about that period, from 'sixty-seven to the early seventies, when so much seemed to . . . shift. And not just in music but the whole counter-culture.'

'And you didn't tell me about this before?'

I can feel my cheeks colouring. I drink more beer. 'Well, it's my boss's thing really. And it isn't finished yet. A lot of it has been focused on the States. You know,

Haight-Ashbury, Vietnam. All that.' I swallow. 'But we want there to be more about here, too. There's some content about the Beatles and TM, and what happened at Redlands.' I look up, meet his eyes briefly before glancing away. 'Transcendental Meditation, I mean.'

'I know what TM is, sweetheart. I was there, remember?' He laughs.

'Well, exactly. That's what I mean. I thought it would be amazing to interview you about those days, but also the thirtieth-anniversary thing is a great hook. It was such a seminal album.' I know he'll like this and, sure enough, he starts nodding. 'And the Y2K gathering just shows how much people still revere those days, that music. *Your* music . . .' I tail off, cheeks burning so that I have to resist pressing the cold bottle to them.

His blue eyes have completely thawed now. 'Sounds good to me, Rainy Day.' He pushes himself off the counter. 'You just let me know what you need.' He presses a kiss to my forehead and heads for the door. I catch the scents of him as he goes and, like Ottoline's, they're the same as ever.

He stops at the door. 'I'm glad you're gonna be part of it all, girl,' he says. 'Real glad.'

I stand there for a while after he's gone. The tangle of my emotions is hard to tease apart. Shame, yearning, homesickness and eagerness to please are just the sorry start of it.

When I go back outside, Lennie is nowhere to be seen. It's even hotter now, or maybe it just seems so after the beer and the cool of the high-ceilinged manor. I can feel the moisture rising off the vegetation as it heats up – it must have rained hard here last night. I was still in London, wakeful as usual, but also entirely unsuspecting of what the next day would bring.

I take the old way back to Angie and the cottage. There's a spot where I always stopped to look back at the manor, which seems strange now, prescient. Almost as if I knew I would have to say goodbye to it one day – a last glance in case it would be lost to me for ever.

Movement in an upper window snags my eye and I watch as one of Ottoline's windows is pushed open, just as I pictured it earlier. She leans out and waves at me, blows kisses, and I send one back.

'Come for supper,' Ottoline calls. 'Lennie will adore that.'

I nod, smile, and she blows me a last kiss as she retreats back inside.

People assume Tanglewood is maintained by Karl's music money but in fact there has never been vast quantities of that. A bad recording deal back when he was still doing an early-evening slot at the Troubadour, followed by a series of spectacular fall-outs with collaborators over royalties, put paid to that. The real money, like the estate, came from Ottoline's side.

'She tells anyone who'll listen that it was all Arts and Crafts cabinet-makers and bloody poets dropping in for inspiration,' Angie likes to say. 'But before that, her great-granddad made the family fortune flogging soap flakes. That's what really bought Tanglewood.'

Karl met Ottoline in New York in 1964. She was spending the summer with an uncle and his young American wife, who took her to some scruffy Greenwich Village bar where Karl was playing his guitar. Afterwards, they got talking. Neither of them had ever met anyone remotely like the other. 'It was a *coup de foudre*,' Ottoline once told me. 'A thunderbolt.'

Angie's version is different. 'She lost her head and her virginity. By the time she boarded the plane home, she was pregnant with Caroline. The Mortimers weren't best pleased – they had some chinless minor aristo lined up for her. But, really, what could they do, with a baby on the way?'

I have no idea when Karl started taking mistresses. Needless to say, the whole peculiar dynamic is not something Angie and I can discuss without arguing, and I'd rather die than bring it up with Ottoline. As far as I can tell, the arrangement has always more or less suited everyone. It must do: it's lasted more than three decades. And the other women, those *muses* of Karl who occasionally stray into Tanglewood's orbit, never stay long enough to disrupt the equilibrium.

At least, that's what I've always thought, until now. Willow Green didn't choose to move on. I recall the way I allowed Karl to block any discussion of Willow's death for my own benefit just now, and feel a bit sick.

Back at the cottage, I find Angie reading at the kitchen table.

'I've done your bed,' she says, without looking up from her book. I can't see the cover from where I'm standing but it'll be something from the mind, body and spirit section of the library in Stroud. She goes every week when she takes her washing to the launderette. I asked her once, when I was old enough to notice, why she didn't use the machine up at the manor house or ask Karl to help us buy one of our own. I was savvy enough to know that we didn't have the money to buy it ourselves.

'Oh, Lady O would love that, wouldn't she?' Angie replied. 'No, I'd rather do it this way.'

That meant a mile walk pulling an old-lady shopping trolley of dirty washing to catch the first of two buses, and the same back, only this time with a week's worth of food on board as well. This, and everything else we needed, was paid for by selling shapeless, badly sewn garments she tie-dyed in a bucket, and occasional tarot readings.

'Thanks for that,' I say to her now, for the bed. It used to be me making my own, and hers too most of the time, so this is quite something. A little voice pipes up, *Maybe she does want me here*, but I shove it back into the shadows.

My room remains unaltered, and when I come back for a visit, this is always somewhat unexpected too. There were never any band posters on my walls, only bad-quality prints of the pre-Raphaelite paintings I loved as a girl, after Ottoline introduced me to them via the small but original Burne-Jones hanging over her dressing-table.

An ornate silver-plate mirror hangs among them, a gift from Ottoline, which was made by a famous craftsman from Chipping Campden. In even worse condition than the mirror next to the front door downstairs, it has a crack fissuring across it from north-west to south-east, which happened when it fell off the wall one day, the nail holding it up apparently having failed.

Angie couldn't believe I wanted to keep it after that, what with all the bad luck it foretold, but I put it back up, with a sturdy picture hook filched from one of the lesser-used rooms at the manor. It was only much later that I wondered if Angie might have helped it off the wall, as a small act of aggression towards her nemesis.

Even if you ignore the crack, the mirror is foxed, and it does something strange to my face now. I look darker-eyed, hollower-cheeked, much more striking than I usually picture myself. I pull my hair out of its customary low ponytail and it waves thickly around my shoulders.

I recall again what Karl said, the way he'd looked at me for a long beat as if I was someone else, and I search my face now for signs of Angie. She's definitely, obviously there, in the almost-black hair, the big brown eyes.

Next, I search for Karl, for something in my features that matches the looks the old magazine profiles always described as fine-boned and delicate. Sometimes even pretty. But I don't know. I just don't know.

'*Is* Karl my dad?' I used to say to Angie occasionally, when I had judged the mood to be right. And by that I mean how intoxicated she was on one substance or another, and how they happened to be combining that day according to her mood, the alignment of the planets, her menstrual cycle, the ebbs and flows of her relationship with the man.

'I'll tell you when you're older,' she'd say, with a wink, if she said anything at all. 'For now, you've got me.'

But as the years piled up, she never did tell me. And by the time I was unequivocally old enough to know, I wouldn't give her the satisfaction of asking.

He has the kind of hair the sun lightens in a single day. He's obviously spent weeks out under its hot white eye, the ends that reach almost to his shoulders palest gold against his deep tan. Usually he has it tied back with a red rag. *Usually* because she's noticed him a few times during the last couple of days, as the small crowd who are always just *around* at Tanglewood have swelled in numbers, ahead of the Gathering this weekend.

He's just told her his name is Graham.

'Like Nash,' she says, to soften her smirk. 'Didn't really suit him, either.'

He turns to stare at her. 'You've met Graham Nash?'

'Might have.' She winks.

She has, actually. Just once, at Braziers Park, though it didn't go further than a charged glance over a lit joint, which she could say about a lot of men. She thinks of saying she slept with him. It isn't like anyone can disprove it; there's no way anyone can keep track of that many conquests, if the rumours about him are true.

But she doesn't like to lie about that kind of thing, even if it makes for a good story. Something of her upbringing remains. A vestige of decorum. A last button still done up.

'I'm one of the crew,' the Graham sitting beside her in the long grass says now. 'For the documentary. We're here early to set everything up.'

He says this with such pride that she hides her smile. The documentary is just one strand of Karl's carefully orchestrated *happening* around the release of his debut solo album. Its first-ever live performance will take place on Saturday night, which is happily also the Fourth of July. 'It's my own Independence Day,' he said to her. 'No one's name on it but mine.'

She hasn't heard all the tracks on *Lady of the Valley* yet, though he's hinted that at least one was inspired by her own return in early spring, after a couple of months in Morocco. She was surprised he'd even noticed; there were always so many people clamouring for Karl's attention. So many women.

He's also been tight-lipped about details of the Gathering, though apparently there are plans to stage the main performances within Tanglewood's ancient trees.

'I've seen you around with your camera,' she says to Graham now. 'And that intense bloke with the big beard.'

'Bill. He's the director. It was him who talked Karl into doing it.'

'I doubt he needed much persuasion.'

He's looking sideways at her again. 'You know Karl too, then?'

'Yeah, I know Karl.' She lights another cigarette, knowing she does it prettily, that it suits her mouth. It's a posh one with a gold filter; Karl brings them from the manor house for her. She knows they're Lady O's.

Whatever anyone else thinks – and people whisper about it, for all their talk of shucking off convention – she isn't here just for Karl. She who has always found it easy to move on, sanguine about cutting her losses and not looking back.

People are always talking about the counter-culture – how they're breaking away from everything that's old and staid. But when you really get into it with them, they always generalize, which makes her think they don't really mean it. That they hadn't really felt the visceral need to blow everything up.

She can only explain it in terms of her own specifics. The bleak, interminable Sundays after her father died and before she left home; the radio chuntering on and the smell of singed dust as the two-bar fire in the back room heated up. The love spoons and china shepherdesses and miniature brass kettles that crowded the mantel over it. The bleed of her mother's coral lipstick. The way she chewed her meat.

It was for all this that she'd taken down the cardboard suitcase kept on top of the wardrobe – the one that had only ever been used for holidays to meanly appointed boarding houses on the south coast – and left without a backward glance.

'I don't know where you sprang from,' her mother used to say sometimes, as though her father hadn't contributed anything to her existence. 'There's nothing of me in you. Perhaps there was a mix-up at the hospital.'

It hurt but she was glad of it, too, when she left. It strengthened her resolve. So her mother thought she was a changeling. Well, fine. Better than being a chip off the old block. *My fairy queen*, Karl calls her.

Anyway, once she left the house she grew up in, she found it hard to stop leaving. Until Tanglewood. There's something about this place that makes it physically difficult for her to go. Karl says it's the ley lines that criss-cross the valley – some mystical confluence of good energy that draws people in and makes them reluctant to leave.

He has this theory that the space-time continuum here is subject to disruption by something deep in the oolite under their feet – that this makes the membrane between past, present and future especially thin, prone to warping and bending back in on itself. That's mainly the acid talking, of course, but there's something real in it, too, she thinks.

She's seen things here she can't explain. Felt presences behind her only to turn and find nothing there. Slippage, is how she thinks of it. It seems to fit the topography, the land so steep in places that it's easy to lose your footing.

But it's not the only thing that makes it difficult to go. It's also the quality of light on the golden evenings, and the strange song of the skylarks as they hover above the sun-bleached grass. However hard you look, your eye never catches on anything ugly or garish. Like nowhere else she's ever been, this place slows her blood. It soothes the itching in her bones.

She is pondering all this, the little square of LSD she took earlier starting to prise open her mind, when Graham's thumb creeps over hers and begins to stroke. She'd actually forgotten he was there but now considers what will happen if she lets him make love to her – if it will offend Karl. She hasn't given him reason to be proprietorial, not yet, but she's witnessed what it is to fall out of his favour. *The king is displeased.* It isn't something you play games with if you don't need to.

Then again, it's not like he doesn't openly admire other women in front of her. There's a new one who looks a bit like Marianne Faithfull. She knows it, too, all sandy blondeness and limpid eyes. She turned up unannounced last week, just as she herself had the first time, the advantage of novelty belonging to her then.

She isn't jealous, not really. She genuinely believes that monogamy is unnatural and stunting, that nobody can own somebody else and still call it love. By the same token, she doesn't owe Karl any kind of exclusivity either.

From a slight and woozy remove, she observes herself standing and holding out her hand. The smooth lines of her arm shimmer and rainbow sparks dance through the air between her and the man on the grass.

'Let's go,' she says, and the answering expression on his face makes her laugh. Not at him, but from the bubbling pleasure that fills her as she watches his face light with a pure kind of gratitude. She can suddenly see the small boy he once was. She can see the old man who will remember this encounter with her for ever. And if that isn't a kind of love, then what is?

He takes her hand and she leads him away, across the Great Meadow towards the dark embrace of the woods. She doesn't look back to see if Karl notices them go from where he's holding court by the bonfire. In that moment, full of light and certainty, she doesn't think to.

Chapter Six

Voices from downstairs rouse me from a state that's half doze, half teenage self-absorption. My childhood was unique in so many ways but I still regress when I go home, just like everyone else.

I sit up in bed and look out of the window. The way the light is thrown across the valley says it's four fifteen, half past at the latest. Angie doesn't have clocks in the house because they stress her out, and I've never lost my wolf-child knack of using the sun to tell the time, backing that up with my internal clock. Dan tests me on it sometimes, like it's a party trick, shaking his head with wonderment when I'm bang-on.

I go to the top of the stairs and, though I can't hear any distinct words, I can tell that Angie is on the defensive, voice rising, intonation hardening. Every earth-mother I've ever met is exactly the same – the minute you cross them all that bosom-pressing warmth and wisdom vanishes into the ether like smoke.

I get downstairs to find a lean Black woman in a well-cut suit sitting at the kitchen table, apparently quite at ease. The impression of her clothes and understated make-up is complicated by the array of piercings in her ears and the delicate tattoo visible on her inside wrist as she reaches for a pen. I didn't hear her drive up, so maybe I do occasionally fall asleep.

Angie doesn't know what to make of her at all. I can tell this by the groove between her eyebrows, and the way the muscles are working in her jaw. Next to the composed interloper, she looks ravaged. The henna she's used on her hair for ever is now a lurid burnt orange where the grey is coming through underneath, and the skin around her mouth is deeply lined, as though it's perpetually pursed for the next roll-up.

'And who's this?' the woman in the suit says easily, when I walk in. I notice her small notebook and realize in a rush that she's police. And not just any old country copper. A detective and a high-ranking one, too, judging by her smooth confidence. Not many uninvited women would feel as laidback in Angie's domain, especially when Angie is radiating so much hostility that the air seems to vibrate with it.

'This is my daughter, Rain,' she says, spitting the words. 'I mentioned her to one of your lot on the day the body was found. Young lad in uniform, looked about fourteen. Drowning in Lynx.'

The detective smirks and, without getting up, holds out her hand for me to shake. 'DI Harkin,' she says.

'Willow didn't ever set foot in here,' says Angie. I'm trying to remember the last time I saw her so rattled. Her hands are shaking even harder than they were earlier. 'And I've already told you everything I know. I don't understand why you're wasting your time when you could be out—'

'Out there catching real criminals,' finishes Harkin. 'Yes. But catching criminals requires thoroughness, which is exactly why I'm here.'

She gestures for me to take the chair next to her. Angie glowers at the two of us from the position she's taken up next to the sink. It's obvious she doesn't want to be within six feet of the detective and, although I've grown up with her banging on about police brutality and the patriarchy to anyone who'll listen – the latter with no apparent irony despite her and Karl – this is such a visceral reaction that it feels bizarre.

I can tell her fingers are itching for a cigarette, so I chuck her the tobacco pouch, which she almost fumbles, making my heart contract unexpectedly. *She looks so old*, I think. Older than her fifty-eight years.

Harkin turns to me. 'I was saying to your mum that some new information has come to light that we need to follow up on.'

Angie can't contain herself. 'And *I* was saying that if she's talking about the ravings of Graham Warner, the police are no better than the tabloids.'

Harkin doesn't immediately reply to this and I realize she's enjoying herself, especially the waves of fury rolling off Angie. Again, I wonder why such an extreme response. It seems disproportionate. Then again, Angie's never knowingly underreacted in her life.

'Of course, our focus is on Ms Green,' says Harkin, after a weighted pause, 'but obviously we wouldn't be doing our jobs properly if we didn't follow up on the possibility of another death here, however cold the case might be.' She looks at me. 'You must have been a little kid in the summer of 1970.'

'I was eight,' I say. 'I can't really remember that far back.' I glance over at Angie, who has rolled and lit her cigarette now, face wreathed in smoke. She gives me a nod, as though I'm saying the right thing to the *establishment*, to the *pigs*, when it's actually just the truth. I wish I *could* remember more.

'What – nothing?' says Harkin, one eyebrow cocked.

'She was a child,' says Angie. 'I protected her from things like that.'

'Like what?'

'Oh, for fuck's sake. And you wonder why people don't like dealing with you lot.'

'So, you definitely don't remember hearing anything about this . . .' – she consults her notebook – '. . . Astrid, then?' While Angie huffs, Harkin keeps her eye on me. It's as if Angie isn't there, and it's thrilling and awful at the same time.

Because of this, hearing that name aloud for the first time doesn't so much hit me as settle like fine rain. *Astrid.* It's strange: familiar and fresh at the same time, like turning on the radio and hearing an old song you once knew well but had forgotten existed. Like something that's been waiting for me quietly in a dark room for a long, long time.

'There's something about it . . .' – I catch sight of Angie – '. . . but no. I don't remember anyone called that.' I spread my hands, gesture in the vague direction of the manor up the valley. 'There were always people coming and going when I was growing up here. Staying for a bit and then moving on. That's just how it was. And I guess even more so if there was a Gathering happening. And a documentary being made.'

'Yes, Graham Warner told us all about that,' Harkin says, writing something I can't read in her little book.

She's left-handed, like me. She finally deigns to glance in Angie's direction. 'Says he might be able to dig up some old footage.'

'Even if he does, which I seriously doubt, there won't be anything useful on it.' Angie's mouth is set in something close to a snarl now. Even with the smoke-marbled afternoon light behind her, her cheeks are approaching coronary levels of crimson. 'And that's because Warner never found any dead body.'

Harkin gets to her feet. She must be at least a head taller than me and Angie.

'Well, let's see what *we* turn up, eh? And, in the meantime, do let us know if you remember something, won't you?' She's looking at Angie. 'Transparency's always the best course, I think.' She touches her hand briefly to my shoulder. 'Thanks for your time, Rain. Angie.'

'It's Ms Valentine to you,' Angie says, and Harkin meets my eye for a brief moment, the ghost of a conspiratorial smile passing between us before I catch myself.

She's good at this, Harkin. Really good. And even as I'm thinking it, I'm accepting the business card she's produced, like a conjuror's trick, from somewhere on her person. I'm wholeheartedly glad I'm not hiding something from her because she's the sort who makes you wonder if you somehow broke the law without noticing. Who makes you mentally turn out your pockets and put up your hands even when you were a hundred miles from the scene of the crime.

She's almost out of the door when she turns. 'You don't live here on the estate now, do you? You weren't on the list.'

'I live in London. I only came down today.'

'So someone could corroborate where you were late on Thursday night, then?'

I think back, chest tightening because I spend most of my free time on my own, in my flat, but then remember Dan had asked me to stay late to do a last-minute phone interview with someone in America. A couple of our regular researchers who were also in had persuaded me to go to the pub after.

'I worked late, then went out for a drink with colleagues.'

She nods. 'Okay. I'll come back to you if we need to check that out. Why did you come down here today?'

'It was a free country, last time I checked,' Angie puts in from behind us. 'Rain can go where she pleases, but for your information she wanted to check I was all right, seeing as someone just turned up dead on the estate where I live.'

Harkin's still looking at me, so I shrug. 'I saw the *Mail* article and got straight in the car.'

'So you didn't know about it until today?'

'Her phone was playing up,' says Angie. 'I couldn't get through. Look, I'm telling you now, you're wasting your time and taxpayers' money with Graham Warner.'

Harkin smiles dangerously. 'I wasn't aware you paid any tax, Ms Valentine.'

Angie ignores that. 'He's a bloody fantasist. He must be obsessed with this place to stay so close all these years. He's saying what he's saying because he's got nothing and no one in his life.'

'And if he's obsessed with Tanglewood, why would that be?' says Harkin. 'Because something shocking happened to him that he can't get past, perhaps?'

Angie tuts. 'Look, there wasn't anything funny going on back then, and there's nothing funny about what's happened to Willow Green now, either.'

'No one is saying it *is* funny,' says Harkin, and Angie finally looks chastened.

'Look, I meant *suspicious*. Maybe I sound harsh, but I've been around long enough to spot Willow's type a mile off. They can't cope with real life. They're too . . . reckless. It's like they've already got one foot in the next world. She should never have had that poor . . .' She stops dead.

Harkin raises a groomed eyebrow. 'That poor . . . ?'

'That poor gardener wrapped around her little finger like she did. Him that found her.' I can hear the quaver in Angie's voice, the wobble as she wheels back from the cliff-edge she's nearly launched herself over. 'That's what I mean about reckless. That and the drugs. She liked flirting with him, leading him on a bit, but anyone with eyes in their head could see she was besotted with Karl and Karl's music and only that.'

Harkin regards Angie for a long moment. 'Well, I'll be sure to follow that up,' she says eventually. 'Mark Jenkins is only eighteen, of course, and Willow Green was thirty-three. Plus, he'd only been in the job a few weeks. Doesn't seem very long to form such a strong . . . attachment. But I suppose stranger things happen. Much stranger. So, like with Astrid, we'll look into it. Either way, forensics will be back from Ms Green's body soon. From the inside of her bus, too. That'll tell us more.'

She turns and picks her way along the unkempt garden path, past lolling foxgloves and roses bristling with thorns, to the little green gate, where she raises a hand without looking back. Angie and I watch her execute a deft three-point turn in her convertible Audi and accelerate smoothly away.

When the sound of the engine has been subsumed by the pigeons squabbling in the wisteria boughs above the porch, I turn to Angie. 'Presumably you realize how totally, mentally suspicious you sounded then.'

She's reaching over to stub out her cigarette in the old bird bath, but whips round to face me instead. 'What the hell do you mean by that?'

'If you want her to come back with more questions, you've gone the right way about it.' I sound exactly like Angie, and I've only been here half a day. Sometimes, usually when I'm on my way back to London after one of my rare visits, I regret how tetchy I've been in Angie's presence, but right now I feel like indulging myself. 'What have the police ever done to you, anyway?' I say. 'Apart from a caution for possession? Or putting you in the back of a van for being gobby at a protest eight hundred years ago?'

She pushes past me to go back inside, her neck blotchy with temper, too, but this is not the usual anti-establishment side of Angie that sees her flogging the *Socialist Worker* in town while her clothes are turning in the launderette. There's something dark and festering behind the bluster and I've seen it so rarely that it takes me a moment to recognize it.

She's afraid. And I can't work out why that would be. I'm not sure I want to, either. Just like I'm not sure why I didn't tell DI Harkin about Lennie. Why Angie stopped herself doing the same, when surely the only person it would piss off is her long-time nemesis Ottoline. Why I've been back at Tanglewood for five minutes and I'm already complicit in something, I don't understand.

I stand there in a patch of sun, the pigeons mollified and cooing now, despite the mood on the ground. The garden is offering up its scents in the soporific heat of mid-afternoon and though it's beautiful, so beautiful it's like something from a dream, I can feel the ropes of the place inching towards my ankles. If I don't get moving soon, they'll coil around me, and all the years I've worked so hard to disentangle myself will have been in vain.

Chapter Seven

Instead of going back inside, I make my escape for the second time today, striking out across the fields. Otherwise Angie will gather herself and come back out for round two, and I haven't got the energy.

This time, I don't head uphill to the manor but down to Tanglewood's biggest stream. It's just the same as it's always been and, somewhat against my will, it makes my heart sing. At this point in its journey through the valley, the water runs fast and clear through a broad and silent avenue of trees. The grassy banks are so green they hurt my eyes. I'm not convinced a single soul has set foot here since I was back for a mere twenty-four hours at Christmas, when frost silvered each blade and made the ground crunch cleanly underfoot.

The air feels expectant, pleasantly surprised by my arrival, like a neglected maiden aunt answering the door. The vetch and fairy flax have been growing unhindered since spring and the grass is knee-high and dew-damp, despite the height and strength of the sun.

It's not just that Angie would have come back out recharged and ready to rant about the bullying tactics of the police. It's also that I need to be by myself. I can't believe I've only been here about five hours.

I spend a lot of time on my own in London, probably too much, and one of the side effects is a lowered tolerance of other people – even those whose characters are far less overbearing than Angie's. Even people who are outwardly quiet, like me. It's like I can hear the systems of their bodies and brains grinding away, and it disrupts my own private frequency to the degree that I can't think straight.

I don't know what I was expecting to return to – my head was curiously empty as I drove on autopilot up the M4 – but it wasn't Angie being so peculiar, even with the knowledge that two people might have died suspicious deaths here.

I find a big chunk of limestone to sit on and try to separate the strands. It's not as if the dynamic at Tanglewood has ever been straightforward. As soon as I moved into halls at university, having enrolled myself for the A levels that got me a place there, I understood the full extent of how fundamentally odd my upbringing had been – which meant I learnt very fast never to talk about it.

Instead, I concocted something much more conventional and suburban, a version of myself that persists to this day and is now so well-worn that I believe it myself most of the time. It's what Dan accepted without question, and what various Dans before him accepted, too. Anyway, it's not like it's tested much. It's always amazed me how little men press you on the details of yourself. Women are much more difficult to fool, which is why I don't have many in my life. Except here, of course. Look, I'd be lying if I said I wasn't lonely in London sometimes. I seriously considered a proper relationship with Dan after our kiss, despite a messy separation from his wife last year, and it wasn't because I was falling for him.

It was because I'd come to dread Friday nights, staring down the barrel of another interminable weekend on my own. But, in the end, I decided it wasn't worth the trouble. As I said to the campus therapist before I left for good after half a dozen sessions, I'd rather rely on myself. That way I always know what I'm getting.

The trouble with Tanglewood is that it lives on in my bones and my blood, however deftly I manage to avoid thinking about it when I'm away. The fact is, I feel more like myself here than I do anywhere else – than I probably ever will anywhere else. I also feel known, and somehow more substantial, like I've taken off my London cloak of invisibility. I tend to forget how potent that is.

But never mind all that. Unlike the grass under my feet, it's well-trodden ground. What's really unnerving me is Angie. Even allowing for her pathological aversion to anyone in authority, she's being really strange. I think I'm right that it stems from fear, but there's something else in the mix, too. It's circling, dark and predatory, and there on my rock, the stream burbling below me and the beech leaves whispering above, I allow it to land. *Guilt.* She seems guilty.

I jolt as my phone begins to buzz in the pocket of my jeans. I must have stopped by chance in a rare window of signal. I pull it out to see it's Dan. I drove him mad for weeks when it was new by leaving it on silent, right at the bottom of my bag. The compromise we came up with is that it's now set to vibrate. My finger hovers over the button with the little green phone symbol, hesitating for so long that it stops before I can persuade myself to press it.

I know what he's going to say, anyway. *Have you tracked down the bloke from the* Mail *yet?* If he knew about the possibility of lost documentary footage, he'd be seriously excited. That sort of thing – lost for years and highly visual, perfect for breaking up any modern talking-head segments – is brilliant for generating publicity. As there was no mention of it in the *Mail* piece, Graham Warner kept back that little grenade from the papers for a reason I can't fathom. Either way, it might make an exclusive for the documentary. As conflicted as I'm already feeling, even I can see that would be a bit of a coup.

The urge for another drink eddies through me. Not just a bottle of Karl's lager, either, but a large vodka and tonic. There's a good pub a mile or so up a footpath, complete with a picture-perfect cottage garden that's been used as a filming location multiple times. Last time I was there, also to escape Angie's wrath, the floppy-haired land-management student beside me at the bar told his companion that he couldn't watch the rugby later because he was taking his grandmother to get her pearls restrung.

Posh or not, it's far enough from Tanglewood to be out of its emotional range. The vodka and I might be able to work out if what I really need to do is get straight back in the car and return to London, whatever Dan would think about that, especially after the professional year we've had, when one project after another has fallen through, or somehow fallen flat.

You might just bump into Graham Warner, if you go to that *pub*, says an annoying voice in my head, which could be Dan's but is probably just me – the me who has a genuine hunger for investigative research. A hunger whose origins undoubtedly lie in the very documentary Warner worked on before it was cancelled. The same documentary that coincides with the big ol' void of my childhood memories.

Even though I spent approximately four and a half hours with her eighteen years ago, I feel as if I know exactly what my old therapist would say about my life choices. Of my career, she'd say I'm subconsciously hoping that if I uncover enough answers to other people's mysteries and contradictions, then eventually I'll get to the bottom of my own.

And, of course, Warner's in the pub, propping up the bar, as though the cosmos has sided with Tanglewood and Dan, and doesn't want me going back to London either.

Then again, I clocked the alcoholic's nose in the picture of him in the paper and there's no other pub in this village, so perhaps it's hardly kismet that he's here.

He's glancing around furtively when I spot him, probably angling for attention and questions about the article, and witnessing it hardens me. I'm right, too, because when I approach and he turns to inspect me, there's an eagerness in his faded eyes that has little to do with getting justice for any dead woman. *Women*.

I think back to what Angie said about him being a fantasist and I realize that what's most interesting is not the possibility that he is – though obviously it's worth bearing in mind – but that she apparently knows him so well, or did once.

I adopt a perplexed expression as I clamber onto the stool next to where he's planted himself, glancing over, then away, and back.

'You might recognize me from the paper,' he says, after about four seconds.

I make my eyes go wide. 'Oh, yes, of course. I couldn't place you for a minute. That poor woman.'

'Which one?' he says pointedly, and I watch the tip of his tongue flick out to wet his lips.

I order my drink, making it a double, and resist offering him one because he's not a source or an interviewee, not one who knows he is, anyway. This is not how I would normally operate, but there's nothing normal about me being here. Anyway, apart from all that, he's only a third of the way down a pint of cider that definitely isn't his first.

'They didn't put in half of what I said,' he continues, unprompted.

I take my first freezing sip of vodka, shoulders lowering a couple of inches. 'Sorry?' I turn to him with a bland smile.

'In the piece. I gave them all these details about how it was back then and they cut most of it out. Made the whole connection seem less . . .' – he pauses, drinks and sets his glass down – '. . . less convincing. More of a curiosity and less like it might be a double murder. But I knew in my gut as soon as I heard about the flowers and the dress. And then when I talked to the lad . . .'

'The gardener?'

'Yes, him.' He waves his hand. 'He's only a youngster. Not much of a talker. I had to drag it all out of him. You know, the specifics of it. How she looked, how she was . . . left.'

A chill inches along my spine, which I tell myself is down to the ice in my drink. 'It said in the paper she was wearing a flower crown,' I say. 'Is that what you mean?' What the feminist in me really wants to ask him is why. *Why did you* want *to drag it all out of him?*

'My point is that it was much more specific. They left out the best bits. Well, not the best bits.' He has the grace to colour, cheeks darkening to match his nose. 'The important bits, is what I mean. The flowers for instance. They were *exactly the same.*'

He finishes his drink and signals for another. 'Pretty, they were. She looked like a . . . like a fairy queen.' He flushes, looks grateful at the arrival of the new pint. He reaches for it with an unsteady hand and drinks half of it in one.

He's quite drunk now – one of those drinkers who are fine for ages and then suddenly aren't, like a switch flipped. Quite abruptly, he's having to concentrate on the fine motor skills required to lift his glass and stay upright at the bar. Still, he's definite enough when he turns and looks me straight in the eye.

'Both of them were the same. That's what I'm saying. It was just like before.' He drops his voice. 'I didn't say to the press, I didn't like to, but the rose thorns in the crown had made her forehead bleed, and the lad, Jenkins, he said it was just the same. I'll never forget it, the sight of it, and he won't, either. It was the only damage on her. She was . . . perfect, otherwise. Looked like she was sleeping but for these two lines of dried blood down her face. They were like tears.'

He shudders then. A whole-body quiver that makes my bare arms goosebump in response, the hum of the pub falling away.

'Why didn't you speak to the police back then?' I say.

The vodka is already seeping coldly into my bloodstream, and I haven't eaten since London, but my voice is steady.

He shrugs. 'I said in the papers, I didn't want her name dragged through the muck. The police wouldn't have cared. They would have made out like she brought it on herself if it was an overdose, and that she asked for it if someone did it to her. Either way, they'd have made out she wasn't a nice, respectable kind of girl.

'Besides, Bill – he was the director, mates with Karl Lund – he said to leave it, to tell no one. Said there was nothing suspicious about it but it had to be kept under wraps if we didn't want the papers getting hold of it or the police and coroners and what-have-you cutting her up. I think Bill thought she might've, you know, done it to herself, which I never believed for a second. But I looked up to him. I wanted to believe it was a horrible accident so I let him convince me that she'd taken too much, or mixed the wrong things. I didn't know much about drugs then. I was pretty green.

'In any case, people had seen her acting strangely that night. Like she was out of it. It wasn't until I came down here for a pint last week and heard that Jenkins had found some poor girl just like I had that I started thinking my first instincts were right and there was something funny going on.'

He stares down into the depths of his glass, far away in memories and intoxication.

'Wasn't she missed by anyone?' I say gently, trying to steer him back to the present. 'I mean, if it was all hushed up? She must have had friends, family, people who noticed she was gone?'

'Only a handful of us knew. For the rest, they put a rumour about that she'd left in the night. That she'd cut loose and gone abroad. Spain or North Africa or somewhere. Like the rest of them, she was the free-spirited type, so no one batted an eyelid. You won't understand, but that's just how it was at places like Tanglewood then. People came, people went. No one was tied down. I s'pose that was the point, really.'

He must mistake my rueful expression for scepticism – I know that transient scene only too well – because he leans in closer, so that I can smell the souring cider on his breath and the stringy, colourless hair that needs a wash.

'Look, I wasn't just there to party,' he says, getting out his wallet. 'I had a job to do.' He slaps a business card down on the bar, pushes it towards me. 'I was the youngest on the team and I wanted to make a good impression, which meant keeping my eyes peeled.' He gives me a fierce look. 'Anyway, what would you know about any of it? You weren't even there.'

But I was, I want to say. In so many senses, including the literal, I *was* there.

If a memory is ever going to resurface, it's now. I let my eyes unfocus on the complicated facets of my highball glass. What comes is not that long-ago summer but a vision of Lennie at the window of a lost girl's bedroom, pale and sharp against the shadows behind her.

Chapter Eight

I'm tempted to keep drinking after Warner stumbles out. Just as abruptly as he'd flipped from sober to drunk, he went from garrulous to clammed-up, his hand going up to silence me when I tried to ask why he was still here after all these years, although I was pretty sure it was because he's never really got over what he stumbled across one dawn thirty years ago. The light in his eyes guttered out completely, and I hardly needed to wonder where he'd gone. Back to 1970, seemed the likely answer.

I can't tune out the noise of the bar once he's left. Or maybe it's just got louder as evening approaches and the collective boozing does its thing. Even as I'm weighing up which it is, a load of agricultural students floods in, like a spring tide around the lone rock of my bar stool, ruddy cheeks matching their trousers. They're enormous to a man and have so much tousled hair that it makes you wonder what they were fed growing up.

I grab my glass and duck under them to head outside to the garden, which is pretty much empty despite the last honeyed pools of sun. I spot a rickety table in the deep shade of one corner, overshadowed by a huge lilac bush. It looks like the most likely place to be left alone.

Even before it was Farrow-and-Ball'd, this place was too chichi for Angie's taste, but Karl graces it with his presence now and then, and there's a signed picture of him in the back snug to prove it. More than once, in the years when I was to-ing and fro-ing between here and university, he had me in tow. You think I'd remember summer nights like this one was gearing up to be, but actually it's those nebulous days between Christmas and New Year that I associate with being in the pub with him. Days when it felt like the sky's light-bulb needed changing. When I made sure I stayed mildly pissed so nothing could really get to me.

Tucked away under the lilac, I take a big gulp of my drink, which is going down much too easily. Thanks to Graham Warner and what he'd dragged out of Jenkins the gardener, I now have a new, indelible image of Lennie's mother in my mind – and it's in serious danger of rubbing out the carefree one from the paper.

I try hard to see Willow as she was in that photo – the long, lit-up hair and the brown skin – and wish I'd thought to bring it with me from the car. It doesn't really work, though. I can't picture her now without also seeing her crown of thorns and flowers. Her eyes spilling rust-red tears. That detail, more than any other, will haunt me as I try to sleep tonight. Because I can't help trying to picture the other one, too. *Astrid.* Her and Willow, shadowy twins despite the three decades between them, spinning together in my mind. I really wish I'd asked Warner if he had a photograph. If there *was* any old documentary footage.

And then it strikes me: if hardly anyone knew about Astrid's death and the manner of it, Willow Green can't be an accident. It would be too much of a coincidence. It couldn't be some sort of copycat by a random person, either; some kind of creepy homage. Maybe the vodka is interfering with my sense of logic but I think this means that Warner was right about foul play. And that whoever was involved in Astrid's death was also there for Willow's.

The air has thickened and dimmed way beyond dusk by the time I force myself to move from my secret corner. It's much brighter inside the pub than out. Above the shingles of the roof, the sky is mauve and Venus is winking between the chimneys, or maybe it's Jupiter. Ottoline would know.

In order to stop thinking about dead women, I've sunk another large vodka-tonic and, like Warner earlier, I have to concentrate to stand and push back my chair without mishap. When I'm far enough away from the pub's open kitchen door that my stomach stops fizzing with hunger, the countryside creeps back into the air, the scents of midsummer nights just as my DNA remembers them. Of honeysuckle and old things, of mossy stone and damp grass. Of an ancient England that I lose my grip on in the city, except for those brief moments when I'm by the Thames and there isn't a siren blasting away the past. The alcohol means that this makes me teary, which in turn makes me vow to leave the next morning, whatever anyone else might have to say about it.

The thought of Dan makes me check my phone. He's called again and I automatically press the button to call him back, then cancel it before it can ring. He's not a part of this place. I seriously consider shoving it inside a perfectly groomed hedge but push it into my pocket instead, first patting around to make sure the battered business card Warner gave me is still there.

Photographer and Cameraman, it says, but it looks as if he's been carrying it in his wallet for years, the paper soft at the corners. This makes me maudlin, too – for the hope and optimism that went into ordering those cards and for the years that followed, when none of it really came to anything, as far as I can make out. I can't know for sure, but I think Graham Warner got hooked on that summer thirty years ago and has never managed to pull himself free.

There's an address on the card and I hesitate at the turning for the path back to Tanglewood. He lives in one of a row of tiny almshouses and it's only a minute's walk past the church. I'm halfway there before I really make the decision.

I don't even need to check which is his. He's left the curtains open and the big light is on, starkly showcasing the living room I recognize from the paper, devoid of anything homely or personal.

He's put the telly on. I can see the cold blue flicker of it on the bare magnolia walls. I move closer and the man himself comes into view, or at least the back of his head does. He's sitting in that horrible, overstuffed armchair and looks shrunken in it, old and vulnerable, his hair thin at the crown. But then I've always had a weakness for lonely old men. Not in that way, obviously. In the sense that when I see the meagre contents of their baskets in the supermarket, it makes me want to weep.

I check what he's watching, in the daft hope that it's the unearthed documentary footage. But it's a cosy detective drama filmed here in the Cotswolds, which seems rather ironic, and makes me wonder for the second time if Angie has a point. Maybe he is a fantasist. Maybe he believes he's inside his own Cotswolds police procedural like this one, which has been running for so long that the murders have become ever more lurid and absurd. Because it's so unlikely, isn't it? That two women would be killed thirty years apart in some weird, ritualistic way involving white dresses and flower crowns?

I haven't moved, haven't made even the smallest noise, but some animal sense must be prickling the back of his neck because he suddenly whips round in his chair, looking directly at the spot where I'm hovering, like a spectre, on the other side of the low wall of his weed-blown front garden. We stare at each other, my feet rooted to the spot even as my brain prepares sentences.

Sorry if I made you jump. I just wanted to ask one more question.

I hope you don't mind me swinging by, Graham, but I forgot to say . . .

But he's not moving and he doesn't get to his feet, and I realize he can't see me. It's too dark out here and too bright in there. He can probably only see himself, silhouetted in the reflection of his own sterile room.

Chapter Nine

I walk fast towards the path, past the church, which seems to be tilting oddly over the graveyard now that the moon has risen behind it, backlighting it, like an atmospheric establishing shot from that detective show. A bat flits past me, low, and so fast and close that it disturbs the air on my face, moving my hair and making me gasp in the silence.

The path, flanked by summer-tall hedgerows, is so thick with shadow that I can't see my feet. I'm only thirty yards down it when it happens.

It comes at me, a couple of hours later than expected, looking and feeling like a dream. Me, who never dreams. Who is never far enough beneath the surface of sleep to get lost in some bizarre narrative thrown up by my subconscious. And because I'm awake and walking surprisingly surefooted through the deep dark, as though Tanglewood is pulling me back towards her like a tractor beam from the mothership, I understand it's a memory. It's real. Or was real, once.

I can see him as clearly as I just saw him through the window, except he's young now. Young like he was when he found the first body that summer. Tanned and easy in his body, unbowed by the years, his hair thick and gold and tied back with a torn-off strip of red cotton. The details of him are so sharp and three-dimensional that I know this is not some version of the photo in the paper.

This version of Graham Warner is moving, animated. He's alive.

I stop walking to focus and see him press the heels of his hands to his eyes. They come away wet. He's making a strange noise, sort of choking and gulping and moaning all at once.

And there's something else that convinces me this is real: my own vantage point in the memory. The height from which I'm regarding him as he cries means I only came up to his elbow at the time.

It's that summer. I'm eight again. This is now my earliest memory.

I blink and the darkness of the new night pours back in. I file the memory away so it doesn't start to degrade, because I know it's important. That it somehow means something.

I wonder if there'll be more. Now the first has sidled in, I'm pretty sure others will follow.

After that, I feel exhausted, but I still have half a mile to trek through the pitch-black tunnel of trees, all the while trying to ignore the animal-prickling on the back of my neck. If I allow myself to start checking the shadows behind me, I'll have to run. And with terrain this steep and rolling, that'll end in a broken neck. It's not until my stomach sends out another rumbling protest that I remember I was expected at the manor for dinner. Unless my instincts have been thrown off by a strange evening, it's already past nine.

As the manor comes into view, it looks like every available lamp has been switched on. The effect in the lightless valley is one of suspension, a galleon gliding weightless through a calm black sea. The moon abruptly pulls free of cloud and catches the pale stone of the Dark Ride, turning it into the slow, briny roil of the ship's wake.

I'm not scared now. The last of it has been crowded out by the old anticipation I've always associated with the manor. About being part of it; of being wanted and expected there. Angie could always smell it on me and gave me stick about it. Of course, I could have turned around and said she was just the same about Karl, but I never did. Back then, it was always me who swallowed my words rather than her, despite my being the child and her the adult.

I pick up the pace, the tractor beam irresistible now, but then my phone buzzes through my hip bone. It'll be Dan again, following up with a text because he can't get through. I open it, expecting something short and shitty about me never answering. But it's not.

Good news. LK got stay of execution. Got it on tape and might be able to move flight to Friday. If so, will join you on home turf in time for Sat!

I swallow, push away the uncomfortable notion of Dan being here, and realize simultaneously that, if I'm thinking along those lines, my faithless heart has already decided I'm not leaving tomorrow.

Chapter Ten

They're not in the dining room, though the detritus from one of Ottoline's cold collations is. I rip open a roll, stuff it with roast chicken and eat it standing up below the gilt-framed portrait of Grandmother Adaline. She's a smaller, softer-limbed version of Ottoline, with the same ash-blonde hair and high forehead, the same slightly hooked nose. There's a tear at the very bottom left of the canvas if you know where to look for it.

There are conflicting reports about how it got slashed, and by whom, during the first Gathering back in '67. That one, according to Angie, was a much more intimate affair than they had become by the last, in 1970. More like a house party, and much more genuinely debauched than anything the Stones and Marianne Faithfull were supposedly up to when they'd got busted at Redlands earlier that same year. The Gatherings got bigger each year until what had begun as an intimate party for friends in the music and art worlds had become something closer to a days-long festival: scores of people turning up with their tents and campervans, the party spilling out of the manor and across the Great Meadow. The Gatherings are so much part of Tanglewood lore – and so representative of a time before I can remember – that I can't quite get my head around them being resurrected in five days' time.

When I've finished eating, I go to the bottom of the

stairs, ears pricked. The inevitable thud of bass is coming from the cellar, which is one long vaulted room Karl turned into a private nightclub when I was about twelve. These days it acts as a kind of after-dinner retiring room for visiting (male) musicians. There's even a billiards table down there.

I go upstairs instead, trusting my instincts that I'll find Ottoline and Lennie there together.

I hear the singing when I get to the landing, and it stops me in my tracks. I catch the expression on my face in the huge mirror over a lamp table and it's oddly stricken, though with exactly what emotion I'm not sure and don't want to get into right now.

I know that song, though. It's an old folk lament, haunting and sad, intended to be sung in the round, though it's effective enough with just two voices weaving through each other. Ottoline's has a slight quaver that I don't remember from the past and must have come with age, but Lennie's voice is pure and sweet. It reminds me of the stream, and maybe it's the thought of water that makes tears rise so that my eyes are brimming before I have time to tamp it all back down to wherever it came from. *This* is why I don't listen to music. It gets me between the ribs, so swiftly and sharply I don't even feel the blade going in.

I creep silently along the passage towards them. Towards Caroline's room. It's darker here, away from the sconces of the main gallery and staircase, and the light from the half-open door to her room is a narrow spill of warmth and comfort. I feel like a Dickensian orphan about to press my cold nose up against the bottle-glass of a happy house at Christmas.

In fact, it's a much more intimate scene. A much more poignant one, too, somehow. Through the gap in the door, I can see the two of them reflected perfectly in the cheval mirror set into the huge mahogany wardrobe. Lennie is tiny in the four-poster bed, her hair loosened from its plait and brushed out on her shoulders, lamplight catching in the ripples. Ottoline has pulled up the dusty-pink nursing chair to the side of the bed and is leaning towards her with her elbows on the counterpane, an old book between them on the cover. I bet I know which one it is.

Caroline would be in her mid-thirties now, the thought so arresting and strange that I can't get my head around it. There's a portrait of her in Ottoline's room, which I always found difficult to look at once Angie had told me, with some relish, that it had been painted after she died. 'Look for the hourglass and the apple,' she said. 'It's one of those macabre *memento mori* things. The sand's all at the bottom and the apple's half rotten. Means someone's already gone.' I could never unsee it after that.

Caroline died of natural causes when she was four. One night her heart just stopped beating. She never woke up to see another morning in that lovely room. The sheer random bad luck of it, and the lack of any warning, did nothing for my ability to sleep. What was it Poe called sleep? *Those little slices of death.* I was scared to let myself cross that threshold into unconsciousness in case, like Caroline, I never came back.

Ottoline found her. She only spoke about it directly once in my presence, during one of those dreamlike times when I used to sneak upstairs to her rooms. Looking back now, I can see she was almost catatonic with grief that day. She didn't say a word to me until that point, and I just kept reading, one page after another, concentrating hard so I didn't stumble. Occasionally, I'd glance over and, though her expression was frozen, tears would be leaking out of her eyes, like one of those Catholic miracle statues.

That day, I was reading *Snow White*, by the Brothers Grimm, and there was a passage in it about how perfectly still and pale she looked in her glass coffin. Ottoline said something, too low for me to catch, and I broke off reading and waited for her to say it again. Held my breath so I couldn't possibly miss it.

'She was so cold,' she whispered, when I was just about to run out of oxygen. 'She was so much colder than the air in the room. Like the cold came from inside her.'

The title in the original German was *Schneewittchen. Wittchen* meant white, but it sounded like witch, so it became that for me from the moment I heard it. I was half afraid of, half fascinated by Caroline. I was terrified to share her fate, even as I wanted to turn into her, for Ottoline's sake mainly but maybe my own a little bit, too. It wasn't long after that day that Angie found out how much time I was spending with Ottoline in those rooms and put a stop to it.

It was rare that Angie ever set foot in the manor. I can count on one hand the other occasions, and none of them took place when there weren't dozens of other people around to soak up the tension.

While I'm thinking all this, a much older part of my brain registers something behind me in the dark hall. I whip round, fully expecting a transparent Caroline in a white nightgown, but it's only Karl. He looks cadaverous in the low light, all his boyishness gone to reveal something almost sepulchral.

'You spying, Rainy?' He says it quietly enough that Lennie and Ottoline won't hear him. 'We missed you at dinner.'

He gives me a warm-looking smile then, and it transforms him into something more familiar. The other one, though, I can still see, flickering behind. My heart feels as if it's going to stutter out of my chest, but maybe some of that – the paranoia too – is down to the vodka I don't usually drink because, having witnessed it so often in the past, I don't like loss of control.

He reaches out, making me flinch, but it's only to pat my arm before putting his head round the door. 'There's someone here who wants to say goodnight, Lennie.'

I find myself gently pushed inside the room. Lennie gives me a little wave and I take in the space properly. And, just like that, I'm a child again.

Back then, this was exactly how I imagined little rich girls' bedrooms to look. Everything was plush and pale, creamy coloured, with soft rugs my toes disappeared into. The bed was high, 'Princess and the Pea' high to me. Old lace edged the fine cotton pillowcases, and a small easel was placed in the corner by the window with the best view.

In a deep alcove next to the fireplace, there were shelves lined with Caroline's stuffed toys and dolls. The only other time I was here, I didn't have time to do much more than covet them as a whole collection. I was astounded by their number. I, who only had a few teddies. It went without saying that they weren't to be touched, that *nothing* was to be touched, as if a red velvet rope was strung between brass posts across the room. But now all I can see are their eyes, oddly luminous and alert in the shadows.

Though Lennie's too old for it, Ottoline has put on a nightlight – a rotating toadstool house with lit-up windows – and, as it turns, the effect it has on the toys is a brief, unnerving flaring into animation. Even the knowledge that it's a trick of the light doesn't diminish the sheer uncanniness of it, those twitches of movement followed by perfect stillness and back again, like they've grown more impatient and daring in the years of waiting for a little girl to inhabit the room again.

'Oh, here you are, darling,' says Ottoline, breaking into my creepy little reverie. 'We wondered where you'd got to.'

'I'm so sorry. I went for a walk, ended up at the pub and . . . I don't know where the time went.'

Ottoline frowns. 'You didn't come back along that path on your own in the pitch dark?'

'It was fine,' I say. 'I could do it with my eyes closed.' But then I realize she probably didn't mean it like that, that she's probably thinking of Willow and what happened to her out there. I remember the phone ringing earlier, and Ottoline's reaction to hearing it, and wonder if my instinct that it was the police was right. And, if so, what they'd had to say.

Karl has come in behind me to sit on one of the deep window-seats. No one has closed the curtains yet and it's now so entirely dark outside that the room is reflected perfectly in the glass. It reminds me of Graham Warner, blind at his own window, and me no more substantial than mist on the other side of it.

One of the casements is open and the summer smells that got to me on my walk are insinuating themselves into the room. There's a honeysuckle bush in the deep flower-bed below and I can smell it distinctly now I've noticed. It's heady, verging on sickly.

'We were discussing the Gathering over supper,' says Ottoline. She squeezes Lennie's hand. 'How wonderful it will be to share the estate with other people again.'

I glance at Lennie, who seems not to react.

'Don't you think, darling?' presses Ottoline, when I don't answer.

'Are there going to be lots of people coming, do you think?' I say awkwardly, perching on the velvet ottoman at the end of the bed. The absence of Willow from this narrative is uncomfortably loud. Ottoline's enthusiasm is odd, too. She's been reclusive for so long.

'Goodness, of *course* there will be lots of people,' Ottoline says. 'Karl's masterpiece is thirty years old. It's the first summer of the millennium. And our darling Lennie was sent to us as a special blessing. We couldn't ask for more to celebrate.'

This seems so cringingly oblivious that I can't think of anything to say. Ottoline's manners are usually impeccable, her sensitivity to others' feelings acute. I study the little girl in the big bed again, looking for any reaction to Ottoline's redrawing of a tragedy – as though her mother was little more than a delivery service who did her job and conveniently died – but her eyes are cast down to the book she's taken onto her lap, small fingers tracking the gold flourishes of the embossed leather cover.

'I've been talking to Caleb since you two went up,' Karl says to Ottoline.

My head goes up at that name before I can stop it, but Ottoline only smiles absently and reaches out to stroke a hank of Lennie's hair.

'He assured me he'll be around on Saturday.'

'How lovely,' Ottoline murmurs.

I try to calculate how long it's been since I've seen or even thought about their son Caleb, who's a year younger than me. It's long enough that I give up pretty quickly. The last I heard, he was in Sweden, living in a remote cabin deep in the forest.

My last clear memory of him is from one of those times Karl spontaneously decided that everyone would go to the pub. Caleb was painfully skinny back then, everything out of proportion, a smattering of spots along his jaw that he kept ducking his head to hide.

It's easy to forget that Karl and Ottoline have another child. After Caroline died, I don't think Caleb could ever make a dent in the thick castle keep of Ottoline's sorrow. And Karl's attention span was always pretty limited; music and women were always going to be more interesting to him than a silent kid who seemed to have inherited none of his father's charisma or his mother's easy grace.

He didn't possess the gifts children set so much store by either: sporting prowess or natural leadership. I guess it was an admirable kind of meritocracy we were operating in that his parents – the undisputed king and queen of our enchanted lands – conferred on him no special status at all.

He was sent to boarding school when we were still quite young – the same place Ottoline's father attended.

One day he was at Tanglewood, and then he was gone, and because we were still in the thick of the estate's transient years – people dropping in and staying for months, camping in the grounds, or maybe doing work on the land or outbuildings in exchange for a bed in the manor – his absence didn't feel unusual. There were whole tribes of children running wild, coming and going with the seasons, and Caleb being gone barely seemed to register. I'm not convinced it registered with his parents, either.

This is the first time it's ever struck me how profoundly sad this is. In my defence, I had my own mother issues to contend with. The only fleeting interest I ever had in him as a boy was connected to my suspicions about who my father might be, and who his sister had been.

But I remember him from the pub that time because that was the holiday when he finally blasted onto everyone's radar at once by getting expelled. I had just left for university, while he was in his last year of school. The reasons for the expulsion were unclear, or deliberately withheld, but they were serious enough that Ottoline took to her bed. She made it downstairs only a couple of times while I was back for the holidays – and because the privileged years of me sneaking in to read to her were long gone, I had no special insight into what was going on behind the scenes.

Whatever he'd done, it was clear he'd also turned mean. It gave him real presence for the first time, even with the spots, and not in a good way: his lip was permanently curled in a sneer. He was particularly contemptuous of Ottoline when she was there, which made me despise him. He made fun of her harmless little whimsies until her face closed completely.

I took him aside at the end of that pub evening, told him to stop being such a dick to everyone. He let out an ugly crack of laughter.

'Pretty fucking rich, coming from you,' he said, without missing a beat. 'Maybe sort out your own excuse for a mother before you start interfering with me and mine.'

I can still remember the force of it, and how for the first time it made him resemble his father.

'I thought he was off-grid in some Swedish cabin,' I say now. 'Does everyone in the world have a mobile phone now, or what?'

I'm smiling but Karl looks perplexed. 'Mobile? I walked up to his van.'

Van? My brain ticks over, the vodka slowing it.

'He came back in the spring, darling,' Ottoline says. 'Of course, you haven't been here since Christmas so you wouldn't know.'

'He's here? At Tanglewood?'

Karl snorts. 'This house ain't good enough for him, apparently. Said something about *boundaries*. He's camped up in the woods on the western ridge, pretending he's a real backwoodsman when he's still taking food and beer from my fridge.'

'But I want him to feel like this is his home,' says Ottoline softly, her eyes briefly meeting mine. I can't read them in the low light but I remember the unease shimmering in her face when I said I'd walked back alone through the dark valley, and I wonder now if the two things are connected. Which makes an unease of my own go through me like a cold draught.

Chapter Eleven

'You didn't tell me Caleb was back.'

'Evening to you, too.' Angie is lying full-length on the ancient sofa. A Crosby, Stills and Nash LP is on the turntable and it's 'Guinnevere', which Angie once declared was based on her, in total denial of the lyric about green eyes. They came here one summer, apparently, although Angie says a lot of things and I've learnt to be sceptical.

She's nearly at the end of her book and the room would be thick with smoke if it wasn't for the wide-flung window. I surprise and unnerve myself by finding the whole scene rather comforting.

'How was *supper*?' she says, raising the sardonic eyebrow she keeps especially for digs at Ottoline, but for once there's no real malice in her tone.

'Actually, I missed it. I went for a long walk, lost track of time. I just called in briefly.'

She doesn't say anything to that, caught between disapproval of my loner tendencies – which she thinks are worryingly antisocial, even though she's lived on her own for decades – and deep satisfaction that I forgot to attend Ottoline when I'd been summoned.

'You drunk?' she says instead, smiling. It looks almost affectionate, though it might be the light.

'A little bit,' I say, sitting down on the rug in front of the fireplace. 'I walked to the pub in the village. Felt like

I needed a break, having been back here for five minutes.'

I see her decide not to rise to that one. I still know all her faces, just as she knows mine.

'See anyone interesting?' she says, and I wonder if she's making conversation or if she means Warner – a little barb about my ulterior motives here.

I shake my head. 'Only the Hooray Henrys.' I couldn't honestly say whether I'm lying by omission because I feel disloyal for poking around, or out of habitual contrariness.

'Oh, Christ – them,' she says, rolling her eyes. 'More middle names between them than brain cells.'

I laugh and she grins. It takes ten years off her. It won't last, this ceasefire, but it's nice in the moment, like Christmas Day football in no man's land.

'Caleb came back in February, I think it was,' she says, 'to answer your question. Though he's not always around. He comes and goes, sometimes for a week at a time, who knows where? He's got this VW campervan, not new but it's been done up inside. No doubt his mother footed the bill for that.' She sniffs.

'What's he like these days, Caleb? Has Sweden mellowed him?'

'Don't know about mellow. He's grown into his looks, though.' She gives me a sly smile I decide to ignore. 'You'll see what I mean.'

'Was he around when . . .?'

Angie nods.

'So I guess the police talked to him, too?'

'I can't imagine that they didn't. Not if that Harkin madam had anything to do with it.'

'Well, she doesn't know about Lennie, does she?'

Angie shrugs. 'I s'pose. Caleb's probably pretty well hidden up on the ridge.' She pushes herself up into a sitting position. 'How was Karl when you saw him?'

'I talked to him a bit about this new version of the Gathering. He assumed I was talking about that when I tried to bring up Willow. It's like he's blanked the whole thing out.' *It's like everyone has*, I resist adding.

'Well, that's how he copes with difficult things, isn't it?' Angie is saying. 'He's always been the same. Has to shut down to keep the hurt at bay. And, to be honest, I don't know how strong the connection was between him and Willow anyway. No disrespect to the dead, but I think he was beginning to move on, spiritually.'

I open my mouth to say something scathing, then close it again. Exhaustion is beginning to roll over me in waves and, besides, I don't want to ruffle the cottage's peaceful atmosphere. It's easy to remember the bad stuff, but it wasn't always like that. Sometimes it was easy, comfortable, like we were on the same side, especially when I was younger. It feels a bit like that now. Like home, I guess.

I go up to bed before it can go wrong, and when I come downstairs a little later, suddenly thirsty for a glass of the cold tap water that tastes better here than anywhere else, Angie has fallen asleep on the sofa, book splayed open on her chest, mouth slightly open. She'll be snoring soon.

I shake out the old patchwork quilt I associate with every childhood illness I ever had and reluctantly recall Angie bringing me soup. As I tuck it in around her, I pray she won't wake up and catch me at it. She won't remember she didn't do it herself by morning; the bottle of red on the side is empty, her lips blackberry-dark.

It's mainly drink, these days, and probably the odd spliff with Karl, if he really is still visiting with any regularity. I'm pretty sure the days of the more hardcore stuff are over. Angie claims they are.

As a child, you don't understand addiction. Especially in a place like Tanglewood, where the baseline of what's considered normal is already skewed. I was thirteen when Angie stopped trying to hide it from me. Or maybe she just sank further into it and couldn't keep up appearances any more. And because there's never any in-between with her, she went from being this all-powerful goddess I felt entirely safe with to this creature I hardly recognized, whose great needfulness only ballooned as the years went by. Eventually, I began marking off the days until I could leave for university on a hand-drawn calendar. I started it even before I'd picked my A levels, like I was approaching the last two years of a prison stretch.

I never showed it to her. It wasn't like I had it scratched into my bedroom wall. I don't think I've ever been deliberately cruel to her. But she found it one day, going through my stuff when I was up at the manor. She didn't rage at me, as I would have expected. Instead she turned mean and chilly, like Caleb did that time.

I had to leave her to save myself, and I don't think she's ever forgiven me for that. But then again, I don't think I've ever forgiven her for letting me see behind the curtain of who she really is. Fallible and selfish, someone who chose drugs and drink and undeserving men over her child.

But tonight I don't feel like raking that up. It's been a long time since I glimpsed the old Angie and I'm tired enough to let everything go for a while, tired enough to sleep, even. The strange guilt and fear I thought I saw on her face earlier tries to worm its way back in but I slam the door on it. The night air steals in through the open windows, cool green fingers slowing my thoughts and my heart.

Chapter Twelve

Tuesday

I was so exhausted by the time I got to bed that I had high hopes of sleeping and maybe I did, for a while. But there's no denying that my first night back at Tanglewood was a long one. I'm not a wanderer as an insomniac, flitting around the house dusting or eating cereal straight from the box. I don't know whether it's optimism or masochism that keeps me stubbornly in bed but, most nights, I don't even turn on the light and read. I lie there ruminating in the dark, slipping uneasily in and out of daydreams and, on the particularly bad nights, spiralling down towards cold black doom.

There wasn't much of that this time, to be fair, considering where I was. It was actually a half-decent night by my low standards. I spent it combing the past for treasure, by which I mean anything that could constitute a memory I haven't had in the banks for ever. I went over the vision of Graham Warner that hit me like a brick in the dark after the pub, though not so much that it would get dog-eared and fuzzy and I would start to doubt that it was real. I lay there under the striped duvet of my childhood, fine with age and a thousand launderette trips, and willed more memories to come. They didn't. Eventually, I gave up and thought some more about whether it was conceivable for two women to die in similar circumstances almost exactly thirty years apart and it *not* be suspicious, all the while resisting the temptation to pull back the curtains and check for nuns.

I'd forgotten how slowly the dawn reaches the cottage, even in high summer. The steep escarpment does a thorough job of blocking the eastern sky, so when the sun does arrive, it's more of a sidling-in on tiptoe, a gradual brightening of the slope opposite until the greens are dialled up to eleven and light finally pierces the thin curtains in narrow shafts. It's nearly eight by the time I blink out of the shallow doze that found me about three hours earlier.

I'll ring Dan back today, I think, as I swing my legs out of bed. Even as the resolution takes shape, I know I probably won't. Even as the documentarian in me knows that what's happened here – now and thirty years ago – is great material, the rest of me wants to keep it private. I want answers, but not for Dan.

I'm quiet on the stairs – I still know every creak – though an earthquake would struggle to rouse Angie before ten. The water I drink straight from the tap is teeth-achingly cold, and I follow it up with a banana, eaten on my feet in four bites. If I don't head out quickly, I'll change my mind.

I know exactly where I'll find Caleb's campervan. As soon as Karl said it, I could picture the glade among the beeches that forms a natural campsite, complete with its own spectacular view across the rolling valley. It's not as steeply dramatic as the one from Ottoline's windows, but it's bucolic enough. There isn't a single telegraph pole to indicate that the last couple of centuries have even happened, and I'm guessing that will appeal to someone who's spent the last few years in the back of the Swedish beyond.

I smell smoke before I see anything. Not tobacco or weed but good old-fashioned woodsmoke. Caleb must be awake and making breakfast. There's no other reason to bother with a fire, the morning air already as warm as a bath.

I become aware that I'm approaching like an assassin and make myself walk normally, so that twigs snap and give him some warning. It must work because when I get into the clearing, he's already on his feet and looking in my direction, body as tensed and alert as an animal's.

There's a beat as he processes who I am and I wait, trying to read the weather of his expressions, expecting irritation and dislike but getting something that looks suspiciously like pleasant surprise.

'Holy shit, it's you,' he says, getting to his feet. 'I thought it was Dad back again.'

You. It's weirdly intimate. He hasn't seen me for years.

'It is me,' I say, like an idiot.

He steps towards me, arms lifting as though he's going to pull me in for a hug, but then he stops, and I wonder whether something in my face changed his mind. I try to recall if we've ever touched, at least on purpose, but all I can think about is Angie saying how he'd grown into his looks.

He's got Karl's blue-blue eyes and dangerous smile, but otherwise the full-grown Caleb standing in front of me is a genetic arrow fired straight down the line from

Ottoline's side. Where Karl was slight even in his prime, Caleb is broad-shouldered and long-limbed, like the old photographs of men in army uniform and cricket whites at the manor. But the change in him is more profound than just looks. There's an openness that wasn't there before. That guarded suspicion, the readiness to lash out – all of it seems to have dissipated with the years.

'It's been a while,' he says, and we smile at the understatement.

'I was trying to work out exactly how long,' I say. 'I think it might have been at the pub back when you'd . . . When I was at uni. We had a spat about our mothers.'

He closes his eyes briefly. 'Oh, God, yes. I remember that. I was revolting back then, wasn't I? I hated everyone and everything. I blame the acne. And that bloody boarding school. But that wasn't the last time, actually. There was a Christmas a few years later.'

I frown, trying to retrieve it, but my brain offers up nothing.

'You'd graduated and moved to London by then,' he says. 'There was a boyfriend who was going to come but then didn't, for some reason. I remember that.' He looks at me, nose screwed up bashfully, which I assume is a Karl-style contrivance until I notice the slight flush along his cheekbones. 'My mother did the full works on Boxing Day, enough food to feed the five thousand and all that, and you were there in this big red jumper, sleeves pulled over your hands.'

'Impressive recall,' I say, and it comes out sarky because I'm embarrassed. 'I loved that jumper. I wore it into holes. Had to chuck it away in the end.'

He looks down, scuffs his boot in the earth. 'The reason I remember it so clearly is because I was working myself up to apologize to you for being such a shit before.'

'Well, I'm guessing you didn't because, no offence, I don't even remember you even being there, let alone any apology.'

'Yeah, I did my thing of retreating into the shadows. Bottled it, basically.' He grins. 'You looked pretty fearsome as it was, but then I spotted Angie. The combination scared me off.'

'God, that's right, she *was* there. Only to freak me out, of course.'

Now that I've grasped it, I can remember it in excruciating detail. I'd been winding her up, saying she was intimidated by the county set who were coming to Ottoline's parties by then, and she'd decided she'd show me she wasn't.

I don't think I breathed properly the whole time we were there. I was just waiting for her to do something awful – get so drunk that she called someone a Tory bastard or take off her clothes. Instead, she held court with the crusties next to the bar, banging on about Thatcher while she drank Ottoline's champagne. If she hadn't been my mum, I would probably have admired her nerve. But she was, and I wanted to die.

In the end, I pretended I'd got my period and that it was a bad one. It was rare I ever gave her the chance to nurse me – for so long it had been the other way round – and I knew she'd be unable to resist. Sure enough, she took me straight back to the cottage, the ordeal at the manor over.

'Anyway, it wasn't just you,' Caleb is saying. 'I don't think anyone really noticed me. I've always been good at keeping a low profile. And I don't like big crowds, can never think of anything to say.'

'Not an ideal place to grow up, then.'

He laughs. 'No. Hence the cabin in the Swedish wilderness. I needed a decade of decompression by that point.'

'But you're here now. Angie said you came back in February.'

'I wasn't planning to stay long. But then . . .' He breaks off, looks out across the valley. In the clear light, I can see that his eyes are different from Karl's after all. Caleb's are paler, with narrow navy rims that make them even more arresting.

'But then the old Tanglewood spell worked its magic,' I say.

He turns back to me, rubs his chin. 'Yeah, looks like it. You'd better tread carefully or it'll get hold of you, too.'

I reach up and pull my ponytail tighter. 'Nah, I'm immune these days. Shook that habit years ago.'

'Shame,' he says. 'It'd be nice to have some company round here. Relatively sane company, I mean.' He gestures towards the fire, the battered metal kettle he's propped over it. 'Do you want a coffee? I was just making some.'

I start to shake my head, find myself saying yes instead.

'I hear you're producing documentaries these days,' he says, when the coffee's ready. It's surprisingly good. He's brushed off a log to sit on, having given me the one camping chair.

'I was a runner for one of the big film studios for a while, but it's impossible to do that for long unless you can live rent-free in London. Or there's a handy trust fund to dip into.' I take a burning too-big gulp of coffee because I didn't mean it like that. I didn't mean him. I have no idea what money he gets from the estate, though I've heard Angie speculate enough about it.

'I'm sure my parents would have helped you out,' he says, and there's no edge to his voice.

'Yes, maybe, but . . .' I trail off.

He lifts his chin. 'I get it. Whatever Dad says to the contrary, I've also got my pride about taking money from them.'

'Yes, but you're their son. Their only child. That's different.' The unspoken rest of it swirls in the air, glitter motes in the wood smoke. Not just Caroline, but my own beginnings. It's surely somewhere between unlikely and impossible that Caleb has never wondered if I'm Karl's too.

'So, have you come back for the Gathering or because of what happened to Willow?' He gives me a sad smile to soften it.

'I'm so sorry about that. It was a shock to see it in the papers. Did you know her?'

'Yeah. I wasn't here when it happened. I'd gone up to Edinburgh to see old friends.'

'I'm back because my boss Dan wanted me to cover the Gathering this weekend,' I say. 'To be honest, he knew I was from around here but I never told him about growing up on the estate.'

'Yeah, I don't tell people either.' He gives me a rueful smile. 'It's just easier not to, isn't it?'

'Dan's been working on this documentary about the

whole scene that Tanglewood was on the periphery of at the end of the sixties. It's virtually finished, but when he saw the news about Willow and it mentioned the Gathering being resurrected, he thought it might make an interesting extra segment – something more current. He'd have come himself but he's out in the States on another project. I mentioned doing an interview to your dad and he seemed amenable. Of course, I also wanted to check everyone was okay.' It sounds inadequate but Caleb is just looking thoughtful.

'I'd be lying if I said the parallels between what happened to Willow and what supposedly also happened in 1970 weren't the kind of thing documentary makers dream of,' I go on. 'The kind of thing my boss dreams of, anyway.' I stop when I see he's gazing at me blankly. 'Ah. You haven't read yesterday's *Daily Mail* then.'

He gestures around at the trees. 'I'm not sure I'd know the world was about to end up here, which is kind of deliberate.'

I blow out a breath. 'Do you remember they were planning to make a documentary about the Gathering in 1970 but it never got finished?'

Caleb raises his eyebrows. 'Blimey, that's going back. I must have been, what, six? I do remember bits about that Gathering, probably because it ended up being the last. I've got this memory of the stage being built in the woods.' He smiles. 'I loved all that – typical boy. And I remember waking up at dawn and the music was *still* going.

'I'd forgotten about the documentary, though, and I don't think I've ever heard Dad mention it. I do remember the cameras. If there were gadgets and tools involved, I was into it. One of the camera guys let me hold his boom mike.'

I sigh. 'Well, one of those camera guys went to the papers when he heard Willow had died. He's saying the same thing happened back then – that it was him who found her, just like the gardener found Willow this time. That's what I mean by parallels.'

'Jesus, I thought you were going to say there was a puff piece in there. Some well-placed PR for this *Y2K Gathering*.' He does air quotes. 'Not that someone else died. That's awful.' He glances sideways at me. 'Is it definitely true?'

'Angie says he's made it up, but the police came round yesterday to ask about it, so they obviously haven't completely discounted it as a possibility.'

I watch Caleb carefully but he seems genuinely shocked. 'So, who was this woman before, then?'

'Her name was Astrid.'

He frowns, eyes on his boots. 'I mean, that might ring a bell but it's kind of one of those names, isn't it? There were hundreds of people here that year. It felt like an invasion. God only knows how big those events would have got if they hadn't stopped.' He looks up. 'Do you think that's why they did? And why the documentary basically came to nothing?'

I shrug. 'Maybe.'

'In as much as I've ever thought about it all, I assumed my dad had a tantrum. Changed his mind about people trampling all over the place. You know what he's like: he wants the attention, the adulation, but it has to be absolutely on his terms. Without the Astrid element, I would've guessed the documentary was canned because he lost his rag with someone. That it was just another Karl Lund bust-up.' For the first time, something of the old Caleb surfaces, bitterness set cold and hard in his face, but then it's gone, and I can't see anything but sadness.

'I guess it could be a coincidence,' he says, after a while. 'I mean, if the Astrid thing is even true. We both know now that it was a druggy scene here back in the day.'

He gives me a look and I will him not to say anything about Angie. It's not like I need reminding.

'And Willow liked a bit of a smoke,' he goes on. 'She might have dabbled with other stuff.'

'Yes, but the thing is, the similarities are more specific than that. They were dressed the same, in long white dresses, and wearing these flower crowns.' I think about the trails of dried blood on their faces but can't quite bear to say it aloud.

'That's seriously weird,' says Caleb.

'It's not just me being sensationalist, is it?' I say. 'It's a stretch thinking *that* could be a coincidence, surely.'

He doesn't say anything. He's probably trying to find logical answers that would explain this away, just as I have.

'Did you know Willow well?' I say, after a while.

Something complicated crosses his face. 'Not that well,' he says eventually. 'I mean, she tried.' He catches my expression. 'Oh, God, I don't mean she was after me or something. We weren't exactly each other's type, to be honest. I got put off the woo-woo ones a long time ago.' He spreads his hands. 'That sounds insensitive. I just mean she was a really open sort of person and expected everyone else to be. In a good way. She was really friendly and . . . spirited. Interested in everyone's story. But it felt weird to be friends.' He looks up at me, tries and fails to smile. 'I mean, she was sleeping with my dad. Only my mother goes along with that game.'

Angie hovers in the air between us again, or at least her peculiar status at Tanglewood does. Sometimes I see it afresh, like a stranger would, and it makes me cringe. Why did she want to stay here, as second best? Why has Ottoline allowed it all these years? You don't think to question these things as a kid. But now . . .

'If we take Astrid out of the equation for a minute, I honestly thought something just went wrong for Willow,' he says, changing the subject back, to my relief. 'I thought it was an accidental overdose.'

'Angie said she mixed things. That she wasn't . . . careful.'

He sighs. 'That's a fair assessment. I don't think she drank that much but I'm not sure anything else was off-limits. Dad's been *researching* hallucinogens for a few years now, and Willow was really interested in that.' He rolls his eyes. 'And there are mushrooms here, too – if you know where to look. I reckon it'll turn out to be something like that, maybe on top of a bad pill.'

'Not suicide?'

'No,' he says, and he's definite. 'She seemed pretty happy-go-lucky.'

'Sometimes the mask can be really convincing.'

'No, honestly. She was – and this is going to sound a bit *far out, man*, which I'm basically allergic to – but she had this energy about her. If I believed in auras, which I totally don't, despite my childhood's best efforts, hers would have been all, I dunno, sparky or like fireworks. And anyway, there's Lennie. She wouldn't have left her.' He glances up at me, smiles properly. 'Have you met Lennie yet? She's a sweetheart.'

'We went for a walk in the woods yesterday. She seems to be coping really well. I wondered if . . .'

'She was coping too well?' Caleb swirls the dregs of his coffee around. 'Yeah, I've wondered that too. I'm not sure my mother's left her any room for grieving.' He frowns again. 'I'm just speculating about her mum, really. What she might or might not have been taking. None of that stuff is my bag.'

I give him a half-smile. I know what he's leaving unsaid because it's my own experience, too. We've rebelled against our parents in the same way, Caleb and I. By staying firmly on the rails, give or take the odd vodka-tonic blackout in my case. Or, as Angie would probably have it, by being repressed and uptight, tragically closed to experience and expanding our minds.

I say no to a second coffee, and as I'm walking back down the path, sunlight speckling the roots and fallen branches like scattered pennies, I know that I mainly refused because I wanted to stay. It's become habitual for me to pull away when I feel like that. I glance back, but I can't see Caleb's encampment now. The beeches have closed ranks around him.

It's a strange comfort to find someone in such a similar position to me; someone who was also here in 1970 but apparently as much in the dark about what might have gone on as I am. When I told him about the coincidences between Willow and Astrid, his shock was genuine.

Other than his obvious contempt for Karl, Caleb seems completely changed. I can't put him and the teenaged version together and make the same person at all. And though I really like him, the suspicious little voice that always pipes up inside my head when I'm drawn to people reminds me that, despite everything we've got in common, maybe even half our DNA, I don't know Caleb. Not any more. I don't know him at all.

Chapter Thirteen

Angie is in the garden when I get back, doing something ineffectual with secateurs to a blowsy hydrangea.

'You're up early,' I say.

She nods towards the open cottage door. 'Someone's here for you. Woke me up knocking on the door.'

Graham Warner is the first possibility my mind goes to after last night, but there's no way Angie would be so unruffled if it was him. And that rules out DI Harkin, too.

She's sitting in the battered old carver's chair at the head of the kitchen table, her hands clasped around a mug of tea that's not much smaller than her head.

'Lennie,' I say. 'This is a nice surprise. What're you drinking?'

'Ginger and turmeric.'

'Is it nice?'

She regards her mug. 'It's like pond water but . . . spicy.'

I laugh, pour myself a glass of water and join her at the table. Someone, presumably Ottoline, has redone her plait and the dusty light shows up all its different colours: palest gold, silver and mink. Whoever her father was, she inherited her colouring from him. Willow was much darker – all those burnished red strands in her hair in the photograph, and the brown eyes, like mine and Angie's. As I said before, Karl has a type.

'I've just been up to see Caleb,' I say. 'We haven't seen

each other for a long, long time. We were kids together here, about a hundred years ago.'

'How old *are* you?' she says, in what I'm starting to gather is her usual frank way.

'Thirty-eight.' I can never reconcile the number with how I feel inside. I haven't been able to for at least ten years.

She rubs her nose – her fingers are filthy. There are marks on her faded T-shirt too. 'You don't seem it. That's five years older than my mum.'

I open my mouth to say something about that because, again, I feel like I really ought to: Lennie is just too okay about this. Which sounds as if I'd rather she was crying, which is obviously not the case. It's just that I don't want her to be on her best behaviour with everyone, if that's what this is. I hate the thought that she's keeping everything bottled up tight inside her, just so that no one thinks she's any trouble. She's too young to be making that sort of calculation and I would know. But before I have a chance to choose my words, she's talking again.

'I like Caleb. I went up to his camp when it was the solstice and we put marshmallows on sticks. Then we held them over the fire till they went all melted and stretchy.'

'You, him and your mum?'

'Just me that time. I had the pink ones and he had the white ones. Mum didn't come because Karl wanted her to go to the studio and listen to his music.'

'Right.'

'That's exactly what Caleb said, too, funnily enough.' She takes a sip of her tea and swings her legs, making the table judder slightly.

'We'd better make sure we've given your hands a wash

before you go back to the manor,' I say. 'What have you been doing? Digging?'

She holds them up, studies them, face intent. 'I went back to our bus to check on my seeds. There was dirt everywhere.' Her voice cracks on the last syllable but she heaves a big breath, gets hold of herself. The effort hurts me to watch. Her big grey eyes fix on the window, unseeing and shiny with tears that don't quite spill.

I suddenly work out what she means. 'The police. They must have fingerprinted it. Was it a black dust?'

She nods and swallows, blinking fast, while I wait for her, pretending to be interested in my glass of water. It takes a while.

'Ottoline said last week that I mustn't go there but I *had* to,' she manages to say, after a while. 'The seeds have to be watered or they'll die.'

The word comes out strangled.

'Of course,' I say. 'Were they all right?'

Her face clears slightly. 'Yes, I think so. There was a shoot on one of them. But . . .' A tear finally spills over. She swipes at it, leaving a smudge on her cheek, which nearly sends me over the edge.

When I reach over to lay my hand on hers, I expect her to pull away. I would have done, when I was her age. But she doesn't. 'What were you going to say?'

'I ran away before I got the water. It felt funny in there. Like the air was too thick. I didn't like it. So I ran. Came here.'

'Do you want me to go and do it? Or we'll both go together and you can show me?'

Her head snaps up at that. 'Can we? Can we go today?'

'We can go right now, if you like.'

She smiles then, and it lights her up so that she's suddenly golden among the slow-spinning dust motes.

The day is shaping up to be another hot one. The blue of the sky above the valley slopes is already deep and true. Once your eyes tune into it, life is everywhere, the air full of tiny specks of insects, the grass trembling with unseen creatures.

The bus is parked in a dead-end cut-through among the sparse trees behind the house. If the manor were a stately home open to the public, this would be where they built the toilet block. The bus is entirely what I pictured it would be: a dilapidated old double-decker painted in swirls of faded rainbow colours, CND stickers peeling off the windows and wind chimes hanging from one of the wing-mirrors. There's no discernible breeze today but they're still tinkling restlessly enough to set my teeth on edge. Above the windscreen, the old destination board is stuck on *Golders Green.*

I become aware that Lennie is sneaking looks at me so I arrange my face into a smile. 'Did you really live in here? That must have been amazing.'

She nods, pleased. 'Yes, it is. It doesn't go over forty-five but that doesn't really matter because we don't move often. Once, we broke down on the M4, but a man came and towed it for free. Me and Mum sat up with him on the front seat of his truck and he gave us a pasty to share. I was scared the rope would break or that the bus would turn over when we went round corners, and that all our stuff would fall off and smash, but thankfully it was okay.'

It smells of Willow inside – or what I presume was her, the scent much too womanly to be Lennie's. Jasmine and something warm and amber-y. Underneath it, dimly, there are notes of burnt rubber and vinyl seating, curling sandwiches and sherbet Dip-Dabs, ghostly vestiges of the bus's formative days, trundling up and down the streets of north London carrying old ladies and schoolboys.

'We probably shouldn't clean off the dust just yet,' I say. 'Not until the police say we can. But when they do, I'll help you, okay?'

'Yes, but you mustn't say about me to the police. It's a secret. Otherwise they'll take me away. We had to carry my stuff to the manor so they wouldn't guess there was a child.' She shrugs her small shoulders. 'The seeds were okay to be left. They're a hobby for any age.'

'Did Ottoline tell you to keep everything secret?'

She nods, and fills a mug with water, which is down to a trickle by the time it reaches the top, the tank Willow must have kept filled now running dry. I watch Lennie attend to her little flowerpots of seeds, which are arranged in a line behind the sink. In fact, two now have shoots. This corner of Tanglewood might not have a view but it still gets the morning sun, the air of the bus already as warm and close as that in a greenhouse.

'I tell you what, why don't we . . .' I stop.

'Go on,' she says, sounding strangely old for her age, as I'm starting to understand she often does.

'Well, I was thinking we could take them back to Angie's cottage. It might be easier to keep an eye on them there.'

She looks around the bus, and I see what she meant

about the air in here. It sounds fanciful but, in that moment, it feels like it's swirling thickly with memories. All the years Lennie spent with Willow here, the in-jokes and routines that won't mean anything to anyone but Lennie now. She shouldn't be old enough to understand that, without warning, an era of her life is over. But she does, I just know it.

'Don't worry,' I say, as lightly as I can manage, 'it's a daft idea. It's just as easy to come here and water them. It's probably nearer the manor actually, and—'

'No.' She cuts me off. 'Let's take them. They're safer if they're with you and Angie. And it's only four minutes to your cottage if I run. I timed it.'

Outside the bus, I stand there clutching half of the pots while Lennie checks the door is properly closed. There's no lock, of course, only a makeshift hook and eye on the inside. When she's satisfied, she pats the door, small hand lingering on the dusty glass. Then she retrieves the pots she'd put down carefully on the ground and sets off, back towards the main path. She doesn't look back.

1970

It's American Independence Day tomorrow, when the Gathering will reach its Saturday-evening climax with the first showcase of Karl's new album, ahead of its commercial release on Monday. The Gatherings, which have grown exponentially over the last few years, have always been held around this time of year, but the fact that this one landed on the Fourth of July seemed particularly auspicious. *Lady of the Valley* is the first Karl Lund solo project.

He hasn't spoken to her since yesterday morning. She's barely even seen him. He's been busy, she knows, the evidence all around them, but she can't help suspecting he's found out about Graham on the grapevine.

She doesn't regret sleeping with him. It was sweet and tender between them in a way that took her by surprise. It was very different from how it is with Karl. But, still, she can't imagine Graham not telling someone afterwards. He's the least confident of the documentary men, as she thinks of them – the least certain of his place in the pecking order. She would have bought him some credit he might've been unable to resist cashing in.

People have already started to assemble in proper numbers now. There's a hum in the air that isn't coming only from the cars and vans crawling up the Dark Ride, or from the conversations between those who have already set up camp, who know each other from previous happenings like this one, though everyone agrees there's nowhere quite like Tanglewood – that there's nothing quite like the energy that seems to collect and intensify in the deep bowl of the valley here. No, it's that, already, anticipation is running through the place like a live wire. You can't exactly hear it in the air – it's beyond or perhaps beneath that. But you can definitely feel it, a current that sings in the blood.

She stands apart from the crowd in her favourite wine-red blouse, with its deep neckline and tassels strung with tiny silver bells. She hasn't decided exactly how she feels about this . . . this incursion, though, of course, she's only been here a few months. It's hard not to be infected by the hum, though the quality of that feels different today. Part of her, maybe most of her, is more uneasy than excited.

The wrong feeling began yesterday and she's been trying to visualize it in the hope that that might shrink its power. The closest she can get is a dank fog that has wrapped itself around her. Or a cold pebble of dread, right in the heart of her. Yes, that's getting nearer to it.

When it crept up on her yesterday, just as the daylight faded, she took something to chase it away. It seemed to make it worse, though: larger and colder. She's decided not to have anything today, even a drink, though the sharp clarity of this new sobriety is tricky in its own way. She keeps flinching when people get too close.

She catches sight of Graham in the distance, standing with the bearded director. They're talking to a trio of women who have just arrived in a battered yellow Mini. Their hair shines in the sun. They look at ease, as light as air. As if they've never been gripped by a frightening thought in their lives.

She's been avoiding Graham. Just as she'd predicted, he was the intense type, who looked at her like he was falling in love within hours of meeting her. She thinks he might even have muttered it, when they were having sex in the woods, when he was close, although that never means much with a man in that state.

Right now, though? Right now, she wishes he would spot her standing alone and come over. It would be nice to have someone take her mind off the way the pebble is turning over and over inside her, the way the beat of someone's drumming fifty feet away is making her teeth itch.

She hasn't even glimpsed Karl yet today and, though she's been telling herself that he's the sole source of her unease, she's got this feeling – growing by the minute – that something bigger than him is barrelling towards her.

She's well aware of the pattern that forms in her relationships with men. The groove she finds herself stuck in again and again, like the needle skipping on a record.

Karl would appreciate this analogy more than most. He would also be insulted by it – not only because of its implied criticism of him, but because it would remind him that he's not her first, that there were men in her bed before him. The fairy-queen persona he's given her is a double-edged sword. She loves that he sees her like that, just as she knows she can never live up to the unearthly expectation of it.

It was his idea to change her name, and she was glad to. The one on her birth certificate had been her mother's choice, and getting rid of it felt like cutting the final string. She still misses her father, still writes him postcards she can't send, just as she did when he died, but the rest of it? No. She wouldn't go back for anything. She came up with the new name herself: Astrid, meaning 'star'.

'A little bird told me something about you.'

She jumps. She's been looking out for Karl all day and now he's suddenly right next to her, smiling, but coldly. He follows the direction of where her gaze just was, and her breath hitches in her chest. Graham's fair hair is so bright in the sun.

‘I thought I knew that girl,’ she says, too fast. ‘The redhead by the Mini.’

‘Yeah?’ he says, playing along, shielding his eyes against the sunlight, pretending to assess her properly. ‘She looks pretty cool. You know what they say about girls with red hair. Maybe you can introduce us.’ He looks back at Astrid, mouth twisting into a smirk, and reaches for her hand. She’s wearing a silver ring he gave her, like a tiny wreath of woven branches, and it hurts her fingers as he squeezes them together.

‘Ain’t you gonna ask what I heard?’ It rarely augurs well when Karl sounds more American.

‘Where’ve you been?’ she says, as lightly as she can, reaching out with her other hand to stroke his collarbone. ‘I’ve missed you.’ This had worked for her once before, gliding past an accusation as though she simply hadn’t heard it.

‘Have you? Missed me? I’m not so sure.’

He adjusts his grip so he’s got hold of her wrist. Her silver bangles tinkle, as if in alarm.

‘You shouldna done what you did,’ he says close to her ear, breath hot and whisky-sour. ‘You’re gonna make it up to me.’

Chapter Fourteen

I don't even hear the car until it's nearly upon us. I say *us*; when I turn to Lennie to warn her that it's DI Harkin – apparently already complicit in Ottoline's conspiracy of secrecy and deciding I'm comfortable with it – I find I'm already alone.

It's uncanny, actually, how quickly she vanishes – absorbed into the green velvet folds of the valley as if she was never there. As if she knows all the places where time has worn thin enough to slip through.

Meanwhile, Harkin has pulled up and is already out of the car, hand raised in greeting. 'I was hoping to catch you,' she calls, a choice of phrase that brings handcuffs to mind, and is probably deliberate. Still, she seems laser-focused on me as she approaches, which must mean she didn't catch sight of Lennie.

'I think I mentioned yesterday, I'm not sure I'm going to be much help to you,' I say, spreading my hands. 'I wasn't even here.'

She smiles. 'But you're here now. And apparently you were deep in conversation with Graham Warner at the pub last night. I find that quite interesting.'

There's a painful pause until I remember I can speak to whom I want, that I really did have nothing to do with whatever happened to Willow Green. The lie of omission about Lennie is clouding my sense of logic.

'There's nothing very strange about that, I'm afraid,' I say, normally enough. 'I went for a walk and ended up at the pub. Graham and I got talking at the bar. It wasn't like I sought him out. He was standing there, looking around hopefully for people before his fifteen minutes of fame ran out.'

'Oh, sure,' she says, waving her hand dismissively. 'It's just that when you put that together with your documentary-making . . .' She lets that settle, looking thoughtfully into the middle distance.

My mind whirs: did someone on the estate tell her what I do for a living? Did I, when she came to the cottage and I was still half asleep? I don't think so. Maybe she's looked me up on some database.

'It made me wonder if you were starting up your own investigation into Warner's allegations,' she continues, 'because that really wouldn't be advisable right now.'

She tips her head on one side, eyes me shrewdly. 'I guess it was the 1970 documentary that inspired you to go into your line of work in the first place. Was it?'

'I don't know. Maybe.' It comes out too fast and too defensively, making my cheeks flare, helpfully.

'And yet you can't remember anything about that summer. Funny to be inspired by something you didn't even know about.'

My cheeks heat again. It's obvious now, where she's leading me. 'I did know about it. I just don't remember it. I'm not making that up. I wish I could remember, and the years before, too. So, actually, if something did put me on that career path, it was probably the *not*-remembering – as opposed to some dark secret I'm inexplicably keeping from when I was eight years old.'

She looks sceptical but I push on, even as my internal voice tells me to *stop talking*.

'With documentary-making we have to gather evidence, piece things together, try to make objective sense of something for people who weren't there. It's not that different from what you do, really.'

I'm rewarded with a little smile. 'Okay, fair enough. And I get that you were a hundred miles away when Ms Green died. She's my priority here but, as I said before to you and your mum, we've still got to look into Graham Warner's claims. While I do that, I don't need you muddying the waters on the side.

'I can totally see the appeal from your point of view if he *is* telling the truth: two dead women, found in eerily similar circumstances thirty years apart. An old, unfinished documentary that may hold some of the answers, if only the footage could be found. I mean, a *new* documentary about all that, plus an opportunity to film at this gathering thing on Saturday?' She spreads her hands wide. 'Sounds pretty hooky to me.'

I make myself sigh. 'I *am* going to stay on this weekend. It would be daft not to cover it when my boss has been working for ages on something about a music scene that Karl Lund was part of. It might make it in as a short segment or it might not. But as soon as that's done, I'll be heading back to London.'

'It's a juicy angle, though, isn't it?' Her voice is soft, coaxing. 'You've got to admit it. Adds to the sex, drugs and rock 'n' roll vibe. I mean, I'd put it in if it was my documentary. But I can see that might be tricky for you. All very close to home, isn't it? It's clear your mum isn't happy reliving old times. What about you?'

I can feel every one of the minutes I didn't sleep. 'Look, I'm here for the music. I'm keeping my own connections to this place out of it. I don't usually tell people I grew up here, strangely enough.'

Harkin looks puzzled. 'Why strangely enough? It's quite cool, isn't it, to have grown up in the middle of some cultural moment?'

I can't tell if she's being facetious. 'Not to me,' I say. 'That's all people see then, and I can't possibly live up to it. I'm not some hippie wild-child. I never was.' I gesture around me, at the valley's lush and traitorous beauty. 'I haven't been part of all this for a long time.'

Harkin doesn't take her eyes off me. 'And yet here you are now.'

'I've explained that. And, anyway, Angie's still my mother, even if she does drive me insane.'

She laughs, and it's a good one, open and easy. It makes my shoulders drop half an inch. 'Okay, I hear you. I'm fifteen again within five minutes of going home. Slamming doors within ten. It's comforting but it's also . . .' – she casts around for the right word – '. . . claustrophobic.'

'Yep.' I pause, wonder if it matters if I ask her something, then decide to do it anyway. 'So, does it look like there's any truth in what Warner's saying?'

Harkin's face turns serious again. She regards me, chin lifted, five tiny studs in her left ear catching the sun. 'Obviously this is off the record, in case you do go down that road, but there are some details he's told us about

1970 that match up with our present-day victim. Things he didn't hear from the gardener, and that we have kept back from the press. When you put them together, they're rather . . . striking.'

I wasn't expecting that kind of candour. My mouth has gone dry. 'What sort of details?'

'Obviously I can't go into that.'

'Presumably detectives don't really do coincidences.'

She smiles. 'Not this one.'

I stand there, gazing at the ground while my mind turns it all over. When I look up, she's halfway back to her car.

She turns before she gets in. 'No more digging around, please. Leave Graham Warner and those two women to me. Stick to the music, yeah? And if, in the meantime, a memory does happen to resurface, give me a call. You've got my card. I'm sure we can come to some agreement down the line if you leave us to it now, okay?'

Like Angie, she must be able to smell my interest in Willow and Astrid. She doesn't believe any documentary-maker worth their salt would be able to leave the unsettling mystery of them alone. I probably wouldn't either, in her shoes.

I watch her fold her long body into the sporty little Audi, the door closing with a *thunk* and the engine firing, gunshot-loud in the silent valley.

Chapter Fifteen

I wait a while after Harkin has driven away but Lennie doesn't emerge from any hiding place. She must have flitted back to the manor. I head downhill towards home – *Angie's cottage* – the birdsong so deafening that I can't tune it out. As well as a dozen crows screeching after a buzzard, a woodpecker is going hard at some unfortunate beech trunk, loud enough that it might as well be making a hole in my head.

My visits are so sporadic that I forget how strange the acoustics are in the valley. Karl always said it was a natural amphitheatre, but it's more than that. In some places sounds are thrown further than they should be, and are oddly absent in others, like the heavy-pressing quiet of the woods after I left Caleb.

Angie is no longer pottering in the garden where I left her. And the instant I take that in, the silence rushes back, as though the birds never existed. An image blooms in my mind, as vivid as the memory from last night, only it's not a memory this time, which makes it feel instead like a horrible premonition: Angie, collapsed on the faded old rag-rug on her bedroom floor, face waxen and still, lips blue.

I take the stairs two at a time, shouting her name, and almost fall through the doorway of her bedroom, I'm going so fast. She turns to me from where she's rooting through the drawers of her dressing-table, the rickety old stool groaning as her weight shifts, face slack with astonishment. For a second, I can't process that she's sitting up and apparently fine, though her half-done eyeliner – one side Cleopatra-dramatic, the other naked and small, mole-squinty in comparison – makes her look deranged.

'Bloody hellfire, Rain, you nearly gave me heart failure,' she says.

'I thought you had . . .' I tail off. 'I thought you were . . .'

'You thought I was what?'

I sit down heavily on the bed, my adrenaline-twitchy hands clutching at the rumpled layers of batik and blankets while I get my breath back and my wits together. The hot clashing colours and busy patterns, everything smelling faintly of *nag champa*, aren't helping. I close my eyes and picture my London bedroom with its Edwardian sash window overlooking neat stripes of lawn, everything inside it white, dove-grey and neat as a pin, from the plain cotton duvet pulled straight and smoothed carefully over the mattress to the hospital corners of the sheet underneath. Thinking about it when I'm here always calms me down.

'Rain?' Angie interrupts. 'What did you think I was?'

'It doesn't matter.'

'Well, it's me who should be in a state, anyway, not you. While you've been off gallivanting with Lennie, I've been fending off that bloody Harkin woman again.' She seems to catch sight of herself in the mirror and picks up a kohl pencil.

I notice then that her hand is as unsteady as it was yesterday – the combination of that and her sitting up at her dressing-table taking me straight back to the days when she would pair her morning routine with half a mug of gin.

I sigh. 'I saw her too. She didn't say she'd been here first.'

Angie's face sharpens in the mirror. 'What did she want with you?'

'Not a lot.'

She swallows. 'She was asking about my readings. Asking how often I did them, who my regulars were.'

'Your *tarot* readings? Why would she be asking about those? I didn't even know you still did them.'

Angie goes to shrug but it turns into an all-over shudder. 'Well, I told Harkin I didn't. And, to be honest, I don't very often these days, although Karl said he might want me to at the Gathering. Maybe auras, as well, though they were never really my forte.' She exhales shakily and puts down the kohl, which rolls off the dressing-table and lands on the bare boards with a clatter.

'Why did you say you don't do readings if you do?' I say.

She isn't listening. 'Do you think she was asking because I've always done it cash-in-hand? What was it she said about tax yesterday?'

'It won't be that,' I say. 'You've never earned enough to pay any tax.' I look around, something about the room snagging my eye. 'Where's the rag-rug gone?' I can still picture her lying on it, eyes closed, mouth turned that horrible blue, as though she'd been chewing a pen or packed under ice.

She waves her hand. 'Oh, I had to chuck it. Covered in slug trails. You could see them shining in the mornings.'

I close my eyes briefly, and when I open them she's

looking at me with a little smile. 'When you came rushing in, do you know what you were shouting?'

I don't answer. Now that my panic is wearing off, this tarot business is beginning to niggle at me.

'You were saying *Mum*.' She nods triumphantly. 'You were in such a state you forgot to call me Angie. Which made a nice change.' But then she frowns. 'Are you sure Harkin didn't say something to you about me?'

I pull the elastic out of my hair, rake my hands through it. It's hot and airless in the bedroom, and the back of my neck is damp. 'I just said she didn't mention you.' I blow out a long breath. 'I had a bad feeling, that's all. But it was obviously nothing.'

I see the moment the penny drops. 'Oh, God, you thought I was dead, didn't you?' She claps a hand to her breast. 'You thought I'd dropped dead.'

'But you haven't, have you? Clearly.'

She gets up and goes over to the wardrobe, flinging open the doors and kneeling with much creaking of joints, and starts going through the bottom, enormous backside the only visible part of her. 'I told her I hadn't done a reading in years,' she's saying, voice muffled by the swathes of clothes she's deep inside. The rail of harem pants and blanket ponchos and cheesecloth dresses sways. Dust billows. 'Said I didn't have the foggiest where the cards were. It's been so long that, for all I knew, they might have gone off to the charity shop last time I had a clear-out. Of course I knew full well they were in here somewhere, but I wasn't about to let on, not to the likes of her.'

'Why would you lie about that?' I try again. 'And why was she asking, anyway? Seems weird.'

She sits back on her haunches, cheeks red from her exertions, and puffs her hair off her forehead as she holds up the dark blue velvet pouch. I know it instantly. Inside is the tarot deck she's had for ever. Surprisingly, the pouch looks as good as new, the nap flawless and the drawstring bright white.

Even before she opens it and pulls out the cards, so carefully and reverently you'd have thought they were sentient, I can recall exactly what each of the major arcana cards looks like. My favourite as a child was the Knight of Swords. Not because of him but because of his galloping white horse, mane and pennant flying.

'So, why are you getting them out now, then?' I say. 'If she's gone?'

She pauses, and when she looks up at me, there's something in her eyes that reminds me of the bad old days. 'To do a reading, of course,' she says, after a beat. 'For myself. To see if what you had was a premonition. If my number's up next, I'd like to know about it. I always thought you had a touch of the sight. You're so bloody-mindedly resistant to all things alternative that you must have.'

I roll my eyes but I'm still wondering about Harkin. 'Did you ever tell the police you used to do readings?' I say. 'I don't mean Harkin, but the first lot who came here, just after Willow was found.'

'No,' she says. 'They didn't ask and I didn't tell them. Harkin just said it out of the blue today. Do you think . . . ?'

'What?'

But Angie shakes her head. 'Nothing. She's just got me in a flap, coming round again, that's all.'

'Maybe she made an assumption about the hippie

alternative woo-woo thing.' I'm trying to sound reassuring so Angie doesn't wind herself up to the ceiling. Possibly I'm trying to reassure myself, too, because Harkin wouldn't be making random enquiries for fun. She's obviously worked out some connection between Willow and tarot cards, though I can't imagine what. 'Let's face it,' I continue, gesturing at the textbook contents of the open wardrobe, the dreamcatcher over the bed, the huge, wobbly purple triskelion daubed on the low ceiling by a lodger she moved in during the winter I was twelve, doubtless to make Karl jealous, 'you tick all the other boxes.'

'Bloody cheek,' mutters Angie, but she's calmer now, her hands steadier as she shuffles the cards. The interwoven pattern on their backs – of green moons, oak leaves and wide-eyed hares – blurs as she gets into her rhythm. 'Shall I do you first, seeing as you're here?'

I stand, pull my hair into a ponytail again. 'No chance.'

She fans the cards, holds them up to me. From her position on the floor, she looks disconcertingly like some sort of penitent. 'Come on, don't rush off yet,' she says, with a smile that might or might not be sly. 'I know you're allergic to all this stuff. To me, really. But I've hardly seen you since you got back.'

For a fraction of a second, I'm tempted. The image of her lying there so bloodless and immobile will still be there if I close my eyes. But that's what's stopping me, too. I wouldn't let on to Angie for the world, but a daft part of me is worried that it *was* some sort of premonition. As I've often said before, no one emerges from a childhood like mine without being a bit nuts. And that part is disproportionately vocal when strange things are setting off my internal alarm bells. Right now, it's doing a pretty thorough job of drowning out the rational 95 per cent.

I don't trust those cards not to reveal something horrible, and not just *to* Angie. There's also the possibility of glimpsing a terrible thing she's *done* to someone else.

Chapter Sixteen

We have dinner together that night, Angie and I. She hasn't pushed the tarot thing again, though the cards sit on the table next to us like a third guest, or a beloved pet. She can't help glancing at them every so often, as though they've chipped in with an observation that only she can hear. In the end she didn't do a reading for herself, and I'm still wondering what that was all about – on Harkin's side and on Angie's. The latter is definitely keeping something back, too.

For my part, I resolutely ignore the tarot's presence, not easy when it's shimmering in my peripheral vision like something in the distance on a hot day. It's probably just the lack of sleep, though you think I'd be used to that. Anyway, Angie has apparently taken the hint, and I'm grateful for it.

I finish my second helping of sponge pudding and custard, both from tins and both delicious. She nods towards her own, hardly touched helping, but I shake my head. She's still preoccupied, then. Angie never leaves her pudding.

'You know you said to Harkin yesterday that Graham Warner was a fantasist?' I say. We've drunk a bottle of heavy red, which will probably seem like a bad idea in the morning.

'I knew it wouldn't take long before you started picking at that,' she says, reaching for her tobacco. 'If you're staying on here for research, does that mean I'm going to meet Dan? Is he good-looking? Is he a good snog?'

I've never told Angie about me and Dan. She just always seems to know these things.

'I keep wondering why he'd make it up,' I say, ignoring her.

'There doesn't have to be a why, if you're a fantasist,' she says. 'That's the whole bloody point.'

'Okay, then why stay round here? Why didn't he move on with his life unless he was . . . I don't know . . . *haunted* by something that happened to him that summer?'

'You sound like Harkin now.'

I'm still reluctant to mention I've seen Warner for myself, and that, whatever I thought of him, I don't think he'd invent Astrid from scratch. 'I guess if he can dig out some film of this woman, it would at least prove she existed,' I say eventually, rubbing at the wine ring my glass has left on the table. 'I mean, he *was* a cameraman. I guess he might have kept some footage.'

'It would only be his say-so, though, wouldn't it?' says Angie. 'He could be pointing out anyone and saying she was Astrid. It's interesting he doesn't even know her surname, isn't it? She was probably some bird he took a fancy to one night and she turned him down. He's spent the thirty years turning it into this big tragedy.'

I blink, wish I hadn't drunk anything. 'So you're saying there might have been someone called Astrid now?'

'I never said there wasn't.' Angie raises her chin. 'I didn't know every Tom, Dick and Jane who rocked up here, looking for a good time. All I said was that no woman called Astrid *died* here in 1970.'

'I'm sure you said . . .' But, actually, I'm not now. I try to think back but my usual insomniac brain-fog is conspiring against me with the wine and winning.

'Like I said to Harkin, the crew were indulging as much as the rest of us. Graham was only twenty or so, and pretty green. He didn't know his arse from his elbow with the technical stuff, either – he was learning on the job and probably being paid peanuts. I remember he was driving the director nuts, making mistakes when they were setting up ahead of everyone else arriving.' She looks thoughtful. 'I would've thought if anyone had kept any footage, it would have been him.'

'Who was the director? Did you know him, too?'

Angie taps her spoon on the oilcloth. 'God, what was his name? He was a funny bloke. Swarthy as a pirate, with his great big beard. Some of the girls thought he was sexy but I didn't like the cut of his jib. I said to them, I said, "Watch that one, he's cruel, he'll hurt you." I could always spot the ones with a sadistic streak.' She lights her cigarette.

I allow myself a glance at the tarot cards, which seem to be pulsing now. I cover them with a tea-towel, as subtly as I can. 'So, if you thought he might be dangerous, and you're saying there might have been someone called Astrid, isn't there a small chance that Warner is telling the truth and you just didn't know about it?'

Something complicated crosses her face. 'No way. There's nothing I don't know about this place.' She sighs. 'Look, let's not dwell on all that. It's so long ago and, whatever conspiracies Harkin is cooking up, there's nothing connecting back then with poor old Willow. Maybe she's hoping for a serial killer or something to make her name. Good luck to her in the bleedin' Cotswolds. She's not going to get another Fred and Rose in this part of the county. Aliens coming down to make crop circles in the middle of the night are more likely.'

She shuffles to the side and holds up a second bottle of red like a prize. 'Let's open another, shall we?'

I nod. I'm not going to figure any of this out tonight and, besides, I'm approaching the point when I'd agree to lots of things I wouldn't dream of sober. In the right mood, I quite like it. It's like letting go of the railings, enjoying the wind on your face on the way down. It's moments like this when I really feel like my mother's daughter.

While Angie does the honours with the corkscrew, I sit back in my chair and look around the kitchen, whose dimensions and shadows I know better than my own reflection in the mirror: the low lamplight cancelling out the sticky cooking-oil dust and clutter, the fragrant air stealing in from the twilit valley to overpower the ghosts of a hundred lentil stews past, one of Angie's less strident joss-sticks issuing a pencil-line of smoke into the air. The entire scene is so redolent of the summers before I turned cynical that it wouldn't take much for me to burst into tears.

'What were we talking about again?' Angie says, sitting down with audible relief and filling my glass to the brim.

'The director with the sadistic streak who would've had all the footage.'

'No, I said we should leave all that alone. Nothing to tell there. Come on, now you've let your hair down for once, let's give you a reading.'

She whips away the tea-towel and, in the soft light, I can see what Karl and the rest of them saw in her. Angie couldn't be boring if she tried. I've always assumed she's also just the right side of dangerous. That there's surely nothing mad lurking in those brown eyes, just hedonism and fun. *I-won't-tell-your-wife fun. I-won't-lose-the-plot fun.*

Go to bed, I tell myself, so forcefully that my lips move, forming the words, like someone who only reads when they're made to at school. But the wine is flowing freely in my blood, and I want some more. I pick up my glass, drink half of it. Dimly, it occurs to me that it feels oddly like Angie and I are playing poker, like we both have skin in the game, only I've never really known the rules.

'Can I ask one more question?' I say, in a last attempt to steer the conversation.

'Only if you let me do a reading.'

I exhale. 'Okay, fine. Do you promise you're telling me the truth about all this? Not the police, *me*?' I watch her closely, though I'm scared to see further signs of fear, like yesterday, or earlier, when she was pulling her room apart. I'm scared to see guilt.

She doesn't say anything or even move for so long that I think she's decided to ignore me. But then she looks me straight in the eye. 'I promise I'm telling you the truth,' she says. 'Right, now your side of the bargain.' She opens the velvet pouch.

'Well, hang on, I . . .'

'No, that was our deal. Now, ask a question while you give these a shuffle.' She holds out the cards.

I raise my hands. 'I don't have a question – not about me, anyway. This was your idea, remember.'

She rolls her eyes. 'Oh, come on. You know how it works. You don't have to say it out loud. Just think it. The cards'll hear you.'

I go to say something scathing about cards not being sentient and then realize she's winding me up, eyes glinting.

I knock back some wine and shuffle the cards inexpertly, refusing to make eye contact with Angie because part of me still worries, as I did when I was a child, that she's capable of reading my mind. I don't want to play this game and, anyway, any questions I have are about other people – chiefly Angie and what she knows but isn't letting on, despite her assurances. But then one appears in my head anyway, and so cleanly it's as if someone blew it into my ear. I concentrate on it as my fingers move more deftly through the cards.

It's simple enough, and ironically the title of one of Angie's favourite songs, one she used to like to blast out in the mornings to get her going after a particularly heavy night. *Should I stay or should I go?*

I hand back the cards and she lays them out in the Celtic Cross formation. Her rings flash as she turns over the first.

The Fool. Of course it is.

I bark out a hard laugh. 'Maybe there is something in this after all. I knew it was a bad idea coming back here. I should have told Dan to fuck off.'

Angie raises an eyebrow. 'So that *was* the main reason, then? I knew it. But, as for the cards, don't you think you might be being a bit literal?'

'I know the Fool means folly and I also know that the first card is about someone's current situation. I did take some of this stuff in, you know, whether I liked it or not. The question I asked was whether I should stay here longer or go back to London. How else am I supposed to take that?'

Angie fills my glass again. 'The Fool can also be interpreted as a return to somewhere old in order to embark on a fresh cycle there. An opportunity to begin a new phase.'

'How can anyone do that somewhere old? How can I begin a new phase *here*, of all places? It's absolutely heaving with ghosts from my past and everyone else's.'

'Best place, if you ask me,' she says. 'If you're always moving on to the next place, you never have to begin a new phase *yourself*, internally. You're just changing the scenery and pretending it's progress.'

She turns over the next card. 'Hmm.' She sits back in her chair.

It's the Six of Cups. I can't remember what it means. 'Do people pay you just to freak them out?' I say, when she still hasn't spoken after an interminable ten seconds.

She shakes her head, as though clearing it. 'It's all right. I wasn't expecting that but it actually ties in very nicely. The second card can reinforce the first and the Six of Cups is all about nostalgia.'

'So much for a new phase, then.'

She gives me a wry look. 'It's a lovely card, very positive. A big part of moving on is coming to terms with what's been. Maybe it's time you understood that it wasn't all bad, back then, here with me. Anyway, if ever there was a pair of cards telling someone not to go back to sodding London yet, these are the ones.'

I roll my eyes. 'Yes, okay, fine. And let's hope number three is a bit less on the nose, eh?'

She turns it over. I try to laugh again but nothing comes out.

It's the Tower, and that card, unlike the others – which as a child I always thought were pretty or at least intriguing – genuinely frightens me. And not just me. It's not included in some decks because it's difficult to cobble together any positives out of the doom and chaos it represents. The card's illustration always seemed pretty unequivocal: flames licking around the tower windows and people falling head first towards the ground. The skeleton knight of the Death card is cheery by comparison.

'Excellent,' I say, standing up and knocking against the table, making the wine glasses wobble. 'I think this is my sign from the universe to call it a night.'

Angie doesn't seem to hear me. She's focused on the card, the frown lines on her forehead so pronounced in the low, wavering light that I can see what she'll look like as a really old woman.

I deliberately scrape my chair as I tuck it under the table and that finally rouses her.

'Hold your horses,' she says, blinking fast as though she's just been shaken awake. 'We've hardly got going yet.'

I hesitate. I can't think what the third card refers to. The Tower itself is enough for me.

'It's your past,' Angie says uncannily. 'The third card is your past.'

I take myself to the door. 'Can we finish this tomorrow?' I say, though I have no intention of letting that happen. 'I'm not sure I'm up to knowing my future on card four.'

To my surprise, she doesn't protest. She doesn't say a word. She sweeps all the cards into a pile and keeps her hands on them, palms down and eyes closed. Which is significantly more unsettling than anything she might have told me.

Chapter Seventeen

Wednesday

It's rare for me to drink two nights in a row, and I wake the next morning feeling like I've slept better than I have in a long time. No doubt it was bad quality but, when you're a lifelong insomniac, even passing out from too much rough table red feels like a spa break.

Without getting out of bed, I pick over the evening with my mother but there are no rows to recall and regret, just a lingering unease over the tarot cards. Not so much the reading, although the Tower thing was pretty unnerving in the moment, but Harkin's quizzing Angie about them, and that she's made two visits in as many days. Whatever Angie might have promised, I know she's keeping something back.

It's still early, judging by the faint light behind the curtains, but when I rouse myself enough to sit up and pull them back, the valley is hidden behind thick white mist. It's the one type of weather that interferes with my time-telling skills, and sure enough, when I dig in my bag for my mobile to check, it's well after nine. I click the screen off before it can find some signal and start stacking up all the calls and messages I might have missed.

Downstairs, I clear up last night's detritus and consider going up to see Karl about our interview but, like Angie, he's hardly an early bird. I catch sight of my car keys, and the urge to escape Tanglewood, at least for a little while, is overwhelming. Knowing the microclimate of the valley, it'll probably be sunny as soon as I pull clear of it, too.

I go along the Dark Ride this time, crawling at ten miles an hour because I can't see anything beyond the bonnet but swirling white air. I don't want to hit a deer. At least going this way I won't have to get out and wrestle with any padlocks. The big main gates will swing open for me automatically. I don't like fog, the blindness it brings. I never have. I don't want to be out in it.

She materializes out of the pale nothing with no warning, veering in on the passenger side, eyes wide and skin so colourless it looks see-through, making me scream as I slam on the brakes. For an irrational split-second before reason gets hold of me, I go to hit the central locking so she – *it* – can't get in.

But, despite all appearances, it's nothing spectral, only Lennie.

She pulls open the door and climbs in, breathing hard. 'Morning. I heard the engine and thought it must be you. I was running but then I couldn't see where the drive was and almost got myself flattened.' She grins.

I'm gripping the steering wheel so tightly the bones of my hands hurt. I force myself to relax by flexing my fingers. 'Hi, Lennie. You gave me a bit of a fright there.'

'Oh, sorry,' she says, clipping on her seatbelt. 'Where are you going? Can I come?'

I heave in a deep breath. 'Looks like you are. But . . .'

'Ottoline's still asleep. She was up all night checking on me, so I reckon she'll be out for ages yet.'

'What do you mean, checking on you?'

Lennie shrugs as I let the brake off and we wind slowly towards the gates. 'She comes in when she thinks I'm asleep. Sometimes I am, and she wakes me up. I always keep my eyes shut because I don't think she wants me to know she does it. I think she's quite a . . . a worried person.'

An oak looms out of the fog and I correct my steering. 'Well, after . . . I mean, the thing is, when you've lost . . .'

'Oh, I know it's because of Caroline. She's just checking I'm not dead and stuff. It's fair enough.' She folds her hands neatly over a small coin purse in her lap that's shaped like a cat's head.

I adore Ottoline, but that sounds a bit odd – especially on top of Lennie's very existence here being kept secret.

I turn onto the road that will take me through the village and past the pub, out onto a bigger A-road and eventually to Stroud. As predicted, it's shaping up to be a glorious day once we're up on the ridge between Tanglewood's valley and the next. The fog-bound valley feels insubstantial already, like a setting in a dream, already falling to dust.

'Well I never,' says Lennie. 'Who'd have guessed it would be like this up here? It's like a different day.'

I suppress a smile at her old-fashioned turns of phrase. 'It's called valley fog,' I say, putting my foot down and enjoying the relief of leaving the strangeness behind. 'It's an actual thing. It happens when colder air settles at the bottom and warm air passes over the top, trapping it in. Something like that, anyway. It'll burn off in a couple of hours.'

'Good knowledge. Did you go to school round here?'

'I didn't go to school.'

'But Ottoline said that before you lived in London you went to university, and you can't go to university without doing A levels. Were you home-schooled?'

'If you count me teaching myself from second-hand textbooks.'

'Didn't Angie teach you? Isn't it supposed to be your parents who do home-schooling?'

'Angie's a graduate of the university of life. She thought that was enough for anyone, including me.'

Lennie opens the window six inches and sticks her hand out, waggling her fingers in the warm breeze. 'I think my mum went to that one, too.'

'What about you?' I say, after a while. 'Did you go to school before you came to the valley?'

'Sometimes.'

'Do you miss it?'

'No. I liked it when the teacher read to us but I always got called names because of my clothes. Mainly Pikey, but one boy called me a tramp. On balance, I'd rather not go again.'

'Little shits,' I say, without thinking, and Lennie laughs.

'Little shits,' she yells, out of the window, which sets me off.

'I like Angie,' she says, when we've both calmed down.

'Yeah?'

'She doesn't talk to me like I'm a kid. Just a normal person.'

'That can work both ways, though,' I say, more to myself than her.

But Lennie turns in her seat. 'What do you mean?'

'Well, sometimes I just wanted to be a kid. I wanted her to be in charge. And she wasn't. Sometimes it felt like I was.' I swallow. Hangovers always make me say too much.

'Like how?' says Lennie.

I brake for a pheasant that has apparently been waiting at the verge all morning for me to come along and run it over.

'You mean drugs, don't you?' she says, when I still haven't answered.

'That was part of it.' I pause – in case she wants to offload something similar about Willow and, in the gap, my mind presses play on a helpful montage of Bad Angie Moments. Refusals to get out of bed for days on end because of Karl. Every single piece of crockery and cutlery we owned piled up in the sink and the bin stinking. Harsh morning light on overflowing ashtrays and wine rings. A whiff of vomit in the bathroom. I remember the Six of Cups card from last night. Nostalgic is not the word I'd choose.

But when Lennie does speak, it's not about her own mother. She's still on me. 'It must have been a lot,' she says carefully, 'having Angie as your mum and then Ottoline as well.'

'What do you mean?' I glance sideways at her and see she's coloured slightly, a small frown between her brows.

'Well, it's just that Ottoline . . .'

'I won't say anything.'

'It's like what I was saying before. She's *so* nice. She's a really good person. But sometimes she acts like I'm a baby. Or like she wishes I was *her* baby.' It comes out in a rush, and it takes me straight back to something I haven't thought of in years. That maybe I've never thought of properly since I actually *lived* it in the moment.

I caught a chill one winter because Angie hadn't bothered getting any firewood and I'd been dressing myself in clothes I'd washed in the sink and failed to dry properly. Feeling sorry for myself, I went up to the manor and Ottoline – in one of her up-phases – swooped down on me, ran me a bubble bath and had my clothes washed and dried properly. I was propped up against white-white pillows in her own bed while she fed me chicken broth. I pretended I was Mark Lester as Oliver Twist in the film, having just been rescued by Mr Brownlow.

'And it's tricky trying to be her baby,' Lennie is saying, with a sigh too heavy for her years. 'Because the thing is, I'm actually ten. I haven't been a baby for a long time. Plus I'm an old soul anyway. Mum always said so.'

Just as I've never acknowledged the present tense with Lennie before, I don't acknowledge the past now. I reach over to pat her hand, and hope she'll say more when she's ready. We drive on in companionable silence, through the undulating fields of green and gold. It's as easy as being by myself.

It's busy in Stroud. There's probably a market on. When I come back from paying for a ticket in the car park, taking a while because it's next to the police station and I was trying to spot Harkin's Audi, Lennie is holding up my mobile.

'It went off in your bag and I answered,' she says. 'It was a man called Dan.'

'Oh, God.'

'He said . . .' – she pauses to get it right – '. . . "Can you please ask Rain to give me a ring back ASAP if it's not too much fucking trouble."'

'Charming. Look, I'm sorry about that. Lots of swearing this morning.'

'In fairness, I don't think he knew he was speaking to a child. What does ASAP stand for?'

'"As soon as possible". Annoying people use it to sound important.'

'Oh.' She reaches up to take my hand as we cross the road, which makes me jolt with surprise. It feels small and warm. 'Is he your boyfriend?'

'You're as nosy as Angie.'

'Well, is he?'

'No, he's not.'

'That's a relief. He sounded like hard work.'

I snort. 'I'll tell him that if I ring him back.'

'*If*,' says Lennie, with emphasis, and turns to me with an eyebrow raised, which makes me laugh again.

It's bustling on the main shopping street, which tips steeply down. In the background, the hills rise sharply up again, like a green wave. Although it's nothing compared to London, it's still something of a sensory assault to be suddenly among so many people and their attendant noise.

'It's absolutely heaving,' says Lennie. 'Do you think it's going to be this hectic at the Gathering?'

I'm just wondering whether I should ask how she feels about it going ahead so soon after her mum when my phone goes off again. I pull it out, fully expecting Dan. But it's the cottage landline. I still have it saved as 'Home'.

Angie's already talking when it connects. 'Slow down,' I say. 'I can't work out what you're saying.'

'I've got to go in for questioning,' she says, her outrage and fear pulsing down the line. 'Harkin's downstairs. I sneaked up here to ring you, said I needed the loo. She's got hold of the bloody tarots, of course. Saw them on the table after I'd said I had no idea where they were yesterday. So, that didn't look great to begin with, but then I tripped up and said she'd finagled me into giving her a reading and, God, if we hadn't had all that wine last night, this would never have happened because I'd have had my wits about me.'

I move away from Lennie, who has knelt to pet a dog in a Che Guevara bandana.

'Hang on, are you talking about Willow?' I hiss down the phone. 'You did a tarot reading for Willow? You *promised* me last night that you'd told me everything.'

'I didn't lay a finger on her, Rain. I swear to you.'

'So why didn't you just tell Harkin about the reading in the first place?'

'Because she'd have twisted it into something suspicious, just like she is now.'

I close my eyes against the busy street, suck in a breath. 'Look, what exactly has Harkin said?'

'That she wants me to *accompany her to the station to further assist with enquiries relating to the murder of Willow Green.*'

'So, she's not arresting you.'

'Not yet, but she wants me on her turf so she can put the frighteners on. She'll probably sling me in a cell for hours to break me down. This is how they operate, Rain. This is what they do.'

'We're in Gloucestershire,' I say. 'They're not the bloody Stasi.' It's a dismissive reflex, which is partly an aversion to Angie's histrionics and partly fear about what else she might have lied to me about. I'm also anxious that her health isn't up to this kind of high drama. I'd be amazed if she didn't have sky-high blood pressure, what with her hot temper, her smoking and drinking, and the weight she's piled on even since Christmas. I can still picture her lifeless on the rag-rug and, who knows, maybe I do have some sort of psychic inkling.

Then I properly take in what she's said.

'So, hang on, it's definitely murder now, then?'

Angie doesn't say anything, but I can hear her breathing, too fast and shallow.

'Right, listen to me,' I say. 'I'm in town with Lennie. I'll take her to Tanglewood, then come back, try to talk to someone at the station.'

'Can't you just stay where you are? Meet us at the station? We won't be long. I want to see you before they lock me up.' Her voice cracks and, in the background, Harkin is calling up the stairs.

'Right, fine. See you soon. And, Mum, deep breaths, okay? Do an omm chant if it helps.'

The line clicks and she's gone.

Chapter Eighteen

'Was that Dan again?' says Lennie, when I get back to her. She widens her eyes for comic effect.

'Actually, no. Look, are you hungry?'

'I'm always hungry. I've got hollow legs.'

'Okay, let's get you something.'

One of the stalls crowding the side-streets is selling cookies and Lennie points to a huge triple-chocolate one, squeaking with delight when I buy it without a word about eating a proper breakfast. She holds the little paper bag with reverence as we climb back up towards the police station.

There's a low wall around the corner and I install her on it. I'll still be able to see her from the entrance.

'Stay there, will you? I've got to go and sort something out.'

She stands, suddenly alert, the precious cookie forgotten. 'What's happened? Has Karl been arrested?'

That stops me in my tracks. 'Why do you say that?'

She lifts her chin. 'I'm not an idiot. I know it's usually the boyfriend. Of course they'd think it's him that hurt . . .' She stops, puts a hand over her mouth, but not before a sob escapes.

Before I can overthink it, I pull her to me, stroking her hair while she cries, her hands tight around my waist. When the grief subsides, I go to step away and give her some space, but she holds on tight, grip surprisingly strong.

I've been naïve to think Lennie has barely taken in her mum's death. By the sound of it, she understands the situation only too well. With a lurch, I remember what she'd been trying to say in the car about Ottoline babying her. Maybe she's felt like she's got to play along, to save her brand new guardian's feelings. Or, much worse, that if she doesn't, she'll be carted off into care.

'They haven't arrested anyone,' I say softly, close to her ear. 'That was Angie on the phone, but they just want to ask her some more questions. They're still trying to work out what happened to your mum and I guess they need to do it officially, which is why they're bringing her to the station. She's a bit scared, though, so I'm going to try to see her before she goes in.'

There's something about this girl that makes it impossible to lie to her, even if at her age it would be better to massage the truth a little.

'I'll come too,' Lennie says. She takes a shuddery little breath and tucks the paper bag under her arm. 'No arguments.'

Angie has to be helped out of the back of the police car by a young officer in uniform, and it *is* a police car, rather than Harkin's little coupé. A hot ripple of anger goes through me.

She looks pretty wrecked, her hair as wild as her eyes, but at least she's got her make-up on. Her armour. She wouldn't feel like herself without it.

Harkin gets out of the passenger side and slams the

door, doing a double-take when she sees me and Lennie standing there.

'Is there any need for all this?' I gesture at the car. The uniformed officer, sensing possible trouble, tries to usher Angie towards the station entrance, without any joy. She's twice the width of him.

'It wouldn't be happening if there wasn't,' Harkin says, and then looks down at Lennie. 'Who's this, then?'

My mind empties and, in the corner of my eye, Angie stills. The sounds of the town fade until all I can hear is my own blood pounding in my ears.

'I'm Lucy,' says Lennie, in a little-girl voice quite unlike her own. 'Rain's my godmother. We've been at the market and she bought me a cookie.' She holds up her paper bag.

'Right,' says Harkin. 'Good to meet you, Lucy.'

Lennie smiles winningly and skips off to the wall, sits down and begins to work her way through the cookie.

'I was in town anyway,' I manage to say. I feel like I owe it to Lennie after that performance, though it's not going to look good if Harkin works it all out. I'm not sure of the legal definitions but I'm probably perverting the course of justice, just as Angie might have done with her tarot lies. 'I was here to see Lucy,' I rush on, 'and, you know, thought I'd give her mum a couple of hours to herself.'

'Lucky you just happened to be passing the police station at this precise moment,' Harkin says, with a pointed look at Angie.

'Rain and I communicate psychically when we need to,' she says, lip curled, and, despite her broken promise, it's good to see some of her old spirit back.

Harkin rolls her eyes. 'Perhaps you could psychically

tell your daughter why, contrary to claims you hardly knew the victim, you actually spent some hours with her during her last week alive, reading her fortune at your kitchen table. Then Rain can pass it on to us ordinary mortals, seeing as you won't.'

She looks at me, catching my glance towards Lennie, to check she's out of earshot. 'And perhaps while you're receiving these messages, you can also find out why your mother keeps changing her mind about what she was doing on the night in question.'

I haven't asked Angie about the night Willow died. In the first place because it didn't occur to me that she could've had anything to do with it. I still don't believe she could hurt Willow – even if she has been shifty since I got back, lying about the tarots to the police and to me. But, like Harkin, I think she still knows more than she's letting on, and that's frightening. Not least because I really thought I knew all her tells. I remember the Fool card from last night, Angie telling me not to be literal about it. I push away the image.

'Right,' says Harkin, when I haven't responded. 'Maybe your telepathic signals need charging. We're going in now and I'll be in touch when we're done. I suggest you go and rejoin your goddaughter.'

I don't know if it's due to not wanting to push her luck because of the lie – yet another – about who Lennie is, but Angie gives me a nod and turns towards the station entrance without another word. I watch the door close behind them. As it does, my heart skips a beat, then another, and not in the exciting way that happens in romances; in a way that makes me think there's something seriously physically wrong with me. That it's me I should have pictured lifeless on the floor, not Angie.

I try to breathe normally, not to think about the muscle of my heart squeezing and struggling in my chest, and then become slowly aware that someone is pressing one of my hands between theirs.

'I think you might be having a panic attack,' says Lennie. There's a smear of chocolate on her cheek. 'Mum had them sometimes. You feel like you're going to die, but you aren't. You have to keep breathing, but slowly. Longer on the out-breath.'

She exhales slowly, gesturing for me to copy, and we lock eyes. I can see tiny flecks of palest blue among the grey of hers and it's this observation that blows apart the worst of the awful feeling into smaller, more manageable pieces.

After a few minutes, when my heart is back to something like its normal rhythm, she leads me to the wall. I sit down heavily.

'I thought I was going to have to give you the bag from my cookie to blow into,' she says.

'Sorry about that,' I say shakily. 'I don't know . . . I've never . . .'

'Don't apologize,' she says gravely. 'It can happen to the best of us.'

I'm too wobbly to smile, but I'm not far off, which is progress. 'Weird that it happened like that, though. With no warning. It felt like it came out of nowhere.'

She turns to me and smiles gently, patient adult to slightly dim child. 'You just watched your mum being taken away from you by the police.'

'Well, yes, but she'll be okay. It's not like I won't see her again.'

I swallow, realize what I've said, but Lennie is looking thoughtfully towards the green slopes beyond the town. 'It's probably old trauma coming to the surface.'

'You really are an old soul. Any particular trauma, do you think?' I'm trying to make light but she rolls her eyes.

'Well, I don't know exactly, do I? I've only known you five minutes. You'll have to have a word with your subconscious.'

I do laugh then, sounding slightly deranged. 'You're ten. How the hell do you know about the subconscious?'

'I'm a really advanced reader. We couldn't always get to a library, so when I'd finished my books, I read all Mum's.'

I take a different way back to Tanglewood, an older way that meanders across the countryside via quiet hamlets you'd never know were there if you only kept to the bigger roads. Routes from when the world was bigger and time had to stretch to accommodate it. When travelling a few miles took a whole day.

I stop on a whim at a particularly pretty one, pulling up next to an old red phone box fitted with a shiny new defibrillator. The car windows are down and, with the engine off, it's silent but for the low hum of bees working on a nearby lavender bush. I let my head fall back against the headrest and close my eyes.

'Rain?' Lennie says, after so long that I'm halfway to dozing. It strikes me again how being with Lennie is oddly like being in my own company.

I turn to her. 'I'm okay. Just knackered.'

'Yes, you will be. It takes it out of you, having a panic.'

There's a character like Lennie in an old book I read long ago but I can't retrieve the title now. She was fondly nicknamed 'Little Mother'. In our different ways, we've both grown up too fast.

'But, anyway, that wasn't what I was going to ask,' she's saying.

I raise an eyebrow. 'Oh?'

She pulls in a sharp little breath. 'I want you to help me.'

'Of course. Help you how?'

'It's nice you said yes first. But I mean a big help, not a little one. I want you to help me work out what really happened to my mum.' She watches anxiously for my reaction, and it's one of the most heartbreaking things I've ever seen.

'Of course. I'll help you as much as I can,' I say. 'But don't forget, that's exactly what the police are trying to do, right now.'

'They've got the wrong end of the stick, though. I don't think for a minute it was anything to do with Angie.'

Guilt crawls over me because I *am* beginning to wonder about that. I go over it all in my head again: Angie's strange behaviour and her uncharacteristic fear. I wish I'd asked her, when I had the chance, what she was doing that night. Then again, she'd lied about how well she knew Willow. Maybe she would've lied about that, too. Even so, I still can't make all of it add up to her hurting Willow, and that's important. 'Me too,' I say, and hope I know that for certain soon.

'Rain?'

I turn back to Lennie.

'Do you promise not to go back to London yet?' She's

gripping her little cat purse so tightly I can see the pale caps of her knuckles.

I resist the urge to agree immediately. I really don't want to promise a child something, then go back on it. Especially this child.

'I'm here till Sunday at least. But how do you think I can help more than the police? Harkin will get to the bottom of it, I'm sure. And you need to be extra careful, by the way, now that she's seen you. We'll have to warn Ottoline.'

She nods, looks away, somehow even smaller than she was a moment ago.

I hesitate, then reach for her hand. 'Hey, listen. I hate to make a promise when there's so much going on. I've got my job in London, my flat. But of course I'll help you. I will.'

She nods again but won't meet my eye. She zips and unzips her purse. It's empty.

'Look, I'll be honest with you,' I say, because she deserves it. 'I'm a bit funny about promises. I don't really trust them. I know how easily they're broken, and I would hate to do that to you because of something outside my control.'

She looks me in the eye again then, half smiles. 'Okay, fair dos. But you'll tell me, won't you, if you do have to go? You won't just . . . leave?'

'I won't just leave.'

Neither of us says anything for a while. The bees drone on. A dog barks somewhere. At the old rectory on the other side of the green, someone is mowing immaculate stripes into the front lawn.

I think about what I haven't had a moment to absorb yet: that the police now believe Willow was murdered. Something has happened to tip the balance away from suicide and accidental death. Surely that can't just be down to Angie's tarot cards.

Until now, I haven't really believed that Willow was killed. Not in my heart of hearts. And that makes me wonder something else: if it's true, maybe it follows that Warner's Astrid story is, too.

Eventually, I make myself turn on the engine. Lennie sighs and, though I agree with the sentiment, we can't hide out here for ever. I drive the two of us back towards Tanglewood in silence.

Chapter Nineteen

Angie is still not back by early evening. When I ring the station, the duty sergeant says it's been a busy day and Angie's interview has had to wait, but she definitely won't be in overnight.

'She's in fine fettle,' he says, in the broad Gloucestershire accent I find inexplicably reassuring. 'We sent one of the boys out to the health-food shop for some funny tea on her say-so. Won't drink nothing else, she reckons. No problem with bacon, mind.' He's still laughing when he puts down the phone.

I'm due at the manor for dinner tonight – Lennie's idea – and I intend to make it this time. I've had a tepid bath – the day showing no signs of cooling yet – and changed into an old green dress of Angie's, which can't possibly fit her now. This is a deliberate choice: I want Karl to be reminded of her because I want him to help me get her out. Like lots of people with money and fame, he has a way of making things happen. I pile my hair on top of my head and put on some dangly silver star earrings, which reach almost to my collarbones. In the mirror, I look like how I remember Angie when I was small. *Ooh, what's your game?* I hear her say in my head, though I doubt it's psychically from the police cell. *Just leave me to it*, I retort, just in case. *I'm doing this for you.* I suppose, after her request in the car, I'm also doing it for Lennie.

It's Karl I see first. He's coming down the stairs as I step over the threshold. He stops to take me in and, again, it feels like before: my appearance throwing him out of time, which is exactly the effect I was after.

'Rainy,' he says eventually, coming towards me and taking my hands. 'Don't you look a picture tonight. You should dress feminine more often. It suits you.'

I roll my eyes but I'm smiling, too. I want him on-side. 'Sexist,' I say, but teasingly. 'It's an old one of Angie's. I was too hot in everything I brought with me from London.'

'Yeah, that's it,' he says. 'I thought it looked familiar.' He glances towards the stairs, and I realize he's checking for Ottoline. 'The green brought out her dark eyes. Yours too.'

'She's still stuck at the police station,' I say smoothly. 'They've kept her all day. Did you see them take her away? They sent a patrol car.'

I can see he's got his hearing aids in, but he's caught a glimpse of himself in a mirror and is minutely adjusting his hair. 'Angie's a tough cookie,' he says. 'They haven't got anything on her.'

'Are you sure about that? I feel like something changed between Harkin coming to the cottage yesterday and today. Like maybe they got some forensics back or . . . I don't know. Harkin herself seemed different: more energized or something. I was there at the station when she brought Angie in.'

'Don't worry about Harkin. She's throwing her weight around because she's new and she's a woman. A Black woman. Can't be easy for her. But what happened with Willow is nothing to do with that and she'll get that when she settles down.' He sounds hard. He must catch something in my expression because he pauses, sighs, massages his temples.

'It was a tragic accident, pure and simple. I wish to God it hadn't happened, but no one was involved except her.'

'But the point is that the police don't think it was an accident, do they?' I say, trying not to sound as frustrated as I'm beginning to feel. 'They're officially calling it murder now. I thought they would have updated you on that.'

He looks at me, blue eyes narrowed, then goes back to rubbing his head. 'They're wrong if they're calling it that, and we just have to wait it out until they realize that, okay?'

He turns and leads me towards the drawing room before I can say anything else. He's got the album on his eye-wateringly expensive turntable. How many copies has he worn out over the years? Dozens, surely.

I sit down on the edge of a velvet chair. I'm adjusting the folds of my dress, brain turning over, when something occurs to me. 'Did you say anything to Harkin about Angie's tarot readings?'

He pauses at the drinks tray on the enormous Victorian console table. 'It might have come up. She asked a lot of questions, Harkin. Stuff that had nothing to do with Willow. I guess she was trying to get to the bottom of our unique . . . set-up here.'

This is the first time I've ever heard Karl reference Tanglewood's unconventional arrangement. And it makes me wonder again: how did it ever get established? How did Angie manage to become a permanent fixture here when none of Karl's other women ever did? And more pertinently now: is Harkin thinking that Angie was feeling threatened by Willow? That she might lose her place to a younger model? It seems like a solid motive. How the tarot cards fit into this, though, I have no idea.

'Martini?' Karl brings me back into the room.

I shake my head, then change my mind. I could do with a sharpener, as Ottoline in 1930s-house-party mode would probably call it.

'Where's Lennie?' I say, while he pours and mixes.

'O's putting her to bed.' He hands me my drink and I take a sip. It's perfect. Clean, cold and very strong.

I glance at the clock on the mantel in case I'm losing my touch. But, no, it's not even seven yet. I remember what Lennie said this morning about not being Ottoline's baby. 'Bit early, isn't it?'

He holds up his hands. 'Not my department.'

'I should probably warn you that Harkin saw Lennie today. She was with me in town when Angie was taken in. I know it's supposed to be a secret but . . .'

'It was O's maternal instinct to keep it under wraps about Lennie, and she was right. That poor kid hasn't got anyone else. They'd put her in care. You wouldn't do that to her, would you, Rain? Wouldn't do that to O, either?'

'No, of course not, and I said to Harkin that she was a friend's daughter. I just wondered if it was the right thing—'

'Caleb should be here soon,' he says, over me. 'You seen him around yet?'

I blink. Does he always do this? Just close a subject when he's had enough? 'I have seen him, yes,' I say, and find I'm really glad he's coming. I would have jumped at the opportunity for a private dinner with Karl and Ottoline, once. Tonight? I'm not so sure.

'Can I ask you something?' I say to Karl. I probably haven't got long until Ottoline comes downstairs. Angie is a *verboten* subject in her presence for obvious reasons.

Karl looks at me consideringly. 'Okay, as long you remember that all that talk before was a hell of a downer, sweetheart.'

'Right. It's just that I don't think Angie has been very . . . cooperative with the police about answering their questions, which doesn't look great. You know what she's like about authority and all that . . .' I gulp down some more of my martini, nervous and simultaneously annoyed with myself for being so pathetically reluctant to piss off Karl. 'Look, she wasn't with you that night, was she?' I say, in a rush. 'Or, rather, were you with her, at the cottage? Is that why she's being so weird? Because you're each other's alibi and she doesn't want to tell tales?'

He knocks back his own martini and sloshes in another measure from the shaker. He hasn't sat down yet. 'We can't be alibis because I wasn't here that night,' he says eventually. 'I was away. Harkin knows that.'

'Oh.' Doubts flood in again. 'I . . . thought it might be some misguided loyalty to you and Tanglewood that was stopping her saying anything straightforwardly. Because, you know, it's not like the police would care about you two . . .' I tail off. 'But . . .' I come to another halt.

'I guess jealousy just sounds like a pretty good motive to them.' He shrugs and, while I know Angie hasn't exactly helped herself, I can't quite believe he's standing there, so nonchalant, when she's been in a police cell all day.

I sit back in my seat, put my drink down too hard. *Jealousy*. I know he's right about it being a good motive. I was thinking it myself a few minutes ago. It's been a good motive since time immemorial. But there's something about the way Karl said it so casually that makes me wonder if he did the same with Harkin. The disloyalty of that possibility floors me.

'You said it was an accident a minute ago,' I say carefully, 'that you're totally certain Willow did this to herself, one way or another. Angie said the same thing to Harkin the other day. That she was fragile, that you could see it coming. But this jealousy thing? You make it sound like you've wondered about Angie.' *Or you don't mind the police wondering about Angie*, I don't add.

'Hey, I'm just speculating about what the police might be thinking, knowing something about the . . . dynamic here, that's all.' He reaches over to turn up the music.

'What about Astrid?' I say, raising my voice. I'm never this direct with Karl. 'Was she fragile too?' My hand, when I pick up my drink, is visibly trembling.

I watch him closely: the slow blink of his eyes, the visible rise and fall of his chest. I'm positive he's heard me. 'You referring to that story in the papers?' he says, when the song comes to an end. 'I heard about that. Poor guy must be sick in his mind. The only Astrid I ever heard of went to live in Morocco. Probably still there. I wouldn't know, hardly knew her.'

He lifts the cocktail shaker with a raised eyebrow. 'Another?'

'No, thanks.' My body has gone cold all over, then hot. Karl has just confirmed there was someone here called

Astrid, which is more than I got out of Angie. I'm starting to feel strange – I haven't eaten for hours. I can already feel the effects of the first martini, liquid heat softening my bones.

Doggedly, I decide to give it one more go, before Ottoline or Caleb show up. 'It's lucky *you* had an alibi, being away. After all, you must have been the first person they spoke to.'

Karl has pulled out another record and is reading the sleeve notes. He looks up. 'What makes you say that?'

'Well, I mean they always look at the person the victim is involved with.'

'Involved with?'

An exasperated noise escapes me. 'Your and Willow's *dynamic*. You two,' I swallow, 'sleeping together.'

He shakes his head, jaw tight. 'She was a kind of collaborator. She helped with my music, had a good ear. We had a connection, sure, but it wasn't like that.'

'But . . .' I stop.

'I told the police that, too,' Karl is saying. 'They made the same assumption you did, that it was all about sex. I said to them, "If you're so set on going down that road in your minds, then you'd be better off talking to my son. Hey, talk of the devil.'

I turn and Caleb is in the doorway, pulling off an old cap and ruffling his hair to unflatten it. He gives me a tight smile. It fades when he looks at his father and nods hello. 'What about me?'

But this is the moment that Ottoline chooses to sweep in. She somehow appears even taller and thinner than usual. She's also deathly pale except for two purplish spots high on her cheekbones that would look like bruises if they weren't symmetrical. She's clutching something plastic, which she places carefully on the mantel before coming towards me with her arms outstretched and kissing the air near my cheek. As well as her usual perfume, she smells faintly of something medicinal I can't put my finger on.

'And dear Caleb is here, too,' she says, though she doesn't go to him, or even look at him.

As if he hears that thought of mine, he looks straight at me. I attempt a smile, but my mind is skittering over what Karl just said. I'm trying to recall exactly what Caleb told me about Willow when we had our coffee by the campfire but the martini is making me blurry.

I look around the room once Karl has mixed everyone a new drink. Angie is stuck in a cell while we're doing cocktail hour and, despite being thrown by what Karl just said, a hot spurt of anger licks through me. Which is odd in itself. I'm more accustomed to feeling cross *with* Angie than on her behalf.

I glance at Ottoline. She's perched on a hard chair near the window, gaze moving restlessly between the garden and whatever it was she placed so carefully on the mantel. It's some sort of gadget and Ottoline is the last person I associate with gadgets. She always seems like she's just been teleported in from the inter-war years. My brain suddenly works it out: it's a baby monitor, one of those with a matching handset. Its pair must be in Lennie's bedroom. I feel suddenly chilly in that big room, and when Karl offers me a drink again a few minutes later, I decide I need it.

*

Dinner is laid in the formal dining room, with Ottoline's best china and the crystal glasses I've seen brought out only a few times. As we take our seats, I glance around, feeling I'm missing something. I catch Caleb's eye and he does a tiny shake of his head as though he doesn't get it either.

I don't know how I feel about him after what Karl insinuated. I'm so used to the latter being Tanglewood's long-time Lothario that it has never occurred to me that Caleb might have been sleeping with Willow. Wouldn't Angie have said something about that if it was true? She loves a bit of gossip. The thought of it unsettles me in ways I'm too tipsy to figure out now.

The drink is probably also the reason I haven't noticed the ice bucket – that is, until Ottoline gestures to it and Karl stands to open the champagne that's been waiting there on ice.

'I see we're drinking the good stuff tonight,' he says, inspecting the label, and, though he's smiling, it feels like a forced kind of bonhomie. 'What's the special occasion, O?'

His smile fades as he takes in her sombre expression. As the daylight at the window has slowly dimmed, the candlelight has been turning her more and more cadaverous.

'It's the first of July,' she says simply. I catch her darting glance at the baby monitor she's brought through and placed carefully on the credenza where the good silver is kept. I'm just about close enough to make out what's on its small video screen. In the middle of the black, something ghostly pale is shifting and heaving slightly, like the soft churn of a calm sea. Lennie, asleep. The green signal-light wavers and then brightens.

Because of this, I'm slow to work out the significance of the date. Karl and Caleb get there quicker. Karl's face is closed, Caleb's stricken.

The first of July. Of course. I know it from the hand-stitched sampler next to Ottoline's bed. It's Caroline's birthday, though inevitably, horribly, it only makes me think of its terrible twin. Her death day: the morning Ottoline found her cold in her bed. The same bed Lennie is being so closely monitored in now.

Chapter Twenty

I leave dinner at the manor as soon as it's possible to do so without seeming horribly insensitive to Ottoline. It's not as though anyone was enjoying themselves, and I'm also itching to get to the cottage and see if Angie's back. Caleb seemed to be stewing about something, reminding me of how he used to look, and I wasn't sure if that was about me being a bit cool towards him, or for more complicated reasons to do with Willow or his father or both. I wanted to ask him about Willow but we weren't on our own for a single moment.

Ottoline and Karl said very little all evening, too, though a couple of memories of Caroline were recounted. The trouble was, they felt worn almost to nothing, every line rehearsed and stilted. Caroline, if she was anywhere, wasn't in that dining room with us tonight. Willow certainly felt like she was, her absence underlined, at least for me, by every movement on the baby monitor's screen.

To my profound relief, every light in the cottage is lit when I get there. Angie has evidently been returned. She can't be much of a flight risk when she can't drive and doesn't hold a valid passport, but surely they'd have kept her in overnight if she'd been charged. If they actually thought she was a murderer. Even thinking that word has me glancing over my shoulder. I wonder if the police have considered a third party for Willow's death. Some stranger who vanished by first light.

It seems far-fetched but so does the escalation to murder in the first place. I still bolt the cottage door behind me. The metal shrieks from disuse, making Angie cry out from the sitting room.

'It's me,' I say, hurrying towards her. 'It's only me.'

But she's already on her feet and standing in the doorway, hand clasped to her bosom. 'Christ, Rain, you gave me a fright. What was that horrible noise?'

'The bolt. Hasn't been used in a while, has it?'

'I've never bloody used it. What possessed you to lock it now? It nearly finished me off after the day I've had.'

'I'm sorry.' I lead her back to the lumpen old sofa where she's made herself a nest out of blankets, cushions and curl-edged old magazines. 'I suppose I'm bit jumpy.'

'*You're* a bit jumpy?'

I put my hands up. 'I know, I know. You're the one who's been with the police all day. They haven't charged you, then?'

'Nope. Not with murder or anything else, though Harkin was muttering about perversion of the course of justice.' She grabs my wrist as I'm tucking the blanket around her. 'You know, don't you, that I would never have hurt that girl?'

I nod, because I really can't imagine that. 'But it doesn't matter what I think, does it?' I say. 'It's the police, and the CPS. The Crown Prosecution Service. But it's good, really good, that they haven't charged you.'

'Well, like I said earlier, getting me in was all about

intimidation, wasn't it? They don't like it when people won't roll over and tell them everything they want to hear.'

'But you did lie, didn't you?' I can't help saying. 'You told them – and me – that you hardly knew Willow. On the day I came back, you said to Harkin that she'd never set foot in here, but you'd read her tarot here.' My voice is rising and I stop, take a breath. If Angie feels like I'm getting at her too much, she might just refuse to tell me any more. 'What was all that about anyway?' I say, more gently. 'The tarot stuff. You weren't making much sense on the phone.'

'I'll tell you, but let me just think about something else for a second, all right?'

She leans back against the cushions propped behind her, then gestures at me to pass her the glass of red she's halfway down. 'I thought you'd be here when I got back,' she says, when she's had a mouthful. 'I must say, it was a bit humiliating pulling up to the place in total darkness, saying to the boy driving me that I'd be all right. He insisted on seeing me in. *Him*, all gangly, with bum-fluff on his top lip but still taking better care of me than . . . Well, anyway.'

I don't want to fall into this old groove now: Angie getting at me, me getting at Angie. 'I think I'll get myself a glass,' I say.

I don't turn the light on in the kitchen. I stand there for a while in the dark, quiet except for the ominous, last-legs hum of the fridge. I can feel it tingling in my limbs: the urge to run back to London, to pretend none of this is happening. I take a deep breath and picture Lennie, then reach into the cupboard blind and pull out a glass.

Back in the sitting room, I pour myself a large measure and top up Angie's. 'Look, I'm sorry I wasn't here when you came back,' I say, 'but it was for good reason.'

'Lady O need you more than me, did she?' Her eyes glitter in the low light. It's not temper but hurt. I wonder if it was always that way round and I just couldn't see it.

'It wasn't about her. I went because I wanted to talk to Karl. I wanted to find out if he knew you'd been taken in for questioning, and what he thought about that. I think part of me was hoping he'd go straight down there and tell them you couldn't have had anything to do with what happened to Willow.'

'And what did he have to say?' She's set her jaw, but I can see the wobble behind it. It's really shaken her, this day alone with her thoughts, Karl conspicuous by his absence. Not much chivalrous riding to her rescue going on here, despite thirty-plus years of loyal devotion.

'Not a lot,' I say, 'except he couldn't be your alibi because he was away from the estate that night. Oh, and also that he and Willow weren't in *that* kind of relationship.' I can't quite bear to spell it out. Angie has always coped with Karl's other women by pretending they don't exist.

She harrumphs. 'That sounds about right. Did he say she was *just a muse*, that she was only *helping him with his music*?'

'Almost word for word.'

'The lying shit.' She says it under her breath, and for a second I can't believe I've heard her right. I've wanted Angie to say something like this for a long, long time.

'I'll drink to that,' I say, and she's enough of a sport

to laugh. It's a good sound in the quiet room, rich and low. I have another of those moments when time judders and I can see how she used to be, when she was young and alluring. I remember how much easier it was between us, too, once upon a time.

'Did he tell you not to say anything to the police?' I say, after a while. 'I'm just wondering if that's why you've been so evasive – why you didn't just tell them about doing a reading for Willow in the first place.'

'He didn't tell me to do anything. And even if he had, I'm not completely in thrall to him. He's not sodding Charles Manson. I don't like the police, you know that. I've always thought it wisest to say as little as possible when it comes to them, stop them twisting it.' She's jabbing her finger at the air, attempting her trademark Angie bluster, but the long day is getting the better of her. She looks as exhausted as I feel. 'Anyway, Karl's right about the alibi thing, and more's the pity,' she says, sinking back into the cushions. 'He went away the day before, I think it was. Some rehearsal session for the Gathering. I was here on my tod that night, giving my crystals a polish.'

'Why "more's the pity"?'

Angie rolls her eyes. 'Because if Karl had paid one of his visits, he could've vouched for me.'

'If it had suited him,' I can't help saying.

She leans forward, almost upsetting the plate of biscuits balanced on her knee.

'I know he didn't show up today, but I like to think I mean something to him after all these years.'

'Okay, fine. Karl would have vouched for you if he could, but he can't, and nor can anyone else. Presumably it's the same for Ottoline, but they didn't take her in for questioning today, did they? They took you. So, you need to tell me why, because there must be something.'

'Oh, they wouldn't haul Lady O down the cop shop, would they? She's much too delicate for that.'

'Angie.'

She puts up her hand. 'Okay, okay.' Finishing her wine, she upends the rest of the bottle into it, knocks that back too. Then she sits up straighter. 'It's the cards, isn't it?' she says heavily. 'Them on top of the lack of alibi. Who'd have thought that, of all things, it's the tarot that might just do for me.' And now her chin really does start to wobble. She shields her eyes with her hand, shoulders beginning to heave.

I reach out to squeeze her knee through the blanket, leaving my hand there. Eventually her breathing slows.

'When Harkin first turned up at the door, I couldn't work out why she was asking about the cards *again*. I was still half asleep, and she was going on, saying she'd heard *from various sources* that I did readings, was known for it, and was I absolutely sure I didn't know where my deck was, and how that seemed strange to her, et cetera. When it first came up, I thought she was looking down on me – doing the whole *Here's one of those Stroudy nutters who can't get out of bed till she's checked her horoscope* and all that. Then I was worrying about not paying my tax.

'But this morning, it was different. I could see the fire in her eyes.' Angie shakes her head. 'She meant business all right and, of course, I knew the bloody cards were sitting there on the table behind me, still out from last night. Possibly I started acting peculiar, I don't know. Either way, she spied them soon enough. Her eyes nearly jumped out of her head. I thought, *Christ, Angie, you're for the high-jump now*. I had to sit down, I was having palpitations, but you could tell she thought I was putting it on.'

'But you could have dug them out, couldn't you?' I say. 'After she was asking you about them? I mean, you should have told them earlier about giving Willow a reading but . . .'

'No, no, it's much worse than that,' cries Angie. 'She had one of them, didn't she? In her hand.' A sob escapes her.

I'm confused. 'What – Harkin did? Harkin had one of the tarot cards?'

'No!' Angie pulls at her hair, and I hate myself for feeling the momentary scratch of irritation that, even now, when she's clearly genuinely distressed, part of her is hamming this up – making a performance of it.

'I'm sorry,' I say gently, to make up for being so uncharitable. 'I'm obviously being dim. Explain it to me again.'

She lets out a shuddering breath. 'Willow. I mean Willow. Harkin told me they found a tarot card folded up in her hand. It was one of mine. I didn't notice last night but it was missing from the deck. She must've swiped it when I did her reading.'

'Oh, shit,' I say, before I can stop myself.

'Well, exactly,' she says. '*Now* you see why I'm worried. They might not have charged me today, but I reckon they'll be back, especially if Harkin has anything to do with it. Of course my relationship with Karl doesn't help.'

What did he say before dinner tonight? That jealousy was a *pretty good motive*.

'No one else knows about it yet,' Angie rushes on. 'Not the press. Not the boy who found her. Even the police who were first on the scene didn't notice it. Rigor mortis had set in, you see, and her hand was in a fist around it. They only spotted it once they got her on the slab . . .' – she stops, swallows – '. . . when they did the autopsy, yesterday.'

'Only yesterday?'

'The custody copper said the weekend might've delayed it, but also that it wasn't a priority, I s'pose because they thought it was an overdose or suicide. Nothing violent.'

I close my eyes briefly, and a disturbing thought sidles helpfully in: *What if Astrid had a tarot card hidden in her hand, too?* If Graham Warner mentioned that detail before the pathologist found the same thing on Willow, it would have given real credence to his story. I've been wondering what tipped the balance from accidental death to murder for the police. Might that be enough?

When I open my eyes, Angie is taking out a fat joint from a tin I thought she kept buttons in. She lights it with a shaky hand and the sickly smoke curls towards me. I've always hated the smell of weed. Or pot, as she calls it.

'Don't give me grief,' she says. 'Something's got to make me sleep tonight.'

'Which card was it?' I say, to my own surprise. 'In Willow's hand?'

Something passes over Angie's face. Fear but also relief. Perhaps because I've asked a question that demonstrates some respect for the tarot she loves and I've hitherto rolled my eyes at. It must feel like a show of solidarity.

'It was the Empress,' she says. 'I'm telling you, she took it. She must've.'

I picture it: a woman with long, rippling hair in a sideways pose on her outdoor throne, oddly like a pagan version of Britannia.

'She wears a crown, doesn't she?' I say. 'Like how Willow was found. And how Warner said Astrid was, too.'

'Actually, it's a crown of stars on the tarot,' says Angie, softly. 'The flowers are on her gown.'

I brush the earrings I chose out of the tangle in Angie's jewellery box earlier.

'I noticed those as soon as you came in,' she says. 'Of all the ones you could've worn, you chose the stars.' She takes a long drag on her joint.

'How did Willow seem,' I say, 'when you did the reading? How close was it to her . . . being found?'

Angie blows out smoke in a long sigh. 'Thursday, it was. The day before the night it happened. She was . . . Well, maybe it's just hindsight, but I thought she was a bit jumpy. Jittery. I didn't want to give her a reading, truth be told. I didn't say this to Harkin but we weren't friends, me and Willow. How could we be?

'She tried being friendly when she first turned up in the spring, didn't seem to know who I was to Karl, or if she did, she didn't care. I found her . . . wearing. She was always banging on about her yoga and meditation and whatnot. To hear her talk, you'd think she'd come up with Tantra all by herself. As though I wasn't doing all that thirty years ago.

'Anyway, the Empress card came up. She knew a bit about the cards, like everything else,' Angie sighs, takes another drag, 'and she was very happy about that one. "Makes sense," she goes, with this funny little smile. I thought she meant being here, at Tanglewood. The Empress is all about nature and she was at some Traveller site on the outskirts of Swindon before here.

'In fact, the card was reversed, which means she had self-esteem issues. I thought that was interesting. It's always the over-confident ones who are the most insecure underneath. Anyway, I didn't mention that, even though she was getting on my nerves. There was nothing else significant, as far as I recall. We finished up and off she went, thank God, saying she had to get back to Lennie. Last I saw of her.' She sits forward, ash falling to the blanket. 'You do believe me about that, don't you?'

'I wish you hadn't lied to me,' I say carefully. 'The police are one thing, but you could have told *me*.'

'I know. I think I was just trying to keep you out of it, like I always have.'

'What does that mean?'

'Like I said to Harkin. To protect you.'

'But that was when I was kid.'

'It was daft,' she says. 'I'm sorry.'

I can't think of anything to say to that. Angie is not one for apologies.

After that, we sit in silence for a long time, Angie smoking and me finishing my wine, though it tastes sour and I really don't need any more alcohol. I keep thinking about Willow. Willow *and* Astrid. For the first time, I wonder what Astrid looked like, and that sobers me up a bit. Apparently I believe she existed now.

I'm just trying to summon the energy to go to bed, telling myself I'll tackle Angie about the Astrid thing tomorrow, when she speaks.

‘I gleaned a bit of useful intel on the way home,’ she says. She’s almost smiling. ‘They were daft putting me in a patrol car with a young lad who’d pegged me as some old hippie nan who bakes her own bread.’

I forget, as someone who has long honed their defences against Angie’s earth-mother act, that people have a habit of telling her things they shouldn’t. Especially if they’re not the sharpest.

‘Apparently Harkin’s having trouble with her boss,’ she continues. ‘I forget the title. Super-something.’

‘Superintendent?’

‘That’s the badger.’ She stubs out the last half-inch of her joint on the biscuit plate. ‘Well, apparently, she’s not popular in the station. Keeps rubbing everyone up the wrong way. *Top brass aren’t happy*, he said. Made me wonder if some strings had been pulled, actually. Someone higher up wanting it to be done and dusted because it’s Tanglewood.’

‘What do you mean?’

‘Oh, the Mortimer name’s carried weight in these parts for many years. Ottoline’s old man was high up in the masons, or so I’ve heard. Some sort of grand master, he was. And you know we never got any bother from the police during the original Gatherings. That was in the days when they were going after people like us, making trouble where there wasn’t any to be found. But here at Tanglewood? Never, not even when there *was* trouble.’

‘What kind of trouble?’

She hesitates, licks her lips, which are stained with the wine. ‘Oh, nothing much. Just the usual when you put a load of people who are out for a good time in a field together. Little scuffles. People needing their stomachs pumped.'

She pulls in her chin. 'So, that's a glimmer of good news anyway. Harkin's got it in for me, or so it feels, but maybe that won't matter if she's pulled off the case. Sent back to HQ in Gloucester for being a pain in everyone's backsides.'

'I guess so.' I'm not sure it's that simple, especially if they're taking the Astrid story seriously now. It can't just be Harkin driving this. That's not how the police work.

'She would have been interested in something Karl said tonight,' I say, after a while. 'It might have given her pause about you for five minutes, anyway.'

Angie looks up. 'Oh? Seems like Karl's had quite a lot to say today, one way or another. Just not to me, eh?'

I don't reply to that. In all the years I've watched from the sidelines of Karl and Angie's bizarre relationship, I have never, ever heard her say anything as negative about him as I have tonight. While the addiction issues were the main reason I distanced myself from her, second prize would definitely go to her unwavering adulation of Karl. It wasn't that I disliked him – as a child I pretty much adored him, even if I was sometimes afraid of his moods – but I did despise what a fool he continually made of my mother. I can't quite believe she's said two negative things about him in one conversation, and don't want to make her back off by chiming in over his shortcomings. As I've said before, we're as contrary as each other.

'Go on, then,' she says stiffly. 'What was it he said? I'm all ears for anything that might throw Harkin off my scent.'

'It was when I was trying to ask him about Willow, about their . . . relationship. He said I'd be better off asking Caleb instead.'

'*Caleb* and Willow?' She makes a disbelieving sound. 'First I've heard. What did you say to that?'

'Nothing. I didn't get a chance. Caleb turned up at that very moment and he was still there when I left.'

Angie shakes her head. 'What's he up to?' she mutters, apparently to herself, and I'm glad I catch it because, really, would she say that if she knew what happened to Willow? I don't think so. But then, I'm so exhausted that I feel like I've been hit with a brick.

'And there's something else,' Angie says, just as I let my eyes drift shut. 'I'm pretty sure Harkin didn't cotton on about Lennie. She didn't say a word about your *goddaughter*. I suppose she had bigger fish to fry, i.e. yours truly.' She gives a mirthless laugh. 'So, that's another positive.'

When I next open my eyes, I'm curled up on the rug, a cushion under my head and a blanket tucked snugly around me. A glass of water is in reach on the side table. Groggy, and still half in dreams of trying to run through trees with cement-heavy legs, I go over to the window to check the moon's progress. It's riding high over the valley, waxing bright and cold. It must be about three. I've been sound asleep for four whole hours.

Upstairs, reverberating through the old plaster and boards of the ceiling, I can make out the steady rhythm of Angie's snoring. Just as I'm feeling sleepy again, a moth flies into the window, making me rear back. It bats its wings futilely against the glass, again and again.

It feels a bit like a sign but the notion of leaving for

London is now an impossibility. I try to make myself picture it: the physical acts of going upstairs to pack my stuff, of getting into the car and simply driving away. I remember the tingling urge I felt in the kitchen to do just that. I'd be back in my little flat by dawn.

It's still so tantalizing in some ways. The trouble is, I know that all I'd be able to see when I got there would be Lennie and Angie's faces, full of reproach and hurt. I'm not going anywhere.

Chapter Twenty-One

Thursday

When I wake the next morning, I lie there for a while, mentally inching my way around my body. I feel strange, floaty and almost disembodied, even as my brain is sharp, information zipping along and connections firing, even as the last remnants of my insanely complicated dream collapse into dust.

And then I realize, and it's so simple: I'm like this because I've slept properly, getting at least another couple of hours even after I came upstairs to my bed. Presumably this is how normal people operate all the time.

The genuine euphoria of sustained rest means it takes me a moment to grasp what's woken me. Voices. Angie's downstairs with a man and hundreds of nights throughout my childhood tell me it's Karl.

In fact, it's Caleb sitting at the kitchen table, working his way through a pile of toast and jam. Mouth full, he raises a hand in greeting. I smile before I can start thinking about the notion of him and Willow again.

'Look at those lovely roses in your cheeks,' says Angie, turning to inspect me from the sink where she's filling up the kettle. 'I've always said a good sleep would transform you.'

'You say that like I'm an insomniac on purpose,' I fire

back, but I'm still smiling, which softens it. Everything feels as clear and as fragile as glass this morning, including the *entente cordiale* Angie and I established last night.

'She never found sleep easily, love her,' says Angie to Caleb. 'Even as a little girl. I used to give her Calpol so she could at least go off all right, but then the chemist in the village started making noises about how many bottles I was getting through.'

Love her. It's a phrase Angie uses about other people all the time. *Oh, love her little heart.* But I haven't heard her use it about me in years. Maybe never. Maybe only in my own prehistoric times, which is as good as never.

I busy myself in the fridge so they can't see my face, which I suspect gives away how pathetically easy I am to disarm.

'Isn't it nice of Caleb to call in and check I'm still in one piece?' says Angie. 'More than his father could rouse himself to do.'

I turn to them, a pot of almost-off yoghurt in hand. Caleb has finished his toast and is watching me closely. His hair gleams in the morning sunlight slanting in through the window, and something about that – its angles and textures – sparks a memory I can't quite get hold of. There's green in it, though: brilliant greens of all hues. And water. I can hear its silvery music. We must be outside, then. Caleb and me, as children.

But then Angie drops a teaspoon on the stone flags and that single shard of recollection shatters. Caleb is still looking at me and I wonder if I've got the nerve to ask him if he remembers it, too. If he can fill in the blanks.

'I've been telling Caleb about the tarot card,' says Angie, before I can. She lowers herself into her customary chair with a groan. 'And that it's murder now.'

'It's pretty sinister,' he says.

'But you don't think it was me, do you?' The need on Angie's face makes me glance away.

Caleb pats her hand. ''Course not. You're a bit weird, Angie, but you're not a killer.'

She throws her head back and laughs more heartily than it warrants. Like she needed the release. Still, like last night, when I got her to laugh too, it's a good sound. Caleb grins at me and, again, I can't help smiling back.

'Before you came down, I was asking Caleb about what Karl told you,' says Angie, eyebrow raised. 'About him sleeping with Willow.'

It's a question I wanted an answer to more than I'd readily admit, but of course it would be Angie who asked it, and so excruciatingly directly, too. It's not just me being uptight, either. Caleb now seems intent on a large, crumb-filled knot of wood on the table.

'He said it's bollocks,' she says, when he doesn't say anything. 'And he has no idea why Karl said that to you.'

'Maybe being a prick is reason enough,' Caleb says quietly, eyes still downcast.

'Oh, come on now,' says Angie, reprovingly. 'He's still your father.' But there's no conviction in it. She's angry with Karl, and it gives me hope.

At that moment, there's a buzzing noise from the side. It's my phone, plugged in at the wall next to the kettle.

'That's been going off all morning,' says Angie. 'Text after text. From Dan.' She raises her eyebrows at Caleb.

'Shame you've got a whatsit on it or I'd have gone in and replied to him myself.'

'Who's Dan?' says Caleb.

'My boss,' I say, at the same time as Angie says, 'Her boyfriend, or so I reckon.'

Caleb laughs and gives me a look I can't quite read.

He makes his excuses soon after that, says he promised he'd show Lennie a fox's den near his camp and he needs to get back before she thinks he's forgotten. When he's gone, I pull my mobile off the charger and head for the stairs.

Angie follows me. 'There's something funny between you two. I could feel it in the room. I think he's a bit sweet on you, my girl.'

I turn, holding on to the banister with my free hand. I still don't feel entirely inside my own flesh and bones. 'Well, that would be a bit bloody twisted, wouldn't it? Even for Tanglewood.'

She frowns up at me, hands on hips. 'What do you mean by that?'

The old anger comes barrelling through me like burning air. 'If he's my half-brother, is what I mean by that.' My voice is too loud in the enclosed space of the narrow staircase.

'Half-brother?' Angie has the nerve to look confounded. 'What are you on about?'

I sit down heavily because my vision is sparking with tiny fireworks, like my blood pressure has just fallen through the floor. 'I asked you time and time again as a kid who my father was,' I say, when the worst of it has passed. 'Whether it was Karl. And you never gave me a straight answer. Never.' I stop because I'm out of breath. My stupid phone buzzes again. Memory full. How many has he sent?

'Did I not?' Angie looks genuinely confused, maybe even contrite, which only makes me crosser.

'No. You didn't. I think I'd remember. It was like a game to you, saying you'd tell me when I was older, only you never did.'

She shakes her head. 'I don't remember you ever asking, I swear I don't. Not in the last . . . Well, God knows how long.'

'I stopped bothering eventually.'

She comes up a few stairs towards me and I stand, ready to turn tail, though I'm still dizzy. She stops, puts up her hands.

'It's all right,' she says, as though she's talking to a nervous animal. 'I'll stay down here.' A breeze finds its way to us through the open front door, heavy with garden scent. The door creaks slightly on its hinges.

'Look, love, I'm sorry if this is overdue.' Angie heaves a great sigh. 'I should have . . . Well, I should've done lots of things, shouldn't I? We both know that. But I can promise you this right now. Karl is not your dad.'

I sit down again abruptly, keeping myself very still as this information lands and sinks in. When the tears come, I'm not expecting them. It's like a water pipe exploding in a flash frost. They run down my face to soak the front of my T-shirt before I've really registered that I'm crying.

Angie does come up to me then, and I'm powerless to fend her off. She pulls me into her and we stay like that, awkwardly – her standing and leaning over, covering me, even as I'm hunched into myself, arms wrapped round my legs – for a long moment.

Again, as with Caleb in the sunlit kitchen, it cracks open something old in me, like a rusty box that's been buried being brought out into the light. All of it is so well-known to me: Angie's complicated smell, the salt-stick of tears itching my cheeks, the damp hotness of my breath inside the curtain of my hair.

She kneads my back with her strong fingers, hard enough almost to hurt, rocking me back and forth, and it's not just familiar in a general sense. We haven't touched in a long time, not properly, not like this, and I know deep inside me that what I'm remembering is the first time she held me like this. Maybe it was the first time I was ever really distressed enough to warrant it. I hadn't just cut open my knee or got into a scrap with some other kid. This was of a different order, whatever it was. *Whenever* it was. Maybe it was the first time I ever felt sad in the existential way adults do, but was still young enough to be comforted about it.

'Come on, cry it all out,' Angie murmurs, and I'm reeling from how the memory isn't getting shattered, like in the kitchen when she dropped the spoon. I'm still in it – more in it, even, than I am in the present. I cry and cry, and when I'm finally done, I'm so hollowed-out that I slump sideways against the cool plaster of the wall, my eyes fluttering closed.

'I'm sorry, my love,' Angie says, and she's still so close to me that I feel the words as much as hear them. 'And not just for this, either.'

'What, then?' I say, hardly more than a whisper.

'All of it. The drugs, the drink. You having to scrape

me up when you were still a little girl. God, it shames me when I think about it properly, which is why I don't. But that's not good enough, is it?'

She sits down awkwardly on the step below me. 'When I was at the police station yesterday, I couldn't do anything *but* think. I was in this bare little room for so long that I saw the sun go right round. I saw the day dying away. Eventually, I came to the conclusion that I've been a crap mother.' And she says it so plainly, with none of the self-pity I can sniff out like a single drop of blood in a whole ocean, that I know she means it.

And because of that, I can say, 'You weren't,' and more or less mean it. Even though, in some crucial ways, she really was crap.

'I was all you had,' she says, 'and I didn't always put you first, I know. I put myself first, or maybe Karl. It's what my own mother did, in her way, and I despise that in myself. It's not an excuse.' She pushes the heels of her hands into the stair, hard. 'I swear it's not, but I reckon I got my addictions from her. Drugs, booze and men for me, the bloody Church for her.'

My grandmother. I think about our line of women – the addictive gene twisting inside our chromosomes – and wonder what my own weakness is. I think about last night, and my first night back, in the pub with Graham Warner, the way I find it difficult to stop drinking for the numbness and near-sleep it brings, which is why I hardly ever do it. Hardly ever do it in London, anyway.

'You haven't got it,' says Angie, in the way I'll never not find unnerving. 'You take after the other side, thank God.' She holds up her hands. 'Look, give me yours.'

I lift my left hand and she places her right one against it, palm to palm. I can feel the heat of her skin, the cold of her rings.

'See what I mean?' she says.

Her palm is square and strong, much broader than mine. Even though we've lined up our fingers at the bases, mine are half an inch longer. I've never noticed.

'You've got your lunulas, too.' She turns over my hand, points out the white crescents at the bottom of my nails. Only the little finger's is hidden under the cuticle. 'Little moons. Means you're creative. I haven't got any.' She tuts, smiles.

'So, if Karl's not my dad, who is?'

She turns to look out beyond the front door just as the shadow of a figure passes along the end of the garden. I know Angie sees it too, from the way her body stiffens. I wait for someone to open the little gate, but nobody does.

'Who was that?' I say, and I'm whispering again, though I don't know why.

'It's her,' Angie says simply. 'She comes here sometimes, especially on summer mornings like this.'

I've already opened my mouth to ask again who my father is, now I know it's not Karl – now that I'm sure I've been wasting my time all these years trying to take his features and overlay them onto my own – but the other side of the genetic coin doesn't seem to matter much any more. Then I properly absorb what Angie's just said.

'Who's *her*?' I say. 'Who are you talking about?'

'I call her the Lady of the Valley,' says Angie, softly, and it slides into place.

She's not talking about anyone real. She's talking about

a ghost. It's one of the many things Angie and I are usually diametrically opposed about. But there's nothing usual about today, and there's nothing usual about the way the air is very slightly humming and shivering in the wake of her.

1970

On the day the documentary crew arrived, before what happened with Graham, before . . . before what happened after, Karl had told her about a cottage, way off in the lower part of the estate, tucked below the beech escarpment, out of sight of the manor. 'I can just see you in there, flowers in jam-jars, little curtains up at the windows,' he said. 'I could get you a piano.'

She'd told him she played as a girl. That she'd had lessons for years and only stopped going when she got into trouble at school. Her mother had threatened to stop the lessons if she ever got into trouble again, so she'd said fine, she'd stop them right now. That she was bored stiff of going anyway.

'Jumped before you were pushed,' said Karl, in a rare moment of astuteness. Because he was right. She had done that. She *did* do that, all the time, with everything. She hadn't been bored of playing the piano, not at all. She still dreamt of it most nights, fingers flying over the keys, mind wonderfully quiet.

She was careful not to react too much when he mentioned the cottage. Instinctively, she knew she shouldn't betray how much she wanted it immediately: a place of her own, at least to a degree. A place of *their* own – her and her child – rather than a tent or someone's van. It would shock her younger self, who had reached the end of her parents' cul-de-sac and not even broken stride as she rounded the corner, suitcase swinging from her hand. But she had lately begun to feel tired in a way she hadn't since before she'd left. The notion of stone walls and a door she could lock against the night was deeply comforting in a way she couldn't have imagined before.

The morning after the night he'd almost promised the little cottage to her, she had woken alone under the eaves of the carriage-house, sun slanting in at forty-five degrees from the skylight in the roof. Beside her on the pillow was a deft little sketch: a woman in a tall crown, stars scattered through her long waving hair. He'd written *FAIry QUeeN* beneath it in the strange mixture of capitals and lower-case letters she'd seen in the notebooks where he wrote down his song lyrics.

She knew she should get back to the others at the encampment on the Great Meadow. They took turns with the children, with making the breakfast and all the rest of it. *They* being the women, of course. The counterculture didn't seem to extend to men sharing any of the domestic drudge-work. Funny, that.

But when she got downstairs – the studio still, thankfully, deserted at this time of the morning – she decided it wouldn't make any difference if she took another twenty minutes for herself. She'd seen the path he'd described, snaking tantalizingly downhill, but had never taken it before. Not many people did, by the look of it. She had to pick her way carefully through some sections, not just where the nettles pressed in, bristling with midsummer vigour, but because it was so steep in places that it made her knees ache.

There were other parts of her that ached; it felt as though each time with Karl was rougher than the last. She had pretended to enjoy it more than she had, and wondered afterwards what that made her. Was it the thought of the cottage that had made her grit her teeth when he turned her over, pushed her into the mattress so she couldn't move and shoved into her before she was ready?

She kept heading down, lost in her thoughts, until the clumps of nettles grew sparse and the way abruptly opened out. Like a curtain going up, the long, sinuous valley showed itself from an angle she'd never seen.

When she left the provincial town she'd spent her whole life in, she'd thought only about going to London – only about going bigger and brighter. Now, standing unobserved in the green velvet valley, a quirk in the topography almost cutting off the music you could hear everywhere else on the estate, she couldn't imagine herself hemmed in by so many roads and buildings that the whole world turned grey.

The cottage was just below another dip in the land, its chimneys visible before the rest because she was approaching it via a steep grass bank at its sturdy back.

When she got round to the front, she found it was a cottage a child would draw, symmetrical and neat, a front door in the middle flanked by leaded windows, two more above them. A feature that a child might not have thought of was the small oval window above the door.

It looked as if it hadn't been lived in for a long time.

The lozenges of the windowpanes were opaque with dust, and a small wooden porch over the front door, bowing under the weight of thick and twisting wisteria boughs, looked like it might collapse at any moment. But when she squinted, the good bones of the cottage shone out.

Even the garden, weed-strangled as it was, still had structure if you looked closely enough. The remnants of a gravel path ran down the centre from the gate, painted apple-green like the peeling porch and still in working order, though the creak when she pushed it open sent a pair of pigeons flapping away in ruffled indignation. In the deep beds under the windows, a few survivors from another era had survived the invasion of weeds: salvias, delphiniums and roses, and what would be some glorious hollyhocks when they opened in late summer.

Silently, she acknowledged her mother for this education she hadn't known she'd absorbed. The admission brought forth a memory that transported her straight to the neat back garden in which she'd taken her first steps, and specifically to the greenhouse where her mother grew tomatoes. The smell of it – rich and loamy, almost-but-not-quite sweet – came back to her and it wasn't just a sensory memory. Here, in this lost Gloucestershire garden, she could really smell it. She could smell her mother's scent of tuberose, too.

She stood there for a long time, not venturing past the gate, but not ready to leave. She was worried it might tempt Fate if she did, her presumption that the cottage was already hers yanking it out of her grasp for ever. But then she did what she so often did when temptation sidled into view, and went ahead anyway. She had just stepped inside the garden when the flutter of movement in the top left window stopped her dead.

A pale face surrounded by a mass of dark hair appeared in the dusty glass. She knew she should duck behind the wall so she wouldn't be seen but she couldn't move. Besides, the face wasn't looking down at her. It was angled towards the view, the long sweep of the valley.

She laid a hand on the gate. The painted iron was cold considering the warmth of the day. The shock of it steadied her. I won't get high today, she promised herself. But it wasn't that, she knew. It wasn't her mind playing tricks. This was something else.

She looked for the face again, but it had gone. The window was dark, empty but for dust and reflected sunlight. Perhaps it was a ghost, she thought, with a swooping kind of elation, even as her skin prickled. Someone who had been there before, who would still be there, just as she would be, in the years to come. The thought didn't make her frightened of the cottage. It only made her want it more.

Now, she looks back at that moment, less than a week ago, and she wants to weep with nostalgia. As though it was months ago, not just days. She hasn't mentioned the cottage to Karl since they briefly went there together, just after that first time, and suddenly it's the morning of the biggest Gathering yet, and she definitely can't pester him for reassurance today. Not unless she wants to push him into confirming he's changed his mind, that she can't have it after all.

The flame of hope that he'll forgive her is the reason she's ignoring the hard pebble inside her. If she just hangs on until everyone leaves tomorrow, she knows she'll be able to win back his adoration. Win back the promise of the cottage. Meanwhile, though. Meanwhile, the pebble is growing bigger and colder by the hour.

It's not just her body trying to warn her. The land itself is telling her to go. She can feel little tremors under her feet. It would take her, what, two hours to pack up and hitch a lift somewhere? But the little flame won't go out, and the cottage is still lit in her mind like hope. She's not going anywhere, not yet.

Chapter Twenty-Two

'I think I've worked it out,' Angie says, when we've been sitting on the stairs for so long that the shadows in the garden have visibly shortened, the sun climbing determinedly towards its highest point. That other shadow, whatever it was, *who*ever, hasn't returned. If I lay down on my bed, I reckon I could sleep for the whole day and through into the next.

'Rain, are you listening to me?' Angie says. 'Just now. I've got it, I'm sure I have.'

'Got what?'

'What I was saying last night, about Harkin. What she was keeping back about Willow, apart from the tarot card. If I hadn't been so caught up in my own worries, I'd have worked it out already. I should have worked it out when she was here for her reading.' She lets her head fall back against the wall. 'Willow was pregnant when she died.'

I straighten up. 'But . . . Are you sure?'

'Sure as eggs. Well, sure as I can be. Like I said yesterday, when the Empress card came up it was reversed, but she didn't know enough about the tarot to realize and I didn't tell her. The Empress card, at its most basic, is about fertility and fecundity. Everyone knows that. So when Willow said, "Makes sense," all happy and secretive, I think she knew she was pregnant and took the card as a kind of *blessing*.' She shakes her head. 'I should've known. It's not like me to miss something like that, but she was getting on my wick and, anyway, when I was her age, I knew to be careful. We got the pill in 'sixty-seven and it was this . . . miracle. I never missed a day. Oh, Lord, that poor girl.'

Girl. It makes me think not about Willow but Lennie – whether, if Angie is right, she knew her mum was pregnant. But I don't think so, somehow. Maybe I'm flattering myself, but I think she'd have told me yesterday, when she wept next to me in the car. I think she would have been excited about the prospect of a little brother or sister joining the two of them in the old bus, and that double loss would have come spilling out of her. There wasn't even a hint of it.

'You could be wrong. Maybe she wasn't pregnant at all.'

Angie looks sceptical. 'It *feels* right, though. You didn't see that secret little smile of hers.'

'Okay, so let's think about this logically. If your instincts are right and she was pregnant, then the police are going to think that might have been a factor. That it might have been *the* factor. Of course, Willow might not have told anyone she was pregnant – I'm pretty sure Lennie didn't know, and she didn't say anything to you, did she? And presumably she wasn't showing.'

'She wasn't. But people go to readings to get answers. Police will think she did tell me, or I read it in the cards and she confirmed it, and that I was so jealous I killed her for it. Oh, God.' She rubs at her temples.

'But does the pregnancy make it that much worse?' I say. 'I mean, what difference does it really make to you? If you were going to be murderously jealous of Willow, you'd have got rid of her months ago.'

'Could have been the final straw,' says Angie, glumly.

'Maybe.' I frown, try to think. 'They didn't say anything yesterday about cause of death, did they?'

'Nope.'

'I wonder if the autopsy showed something other than drugs and drink. Something that points to violence. Something bigger than tarot cards. Of course, if it did, it's much more likely to have been a man who killed her.' I remember those prickles of unease after dark, how I bolted the door last night. 'Are you sure there wasn't someone else in her life? An ex who'd shown up? Who didn't like her being here with Karl? Maybe even Lennie's father.'

Angie considers. 'No one that I heard or saw, and I don't miss much round here. She made no mention of it, if there was. And Karl wouldn't have allowed some old flame of Willow's to be here anyway. The free-love thing only ever worked one way with him. *He* could do what he liked, but he had to be someone's one and only. I know that very well.

'If you get someone pregnant unexpectedly then a baby coming along is usually trouble,' she says. 'Either you're single and staring down the barrel of a lifetime of responsibility for a little one you didn't want, or you're married and your affair is going to come out, and you'll lose your current set-up. The fun is over, whichever way you slice it.'

Her bleak summary feels totally incongruous as we sit there, surrounded by the beauty and enormous privilege of Tanglewood – of Karl's *current set-up*.

I admit the sentence that's been trying to form inside

my head, like the moth batting against the glass last night. Reluctantly, I open the window and let it in: *What if it was Karl?* Another part of my brain counters it immediately: *He's got an alibi. He wasn't even here.* But, now that I've thought it, it's going to be hard to get rid of it.

Angie sighs, grabs the banister and hauls herself up. 'I hate to think of him like that,' she says, when she gets to the bottom of the stairs. 'I can't bear to think he'd have it in him to do something like that. I've loved him all these years. I always will, I suppose.' She goes to the door so that half of her is inside, half out and dazzlingly lit with sunshine. I think of a prisoner reaching through the bars of their cell window to feel the sun on their skin, and it makes me shudder. *It's not a premonition*, I tell myself. Angie didn't do this, so there won't be any hard evidence that conclusively points to her.

'I think it's too late for me to cut myself free of him,' she's saying. 'It's so ingrained, so long-standing, that he's become part of me.'

It's then that I hear it – something different from the bees and the far-off tractor engine I've been dimly aware of for a while, plying up and down some field further down the valley.

'What's that?' I say, but it's louder now, and I know. Harkin. She's back.

Angie knows it too. She retreats inside, out of the glare, as though her animal instinct wants her to hide before it's too late.

'Good God, what can she possibly want with me now?' she says, doing her best to sound only exasperated. 'I've answered all her questions ten times over.' But then we lock eyes, and I see naked fear in hers, dark and pulsing like I've never seen before, even during the last few strange days.

She turns as, first, the Audi comes into view, and then a patrol car, blue lights strobing. 'Oh, for God's sake. What am I, one of the Great Train Robbers?'

I take her hand and it's cold, the palm sweaty. She squeezes mine until it hurts. Harkin doesn't look either of us in the eye as she comes down the path.

'I'm arresting you, Angela Valentine, on suspicion of the murder of Willow Green and in connection with the disappearance of Astrid X,' she says, and it's such a shock that, for an awful moment, I think I might laugh. In one sense because it's so clichéd, so surreal. And in another because it's both women now and I can't get my head round that in relation to Angie.

And then I realize she *has* laughed: an awful kind of shriek that makes her clap her hand over her mouth, as though she could stuff it back in. Her breathing turns shallow and loud, though not loud enough to drown out Harkin as she reads Angie her rights. Behind her is a man in uniform who can't possibly be one of the young officers Angie has mentioned. This is a huge slab of a man, face impassive, eyes small and expressionless.

'I need my things,' Angie cries. 'I can't go without my things.' She sounds like a confused old lady and it cuts through me.

I step forward. 'This is absurd.' My voice is clear and glass-edged. I sound a bit like Ottoline would, if Ottoline was ever to lose her temper. 'You kept her in for questioning all day yesterday and *now* you're charging her, not just with Willow's murder but because of the disappearance of someone from thirty years ago whose surname you don't even know? You thought Willow's death was accidental two days ago. You'd practically closed the case.'

'I'm not obliged to tell you anything,' says Harkin. She still hasn't met my eye. 'But I never thought it was accidental.'

She stands back with her arms folded, making room for the policeman to come forward with a pair of handcuffs. There's no need for them and I expect Angie to protest but she offers her wrists. They're trembling so violently that he has to hold them steady as he clicks them in. He's horribly outsized next to the cottage, next to Angie, his height and bulk so incongruous that it feels like an attack, a real violation.

'I didn't do anything, Rain,' she says, straining round to look at me as he leads her away. 'I didn't lay a finger on that girl. On either of them. You'll tell Lennie that, won't you? Will you promise me, Rain? Will you bring my things? My crystals? I can't do a night in that place without them.'

I promise her, even as my brain is thinking that just a handful of minutes ago I was watching her standing peacefully in her own doorway, the sun bright on her skin. Another part of my brain is whispering about that other thought I had and hoped wasn't a premonition, and a third is ringing alarm bells because she's just mentioned Lennie.

I glance at Harkin, who opens her mouth to speak just as a loud crackle issues from the patrol car's radio. She turns at the sound, distracted, and I jump in with questions before she can think to ask who Lennie is.

'What do I do now?' I say. 'Do I get her a lawyer? Can she be bailed? She's not in good health.'

Most of my understanding of legal process is cribbed from crime shows set in America. I follow Harkin down the path. Angie is already being guided into the police car, the officer's huge hand pushing down on her head. He hasn't said a word. He gets into the front and starts the engine. In the back, Angie is looking forwards, mouth tight. I think she's in shock. I think after her day of questioning yesterday, when nothing seemed to come of it, she'd really thought she was off the hook.

Harkin's got back into her car and I run round to the driver's side just as she closes the door. The window, which was open, rises smoothly.

'I don't understand what's happened,' I say, 'what's changed.'

She looks as if she's not going to respond but then the window goes down again.

'We wouldn't be doing this if there wasn't credible evidence linking your mother with both women,' she says.

I open my mouth to answer, but when I hesitate, afraid to say something that might inadvertently make things worse, Harkin guns the engine and pulls away so suddenly that dust rises from under her wheels.

The only good thing about any of this, I tell myself, as I watch the cars disappear out of sight, the usual noise and spirit of Angie reduced to an indistinct blur on the left side of the back windscreen, is that Harkin missed the Lennie thing.

Except I don't think Harkin misses anything. I think it will have gone in somewhere, and that it'll probably raise its head again once she's got Angie alone in an interview room.

Astrid. The name runs through my head like ticker tape, even while I'm thinking about what's going on right now. The other thought I had – the one I feared might be some sort of premonition – was about the tarot. That there'd been a card found on Astrid, too. If that's true . . . But, for my own sanity, I don't want to go down that road right now.

Chapter Twenty-Three

After Angie has been taken away, I grab my own keys. I get as far as fastening my seatbelt. It's stuffy inside the car, the air thick with the smell of hot plastic, dust and ink from the newspaper that's now lying on the back seat, where Willow's gaze seems to have taken on an air of reproach.

I open the door, undo the seatbelt, suck in fresh air. I could drive to town and ask to see Harkin, but they'll only tell me to wait or go home. It's pointless. I might even make it worse. It's better to wait, take Angie some things later.

I pocket the keys, not bothering to lock either the car or the cottage. In the absence of a clear plan, I do what I've always done when my feelings seem too big and painful to be contained inside my body. I run to Ottoline. She's always been the person who says the right, comforting things, who has the ability to make the real world vanish.

But, of course, she's with Lennie. There's another troubled little girl in her life now. I hear their voices first, like I heard them singing three nights ago, Ottoline's lullaby lilt, Lennie's like silver bells. It sounds as if they're on the terrace above the croquet lawn.

I peep carefully around the corner of the house just as a piece of music starts up. They're sitting dead centre on the terrace, at the Victorian table and chairs Ottoline and I used on sunny mornings. They're made of intricate wrought iron, with curlicues and whorls I would push my small fingers into. Each spring, Ottoline had them repainted bright white. Still does, by the look of it.

She and Lennie are sitting opposite each other, Lennie and her sharp eyes facing away from where I'm now half crouching behind a large pot. But there are four chairs, and in the other two are large dolls I've never seen leave their shelf in Caroline's bedroom. The music is coming from the old gramophone, which Ottoline has moved so it sits in the French windows, brass horn facing out. The sound is distorted and discordant from my angle, or maybe it's about to wind down, but what's playing suddenly clicks: 'The Teddy Bears' Picnic'. The clipped voice is slow, which makes its precision oddly sinister. In fact, the whole scene is so peculiar that everything that's just happened with Angie slides momentarily out of my head.

I watch, transfixed, as Ottoline lifts an empty china cup and drinks delicately from it. The porcelain is so fine that I can see the light glowing through it from where I am.

'How delicious,' she says. 'Isn't a good cup of tea so refreshing on a summer's day, Delia?' she says, turning to the doll next to her.

I remember these games. I haven't thought about them for a long time, but I remember them now. Ottoline and I played something like them in those snatched hours when Angie thought I was in the woods with the other children. In this heightened moment, I can recall exactly how I understood we were pretending even as I simultaneously believed it was real. The cups were empty even as they were full of the finest China tea.

Make-believe. I always found it easy to enter that state

with Ottoline. She was so good at moving to the side of reality – much better than most adults can ever manage, being too self-conscious or distracted by grown-up concerns. For the first time, it strikes me how well this skill must have served her over the years with Karl.

I watch for a while, wistful even, as my old friend disloyalty creeps in, just as it always did when I sneaked off to Ottoline. There's something else, too, now, and I don't know if it's just because I'm witnessing this scene with the jaundiced eyes of an adult, whether it's simply sad, or something really is a little off here. *This is a bit creepy*, my brain says, and disloyalty floods me again.

But I don't interrupt them. I don't even consider it. What could I say in front of Lennie anyway? I'm craving Ottoline's soothing words like a drug but, really, I know where I need to go now, and that's to see Graham Warner. He's the one who brought Astrid out into the light. Maybe he'll have an idea why she seems to have been officially connected to Willow by the police.

It's grown overcast since I left the cottage. I hadn't noticed but across the valley a great mass of cloud has gathered above the escarpment. There's no breeze, nothing stirring the air. The clouds seem to wait, motionless, as if gathering strength before some imminent battle.

I'm about to head downhill for my car when the low rumble of thunder turns out to be a pair of enormous lorries coming down the Dark Ride towards the manor.

'Here they are, right on time,' says a voice behind me, making me suck in my breath and swing round. It's Karl, and I rear back before I can help it. He catches hold of my arm, his grip strong. 'Why so jumpy, sweetheart?' he says.

'Sorry, sorry,' I say, 'bit of a morning,' and he lets go, stands back and observes me curiously.

This is Karl, I tell myself. You've known him for ever. Calm *down*.

I stand there limply while he talks to the driver high in the cab of the first lorry, giving him instructions, gesturing towards the Great Meadow and the woods beyond. There's already activity at the far side: vans and generators and people assembling things. The Gathering Y2K is really happening. I've known Karl would absolutely push on with plans, despite simultaneously not believing he'd really have the gall.

Soon, he's back. 'I gotta make some phone calls, Rainy. Busy day. Those guys,' he nods towards the lorries, 'they just delivered my stage.' He grins. 'Hey, I'll see you later, yeah?'

He's already turning in the direction of the courtyard and the carriage-house.

'Wait,' I say, and he stops, a spasm of irritation crossing his face. 'Let me come with you.'

I hurry after him across the worn old cobbles of the courtyard in front of the carriage-house. There's music playing from inside; he must have left it on. For once, it's not his own. Instead, it's a woman's voice, Joni Mitchell, but the song takes me a beat longer to identify, hovering at the doorway Karl has already disappeared through, not ready for whatever this conversation is going to be. Then it clicks into place. 'Ladies of the Canyon'. Canyons, valleys. The similarity feels significant.

'This is gonna have to be quick,' says Karl, when I make myself go in after him. He sits down on the padded leather swivel chair behind his desk. 'I need to check on progress after these calls and some of the guys are showing up later. I've got a couple of new songs I want to play them. Works in progress, you know.' He reaches out for the guitar propped next to the desk. It's a beauty: a 1972 Les Paul. A present from Ottoline years ago. 'I'm considering playing one of them on Saturday night.'

'I won't keep you long.' I sit down on a hard chair opposite him.

He lets out a little sigh and puts the guitar down again. 'Okay, I'm all yours. How can Karl help?'

Nerves vibrate inside me but I picture trembling hands, wrists swollen by age, already turning red from metal cuffs. 'Angie's been arrested.'

He only partially reacts, dipping his chin in a strange little nod, but his face doesn't alter. Actually, that's not quite true. His expression is like the day outside, devoid of shade and interest. I watch it flatten into uniform blankness.

'They brought her home last night but then came back just now. I don't know whether they've found out something new or whether they've just decided they've got enough to charge. Convinced the CPS.' I'm beginning to gabble, and make myself stop.

Karl's gaze is fixed somewhere over my left shoulder. 'I'm sorry to hear it,' he says.

'I'm really worried about her.'

'Well, like I told you last night, Angie's tough.'

'Maybe once upon a time she was. I'm not so sure now. She was shaking when they handcuffed her.'

He doesn't expect that, which is why I said it. He meets

my eye for a second. His are as blue as the ocean, and just as unfathomable.

'I thought they might have rung you or left a message,' I stammer. Karl never answers the phone when he's busy. Never calls anyone back. 'You know, to tell you about some . . . new development?' I don't know whether I should mention Astrid or not.

'Why would they say anything to me?' he says.

'Because Willow died here, on the estate?' My voice rises and I stop, force myself to breathe. 'I thought they'd be keeping you in the loop.'

Then – probably because I can see I'm not getting anywhere with him, can't fully penetrate the wall he's constructed – I ask him the question that's hovering in the air over us, like one of the clouds across the valley.

'Karl, do you think Angie could have hurt Willow?'

He leans back in his seat, legs out straight in front of him, crossed at the ankle. His face is tipped back so he's looking down his nose at me. It sharpens his face, brings his eyes closer together.

'And not just Willow,' I rush on, nerve beginning to fail. 'Astrid, too.'

He gets up so fast that the swivel chair flies backwards and hits the wall. I watch him pace back and forth, my hands gripping the underside of my own chair. The urge to stand up is so strong that my legs are twitching.

Finally he comes to a stop, kicks the chair back into position and throws himself into it. I realize – late, because I'm rusty these days – that he's intense and wired and jumpy enough to be on something. Karl has always had an incredible appetite for drugs – and an incredible tolerance to match, despite his wiry frame. I've never spent much time thinking about it because I was always kept busy worrying about Angie.

He wheels closer to me. 'See, the thing is . . .' – he smacks the palm of his hand hard against the side of his leg three times – '. . . the thing is, there's a lot you don't know about Angie. Angie then, and Angie now.'

'What do you mean?'

He looks away, shakes his head. It feels performative but maybe I'm too nervy too judge.

'Please don't say that and then not tell me,' I say.

'Okay,' he nods, as if relenting, 'okay, fine. Well, she's using again, for starters. Did she tell you that?'

'She isn't. I'd know. A bit of wine, a bit of weed before bed. That's it.'

He looks at me and, for the first time, there's softness in his face. It might be real. 'Oh, Rainy.'

I can't tell whether I want to cry or hit him. Maybe both.

'It's true,' I say. 'I've seen her at rock bottom and she's nowhere near that. I know her better than anyone.'

'Sweetheart, you've been back, what, four days? You of all people should know how wily addicts are, how good they are at hiding things they don't want you to see. She can't keep it up with me because I'm the one who's always there. I'm her *constant*, you know. Her North Star.'

His egotism saves me; the tears retreat. *Always there*. A memory comes then, not one of the old ones that must be in there somewhere, under psychological lock and key, but one I *choose* not to access.

I must have been fourteen or fifteen and I'd been avoiding

Karl and the carriage-house because he had his musician friends staying and one of them – McQuinn – gave me the shivers, following me round with his eyes and literally licking his lips, which were always cracked and sore-looking. It was as if his thoughts were corrupting his body. I knew without being told that I should never be alone with him. The only small comfort was that his fascination with me was purely down to my age.

Anyway, one night Angie was raging and uncontrollable in the cottage. These were the days when I wished we had near neighbours, so that things were inevitably taken out of my hands and I could go and live with Ottoline.

That night, she was drunk, high and threatening to cut her wrists. Karl had neglected her for days. She was going through the clutter of the bathroom cabinet and smashing everything she could, looking in vain for razors I had already hidden. I decided I needed help and it went without saying that Ottoline was never to be bothered with Angie troubles. I would have to go to Karl.

Nothing awful happened, not really. I went to the carriage-house and Karl said they were in the middle of a crucial session, and that Angie would blow herself out, as though she was weather instead of my crazed only parent, bent on killing herself. The creepy one with the damaged mouth said *he* could help me and all of them laughed.

That was the sum of it, but it spoilt something for me about Karl, though I did my best to tidy it away and never think of it again. Now, I've found out for sure that he isn't my father, and while I haven't had the head space to digest it yet, I know it isn't going to hurt much. Before that time in the studio – when in my nightdress I had to ask him for help in front of seven strange men, one of whom was staring at my bare legs – knowing I wasn't his daughter would have broken my heart. It hasn't today. The softness in his face is a lie.

'You were never there, unless it suited you to be,' I say quietly, my stomach lifting at my daring, like driving fast over a hump-backed bridge.

His pupils flare and I wonder how long it's been since anyone challenged him. The blankness is back, but darker now.

'Okay,' he says. 'If you really want to know, I'll tell you. Angie has a dark side. I always knew it. I was drawn to it at the beginning, if I'm honest.' He almost smirks. 'You don't have a clue what happened that summer. You were just a kid. How could you?'

That summer. Astrid. He's going to tell me something about Astrid.

He propels himself around the desk and gets hold of my wrists before I can react. When I try to pull away, he grips them tighter. 'I'm so scared for Angie, Rain. I care for her so much. She's been this great love in my life for so long, but I'm real scared that the dark side of her has come back.'

'Come back?'

Something passes over his face. He licks his lips, for the first time seems almost uncertain.

'Are you talking about Astrid?' I make myself say. I try to pull away again because, even though I just asked the question, I don't want to hear any more, but he holds me fast, adjusting his grip so he's holding my hands instead. Mine are sweating, his are cool and hard, not really like flesh at all.

'You don't remember that summer, do you?' he says. Any uncertainty, if that's what it even was, has gone.

I shake my head. 'Just a couple of fragments.'

'And why do you think that is?'

'What do you mean?'

He lets me go, wheels back a little. 'Look, I remember stuff from when I was four, five, maybe younger. So much stuff. I remember being a kid this high.' He levels his hand at waist height. 'We used to go to this lake in summer. My uncle had a cabin there. I remember everything about it. Every inch of it. And then there's you. Nothing until you were nine, ten, right? That's not normal. The mind is clever, man. It's protecting you. But you've got to ask from what, haven't you? It's high time you asked that, Rainy Day.

'If I could get inside that head of yours, unlock it and see what's in there?' He sucks air through his lips. 'I think it'd be pretty bad. I think maybe you saw something back then that your brain didn't let you remember. I've always believed that.'

He fishes in his pocket for a stick of gum, bends it into his mouth unhurriedly. My hands are gripping the underside of my chair again.

'Look, it breaks my heart to doubt Angie,' he says. 'You surely know it does. But I gotta protect my girls now. My *other* girls. You, Lady O; Lennie, too.' He points a finger at me. 'Now, don't you forget that *you* made me tell you this, but last week, the day before Willow died, Angie came to me. Came here, as a matter of fact. She sat where you are right now and she gave an ultimatum. She said if I didn't leave Willow alone I'd be sorry. I said to her that she'd got it all wrong, that it wasn't like that between us. That what we had together was on a spiritual plane.

'But she didn't believe me. She said she knew from the cards that I was lying.' He pauses, lets the tarot reference sink in. I fight to keep my expression unchanged. 'When she left, she looked . . .' He sighs, apparently searching for the right word by raising his eyes to the ceiling, even as his jaws work the gum. 'She looked possessed, Rainy. I'm gonna be brutally honest with you now: I looked deep into her eyes and what I saw there scared me. *She* scared me. She scared the shit out of me.

'I didn't tell the police that part. Only the facts. I had to tell them something else, too. It was only right that I did. Angie was convinced Willow was pregnant. You know how she thinks she's psychic? She reckoned it was mine. She hated the idea of that, hated it. She wouldn't listen when I told her that if she *was* pregnant, then it weren't nothing to do with me, Officer.' He holds up his hands in mock surrender, even in this moment amused by his hillbilly accent. 'Anyway, between those two things, whatever the cops have worked out for themselves, and Angie having no alibi, I guess they thought they had enough.'

Chapter Twenty-Four

Outside the carriage-house, the clouds on the ridge look darker. Or maybe it's just fear telling me so. From the direction of the Great Meadow comes the rhythmic crash of metal on metal. I start walking, speeding up until the back of my top is damp and loose hair is sticking to my face. When I put my hands to my cheeks, they're burning. At the top of a hill I've blindly climbed, mind whirring with everything I've just heard, I stop to rest, bending over, hands on hips.

By the time I've got my breath back, an endorphin-soaked clarity is washing through me. When Angie and I were sitting on the stairs this morning, I genuinely believed she hadn't done anything, and that she'd only just suspected the pregnancy. With Karl in the carriage-house, doubts began to crowd in again, but my gut instinct now is that, of the two of them, it's him who's lying. I know when Angie is in the grip of addiction better than anyone, Karl included. He never had to live with her like that. I did.

Besides, even when things were at their worst between us, Angie never laid a hand on me, or even looked as if she might. She only ever hurt herself. It's true that I ended up with collateral damage, but she never intended that.

So, if Karl *is* lying, he's selling Angie down the river to save his own skin, surely. It was clever of him to bring up the pregnancy possibility with police, to get in there first, handing them the scenario of an Angie deranged by jealousy before they could come for him.

One thing that does look objectively more incriminating for him than Angie is the Ottoline question. A mistress living on the estate out of sight is one thing. A mistress carrying Karl's child might be a very different matter.

Ottoline's parents never came round to Karl while they were still alive. Who knows what arrangements were put in place all those years ago to protect their daughter if she were ever to divorce? Maybe he would get nothing and he knows that. Maybe Willow becoming pregnant with Karl's child almost exactly thirty years after she lost her darling Caroline finally wore out Ottoline's saintly patience.

I keep conjuring up dark scenarios as the clouds build and glower in the sky above the valley. Willow refusing to have a termination. Willow threatening to go to Ottoline and tell her everything. Willow waiting for the summer to wear on so her body revealed the truth for her.

'Rain? Are you okay?'

I spin round to find Caleb standing there. His looks change with the light and his mood but today he looks like Ottoline, and I'm relieved.

'I – I don't know,' I say. 'Angie's been arrested.'

'When? What the fuck?' And he's so obviously shocked, in such contrast to Karl's reaction, that my eyes fill with tears.

'They came not long after you left.'

He shakes his head. 'But they questioned her all day yesterday. Why didn't they charge her then?'

'I don't know. Maybe they had to get approval from higher up. Maybe something new came to light.' I hesitate, then decide to keep going. 'I've just been speaking to your dad.'

'What did he say?' He looks like he's bracing himself.

'Oh, he really went for it. Said Angie has a dark side. That she was obsessed with the idea that he'd got Willow pregnant. That she threatened him in a jealous rage. He said he looked into her eyes and what he saw there scared the shit out of him.'

'Oh, no. Jesus, Rain.'

'He was hinting that she was like this back in 1970, too. With Astrid. He didn't exactly come out and say it. He didn't say much that was definite, actually, but . . . Well, the police definitely think the two are connected now. When they came for Angie, they arrested her for Astrid's disappearance too.'

'Shit.' Caleb has gone pale under his tan.

I swipe at my eyes. 'I don't know what to do. I've been trying to figure it all out but . . .'

I hang my head and he pulls me into a hug. I resist for a second, but then let him. With my head hard up against his chest, I can hear his heart beating fast.

'My father's a born liar,' he says fiercely, voice vibrating through me. 'Angie . . . well, Angie has her faults, but she's not a liar. Not where it counts. And if he's lying about all this, trying to push it all onto her, he's got something to hide.'

Since my first doubts about Angie, my brain has been helpfully gathering a shuffling line of bad memories: all those times she swore she hadn't had a drink, even though

I'd already found an empty bottle of gin tucked into the mouse-chewed cavity in the back of the sofa. Or that she'd been clean for weeks, even as her jaw was working, or her pupils were so dilated there were no irises left. But I realize something important now: I *knew* she was lying then because she was crap at it. I believe her now. Maybe Caleb's logic holds.

Suddenly exhausted, I sit down hard on the grass just as thunder – real, this time – begins to roll around the valley, low-pitched and leisurely, as if undecided whether to bother yet. Caleb sits down beside me, close enough for our thighs to be touching.

'So, apparently we're not related,' I say, after a while. I need a break from thinking about the rest of it.

He lets out a shocked bark of laughter. '*What?*'

I turn to him. 'Did you never wonder about it?'

'Hang on, hang on. You mean you thought Karl might be your father and therefore I was . . . No, I never thought that. Why the hell did you?'

My cheeks heat up again. 'Because I wondered when I was little, and Angie would never give me a straight answer. I thought that might mean he was. Otherwise, why not say so?'

He frowns and I know he's trying to think of something nice to say so I don't feel stupid.

'Yes, I know that sounds daft when Angie would do anything for a bit of drama,' I say. 'But I was young and he was the only man I'd ever known her love. The only man in her life. He's *still* the only man, God help her. And, well, sometimes I've thought I could see something alike about us.' I look down at the grass, pluck at it. 'It's actually completely humiliating, the hours I've spent in the mirror looking for similarities.'

'I can't believe you thought this all these years,' Caleb says. 'That's nuts.'

'Not that nuts. We grew up surrounded by all this free-love bollocks. Angie has been Karl's mistress for years and years, living down the hill from his wife, and no one ever says a word. It's not that much of a leap, is it?'

'I didn't mean it's nuts like that. I meant . . .' He stops, laughs and groans at the same time.

'What? Caleb, I'm confused enough, trying to work out what the hell happened here, without you being cryptic too.'

'Oh, Christ, you think you're embarrassed. Look, it never entered my head you might be my sister. And thank fuck for that, because that would have made my teenage crush on you even weirder than anything our parents could ever come up with.'

I turn to him in astonishment. Thunder rumbles again, and the light has turned a grubby, jaundiced yellow. 'Seriously, you liked me when we were kids? Are you winding me up? Angie said something earlier but I didn't think for a second that . . .'

He squints at the strange sky. 'I'm not winding you up. What did Angie say? I thought I'd hidden it quite well.' He smiles ruefully.

'It wasn't about then, it was after you came round this morning. She said you were sweet on . . .' I grind to an embarrassed halt.

'Oh, right. Cheers, Angie.' Then he realizes what he's said, remembers where Angie is right now, and looks even more sheepish. 'Look, we'll sort this out. I promise.'

'Thank you. But I'm worried about Harkin. She was already determined to prove this wasn't an accident. But now she's been getting a lot of pressure to wrap it up from above – Angie got that much out of someone yesterday. She's not popular at the station apparently. She's probably going to get transferred back. For her pride, if nothing else, she'll want this done and dusted before that can happen.'

'What do you think the connection is to what happened back then? Do you think they've got something solid?'

I assume he doesn't know about the tarot card, and I'm not sure I can bear to tell him and have his expression show me that his belief in Angie has been shaken. 'I suppose Harkin thinks so,' I say. 'She doesn't believe in coincidences, and there are a lot of them.'

'Right.'

A single heavy spot of rain lands on my arm. I rub at it, spreading it across my skin. Another lands on Caleb's leg.

'We should get under cover,' he says, then reddens again.

I get to my feet, rub at my temples because my head is beginning to pound. I don't know if it's the amount of information I'm trying to process, or the pressure of the gathering storm.

'Shall we . . . shall we meet up later?' he says, as I turn to go. 'We could try to figure things out in the pub?' His face is hopeful and it makes something inside me twist and flip.

I give him a tight smile. 'I need to check back in with work. Maybe tomorrow?'

He nods and walks away without another word.

Chapter Twenty-Five

I can't settle in the cottage. It's so full of Angie that her physical absence makes it feel like she's died. I make the mistake of looking up the Six of Cups in a tarot book and see it's connected to childhood trauma, which is all I need after what Karl said about repressed memories.

Before I go to the police station, I need to talk to Warner again – after all, he's the only person who seems to want to talk about Astrid. I don't feel clear-headed enough yet, though.

Slowly, slowly, the sky begins to clear, the storm holding off for now, but the retreating thunder still feels like a horrible portent of what lies ahead.

When the urge to run becomes overwhelming, I get into the car. If I can't be in control of anything else, I can at least take charge of a ton of moving metal. I go the Dark Ride way, forgetting that Karl's lorries are blocking it. Men in hi-vis are unloading scores of long metal poles, laying them out neatly on the flatbed of a trailer attached to a huge tractor. These tangible signs that the Gathering is actually going to happen give me the same feeling in the pit of my stomach as the thunder. It's almost like déjà vu.

Once I've squeezed past them onto the grass verge, I speed up, hoping that if Lennie hears the engine, she won't be quick enough to get to me this time. Not because

I don't want her company but because of where I need to go, the space and quiet I need before I do. And, to that end, I think it might be a good idea to ring Dan. The thought of him sets off a strange feeling, which I identify after a moment as a weird sort of homesickness for his solid presence and certainty about everything.

I hesitate on the other side of Tanglewood's gates, foot on the brake, and watch them swing slowly shut behind me in the rear-view mirror. I turn the wheel left – the opposite direction to the village and, beyond it, Stroud. This way you're hard pushed to get anywhere significant fast. I'd quite relish losing myself in the maze of single-track lanes, which sporadically offer up a shockingly picturesque hamlet you probably couldn't find again if you tried. Meandering along these roads for an hour or so without purpose is exactly what I need.

I pull up in one particularly pretty spot, with sloping fields on one side and an ancient farmstead on the other, so old it's hunkered down into the land like it's always been part of it. An old black Labrador comes to sniff my wheels, then ambles off. There are three bay horses in the pasture on the other side of the wall I've stopped by, and when I wind down my window, I can hear their contented nickering, the slow swish of their tails. The sunlight is glossy on their coats.

Yesterday, despite the barrage of texts, I had no real intention of calling Dan back. Being chased always sends me haring off in the opposite direction. But now . . . maybe I need him.

I check my phone. The little hamlet must be relatively high up or near a mast because there are a couple of bars of reception. Before I can overthink it and change my mind again, I press the button to call him back.

He picks up after a single ring, like he's been waiting.

'Rain.' His voice is cold, flat.

'Sorry,' I say, though it doesn't sound very convincing. 'I didn't wake you up, did I?' Even as I say it, I realize it's the middle of the day in Florida. 'The reception round here is non-existent.'

He doesn't reply. I hear the hollow tap-tap of his plastic keyboard as he resumes typing. From nowhere or, rather, because I've had quite a lot to deal with since coming back to the place *he* sent me, my temper flares.

'I'll go then, shall I?' I say, each word a hard little stone. 'Seems a bit pointless phoning you if you're not going to say anything, especially given how much this must be costing.'

'I've tried you multiple times.' His voice is like flint. 'Texted you. How long does it take to write one message in reply? I've been worried.'

And as quickly as it reared up, my anger ebbs away. 'Look, there's been some family stuff going on,' I say. 'I've been sorting it out, or trying to.'

'Oh.' He pauses and I can almost hear him thinking. 'You should've said. Is everything okay? Is it your mum?'

The sum of what Dan knows: I come from a village near Stroud and my relationship with my mum is . . . fraught; that it was just the two of us when I was growing up, which made it intense at times. I've never told him about her addictions and the mental-health problems that went hand-in-hand, but he's not stupid. He's seen how uptight I am about people having the odd recreational dabble with drugs; how withdrawn and anxious I am on the rare occasions I've got drunk.

'Yes,' I say, because his voice is softer and the typing has stopped. 'She's not ill or anything. But there's a bit of an emergency situation she needs my help with.'

'Okay. Fair enough. If you'd just said that then . . .' He tails off. 'I – I don't suppose you've had much chance to look into the Willow Green case, then?' He sounds so careful that it throws me off guard. Dan gets obsessive about new ideas and I know he thinks this Tanglewood segment would be the icing on the cake. Of course, he doesn't know the half of it.

'About that,' I begin, but alarm bells are going off and I stop. Instead, indecision warping into fatigue, I let my forehead come to rest against the steering wheel.

He waits and I appreciate him not hurrying me.

'Look, there's a lot I haven't told you about . . .' I pause, working out how to phrase it.

'Everything to do with you, ever?' he supplies.

I laugh, then burst into tears.

'Rain?' He sounds as surprised as I feel. 'Are you crying?'

I've never done that in front of him. I have the sense he's holding his breath in case the slightest misstep makes me put down the phone.

'There's a lot going on here,' is all I manage to say, for the second time, and with ridiculous understatement.

'I'm sorry. I feel bad for sending you back there. I never thought . . .'

'You couldn't have known.'

'Do you – do you want to tell me? I might be able to help.'

'I found Graham Warner in the pub.'

'Oh.'

I swallow. *Keep going.* 'Did you know they started filming for a documentary in the summer of 1970?'

'Of course. It's one of those things people like me get all geeky about, speculating on what happened to it.' He pauses. 'Why?'

'Warner reckons he's got some old footage.'

'Holy shit, really?'

'He might be bullshitting. He was pretty drunk, and I think it's become a bit of an obsession, to say the very least.'

'But you're going to find out, right? I mean, if you've got time. Because, you know, if you need some leave, you can have it. And it won't count as holiday or anything.'

'Dan, it's fine. I just feel weird today because I got a good night's sleep.'

'Okay. So, can I help? With the Graham Warner stuff? Obviously I'm still away but I can look stuff up, book a camera guy if you need one for Saturday. Do you need me to get you a press ticket?' He stops. I can almost hear his mind whirring on the other side of the Atlantic. 'What did Warner say about the woman who went missing in 1970? It would be good to have a name, so we can try to track down a photo. Obviously we're all about the music here, but it might be a nice little mystery. Something atmospheric. The dark side of England's Summer of Love. That sort of thing.'

He talks on, thinking aloud, while I watch the horses,

the slow ripple of their muscles as they graze. I toy with the idea of simply telling Dan everything. The notion – the idea I could just open my mouth and do it – makes hysteria bloom inside me.

Never mind Graham Warner and his monomania. I nearly forgot to say that the mother I never discuss has just been arrested for the murder of Willow Green! Turns out she was sleeping with Mum's long-time lover, who – have I never told you this? – is Karl. Yes, Karl Lund.

I cover my mouth with my hand, as though it might all just spill out of me without something physical there to stop it. I'm close enough that I can feel the first words forming on my tongue.

But maybe there's a third way. A way Dan can help without my having to give so much of myself away. I feel like I need the Rain he knows still to exist somewhere for the time after all this, assuming there is one.

That feeling – of brushing up against the possibility of spilling all my secrets – slips away, as quickly as it came. And not just because, like Karl is an ingrained part of Angie, my instinct for privacy is an ingrained part of me. It's also because I can't be sure what might make things worse right now. It's because I don't entirely trust Dan not to use this.

The part of him that's an investigative documentary-maker is much bigger, much more established – much more ingrained – than the part that cares about me. His talk about taking time off for personal reasons doesn't convince me otherwise. After all, it's great material. My own instincts are good enough to know that. The documentaries where the makers find themselves dragged in are special. The objective eye of the camera turned back in on itself. It's always riveting.

'So, what do you think?' he says, breaking into my thoughts. 'How can I help from here? Do you want me to get in touch with Sarah, see if she can head up tomorrow for the weekend, give you a hand?'

'No, no, don't do that. I don't want to scare anyone off.' I stop. I need to give him something. 'Look, I was actually going to drop in on Warner at home. He gave me his card.'

'Okay,' he says eagerly. 'That's a great idea. How are you going to play it?'

'I'll call his bluff on the footage thing,' I hear myself saying. 'It's one thing claiming he's got some when he's at the pub, five pints down. It's another if I'm there, at his house, hinting there might be a broader, more serious place for it than being yesterday's chip paper. I'm thinking that if I play up my local connection, he might be more likely to go with it.'

'Play it up how?'

'Well, maybe tell him I knew the estate as a kid.'

He pauses. 'And did you? Know the estate as a kid? Why didn't you say that on Monday?'

'I mean, I kind of knew it. Everyone round here knew it as the "big house".' I hurry on, before he can ask me to explain.

'Okay, so tell me how I can help. Surely I can do some digging in the background. We've ground to a bit of a halt over here. I've been stuck in my motel room, editing scripts.'

I try to think how I could use Dan's expertise without boxing myself into a corner. He's the best in the business at digging stuff up, unearthing new leads when everyone else has long given up and gone home. It doesn't hurt that new stuff is going up on the internet all the time. One of the runners we used on our last project nicknamed Dan 'Tenacious D' for good reason. If I can prise some more concrete information about Astrid out of Graham Warner, Dan can enjoy trawling the ever-expanding fringes of the net and maybe indirectly help Angie at the same time. I don't know how, only that it feels like something positive that has potential.

'I've got a name for the first woman who died,' I say. 'Astrid.' I catch my reflection in the rear-view mirror, jaw tight with tension.

'Ooh, nice. Did you get that out of Warner?'

Actually, it was the police. 'Yes, that's right. He'd had a few. I thought you could go on those forums, see if she comes up. Even without a surname, it's pretty distinctive.'

After we hang up, I wonder if I've done the right thing. Something else is lurking between the wobbly lines of my own calculations about keeping Dan off my back and helping Angie. It's emitting such a low frequency that it barely registers, like the almost-imperceptible tug of gravity from a distant moon. And that's the pull of my own moth-eaten early childhood. Maybe Dan, oblivious – or as close to oblivious as I can keep him – might help fill in those missing pieces, too.

Chapter Twenty-Six

When I get to the village, Warner's little almshouse looks scruffier than it did by moonlight. This part of the Cotswolds is not as manicured as the Oxfordshire bit, but it's always been picture-postcard tidy here and Warner is rather letting the side down. He probably gets passive-aggressive notes through his letterbox, suggesting numbers for gardeners and dry-stone wallers.

It takes him a while to answer the door. Long enough that I'm beginning to worry it's a sign: that Warner not being in means I shouldn't have told Dan anything.

But suddenly he's pulling back the door, shading his eyes from the sun, like a mole that's surfaced by accident. I wait and eventually he gets there.

'You're the one from the pub,' he says. 'Couldn't place you for a second. Thought you were the police again.'

'Do you mind if I come in?' I say, appearing impressively casual considering what he's just said. 'It's hot out here. It's just that I've been thinking a lot about what you said before, and I wanted to ask you something about the documentary.'

He straightens, and I see it then. A momentary flash of who he used to be. Strong and golden, everything still possible, all his cards still in play. The man in my first recovered memory from back then. As swiftly as it's come, it's gone, and he's an old man again. Prematurely old, too. He stands back and, before he can change his mind, I step past him straight into the living room. It smells of unemptied ashtrays and loneliness.

I hover, unsure whether or not I should sit down, and realize that, now he's not dazzled by the sun, I'm getting another, more thorough, inspection. To an unnerving degree, in fact. Various things ratchet through my head, the most crucial of them being the one that will always occur to a woman alone with a man she barely knows: nobody knows where I am. I've voluntarily put myself inside the house of someone who, like Angie and Karl, was around then and now. Who, for all I know, might be guilty – although going to the tabloids and proclaiming two counts of murder, when the first was entirely buried and the second might have been in time, would take some double-bluffing balls.

'I know you,' he says, so softly I almost don't catch it – as though he's not actually talking to me but is in conversation with some alter-ego of his own. The thought makes the hairs on the back of my neck stand on end.

'Yes,' I say, forcing myself to smile. 'We met at the pub.' My throat is dry and I swallow. It's loud in the silent room.

'No,' he says. 'Not then. Some other time.'

Some other time. It's Angie. He thinks I look like Angie. I calculate as fast as I can, before he can throw me out or lock me in the attic.

'You probably knew my mum,' I say, in a rush. Apart from the fact that I'd rather stay anonymous, I can't think of a good reason not to mention my personal connection right now. 'Back in the day at Tanglewood. I probably remind you of her.'

Something crosses his face. I'm not sure what. He's frowning, even as he keeps on staring. I fold my arms over my chest. 'Angie Valentine,' I say.

'Angie V . . . Yeah, I remember,' Warner says, slowly nodding. 'She all right, is she? I haven't crossed paths with her in a long time.'

I nod. I'm not about to tell him where she is right now.

'Funny old arrangement they've got up there.' He laughs rustily. 'Still, you could argue that it's lasted longer than a lot of marriages do. No offence.'

'I'm actually doing a bit of research on Tanglewood,' I push on, because I don't really fancy getting into the complexities of my mother's weird *ménage à trois* – especially not with Graham Warner and his hotline to the *Mail*.

His face sharpens. 'Oh, are you indeed? You didn't say anything about research at the pub. You a hack then, too, are you?'

'Oh, I thought I did say.' I smile as guilelessly as I can. 'And, no, I'm not a newspaper journalist. I make documentaries. Like the one you were involved with all those years ago.'

'I didn't tell the papers I had footage, and I didn't tell you about it the other night, either. If you know, you must have been talking to that female copper. Harkin.'

'She came to speak to Angie once she was assigned the case. She said something about it, in passing.'

'I didn't take to her much,' he says. 'Harkin, I mean. Nothing soft about her. Women weren't like that in my day. Well, the nice ones weren't. Women were more fun. *Angie* was fun.'

'Okay, forget it. This was a bad idea.'

He puts up his hands. 'Oh, come on, I didn't mean anything by it. Nothing like that, anyway. She was a laugh, Angie, that's all. Life and soul. Everyone liked her. I'm not being disrespectful, honest.'

I decide to give it a bit more time. At the least, I need to see if the police were here yesterday, and what he might have given them if they were. I sit down on the sofa, and Warner, apparently relieved, settles into his armchair. Unintentionally, he's shifted the power balance to me.

'Angie doesn't believe you can have any footage,' I say. 'She reckons none of it survived.'

He smiles. 'She wasn't one of the camera crew, though, was she?'

'So what have you got?'

He sighs. 'Not much, actually. And nothing Harkin thought was incriminating when I showed her the first time. She was in and out in half an hour.'

'There have always been rumours of something surviving,' I say. 'There's this forum on the internet. Most people are sceptical but one person was claiming it's true, said he'd seen it. Was that you?'

He gives a shout of laughter. 'Me, on the World Wide Web? I wouldn't have the first clue. I haven't even got a mobile phone.'

Unless he's lying, I've got him wrong on that front. He might be spending hours alone, staring at a screen in a darkened room, but it's his own cinefilm he's looking at, not the depths of the web.

'I'm not going to exaggerate,' he's saying now. 'It's mainly little snatches of stuff. A couple of minutes here and there where I was testing the light levels and the equipment and whatnot ahead of the real action. There's little that would have made the final cut, but it's definitely very . . . What's the word? *Evocative.* That's it. It gives you a sense of how it was then. A flavour. And, of course, Astrid is on it.'

My skin prickles. Harkin might not have seen anything significant, but maybe she was looking for the wrong things.

'Where did the rest of it go?' I say. 'If you kept some, maybe other people did too.'

'Bill Laing – he was the director, it was him who dealt with Karl – he would have had the rest of it. I heard something about Karl asking for it, said he owned the rights to it and, if it wasn't going to be finished, he didn't want anyone else getting hold of it. For privacy reasons or some such. I wasn't really taking note, to be honest. I was in a state. But it sounds like the sort of thing a bloke like Karl Lund would say, doesn't it? He's dead now, anyway. Bill, I mean – died years ago.' He shrugs. 'I can't tell you more than that.'

'Why have you never sold it?' I say. 'There's always been lots of niche interest in that time. If he was so worried about privacy, Karl might have paid you good money, for a start.'

He shrugs. 'Maybe I didn't want Karl Lund's money. Or his missus'. Nah, it's mine, and I'll never sell it. Everything I've got left from back then is up in my workroom. It was a special time. It was the beginning and the end of things for me, I suppose.' He stands up. 'So, do you want to see it or not?'

Chapter Twenty-Seven

As we climb the stairs, the smell of the house grows more intense. Even someone as isolated as Warner must occasionally have visitors, superficial acquaintances from the pub who stumble back here to keep drinking after hours. Upstairs, though, the air is thick with one person's too-quiet living, like years of stale breath caught and held in the plaster and wood.

The workroom, as he termed it – though when he last earned money from anything in it I can't imagine – is crammed to the rafters. I can see why Harkin – at least at first – might have written him off as a crank whose memories of the past were much more vivid than anything that might be found among the heaving shelves of cardboard box-files, folders of yellowing paper and dusty reels of film. To be fair, a large proportion of the smell I'd attributed to a disappointing life is real and coming from in here. It's so strong I have to fight not to cover my nose.

He unlocks the bottom drawer of the battered old desk with a flourish, checking I'm watching. Angie would be rolling her eyes but it only makes me sad. 'TANGLEWOOD 70' is written in painstakingly neat capitals on the side of a reel.

As he's setting it up, with a deftness that betrays many years' practice, I notice that the longest wall of the room has been left bare for the projector.

'Pull the curtain, would you?' he says, and it must be blackout material because we're plunged into almost complete darkness as I do so, the whir of the machinery louder for it. I question again my decision to be in here with this near-stranger. But then, after a series of blotches and splutters, the scene comes into focus.

I suppose I was expecting black-and-white, but it's colour. Not entirely realistic colour, but something much more saturated with warmth, as though the whole thing has been stained with a golden varnish. The grass is bleached yellow, the sky more green than blue, and a Mini that might have been canary yellow is a strange dirty ochre. Nothing is cool-hued. The camera pans round and, because of the valley's slopes and dips, the angles are weird. It would give you motion sickness if you watched for too long.

The camera settles for a while on the manor house in the distance, so disproportionately small that it looks more like the mansion in a model village than anything else. I can just make out that one of Ottoline's windows is open. It's a dizzying thought that makes the whole thing seem more real: this was a day that really happened, when Ottoline decided to push open that window because her room was stuffy. Or maybe because she wanted to hear the strengthening hum of the crowd gathering outside.

And then I remember: I was there too. I might have been just out of shot in the very moments I'm watching. The feeling of vertigo intensifies. Would I even recognize myself, woozily rendered out of silver salts and light so long ago? Angie was never one for taking family snaps.

As I'm thinking this, a pack of children runs from left

to right across the shot, each one double the size of the toy-like manor above. I scan them as quickly as I can, eyes straining to find the shapes and angles of myself, Caleb too, but they're slightly out of focus and I'm not quick enough. They all look so similar, anyway, little more than an impression of tangled hair and bare skinny limbs, sharp, animated faces. One at the back might be Caleb, hair flashing white-blond in the sun, but they've gone before I can say for sure. Maybe it's the effect of the blackout but it's so close in the room I can feel sweat rolling down my spine and prickling under my arms. My hair is damp at the back of my neck where it's coming out of its ponytail. There's not enough oxygen in the air.

The scene cuts to two or three seconds of fuzzy black and then, instead of a panorama, the whole wall of Warner's workroom transforms into a face caught in profile. For a second, I think it's Angie but then she smiles and I don't know how I mistook her except for the dark hair. The bones of this face are more delicate and feline; the forehead is higher. There's a small beauty spot above her lip.

'Is that *her*?' I say, but I'm not sure it comes out because Warner doesn't reply. I peer at his profile, not that I can make out much in the gloom, and I know he's *there*, deep in those moments when he stood behind the camera capturing this woman, rather than here with me in the present.

I look back at her, and the blood in my fingertips and toes is shooting sparks. She's speaking now, probably calling to someone off-camera, though it's hard to say for sure because there's no sound. Inside the shining dark of her eyes, I think a figure might be reflected, and I step forward to see better, but the heat and the dark are pressing in again and I'm swaying. I put out my hand to steady myself against something but there's nothing, only swirling shadows, and I'm so sure I'm going to fall that I have to grab for Warner.

'I've got you,' he says, surprisingly strong as he takes my weight and guides me into a creaking old office chair. He pulls back the curtain so that light pours into the room again, sending dust motes spinning and briefly blinding us both.

'Deep breaths now,' he says, shoving at the stiff window catch, which screeches as he pushes it open. It's probably not much cooler outside than in but just knowing that fresh air is coming in helps. The room around me steadies.

She's still there, on the projector wall, frozen now because Warner must have paused it, and smiling because whoever she was talking to has replied or is approaching. I look again for the reflection inside her dark eyes but it's too light in the room now to make out any detail, the contrast lost.

'That's the clearest bit I've got,' says Warner, softly. His gaze is back on the woman's smile cast across his wall. 'A few more establishing shots, testing the levels, but that's about it. Nothing of the actual night. Nothing to prove she's who I say she is. At least that's what Harkin said the first time.'

'You thought I was police when you answered the door,' I say. 'Were they here recently?'

'Yesterday. Just as I'd opened a can, sat down to watch something. She'd changed her tune, Harkin. I could tell that straight away.'

'What do you mean?'

'She thought I was a nutter before. I could tell. She's thorough so she came round, took notes in her little book, all that. But I knew she thought it was nonsense. Either cooked up for tabloid cash or because I was actually mad. This time she looked me in the eye, took what I said seriously. And because of that, I gave her a couple of things I didn't before. Didn't *trust her with* before.' He glances down at me. 'I don't see what harm it'll do to tell you. All of it will be coming out soon anyway.'

'What things did you give her?' I say, barely more than a whisper.

'Well, her real name, for starters.' He smiles. 'She came up with Astrid when she left where she grew up in Somerset. Sandra, she was christened. Sandra Margaret Jones. She hated it. Too ordinary, she said. "And who wants to be ordinary, Graham?"

'Of course, she was anything but ordinary, whatever she called herself.' He sighs. 'Didn't save her, though, did it? Being extraordinary. Maybe it's what singled her out.' He gestures at the wall, the light and shadows of a woman I know he's thought of every day for thirty years. 'All that life, and this is all that's left of her.'

I follow his gaze, and we study her together, both of us quiet. Outside, I can hear the soft, melancholy cooing of wood pigeons.

'Well, that and what Harkin was after,' Warner is saying, bringing me out of my thoughts.

'Which was?'

'The card,' he says. 'The tarot card I found on her . . . on her body. I shouldn't have taken it, I know that, but

I wasn't thinking straight. I mentioned it in passing to Harkin the first time and I think she wrote it down, but I didn't hear any more about that or anything else until yesterday, when she came storming in to ask more questions about it. What picture it had on it, things like that.'

'And? What picture did it have?' I ask, even though I'm pretty sure what the answer's going to be and I don't want to hear it.

'It said "The Empress" on it,' he says. 'Woman with long hair on a throne. I asked Harkin, did she want to see it. Her eyes lit up. "You've still got it?" she said, all eager. I said, "Of course I have."' He reaches down to pull open the shallow top drawer of his desk. 'I kept it safe for thirty years.'

I peer inside. There's nothing to see but paperclips, Sellotape and grubby balls of Blu Tack.

'It's not here now,' he says. 'Harkin took it. She wanted it for fingerprinting. I made her write me out a receipt to make sure I get it back.'

Dread settles low inside me. It makes sense now, why Harkin has officially connected Astrid and Willow. I'm guessing she didn't think too much about the tarot card Warner mentioned at first, asking only cursory questions about who might have a deck, then following up by speaking to Angie. It wasn't until the pathologist found an identical card folded out of sight inside Willow's hand that she started taking it seriously.

Perhaps everything they've got on Angie is circumstantial; I'm not sure. But if you keep piling enough circumstantial evidence onto the scales, they'll eventually tip – away from reasonable doubt and towards probable certainty.

'Would Angie have known Astrid?' I say. I'm gripping the arms of the chair, which reminds me of earlier, in the carriage-house.

'Of course,' he says, as though I'm simple. 'There was no love lost between those two.'

'Why?'

'Because of Karl. She didn't mean to step on any toes, Astrid. She told me that herself. She wasn't that sort of person. But I don't think that's how Angie would've seen it, especially when it turned out half the album was written about Astrid, and that he'd put her on the cover, not that she got a penny for it.'

He catches sight of my expression. 'You've never heard about that? Must've cost a fortune to pulp it. Delayed the album's release by a month.'

'I had,' I manage to say. 'I just didn't know it was her.'

I look up at her face again, trace its fine lines with my eyes. She only had a few days left to live. It feels like the more I uncover, the harder the truth is to grasp.

'What do you think happened to her?' I say.

'I think it was him after all,' he says, without hesitation. It's like he's been waiting for me to ask. I wonder if Harkin asked too, then assume that – focused as she was on finding proper evidence – she probably didn't. 'He could do what he wanted, with as many women as he chose. But he didn't like it when he got the same treatment.'

'You mean you and Astrid?'

He smiles sadly, far away again. 'Only the once. But he knew, Karl. Got it out of her, worked it out by himself,

I don't know. She looked scared that last day, like she wanted to do nothing more than run as she stood up there on the stage, him to the side of her, watching her like a hawk. That was the last time I saw her alive.'

Chapter Twenty-Eight

I go to the village churchyard after I leave Warner's. He needs to be alone, I can tell, and I have to get out of there for my own sake, remind myself the world is still turning, three decades on.

I pull the wooden gate behind me, the latch falling shut. I'm not ready to head back to Tanglewood yet, so it's a sit-down here or in the pub, and I don't trust myself not to take things too far today – Angie's bloodline pulsing insistently through me. I'm pretty sure I'm not going to faint again, but I still don't feel right. I think this is what people are getting at when they say they're reeling from something. It also occurs to me that I've hardly eaten, again.

It's deserted among the old stones, some of them listing and sinking into the earth as if to unite with the person they commemorate. I find a bench that looks out over the valley and watch the shadow of a single cloud sweep across it, silent and stately.

I pull out my phone to call Dan, then decide to text him instead: *Can you look up a Sandra Margaret Jones? Connections to Somerset. Likely born 1937–1950.*

I press send. A cynical part of me knows it kills two birds, just as I planned in the car before: potentially throwing something useful up about the past that might help Angie in the present, but also keeping Dan and his inquisitive mind at arm's length.

I mentally tick off all the little bombshells Warner has just dropped on me. Astrid herself, projected onto his wall, moving and alive. Her relationship with Karl; with Warner. Her unintended rivalry with Angie. The Empress tarot card found on her dead body. The ties binding her to the album that may as well be the backing track to my whole life. It's hard to get my head round even half of it.

I can't sit here for ever, but I take the drive back to the estate slowly, deliberately easing off the accelerator as I approach because I'm not sure what to do first. Just before I get to the gates, I pull over in a passing place, hedgerow wildly luxuriant with summer growth, the swathes of bindweed, wild clematis and brambles taller than my car.

I find Harkin's card in my back pocket and copy her number into my mobile. She picks it up after two rings, and as her voice, curt and weary, comes down the line, I'm grateful that at least she can't be grilling Angie right at this moment.

'It's Rain,' I say. No one ever forgets a name like mine, which is occasionally advantageous. 'Is Angie okay?'

'She's sounding off about her human rights, if that's what you mean. You'd think we were pulling her finger-nails out with pliers.'

'Have you charged her?'

'Not yet.'

'Meaning the CPS don't think you've got enough.'

'Meaning,' she repeats, with emphasis, annoyed now, 'that we haven't charged her yet.'

'Have you actually got anything on her that isn't circumstantial?'

Harkin says nothing. In the background, I can hear phones ringing, and the bass rumble of male voices. Her silence may seem to confirm that I've hit a nerve, but that's not how it feels. It feels like the opposite: that, in the aggregate of what she knew about Willow and now knows about Astrid, she's lit upon something solid.

'Have you got her a solicitor?'

'She was informed by the custody sergeant on arrival that she had the right to one, just as she was yesterday. She refused.'

'*What?*'

'She said that, if it came to it, she would represent herself. That at least she could trust herself.'

'Oh, for God's sake.'

'Never have I wished for a suspect to exercise their right to remain silent more,' says Harkin. 'But beyond all the hot air about the police state, she's still not saying anything that helps us with our investigation. And, by extension, anything that helps herself.'

I think I know what Harkin's getting at, and it's that Angie isn't telling tales on anyone. 'Look, please don't hold her for the full twenty-four hours,' I say. 'She'll go mad in there, locked up overnight. Please.'

Harkin sighs. 'We're taking good care of her, don't worry. If we can get somewhere with this today, we will.' She's about to hang up.

'I don't understand why you're so laser-focused on Angie when Karl is the one who – who was involved with Willow,' I blurt, just stopping myself mentioning the possible pregnancy. I don't know that for sure, and if it seems like I do, that might make things worse for Angie. She'd be disgusted if she could hear me, but Angie is proving to be her own worst enemy right now.

Harkin hasn't said anything but she's still there. I can hear the distant wail of a siren ratchet up. A patrol car leaving the station car park.

'His alibi is watertight, Rain,' she says, voice weary again. 'He wasn't even at home. He was with his band ahead of this weekend's performance. They were, and I quote, "jamming" all night. I've spoken personally to every single one of them. It checks out.' She sighs. 'Look, there are things you don't know, and that I can't tell you. You're just going to have to sit tight.'

'I'm coming down to the station soon. I just need to get some things together for Angie—'

'No, you don't,' she cuts across me. 'She's got everything she needs here.'

'But what if she has to stay the full twenty-four hours? What if you charge her?' My voice wobbles perilously on the last word but, when there's no answer, I realize she's quietly hung up.

I drive the last part of the journey on autopilot. Turning into Tanglewood, the sky is such a deep, throbbing blue that it looks sinister, wrong. Like I'm actually trapped inside some English pastoral version of the Matrix. Somewhere the rules are different and the details are off.

I keep driving down towards the cottage, waves of fatigue sweeping over me now, making my vision blur. There's an old wooden steamer chair in the garden that looks like something rescued from the decks of *Titanic* but was probably pinched by Angie from the manor's sheds. I find it, spotlit in a last patch of honeyed sunlight, and lie down to watch the sun sink towards the western slopes. When I next open my eyes, as the landline inside begins to trill, the valley has turned grey and lilac. Where the sun was, thick clouds are beginning to build once more.

I half trip over the doorstep trying to catch the phone and it feels like another bad omen. It's not Harkin at the other end. It's a male detective. I don't take in his name. He tells me in an expressionless voice that 'Mrs Valentine' won't be coming home tonight. As though he's been well schooled by Harkin, he's gone before I can ask any questions.

I replace the handset just as a low reverberation of thunder rolls around the valley. The noisy old fridge lets out a fast series of loud clicks and dies. I stand in the tiny hall of the silent cottage, mind emptied by fear, as rain begins to hiss on the stones outside.

Chapter Twenty-Nine

Friday

My respite from insomnia turns out to be short-lived. I spend the night lying sleepless in my bed, eyes sore and dry as I study the shadows flickering on the ceiling. The storm moves away again before it can really get going but not before the rain has soaked the parched earth. When it stops, around three, the sky clear enough for the moon to be able to cast its cool gaze over the valley, I push open the window as far as it goes. I've always loved that just-rained petrichor smell. It's like outer space: so ancient and elemental that my own fears seem to shrink in comparison.

I wait until mid-morning before I head up to the manor, nerves making my stomach churn because I need to speak to Ottoline and Karl. I need to do it for Angie. I've left three messages with Harkin to call me back. Part of me is desperate to get it over with, but the rest makes the decision to go the long way round, up the Dark Ride, past the swelling hum of activity on the Great Meadow, and around the house to end up next to Karl's Cadillac, which glints tantalizingly in the climbing sun, like the American Dream on wheels. How much of Ottoline's money did it take to bring it over? I didn't always think like this, so cynically. It makes me sad for my younger self, who thought everything and everyone up at the manor house was so wonderful.

A movement in the corner of my eye makes me wheel round. Lennie has appeared out of nowhere and something's not right – though, for a second, I can't work out what it is. She looks neat enough in her denim skirt and white T-shirt embroidered with tiny pink roses, hair in a neat French plait, which suits her much better. Then I realize what's wrong: she's not smiling.

'Lennie? Are you okay?'

She rubs her eyes, which look sore. 'I've got bad hayfever.'

It's more than that, I can tell. She's radiating misery. 'Has something happened?'

'No. Everything's fine. I need to go back in, though. Ottoline said I couldn't be outside long. That it would make me worse.'

'Okay,' I say, though I'm not sure it is. 'You come with me. We'll find Ottoline together.'

She nods and reaches up to put her arm through mine. Her skin is hot, hotter even than the day. We fall into slow step back towards the manor, her weight against me surprisingly heavy.

'I like the hair,' I say, to cover my worry. 'Could you do that on me? All I ever have is a boring ponytail.'

'Ottoline did it,' she says, as though a long way away.

We find her alone in her parlour. Karl is almost certainly in the carriage-house. The old nursery rhyme pops into my head without warning. *The king was in the counting-house, counting out his money. The queen was in the parlour, eating bread and honey*. It's not a million miles away, as a description of them.

Ottoline has always liked to come here on golden

mornings like this one. The light is glorious enough in summer, but on those rare November days when the sky is a crystalline blue and the wintry sun is canted low, it's spectacular. *What it must be to have different bloody lounges for different times of day*, Angie says in my head – inevitably. The thought of her – where she is right now – makes me tense. Each time I remember, it's a shock all over again.

'Darlings,' Ottoline breathes, holding open her arms and gesturing for us to come closer.

'I found this one outside,' I say, as lightly as I can, putting my arm round Lennie, who turns her face into me, so it's hidden. 'I think she's still half asleep.'

'The poor poppet,' Ottoline says, pulling her mouth down. 'Her hayfever is awful. Her eyes and nose were streaming as soon as she woke. It's really quite miserable when it strikes – I remember suffering terribly here as a child. I gave her half a pill, one of mine, but I suppose they can make one feel rather drowsy if you're not accustomed to them. Come and sit by me, my love.' She pats the sofa next to her, and Lennie drifts over and slumps almost immediately over a cushion. 'We'll let her sleep it off,' whispers Ottoline.

'Where's Karl?' I say softly, taking the small armchair that used to be my favourite as a child. This room was always the closest thing the manor had to a normal living space. The upholstery is even worn in places, and there are dog-eared magazines in a basket near the fire – old copies of *Horse & Hound* and *Country Life*.

'He's somewhere around,' says Ottoline, waving a hand. 'He's deep into preparations for the weekend, of course, so I expect he's on the telephone in the carriage-house.

They'll start arriving soon. The musicians and their wives are staying here, of course, and the Gatherers will start arriving tonight, too.'

'Has he said anything to you about . . .?' I pause. It's such an old habit never to mention Angie that I have to battle with myself to keep talking. 'Has he said anything about Angie?' It's a bit like stepping off a ledge into nothing.

Lennie stirs and we both look at her, grateful for the interruption, but then her eyes close again.

Ottoline meets my eye and I give her a small nod. Please don't make me ask again, I think.

'*Angie*?' she says, and even though I must have known on some level that she would do this – inject into those two syllables a combination of bafflement and distaste – it still smarts. And I know myself, and when I'm hurt it tends to warp into anger. That won't be helpful, not to this situation and not to myself. I've loved Ottoline unquestioningly for as long as I can remember. She's always been there for me as a beacon of steady gentleness. My port in an Angie storm. I don't know if I can bear for that to change.

'She was arrested yesterday,' I plough on, my voice only just above a whisper because of Lennie, though she's obviously out for the count and deep in dreams, eyelids flickering now. 'And then they kept her in overnight. I've been ringing to check she's okay, but no one is calling me back.'

'How dreadful,' Ottoline murmurs.

I swallow because my throat is constricting. 'It is dreadful. I'm worried about the strain it's putting her under.' I don't want to be any more specific; it would be a betrayal to mention to Ottoline of all people that I'm afraid Angie's ballooning weight, on top of decades of smoking and the rest of it, must have done her lasting damage. Ottoline's beauty is like a dried wedding bouquet, fragile but still very lovely. You can see exactly what she was, once. Bar the odd, isolated flash in a flattering light, I really don't think you can say the same for Angie.

'She doesn't seem fragile,' I say instead, 'but in her own way, she is, you know?' There's a pleading note in my voice.

But Ottoline doesn't know, and so, in typical fashion, she says nothing, her gaze trained on her exquisitely faded rug. Angie has been nothing but her nemesis for years and years. Her photographic negative. Dark to her blonde, fire to her water. It's hopeless, but I keep talking, I don't know why. My judgement is probably off. I'm totally drained.

'The thing is,' I say, 'I just can't believe she had anything to do with . . . what happened,' I glance towards Lennie. 'Either now or then. I think the police have got fixated on her for the wrong reasons, and I . . .' I put my hands to my cheeks, which have heated up as if I'm running a temperature. Dizziness is slowly creeping over me, just like it did in Warner's blacked-out workroom.

'Darling, I'm going to get you a cold drink,' says Ottoline. She's already risen. 'You've gone the most peculiar colour.'

I stand when she's left the room, legs trembling, on the one hand to reassure myself I still can, and on the other to see how bad I look. In the mirror above the mantel, my face is blotchy and clammy, a sickly olive-grey where it's not flushed. I can't remember when I last ate anything. My time since I got back here is congealing into one strange, disorienting mass.

Ottoline returns with a tall glass of cordial. Ice cubes clink and there's a delicate silver stirrer she's using to mix it. It clinks melodically in the peaceful room. A memory veers in and away before I can grasp it. The liquid is still spinning when she hands me the glass, the dense cordial spreading and dispersing like deep pink smoke. It's so delicious that I gulp it all down.

The hit of sugar clears my mind a little. 'I just wish I knew what really happened. You didn't notice anything that night, did you?' I don't think I'd dare ask this if I wasn't feeling so wrung out.

Ottoline has gone to stand by the window, as though she doesn't want to encourage my questions by settling in a chair facing me. 'My dear Rain,' she says, going over to Lennie and gently brushing a loose strand of hair off her face, 'I wish I could help. But Karl and I saw nothing that night. We heard nothing. It's a terrible thing to think of that poor woman . . .' – she glances down at Lennie and drops her voice – '. . . out there by herself. The notion of it haunts me. It doesn't matter that she was . . . Well, none of *that* matters. It's a tragedy.'

I don't reply. I'm too busy playing back what she just said. *Karl and I saw nothing that night.* He was supposed to be away.

Ottoline minutely adjusts the cushion under Lennie's head. Then she straightens and looks at me properly for the first time since I mentioned Angie.

'You must rest, my darling.' She comes over and takes

my empty glass. 'I wonder if all this – if coming back here – is too much for you. You were always such a sensitive little girl, though you tried so hard to be brave. It made my heart ache to see you. I'm so glad you've come to me today, as you used to.'

I want to press her more but people underestimate the power of extreme politeness. It's almost impossible to chip away at its smooth walls, especially if you're English.

I let her help me to my feet, gripping my elbow with surprising strength. She guides me from the armchair to the sofa where Lennie is now snoring gently. It's easily long enough for the two of us, and when Ottoline gently pushes me down into it, I let her. I'm so tired.

Before I sink into unconsciousness, I have the thought that if I sleep for long enough, I might wake up and everything will be all right. It's childish, but I have always been a child with Ottoline. It's self-centred, I suppose, but it's also an enormous relief just to let go, at least for now.

Chapter Thirty

When I wake, the light has shifted and Lennie has gone. I'm alone. The little gold mantel clock under its glass dome says it's past midday. I've lost hours. Another glass of cordial is sweating on the table beside me, and I gulp it down. My teeth feel coated and sticky with sugar but I need the energy. When I stand up, I see there are people on the Great Meadow. More men in hi-vis. More vans and equipment. It's going to be bigger than I'd imagined.

As I make my way to the carriage-house, I feel clear-headed and determined, though I have no real hope of getting any more out of Karl. I've got something on him now, though, and it galvanizes me. *Karl and I saw nothing.* I think back to the direct look she gave me after she said it, the way she was caring for Lennie: did she hand me that deliberately, rather than making a mistake? Has Ottoline, in her own carefully circumspect way, had enough?

As for the rest of the alibis, Karl's musician mates, the notion of them covering for him with the police doesn't surprise me. People don't cross Karl, and it's not like any of that set have much time for the police anyway, mavericks and rebels as they like to think they still are.

It's a peculiar anticlimax to find he's not there. He clearly *has* been, and very recently – the desk in the small room he calls his cubby, just off the recording studio, is strewn with paper, used coffee mugs and the glasses he never wears in front of other people. The mingled smells of weed and the lemon-and-bergamot cologne that costs two hundred pounds a bottle are faintly discernible. He's worn that scent for ever and it reminds me of what Warner said yesterday, about Karl's money really belonging to 'his missus'.

Karl's family were dirt poor when he was a child. He told the stories often enough when I was growing up that even Ottoline, with her impeccable manners, would glaze over. His father had worked as a lumberjack in Oregon, but after he lost his right foot in an accident, he was out of a job. Apparently, he couldn't or perhaps wouldn't do any other work, so Karl's mother had to go out to earn instead. 'She did some cleaning, dressmaking,' he would say. 'She did everything she could. But there were five kids to feed and we went hungry most of the time. Meanwhile, my pa sat at home, angry. Angry with her, with us, with the whole world, with me most of all, because I answered him back. I couldn't wait to get the hell out.'

He left when he was sixteen, headed south to California, and never looked back, or so the lore goes. I saw a picture of them once – the whole Lund family in the lean, unhappy years after the accident – and it could have been from the previous century. They're standing in front of what looks like a shack with a tin chimney set into the roof. In it Karl is twelve, according to him, but he looks both younger, in the sense of being undersized, and older, with his pinched and wary face. His father looks like he's drunk and gone to seed, the remnants of the good looks he bequeathed Karl barely hanging on. As the only son, Karl took most of the beatings, along with his mother.

I wonder now what the combination of that hard-scrabble start and the vast privilege he enjoys now has made him. 'Ruthless' is the word that comes to mind first.

Part of me wants to leave, avoid having a difficult conversation with Karl when he's hardly going to be receptive. A more stubborn part wants to ask him why he said he hardly knew Astrid, and why he's told police he was away the night Willow died, when – according to Ottoline earlier – he was back.

I'm weighing up the options when my eye catches on the spiral staircase that winds up into the ceiling.

I've barely ever ventured up to the top floor. My footsteps make muffled clangs as I climb into the relative darkness. Up here is where the carriage drivers would have slept when the manor was new and, for a hair's-breadth moment before I turn on the light, the original configuration shimmers in front of me: low sleeping pallets, boots ready to be polished, a distinct smell of grease, oil and men sleeping at close quarters. Then my fingers find the switch and it transforms back into Karl's alternative bedroom for the nights when he's so far inside his creative zone that he can't make it back to the manor to sleep or – at least in the old days – down to Angie to . . . I stop that thought.

Of course, I've always known that this is where he brought other women, too, one of those adult situations that as children we learn by osmosis rather than anyone explaining it to us. It's surprisingly bare, almost monk-like – which seems ironic. There's a low-slung futon in the centre of the polished floorboards, as wide as it's long, made up with navy-blue linen. Apart from a sculptural chrome-and-leather chair and a Japanese-style paper floor lamp, there's nothing.

Except that at the far end of the room, a small door is painted white like the wall so it's not immediately obvious. I didn't notice it in the past, and might not have spotted it now if the gleam of the handle wasn't caught by one of the ceiling spotlights. A stud wall must have been put up across the attic's width to create a separate space.

There's a keyhole underneath the handle and so, when I try it, I expect it to be locked. Instead, the door swings open silently. But why would he bother locking it? This is Karl's domain. No one comes here unless he's with them, and by then they're probably under his spell anyway.

I resented them, too, as I grew up, though not so much for Angie's sake as for my own. Not in any sexual way, the idea nausea-inducing, but because when Karl had a new thing to play with, you couldn't help feeling entirely obsolete: discarded and broken at the bottom of the toy-box. And, of course, in my case, it was a double whammy as Angie raged through the days until he came back to her. To *us*, in a sense.

Ottoline, in her own inscrutable, pathologically discreet way, must have felt the same. Angie has always acted as though her rival is made of ice, but I know how easily Ottoline wounds. How permanently injured she was by the loss of Caroline. Belated anger, that this one man has made all the women in his life feel like this, courses through me. And not just the women. What about his son? As far as I can tell, Caleb never got a look-in with either parent.

This anger with Karl is an uneasy, alien feeling. It's been growing and spreading through me, and by now I despise him. I wish I didn't but, like the light-bulb of a retrieved memory, I can't switch it off; I can't go back. Not only that: I'm embarrassed for my younger self, following him around like a puppy, begging to go for a drive in the Cadillac or to push the switches up and down on the mixing board in the studio.

The room behind the white door is oddly chilly, as though it exists in another season. As a storage place, it's the antithesis of Warner's. Three large filing cabinets stand against the far wall and a desk to the right has nothing on it but a pair of headphones and one of those TVs with an integrated video player.

I pull open the middle drawer of the middle cabinet, feeling like I'm in some soulless-admin version of a fairytale, where the brave hero must choose the right box or meet certain death. It looks completely innocuous inside: a bank of dark-green folders swaying on their rails and labelled with subjects like 'VAT' and 'Contracts'. I open one at random and, sure enough, it's just bills and receipts, bank statements and other correspondence.

I keep going, sifting through folder after folder in a sort of trance, as another part of my brain replays the strange afternoon in the parlour, combing it for evidence of why it felt so strange, even before Ottoline appeared to reveal that Karl has almost certainly lied to the police.

When I find what I suppose I've been looking for, it's not even hidden. Beneath the green folders, in the cavity at the bottom of the drawer, there are half a dozen video tapes. 'Doc 4' is written in Karl's idiosyncratic hand on the sticker of the first I bring out. The next is 'Doc 2'. Doc for 'documentary', surely? If so, he kept some footage after all.

I switch on the TV and push a tape into the slot. I'm about to press play when something makes me go back to the filing cabinet. A strange prolonging of the anticipation, I think, plus the other side of that coin: a fear of anticlimax if there's nothing to see. Or maybe it's just straightforward fear that I'll see something bad – something that will change everything for ever.

I pull out the bottom drawer and grab a folder at random. It takes my brain a second to absorb that I'm not looking at bills any more, but photographs. Large black-and-white photographs of a woman. A naked woman. Some are artfully posed. In one she's caught apparently unaware – her bare back a long cello as she sleeps on her side. A few are just straight-up porn. I don't recognize her, whoever she is, but I do recognize the handwriting on the folder's label, which says 'Patty' in a mixture of upper- and lower-case letters. Jaw clenched against rising queasiness, I walk my fingers back along the row until I clock that he's filed them alphabetically. There's something sinister about that orderliness.

There is no 'O' in front of Patty for Ottoline. I shove the whole lot to the back with a clang and there it is: 'Angie', right at the front. *At least I'm first, eh?* she would probably say, if she was here, and I would have to stop myself pointing out the alphabetical ordering we both understood.

I slam the drawer shut as hard as I can – hard enough that the folders inside rock on their rails with a tinny sound that's almost a hiss. Nothing would entreat me to look at those pictures. Maybe I'll steal them back for Angie, even if it's just to lock them up in the cottage without her knowledge. Maybe I'll take them all. Take all those women away from him. I hate him reducing them to another of his collections, like the Dinky toys, the *Eagle* comics and the model train set he was briefly obsessed with for a while. It says such a lot about him, and the worst of it is that I've brushed up against the knowledge of it since my teenage years. I just never wanted to look it straight in the eye.

When I turn away from the cabinets, the TV's square black eye is waiting for me. I press play, hoping that the arrogance that had Karl cataloguing his conquests without any kind of subterfuge means that 'Doc 1' really is the documentary footage he took from Bill Laing, not some tawdry sex tape starring my mother.

I watch for a while, the footage similar to Warner's: scene-setting shots panning across the valley as the crowd begins to swell, just as it's about to tonight. It's less shaky, better framed, and I assume it was filmed by someone more experienced, who'd also bothered to set up a tripod. I wonder when Karl had all this transferred to video from the original cinefilm, and whether that means he returns to it regularly.

My brain turns like the film inside the machine: there can't be anything incriminating on these tapes, can there? If he had them converted by someone, who would have seen them? As soon as I think it, it seems totally naïve. As if there isn't a thriving black market for hardcore porn and God knows what else. As if there isn't someone somewhere who will do anything for money without asking questions. Besides, I don't even know what I'm expecting. Or dreading.

I eject the tape and put in the first I pulled out:

number four. The view it homes in on without preamble is so utterly familiar that I can't quite compute it. I actually touch the screen because it feels like someone has reached into my head and pulled it out.

It's the cottage: mine and Angie's. I know exactly where the cameraman stood to get this particular angle: in a deep cleft in the hill where I used to read on fine days in summer. If I hunkered down low enough, I couldn't easily be seen from any of the windows, but I was close enough that if something happened to Angie, I could be there in seconds.

Because I'm thinking about this, it takes me a while to notice there's a face at the upstairs window that's been mine for as long as I remember. Between the reflections on the glass from the sun and the dark room behind, I can't make out any features, only that it's there. My skin prickles because for a second I think it might be me. Me from the time before my memories began.

'Open up! Open the window!'

The voice through the speaker is so loud in the room that I physically shrink back from the TV. It's unmistakably Karl – Karl behind the camera. I'd forgotten there was even a possibility of sound after Warner's silent footage. I turn the volume down, heart hammering.

The person behind the glass does as she's told and, as she leans out of the window, I recognize her. It's not my younger self, after all. It's her, Astrid, for the second time in one day.

She waves. She looks happy, as happy as Willow Green looked in that picture splashed over the papers. On the tape, I can hear long-ago birds – wood pigeons and blackbirds. Winged ghosts, as long-gone as her.

'You want it for your own?' he says. His voice is higher than it is now, smoother.

'Yes, please,' she calls, and hearing her voice makes goosebumps rise on my arms. What did Karl say about her? That he *hardly knew her.*

'What're you doing there, Rainy?'

The voice isn't coming from the TV now. I spin round and he's there in the doorway, in the flesh. Karl. Blue eyes cold, face hard.

1970

The ringing, live-wire anticipation of the last few days has dulled but intensified to a low, slow thrum. It raises the pressure in her ears. It feels like literal dread. While she wants to pause time and hold off the shadows she can feel drawing closer each minute, everyone else around her is impatient – itching for the Gathering's main event to begin in earnest. Even the sun seems to be hurrying towards its zenith. Karl's performance is scheduled to begin at ten p.m. Eleven hours left.

The small encampment of tents and campervans that has been her ramshackle home since the spring is deserted. It's been like this all day: wherever she goes, she keeps missing the people she knows, seemingly by seconds. It's not helping the paranoia. The temptation to take something that will soften and smooth it out rises in her like a tide. She counts to herself until it subsides a little. She's been doing so well to keep a clear head. She's had nothing, not even a single drink, for days.

She's got used to the same old faces here over the last few months but, with the influx of newcomers, everyone is a stranger. As she weaves through them, the overlapping smells of them making her nauseous, they smile and smile at her. She struggles to smile back.

Everything feels sinister now, even as the valley has never looked more beautiful. Her presentiment, the stone in her stomach, is even bigger and colder. *Leave*, it tells her. *Go now*. But she can't find anyone she trusts enough to help her to pack and find a lift. She can't even find her child.

A pack of them around the right age hurtle past her, brandishing sticks scavenged from the woods. She searches for a bright-golden head but they're already past her and into the blinding tractor beam of the sun. The sticks were sharpened, she realizes, and the pressure in her head goes up a notch. Is it her imagination or are the children turning ever more feral, like the castaway schoolboys in that book she did at school, with the conch and Piggy? Their parents might be here, but what use are they, tuned out and focused only on their own pleasure? Just as she herself has been.

She climbs away from the Great Meadow and weaves through the woods to the clearing where they're setting up the secret stage. Karl will perform the album for the first time later, just ahead of the official release next week.

It's amazing how much the hired roadies have managed to fit into the space. The stage, shaped like an open clamshell, has been built in front of the giant ash. The raised structure looks as though it's being held – cradled, even – in the spreading branches.

She watches as amps and speakers as big as coffins are

dragged into position. She's supposed to be up there herself tonight, a crown of flowers on her head, stars sewn into her hair and silver paint snaking over her skin. She's smoothed out her white costume and hung it carefully over one of her tent's guy ropes but, even as she did it, she wondered if she would be gone by the time she was supposed to wear it.

Karl had asked her to perform with him and the band weeks ago and she'd been thrilled, had seen it as a great honour. She can't find that feeling anywhere inside her now. The thought of being up there in the glare of the lights – thousands of eyes roving over her as she dances – makes her feel even sicker. It makes her want to run, her feet tingling with the urge – even stronger than her craving to take something to calm her down. *Tick-tock,* the presentiment says. *Time is running out.*

'I've been wanting a word with you.' The low, slightly hoarse voice is so close it might have come from inside her own head.

She spins round to find Angie Valentine standing there, an angry patch of colour high on each cheek. She smells of smoke and patchouli.

She knows who Angie is, of course – everyone knows Angie – but they've never spoken. To be honest, she's always avoided her. She knows she's accidentally usurped Angie's position as Karl's principal mistress. 'You should watch your back, crossing Angie V,' another woman said to her a while back, her eyes bright with the scandal of it. 'You're a braver woman than me. If Ottoline's the queen of Tanglewood, then Angie's the grand sorceress.' She wasn't really joking.

'You're up there tonight, aren't you?' Angie says now. '*Dancing.*' She says it like it tastes bad. 'Look, I know all about you and Karl. I've known a while. Not much gets past me here.' She smiles grimly. 'I don't have a problem with that. What I do have a problem with is the cottage. That was promised to me before you set foot here. I've done my time in the camp, slumming it with everyone else.'

She opens her mouth to reply but nothing comes out. In the silence, feedback screeches from the stage, making her jump.

Angie doesn't even flinch. 'I saw you there before,' she continues, 'nosing round as though it was yours already.'

'That was you, in the upstairs window? I thought I saw someone there.'

'Oh, she *does* speak.' Angie pushes out a laugh, then frowns. 'No, I was up the slope, watching you from above. There was no one inside. It's been locked up for years. Probably a ghost.' She laughs, and it's deep and rich, but somehow without warmth.

'But I . . .' She trails off, looks down. Angie's eyes are boring into her, like she's able to see every thought inside someone's brain if she wants to. She doesn't want to betray her fear, her need to flee. Not to Angie Valentine.

'I did a reading earlier,' Angie says.

She looks up. 'A reading?'

'The tarot. I've got a gift for it. It told me something about you.' She roots in the patchwork bag slung over her shoulder, brings out a card. Before Astrid can see which one it is, Angie flicks it at her, hard. It glances off her chin and flutters to the grass, landing face down.

She'd like to walk away but she's already bending down for the card, unable to resist. She turns it over to find the Empress. She traces her thumb over the crown atop her long hair.

Above her, Angie laughs again. 'You've been caught out, haven't you?' she hisses, pushing her face in close. 'Even if the cards hadn't told me, I'd be able to smell it on you.'

She clutches the card to her chest, starts to back away, but Angie advances.

'I'm right, aren't I? You're pregnant.' She tips her head to one side, narrows her eyes. 'And you haven't told him yet. Want me to do it for you?' She tries to laugh again, but it comes out like a shriek. Her eyes are dull now.

Feedback from the stage screams again. It sounds as if it's coming from the ash. The shock of it gives her the push to turn and run from Angie, out of the clearing, and down another of the dozen paths that snake through the trees back to the Great Meadow. Sunlight flickers and glimmers through the leaves, making her dizzy. Her foot catches on a root but she manages not to fall. Maybe it would be a good thing if she did. Maybe it would dislodge the stone that's growing inside her, the one that might trap her here for ever.

Chapter Thirty-One

It's years since I've seen Karl lose his temper. I suppose I learnt to manage him like Ottoline does. Or, rather, manage myself around him so that no eggshells ever got smashed. Angie never could do that, even for the sake of what she imagined was their great love. It's admirable, really. I just never saw it like that before.

Another thing I learnt was to absent myself when they fought. It helped that Ottoline was always up at the manor, waiting for me. While we played Victorian mother and daughter – ribbons, bone china and crustless cucumber sandwiches – Angie and Karl would be left alone in the cottage. When I ventured back there, she would be quiet and trembling, like a just-broken horse. And, no, I never asked, and she never told me.

I picture her then, and I picture her in the police station now. I do it to stop myself running. To be brave.

'You said you hardly knew her.' I gesture at the paused video as casually as I can, but my quavering voice gives me away.

His jaw starts working. His fists clench. His eyes are startlingly blue in his red face.

I don't realize I'm backing away from the wild-animal sight of him until I hit the filing cabinets with a dull clang.

'You saying I'm a *liar*?' The last word is so loud that my hands twitch to cover my ears. I keep them at my sides because a movement like that might be seen as provocation, might only make him worse.

I shake my head minutely. 'I'm – I'm just confused. I thought you said the other night . . .' I'm not brave enough for this. I can't fight a whole lifetime's habit of avoidance.

Neither of us says anything. It's as though we're suspended, paused like the video. But then he starts to master himself. I actually see it happen and, in another scenario, it would be fascinating: the physical control he exerts over his anger. His face returns to its normal colour and shape, his muscles soften – even his eyes seem to lose some of their cold fire. His hands are the last thing to unclench. I pull in a great mouthful of air.

'After all I've done for you,' he says, in a low voice that's more menacing than the yelling. I freeze again as he takes a step towards me. 'You and Angie. Both of you as ungrateful as each other.'

I'm silent. No words will come.

'I'm thinking it's time you ran back to London,' he says, walking his fingers in the air.

'I can't leave Angie when—'

'No? Never stopped you before. You broke her heart when you left.'

'Lennie, then.'

'Lennie?' He laughs incredulously, a harsh, humourless sound. The gold bridge in his mouth glints. 'O is taking good care of Lennie. She's got nothing to do with you.'

'That's not true. She and I—'

'What you gonna do about Lennie, Rain? Tell the police? Get her taken into care? You think that would be better for her?'

'No, of course not,' I try to cut in. 'I—'

'You think that wouldn't kill my wife? You'd do that to both of them?' He shakes his head as though disgusted.

'I could look after Lennie.' I don't know where it comes from.

He laughs again. 'You? You couldn't keep a cat.' He saunters back to the door and holds it open for me. 'I don't know what you think you've worked out about what happened here. But you're wrong.' He gestures with a flick of his head for me to get out. He's back in control now – of himself and me, too.

I obey him, putting as much distance as possible between the two of us as I pass. I'm almost through the door when he gets hold of my arm. I try to yank it away but his hand is clamped fast around it, tight enough to hurt. He pulls me close, so his mouth is against my ear. I can't move.

'No one is going to spoil this weekend for me, Rain. Especially some stray like you.'

He releases his grip and I run. The stairs ring as I skitter down them and back out into the day. I run until I'm out of sight of the carriage-house and then sit down heavily in the grass. I need to cry but tears won't come so I gasp and rock, face contorted but eyes dry. I knew he had it in him to be like that but the shock of seeing it for myself, his face twisted, his contempt for me, is visceral. If there was anything solid in my stomach, I'd throw it up.

I force myself to stand. I'm still too close to the carriage-house for comfort, though there's no sign that he's followed me. I get up, torn, not knowing where to go. I can't face Ottoline and Lennie like this. I can't go to the cottage, where Angie's absence will be deafening and where I won't even be able to hide in my room without some vestige of Astrid shimmering at me across time – from the cottage Karl apparently offered her thirty years ago, but which Angie and I ended up living in instead.

I head for the woods on the escarpment. My breathing is still not right and I'm soon panting. My ankles keep turning in the deep ruts of the path, my feet catching on tree roots. When the path keeps going relentlessly up, I give in and sit down against a fallen tree covered with moss like lurid velvet. It's deep enough inside the beeches that the ground never really dries out and, though I can feel the damp soaking into my clothes, I can't face moving.

I've been there for a while, flashes of video footage and the way Ottoline smoothed Lennie's hair as she quietly upended Karl's alibi going round and round in my head on a disquieting loop, when the crack of a twig puts me back on high alert. But it's Caleb coming up the path, not his father, and the adrenaline that had me about to run ebbs away.

I raise a hand when he spots me, and watch different expressions cross his face. Surprise, pleasure, concern, guilt, trepidation. They're all there. In the tiny beats as my eyes blink shut, my memory is now offering flashes of what I recalled in the cottage kitchen, when he was eating toast and jam at the table, of him and me as children, somewhere outdoors like this, cool and silvery green. We're holding hands. He's pulling me along by my hand.

'Are you okay?' he says. The memory dims.

He crouches in front of me, hand hovering in the air between us, not quite daring to touch me.

'Do you remember us being together in the woods, years ago? There's this memory I've almost got hold of.'

He frowns. 'We were always in the woods, Rain.'

'Were we?'

He looks down, smiles sadly. 'For a time, yes. Do you honestly not remember? You and me, that documentary summer – the last decent one, I always think of it as – we were always together.'

'I've told you, I've got this big blank. Afterwards I remember everything. But that time and before, it's gone. Apart from a few tiny fragments. Little bits have been coming back, I don't know why, and one of them is you and me somewhere like this, but I don't think it's up here. I think it's lower down in the valley.' I suddenly recall the ash Lennie and I found, the natural theatre of its clearing, where right now they're building a new stage.

His face is faraway. 'We did use to go in those woods,' he says, so softly I instinctively want to move closer to him and only just manage to stop myself.

He shifts round so he's sitting next to me against the log, both of us facing the path that snakes sharply away down towards the bowl of the valley. High over us, the leaf canopy shivers with life, squirrels and birds moving carefully over our heads, unsure if we're dangerous or not.

'Well, anyway, talking of the past,' I begin, and then the whole scene with Karl comes flooding back so vividly that I pull in my knees and wrap my arms around them, making my body as small as possible, as if I was still trapped in the carriage-house with him.

Caleb has tensed next to me. 'Rain?' Slowly, carefully, he lays his hand on my arm. The pressure is firm but gentle, so different from how Karl felt. I can feel the warmth of his fingers through the material of my top.

I heave in a big breath and raise my head. 'I just had a run-in with your dad.'

'What do you mean? Are you okay?'

Where do I begin? *Your father has a filing cabinet full of photos of naked women? He has private footage of the last girl who died here?* I think briefly of what else I might have found in those green files and on those tapes, if Karl hadn't turned up when he did. It makes me go cold.

'I hate him,' Caleb says, in the space I've left open while I try to work out how to tell him what I suspect, or whether I should just keep it to myself. 'I've hated him for so long that I'm worried it's become part of me. That I *am* hateful – hate-*full* – because of him.'

I watch him run his hand over the mulchy ground, back and forth. It's the same shape as Karl's. The same slightly too-prominent knuckles and short, square nail beds.

'I doubt Lennie thinks that,' I say carefully. 'I don't, either.'

'The worst part of it is that before I hated him, I loved him so much. He was everything to me. My mother never knew I existed because I wasn't and never could be Caroline. But it was different with my dad. I think he was excited about having a son. It took me a while to grasp that he just saw me as an extension of himself. When I didn't turn out to be much like him – not as tough, not as definite; I couldn't even hold a *tune*, for fuck's sake – he got bored of me. I was invisible to them both then.'

I don't say anything because what can I say that wouldn't be disingenuous? He's right.

'Anyway . . .' – he turns to me, tries a rueful smile which doesn't quite get there – '. . . I don't want to talk about me. It's old news. I only came back because I love this place. The land. This sounds daft, but I always felt like it gave a shit about me when no one else did.'

'I know exactly what you mean.' And I do. I scan across the valley in my mind: all those hidey-holes and places of refuge I used to run to when I couldn't run to Ottoline, or when – and I have to resist pushing this thought away – I needed to run *from* Ottoline.

A squirrel appears from nowhere, on the ground near us. It's chewing, its tiny paws together, clutching some morsel or other. We hold our breath until it races off again.

'I saw this place I'd forgotten about today,' I say. 'It's a kind of depression in the land near the cottage. I used to sit inside it and read, or just have a think. No one could see me.'

'You mean Angie couldn't see you.'

'Yeah. I felt safe in there, peaceful. The land held me.' I start to blush, but Caleb is nodding, face intent.

'*The land held me*,' he says. 'Yes, that's exactly how it is here.'

I take a breath. I don't know who to trust right now from a rational point of view, but my instincts are telling me to trust Caleb. Maybe it's a legacy of all those childhood hours in the woods together. 'I didn't see it in real life,' I say.

He looks at me, perplexed.

'The place by the cottage. I saw it on film. Or, rather,

the film was of the cottage, but taken from that spot. I recognized it straight away. I spent who-knows-how-many hours looking out from that exact angle.'

'What kind of film?'

'I heard that your dad might have some documentary footage.' I don't want to alienate him by mentioning the research stuff.

'You heard?'

I swallow. 'From Graham Warner. I went to see him because of Angie. I wanted to know if he really did have his own footage. The police wouldn't even know about Astrid if it wasn't for him. I thought he might be able to shed some more light. Anyway, one of the things he said was that Karl might have some footage. But also I wanted to ask Karl about something your mum said in passing earlier. Something weird.' I spread my hands. 'Really, I just want to try to figure out as much as I can for Angie. I don't believe she had anything to do with Willow or Astrid. After seeing what I saw just now in the carriage-house, after seeing how Karl reacted, I'm even more convinced.'

'Oh, Christ, this sounds bad.'

'He did have footage. I found videotapes in these filing cabinets he's got hidden away in the eaves.' I decide on the spot that I'm not going to mention the photos. What purpose would it serve to tell Caleb about them right now?

'Before he came back and caught me up there, I managed to have a look at a couple. The first was similar to what I saw at Warner's: the crowd gathering, panning shots across the valley and stuff. But the second was filmed from the hollow. It was *Karl* behind the camera.

He must have borrowed it from the crew or something, I don't know. He spoke in it and I recognized his voice.'

'And he was filming your cottage? What did he say?'

'He was calling to someone at one of the upstairs windows – my bedroom window, in fact, which completely threw me – and he said, "You want it for your own?"'

'So, it was Angie inside, then?'

'No. You couldn't really make it out at first, just her dark hair, but then she opened the window, leant out, and it was *her*. Astrid.'

'Astrid,' he murmurs.

'She was at the cottage – my cottage – with Karl and he asked if she wanted it for her own, and she said yes. She looked—' I stop, because I'm abruptly on the verge of tears again. 'She looked happy.' I have to force it out.

'But . . .' Caleb tails off and, when I turn to him, he looks confounded and I'm glad. He didn't know anything about this before now. If I had any to spare, I'd lay money on it.

'He told me very clearly the other night that he hardly knew the only Astrid he'd ever heard of,' I carry on. 'He made out like she was just one of a big crowd of strangers. So that's one lie.'

Caleb drops his head. 'What else?'

'This is more recent. The police think Karl has a cast-iron alibi for the night Willow died. He told them he was away somewhere, with his musician buddies, and of course they've all corroborated it. But then I was speaking to Ottoline—'

'You brought *that* up with my mother?' His expression is half shocked, half admiring.

'I know. It was awful. But I had to, didn't I? For Angie.'

'So, what did she say? This is what you meant before about her saying something weird, right?'

I nod. 'She said, "Karl and I heard nothing that night. We saw nothing." And then she gave me this look. Karl was *with* her. He'd come back. And then, when I tried to pick her up on it, the shutters came down again. I couldn't push it any further and I was feeling shit by then, too, sick and dizzy. I basically didn't sleep at all last night.

'Anyway . . .' – I pause to catch my breath; now it's pouring out of me, it's hard to stop – '. . . even if that wasn't pretty conclusive by itself, when Karl caught me in the carriage-house with those videos, he completely lost it. He looked deranged. I've never seen him that angry before. And it wasn't just because someone was challenging his authority. God knows I've seen *that* before, with some new session guy who doesn't know him, or one of the gardeners. But this had a different quality. He . . .' – I stop, tears threatening again – '. . . he looked at me like he hated me, but also like I was . . . nothing.'

'That's new for you?' says Caleb.

His bitterness stops me in my tracks. I turn to face him properly. 'Shit, I'm sorry. Of course, you know better than anyone. But I've barely ever been in the firing line with him, and it shocked me. Like really shocked me. It was so . . . violent, that it made me think he was . . .'

'He was capable of hurting someone. Maybe two people. Two women.'

I sigh, let my eyes unfocus on the flickering greens of the leaves around us. 'Yes.'

For a while, neither of us speaks. Now I've unburdened

myself, I feel as drained as I did in Ottoline's parlour. Again, I'm tempted to lean against him and close my eyes. I suddenly realize he's watching me.

I meet his gaze and attempt a weak smile. 'What?'

He looks sad, so sad that I think he might also be close to tears. I've only seen Caleb cry once, when I was ten or eleven. Karl shouted at him in front of a group of kids, me included. The tears came from anger – anger and injustice and humiliation. This is much bleaker.

'I need to tell you something,' he says. 'I should've done already.'

'Oh, God,' I say, trying for lightness. 'What now? I'm not sure I can take any more today.'

'I don't know why I didn't just tell you straight off. It was only . . . it was only one night.' He looks down, lets that sit.

When it clicks into place for me, I feel much worse about it than I should.

'You slept with Willow.' My voice comes out entirely flat. 'Karl didn't lie about that.'

'It was only once.'

'Yes, you said that.'

'I'm sorry, Rain.'

'I don't know why you're apologizing to me.' My voice is brittle.

He shakes his head and smiles sadly. 'No, I don't either. But, still, I wish I'd told you when we first discussed it.'

'Why did you do it? I mean, she looked as though she was lovely – I don't mean that – but she was sleeping with your *dad*.' I manage to say it as though I'm genuinely non-plussed, rather than as the mean little dig it probably is.

'She came up to see me in the van. We got drunk. She was anxious. I was lonely.'

'Why was she anxious?'

'I'm not sure. I didn't press her on it at the time, but I've wondered about it since.'

Angie's supposed intuition flashes on in my head.

'What?' Caleb looks fearful. He's seen something dawn on my face.

'You know I said about Angie having some psychic notion that Willow was pregnant when she died? I think she was right.'

He goes sheet-white. 'No, no, no. There's no way.'

'Yes,' I say. 'And if she is right, then maybe it was yours.' Another little punishment he probably doesn't deserve.

'No, I mean we were . . . we were careful. I used protection. I wasn't *that* pissed. But even without it, there wasn't time.'

'What do you mean?'

'We— Look, it happened really recently. Less than a week before she died. There wasn't time for her to be pregnant, not in any way that would show up on a test.'

I stand up without planning to. I'm getting stiff on the damp ground, and what I really need to be doing is going back to the cottage to get the car, then driving to the police station. Seeing Angie, if they'll let me. I can try to make Harkin listen to what I think I've worked out.

I look down at him, still propped against the log. He gazes back at me, face wary, eyes pleading. He looks like he did as a boy.

'Do you hate me now?' he says.

'Why would I hate you? It's got nothing to do with

me who you sleep with.' I sound like I do when Angie's wounded me. Cold. Dismissive.

'Okay, fair enough.'

I start to walk away, then stop as something clicks into place in my mind. Willow's genuine happiness in the photograph taken on the croquet lawn. I turn back to him. 'Was it you who sent that picture to the papers? I couldn't work it out.'

'I took it. I didn't send it in.'

'How did they get hold of it, then?'

He shrugs, face miserable. 'She looked so lovely in it. Not anxious like she was later. She liked it so I said she could have it.'

'Are you sure? The tabloids pay good money for stuff like that. I know you hate asking your dad for money.'

His face closes. I don't know if it's an admission of guilt or not.

'Lots of people hate asking their parents for money,' I say. 'That's why they get jobs.'

I walk away so I don't have to see him crushed. I don't want visual proof that I've done that to him. He'd lied to me about Willow, but I'm being cold and hard in a way that reminds me of Karl.

Chapter Thirty-Two

I make swift progress down the hill and on towards the cottage. As my legs carry me along, I try to figure out what I'll say to Harkin, if she'll even see me. But, as I do, what Caleb's just admitted happened between him and Willow keeps stealing into my head. I try to analyse the photo thing – whether it's suspicious, whether I think he was telling the truth and what it means if Willow sent it to the papers – but I know my principal emotion is jealousy. And I really don't want to think about that right now. I have enough to be getting on with.

My phone vibrates in my pocket and I pull it out. Dan. Of course it is. Before I can default to the avoidance, which I'm beginning to realize doesn't get me anywhere, I answer it.

'Holy shit, you picked up.'

'Pressed the wrong button.'

I expect him to laugh – adversarial is how we are – but he only sighs. 'Lovely to hear your voice too.'

'Sorry.' I sound as gruff as a teenager. 'Weird day.'

'You okay? What about your mum?'

'Yep.'

He waits for more, then sighs again. 'Well, look, I think I've got something. About Sandra Jones.'

Astrid. My stomach flips. Their faces – hers and Willow's – are beginning to spin and coalesce in my mind.

Three decades closing in, compressing to nothing. Willow waving at the cottage window instead of Astrid. Astrid reduced to pixels on paper instead of Willow. Long dark hair and lit-up smiles and no idea that Fate was hurtling mercilessly towards them. *What happened to you both?*

'Rain, are you still there?'

'Yes, sorry. What have you found?'

'It's not a hundred-per-cent definite. Jones is not a great surname when you're digging so it was a good job we had a middle name and an idea of where she was from. There's a pretty decent chance I've got the right woman.'

My hand goes involuntarily to my chest.

'This Sandra Margaret Jones was born in Taunton, Somerset, in September 1941. A war baby, maybe conceived at Christmas when the father was home on leave. If he even went to war, of course. I didn't get that far. Anyway, she was the closest candidate by a long way. The only other Sandra Margaret Joneses I could find in the county of Somerset around that period were born in 1934 and 1953. So, either thirty-six or seventeen in 1970.'

'I think you've got the right one,' I say. The woman at my bedroom window definitely wasn't seventeen, and I don't think she was thirty-six either. 'That would have made her twenty-nine, which more or less fits.'

'That's not all.' Dan sounds chuffed with himself, and it grates, though it's my own fault he's got no idea how frighteningly close all this has become for me. 'She had a child.'

I stop walking.

'A little girl. I found her birth certificate. She was registered in Glastonbury, which seems suitably New Age, though of course the festival didn't begin until 1970, funnily enough. Maybe Sandra should have gone there instead of Tanglewood. She might still be with us.' He laughs.

'Anyway,' he hurries on, when I don't join in, 'that's another reason I think this Sandra fits, especially in that era.'

'What do you mean?'

'Well, if it's the same Sandra, she's still got her maiden name on the birth certificate, and where the father's name should be, there's a blank.'

I massage my browbone where it's tender as I try to absorb this, but all I can see is Lennie the first time I met her – newly motherless but already absorbed into the privilege of Tanglewood, no one outside its big iron gates any the wiser. Again, the years seem to collapse, like asteroids nudged into the same orbit millennia ago and finally about to collide.

'What about the old footage?' Dan is saying, making me jolt back into the present. 'Did you manage to see Warner?'

'There's not much,' I say, mind whirring as I calculate how much I want to give away. 'But I think I spotted her: Sandra. *Astrid.*'

'Do you think there's any mileage in it? Any proper connection between the two deaths? Or do we just focus on the thirty-year thing, the big gig tomorrow?'

'Any mileage?'

'Sorry. Documentary head taking over. You know what I mean.'

I sigh. 'What about Astrid's baby? Did you find out anything else about her?'

'Nothing beyond the birth certificate. She vanishes after that. Nowhere in the records, as far as I can see.'

Vanishes. I rub my arms where I feel suddenly chilly, despite the heat.

'What was her name, at least?'

'Actually, this had me wondering if I'd got the right woman after all. As someone who changed her name to Astrid, I mean. But maybe the flower-power stuff got a hold on her later. It's a nice, sensible name: Claire.'

'It means "light",' I say. 'Not that far from "star" for Astrid.'

'Yeah, I suppose so.'

'What do you think happened to her?'

'There are always gaps in the records,' Dan is saying, though I was thinking aloud as much as asking him. 'People move around, get missed. She might not even have been with her mother at Tanglewood. Maybe she was with her father, although that seems unlikely given he doesn't get a mention on the birth certificate. Maybe she grew up with her grandparents.'

'Maybe. Thanks for looking into it. It's really helpful.'

'Is it? It's not like it tells us anything about Willow Green. About what's going on now. It's only a day till the main event. I've been looking that up too. There are rumours Karl Lund is going to play the whole album. Look, sorry to bang on, but do you think we stick to the music, or is there something in the two-women thing?'

I open my mouth to reply, but if I told him all the similarities between Willow and Astrid, I would also have to tell him where I'm from, how I fit into all this. Where I'm standing right now, in the palm of the fabled Tanglewood valley, and how I'm pretty much convinced that Karl Lund, reclusive lord of the manor and folk-rock enigma, who only ever deigned to put out one magical, mystical album, might also be a killer.

Dan starts to say something else, but the signal cuts out. We try again and the same thing happens. He'll want to pin me down as to what filming I'll be able to do tomorrow, at the Gathering, whether I need to get a press pass so I can go backstage, whether there's the smallest chance I might be able to interview someone close to the big man himself.

'I can't hear you,' I say on the third attempt, which is mostly true, and hang up. I'll try him again later, I tell myself.

It's tipped into mid-afternoon now, the sky almost lavender where it meets the hills. There's no visual evidence of Gathering preparations from this angle, but I can hear them in the still air: hammers and drills and the low rumble of a generator. I would've expected it to feel different, knowing there were other people on the estate, but it doesn't. These are Karl's people. Most of them will be in thrall to him. Those who aren't will be in his pay.

But I don't want to think about Karl. Not for a while. I want to think about the women. I want to think about that vanished little girl. *Where are you?* I think. *Where did you go?*

Whatever Dan was suggesting about grandparents in Taunton, I'm afraid she was here that summer.

I'm afraid she never left. That, somehow, she ended up like her mother.

Chapter Thirty-Three

In the cottage's cramped little bathroom, I go doggedly through the cabinet over the sink. As with every cupboard and drawer in the place, it's full of stuff that should have been chucked out years ago. Congealed make-up and lotions, rusted disposable razors, and a dried-up tube of verruca cream are the highlights.

In Angie's bedroom, I get down on my knees to search her bedside table, the dreamcatcher rasping against the plaster above as it's caught in the draught from the open window. Curling paperbacks, crossword books, homemade hand-cream that's gone as hard and yellow as earwax, and some gadget I don't recognize all tumble out onto the floor. The gadget turns itself on, a description that seems appropriate when I realize it's a vibrator. I kick it out of sight under the bed, where it continues to buzz like a dying wasp.

What I'm looking for is medication and I find it in a small cloth bag decorated with a clumsy iron-on sunflower. I don't think the tranquillizers will count as essential prescription drugs when they're six years expired, but there are also some betablockers, which are just about in date. *Fuck you, Karl*, I think, as I clatter down the stairs. Angie isn't using again, or I'd have found signs of it. I never doubted it, not really.

I drive too fast to Stroud. The roads are narrow and

twisting and, even though I could probably anticipate the turns blindfolded, I can't predict the enormous tractor in the middle of the road as I round a particularly sharp bend. I screech to a halt, the smell of scorched rubber rising from the hot tarmac. The farmer gives me a withering stare from high up in his cab and continues manoeuvring at a glacial pace. When I get past him, taking it slower now, I open the window all the way to breathe in the rich scents of grass and flowers, the vestiges of dampness from last night's deluge.

In town, I park as close as I can to the police station and take some deep breaths before getting out of the car. I'm still wound tight and it's not going to help Angie's cause if I lose my temper. It's so not like me, but I'm molten inside now – I don't think it would take much for me to blow. Ironically, Angie would be delighted with this other side to me. *Not so repressed after all, eh, Rainy?*

The custody sergeant spends a long time inspecting the medication. I shift from foot to foot, smiling blandly when he glances up from the close-typed label to inspect me instead.

'I don't know why she didn't take them with her,' I say, in a breezy tone, 'but I suppose she's quite resistant to taking pills. She prefers natural remedies.' I smile again.

After what seems like a whole epoch has passed, he picks up the phone. 'Got Angie Valentine's daughter here with her medication. Says she needs it for her blood pressure. That she's overdue it.'

He scratches at his stubble as he listens, the noise like fingernails down a blackboard in my heightened state. Eventually he replaces the receiver with a rattle.

'Her Majesty herself is coming down,' he says, with a raised eyebrow.

'Angie?' I say, confused.

He huffs out a laugh. 'Harkin. You can wait over there.'

Harkin's suit is still immaculate when she appears, but her eyes are ringed with fatigue.

'You can't see her,' she says. 'There's no provision for visiting suspects in custody.'

'Why haven't you let her go if you haven't charged her? You said you wouldn't keep her overnight.'

'I said we'd try not to, but she still wasn't cooperating, so we had to apply for an extension.'

'The reason she's not saying anything is because she's scared. She'd rather die than get Karl into trouble. It pains me to say it but it's true. Look, can we go somewhere more private?' I nod towards the custody sergeant, who's listening openly.

Harkin sighs. 'Okay, five minutes.'

She takes me to a room with two cheap sofas and a box of tissues on a table between them. She looks so tired that I suspect she's only agreed to this because she wants a sit-down out of sight of her colleagues.

'Why are you still so intent on Karl Lund having something to do with it?' she says. 'I told you his alibi is solid.'

'His alibi is made up. I spoke to his wife and she said he was with her the night Willow died. She knew I'd come to you but she told me that anyway. She said that she and Karl didn't hear or see anything, but the point is he wasn't supposed to be there at all. I think that's as much as she dared tell me. She's scared of him too.'

'I rang each one of those musicians. They all said the same thing.'

'And I'm telling you that I grew up with Karl and those men around, and they're lying for him. Since when do the police take alibis at face value? I believe he was there, at Tanglewood; got back earlier than he said. And if he was there, and he'd just found out he'd got Willow pregnant, I'd say that's a pretty strong motive.'

'How did you know she was pregnant?'

'I didn't. Not for sure. I had a hunch and it looks like I was right.'

Harkin closes her eyes briefly, which should make me feel triumphant, but I'm mainly glad I stopped myself saying it was Angie's hunch, which would probably have sounded suspicious.

'All I'm asking is that you go back to Karl,' I continue. 'Question him again. There's something going on that feels really, really wrong. And it's not just about where he was the night Willow died, either. It's about Astrid. About Sandra Jones.'

Her eyes flare, and I know I've surprised her, that they've found the same birth record Dan has.

'I found a load of naked photos and videotapes among his things yesterday. On one tape, there was footage of the same woman Warner says was Astrid. And not in some crowd scene, either, just Karl and her. It proves Karl knew her well, that there was intimacy between them.'

I'm about to mention the cottage, but stop. Like the pregnancy hunch, it feels too close to Angie, as though I might implicate her in something I don't understand when I'm trying to do the opposite.

Harkin's face is hard to read. She's tapping the end of her pen on the sofa arm and I hope that's because there's something in what I've told her that's catching alight in her detective's brain, some investigative alarm bell starting to clang.

'Where are these tapes?' she says, after a while, and my heart lifts.

'In the carriage-house above his recording studio, up in the eaves. There's a room off the bedroom there. They were in one of the filing cabinets.'

'Right, fine.' She blows out a long breath. 'I'll look into it later.'

'What about now? You could follow me back.'

'I know the way. I'll get over there as soon as I can.' She stands.

'Okay. Thank you. But what about Angie?'

'Angie's fine.' She holds up the betablockers. 'You've done your bit, and I'll follow up, but you need to go now. Leave us to do our jobs.'

I open my mouth and shut it again. For now at least, I think I've pushed it as far as I can.

When I get back, Caleb is sitting on the wall outside the cottage. He looks serious and, as I turn off the engine, I assume it's because he's not sure if we're okay yet, after his earlier confession.

'Any luck at the station?'

I consider giving him the cold shoulder but there are more important things to focus on. 'Maybe. I saw Harkin, told her about the videos. She's said she'll look into it. I don't *think* she was fobbing me off.'

Caleb follows me into the cottage and I get a couple of cold beers out of the fridge. It seems to have come back to life since last night and is now humming away louder than ever.

We take them outside and I lead the way to the cleft of land I remember from the tape. When I sit down, facing the cottage, I see a flash of something at my window, but it's probably just the sun.

For a moment, though, I thought she was there again, dark hair melding with the gloom behind her.

'I went up to the manor,' Caleb says. 'I wanted to see if I could get anything more out of my mother about what Dad was doing that night, what time he got back from his trip if she said he was there. If only I'd been here myself, I might have seen his car.'

I picture the blue Cadillac and it reminds me of earlier. 'Did you see Lennie? Ottoline said her hayfever was bad.'

'No, she was in her room sleeping, apparently. My mother had just come from checking on her.'

'She's doing a lot of that. I'm guessing you saw the baby monitor at dinner.'

'Yeah. She had her blue box out just now.'

'Blue box?'

He smiles sadly. 'A relic of my childhood. It's where she keeps her first-aid kit. Plasters and bandages and all that. She was rinsing off the thermometer when I found her so she must have only just checked on Lennie.'

I have a sip of my beer but it tastes sour now, and I offer it to Caleb, who's nearly finished his. Besides, I feel I need my wits about me.

'Shall I tell you something embarrassing?' he says,

with a sideways smile. 'Just to endear myself to you even more today.'

'Go on, then. I'll enjoy this.'

'I used to pretend to be ill sometimes, when I was a kid.'

I wasn't expecting that. I turn to him, but he's looking down, fingers plucking at the grass.

'It was the only way I ever got any attention from her. Ironically, I never really caught anything when I was here, only when I was back at boarding school and cooped up with the other boys. Here, even when there were kids around . . .' – he glances up – '. . . kids like you, we were always in the fresh air. Anyway, I probably really hammed it up but she didn't seem to realize. Do you remember that scene in *E.T.* when Elliott wants to stay back from school, and he sticks the thermometer against the light-bulb so it reads hotter when his mum comes back to check?'

'You did that too?'

'Yeah.' He laughs shortly. 'We had a trip to the cinema when I was at school – some master who was half human organized it. I guess I was about thirteen or fourteen. I saw that scene and it took me straight back. I'd completely forgotten. It was a real clincher, the fever thing. Once I'd thought of it. Worked like a dream.' He smiles but his eyes are sad.

'You know Lennie's in Caroline's old room, don't you?' I say.

'Yes, she told me. Lennie, I mean. I think she's been a bit overawed by it and I'm not surprised. It's basically a museum. Mine, on the other hand . . .' – he picks up my beer and drinks some – '. . . I came back from school one Christmas and everything had gone. Mother had decided to move me into another room, but apparently didn't see fit to move any of my childhood things into it. Most of it had just disappeared. Been chucked out, I guess. And of course I couldn't complain to Karl, because he never had *anything* as a kid, and what did I want with a load of old toys at my age anyway?'

It comes then, as unexpectedly and completely as the memory on my first night, when I was walking back from the pub in the dark. The blue box against the pink and white of Caroline's room. The cool flannel draped over my forehead, and the nightlight turning slow circles beside me. The curtains were drawn against a bright autumn day. I remember leaves crunching below the windows; one of the gardeners was out there, cutting everything back for the coming winter. The cosseting and the comfort of it, of pretending to be a child who belonged at the manor instead of in the grubby cottage down the valley.

'I remember it, too,' I say, barely louder than a whisper. I lie back in the grass and close my eyes, let the memory come, which it does with pin-sharp clarity.

It was her voice I heard first, much louder than the brittle leaves being crushed underfoot by the gardener outside. Half asleep in my warm cocoon, it took me a long beat to understand it was *Angie*'s voice, because Angie never set foot inside the manor. In that beat she must have pushed past Ottoline and scaled the stairs. I remember the air as she came in – a cold rush of it, as if she'd brought the outside in with her, the valley itself her own flanking army.

I must have been nine, but she flung back the covers and scooped me into her arms as easily as if I'd been a child of four or five. As she rushed me to the door, the flannel slid off my forehead and dropped silently to the thick carpet. The nightlight spun on.

Ottoline didn't say anything as we came down the stairs towards where she was frozen at the bottom, me clinging to Angie like a monkey because I was afraid she was going to trip or drop me.

As I was rushed towards the front door, I locked eyes with Ottoline over Angie's shoulder. She stretched out a hand towards me and I did the same, reaching back for her. Tears coursed down her lovely face. My own cheeks were wet.

'*I'm* your mother,' Angie said, as we went downhill to the cottage. After the heat of Caroline's bedroom, the air was sharp, like needles, on my salt-dry face. My right arm hurt in its socket because Angie had set me down on my feet, grabbed hold of my hand and was now wrenching me along by it. 'Do you hear me?' she said. '*I'm* your mother. She's not having you.'

Unlike the earlier ones, this was a memory I chose to forget.

Chapter Thirty-Four

I stand. Caleb squints up at me. I don't know how long I've been lost in my past but he's finished my beer as well as his own.

'I want to go and talk to Ottoline. I want to see Lennie, too. Will you come?'

He nods and I put out a hand to pull him up.

When we crest the hill above the cottage, it becomes clear the Gathering has stepped up another couple of gears. In a few hours, people will start to arrive, start setting up tents.

'It feels wrong,' puffs Caleb, next to me. We're both breathing hard. The afternoon light has mellowed but the land has been absorbing the sun all day. It's hotter now than it was at midday. 'It's too soon. All this. She only died a week ago.'

'Did you . . . love her?' I don't look at him. It's easier that we're walking, both of us facing ahead.

'No. But I liked her a great deal.'

'Do you think . . . ?' I hesitate.

'Do I think my father killed her? I don't know. I'm probably the last person to give him the benefit of the doubt but I don't want to believe that's what happened. He's got it in him to be violent and I don't think he gives a shit about anything but himself, but what's his motivation here? So he gets someone pregnant. He's cheated on my mother for decades. I actually feel he'd be more pleased than anything else. He'd get to join the ranks of ageing rockers who've knocked up a woman young enough to be their daughter.'

'So maybe she crossed him in some way?' I say. 'Like with the photo you took and gave to her. If you didn't send it . . .'

'I didn't. I swear.'

'Well, maybe *she* did.'

The manor is in view now. The windows of Caroline's bedroom are closed and curtained, white eyes blind to the sweltering afternoon. 'He was frightening earlier, really frightening. Maybe she was after some fame, some attention ahead of the Gathering.'

'So, she went to the tabloids behind his back,' says Caleb. 'And then he found out and just lost it.'

Picturing him as he was in the carriage-house, I can believe it. Maybe all the years of everyone saying yes, the years of ruling his own little fiefdom without outside interference, have accumulated to the point that he's forgotten the rules.

Inside the manor, all is quiet. Caleb goes in search of Ottoline on the ground floor while I pad upstairs as quietly as I can. I expect Caroline's bedroom door to be closed but when I turn the handle and it's locked, I don't want to believe it, twisting it this way and that before I have to accept that Ottoline's anxiety has made her imprison a healthy ten-year-old girl on a glorious afternoon.

I knock as quietly as I can. 'Lennie,' I call, ear to the thick wooden door, 'Lennie, can you hear me?'

I kneel to look through the keyhole, but I can't make out anything except the faint outline of light around one curtained window. The angle is all wrong to see the bed anyway.

As I straighten up, two things happen at once. Caleb appears at the top of the stairs and the door to Ottoline's suite of rooms opens. With the light behind her and the hall dim by comparison, the long silk robe and the turban she's wearing turn her silhouette dramatic. She looks like the Sorceress of Angie's tarot cards.

'Why's Lennie locked in?' I say.

'She mustn't be disturbed,' she says, and her voice is as smooth and modulated as ever, except there's also a thread of steel running through it now. Or maybe it was always there, and I just didn't want to hear it.

'May I have the key, please?' *May* I, not *can* I. Ottoline taught me that long ago. I am as much a product of her as I am my own mother.

'Come and sit with me a while,' she says, standing back to usher me in. 'Then we can see Lennie. Let her sleep a little longer. She's very tired.'

The fine hairs on my arms have lifted but I go towards Ottoline as if magnetized. Caleb does the same.

'No, darling,' she says firmly to him. 'This is between us girls.'

'Go and get those videos,' I say, in an undertone. Harkin might be hours yet. I curse myself for not thinking to do this already.

He hovers there, and I slide in and back out of that memory again. The silvery green one. Ottoline, taking my hand, shakes me out of it.

'Go on,' I say to Caleb. 'And when you've got them, take them to the cottage.'

Ottoline's bedroom is just as it was when I was young. It doesn't even look smaller to me, like they always say of exalted places from childhood. I can smell the roses, which means that somewhere, in some sense, Grandmother Adaline is with us.

This room has always had a soporific effect on me and I drift over to the biggest central window to gaze out, my sense of urgency already blunted. It's the one that Ottoline opened thirty years ago, a tiny act caught by Warner's amateurish camerawork. Now I'm on the other side of it, looking out as the same scene begins to play.

A huge marquee is being set up on the croquet lawn, presumably for any VIPs, white canvas not yet secured but unmoving in air like hot syrup. Out in the dead centre of the Great Meadow, metal scaffolding is taking shape. Cars, maybe two dozen, are now parked on the margins of the Dark Ride, glass and metal flashing as the sun glances off them.

'What's that for?' I say, pointing at the scaffolding. I feel swimmy, sleepy – as if I drank the beer I gave to Caleb. 'What are they building?'

'Ah, that's part of Karl's surprise.' Ottoline comes over to stand next to me. 'All will be revealed tomorrow night.'

'It must be strange, seeing it like this after so long,' I say. 'It must take you right back to the last time.'

'I suppose so.' Her tone doesn't betray her, but her face does.

'It wasn't long after Caroline, was it?' I keep my voice as soft as hers. 'Only six or seven months.' I can see the sampler in my head, the second date picked out in shades of dusty pink and sage: *24 December 1969*.

'She was such a sunny child,' she says, the words as soft as breath. 'Of course, she must have had days when she was out of temper, but I simply can't remember them.'

The low-angled sun is unforgiving on her face. She's almost translucent: just a single sheet of tissue smoothed over fine old bones. Her eyes are sunk deep in her skull, their blue almost washed out.

'I didn't know, you see.' She smiles grimly. 'What a fool I was. It was only when I heard Karl and her talking about it, when I heard him confessing what he'd done to her, that I understood.'

I hold myself very still, in the hope that she'll explain, but she's not looking at me now. Her eyes are fixed just over my shoulder, near where the portrait of Caroline hangs. I hold my breath as her gaze locks on something – or someone – who is clearly visible to her.

'When they said it was her heart – that it had simply stopped in the night, that sometimes this happened to children who seemed entirely healthy but who were all the time carrying this . . . this *fault* around with them.' She cups her hands, as though holding something precious. 'A ticking alarm clock inside her, but not waiting to go off. Waiting to just . . . stop.

'She wouldn't have known a thing about it, they said. She would have just gone to sleep and eventually, at some unknown point, she would have drifted out, beyond her dreams, to a silent place too distant to return from. *Aye, there's the rub!* Cruel for the parents, but easy on the child. That was something I tried to cling to.'

She lapses into silence and I watch her eyes moving around the room. Her face is a mask of longing, almost hunger. It frightens me, even as sadness washes through me and makes my eyes blur.

'You said you overheard him confess,' I risk. 'What did Karl confess?'

She blinks, startled, and I'm afraid I've jolted her out of wherever she's gone to, but then she sighs. 'It was just before the Gathering began.' She gestures towards the scene below us. 'It was a day like this. A film was going to be made about it so everything had to be grander, more . . . outlandish than it had been in previous years.

'The two of them were in her bedroom. In Caroline's bedroom, where he never went. I think he was giving her a tour of the house.' She tries to smile but it turns into a grimace. 'I had been looking for Karl because Bill Laing had telephoned urgently, and I couldn't find him anywhere. He wasn't outside where people were arriving, and he wasn't in the carriage-house. I stood on the landing out there to think, and, in the same moment, noticed Caroline's door was ajar when I always closed it. I would go in there when I was missing her most acutely and I always closed the door after me. But I could hear their voices coming from inside.'

Who? I want to say. *Who was with him?* But I'm afraid to interrupt. Besides, after seeing the film of the cottage, I think I know.

'I was about to call when I clearly heard a woman's voice,' Ottoline says. 'That stopped me cold because he never brought women inside the manor. That was one of our unspoken rules.

'I shouldn't have done it, of course. Eavesdroppers never hear anything good. But I crept to the door and I listened. I listened while he told her what he had kept from me about our daughter's death. And then she told him something in return.'

1970

It's only the second time she's been inside the manor house. The first time was in winter, when she'd not long arrived at Tanglewood, just before Karl and Ottoline's little girl died. She wonders what she'd be doing now if she'd gone back to Morocco and never come back here at all, her hand going automatically to her stomach. Still, it's only an idle thought. Everything feels blessedly distant now.

After her run-in with Angie, she found a man selling pot. He even rolled it for her. It's made her feel like she's floating just outside the confines of her own frightened body, which is exactly what she needed it to do. She's kept the Empress card, decided to view it as a talisman rather than a curse. It's tucked into the pocket of her skirt.

She tiptoes down the hall. It smells of old Turkey rugs beaten outside each spring. Of wax furniture polish applied in infinitesimal layers over many years. Of heavy-bottomed bowls of roses – an old variety, something classy like a damask – cut and brought in from the garden. Of Ottoline's lily-of-the-valley scent.

It smells of wealth.

Somewhere upstairs, Karl's preposterously named wife

will likely be getting ready for tonight's concert in the rooms that look out over the great sweep of her land. Perhaps her parents hoped she would be a boy. Perhaps there was German blood in the family. Certainly she could pass, with her fair hair and pale eyes, but there's nothing else of the Valkyrie about Ottoline. She looks like she would blow away in a stiff breeze, a dandelion clock of a woman; a ghost of what once bloomed. Still lovely but insubstantial. Bloodless.

She spies the huge hatstand in the hall, though the name hardly does it justice. It must be Victorian, some enormous thing of carved mahogany, with dedicated compartments for hats and canes and shoehorns, plus a seat to ease the tying of laces. There's a spotted mirror set into its middle and she catches sight of herself – catches the gleam of curiosity in her eyes as another person might see her. Though it's not just curiosity. Some strange blend of envy and avidity can be read there, too. *This isn't mine, but he is.* With her earlier dread now at a remove, she's recalled that half of tonight's set list are songs written for her, written *about* her – or so he claims. Of *course* she still has power over him.

She runs her fingers through her hair to tidy it and a couple of strands pull loose and tangle around her fingers. *Grubby little gypsy, didn't take after me*, her mother whispers in her head, as though anxiety is trying for a fingerhold in a different, undefended part of her brain.

She lets the hairs drop and they catch the last of the sun angling into the hall as they drift to the tiles. She wonders how long it'll be before they get swept up by some servant or other. Maybe a draught will blow them under the hatstand, and a part of her will stay here in Ottoline's house for ever, undetected.

'Meet me at the hatstand in the hall,' Karl had called to her when she'd seen him a couple of hours ago, he and his entourage of male bandmates and hangers-on moving like a pack of jackals through the round-eyed crowd. He'd seemed jittery, his right eyelid flickering as though he hadn't slept. 'Come at three. O will be busy.' There was no expectation of refusal. He didn't introduce her to the men she didn't already know.

'I want to show you the parts of the house you haven't seen,' he said more quietly before he moved away, getting close enough to her to run his string-calloused finger down the inside of her arm. 'I want to see you inside it.' One of the men sniggered as they went. Another leered.

The joint started to take effect soon after. Fear slid out and relief took its place – relief that Karl had apparently got over the Graham thing. She'd had a last couple of drags, and then curiosity to see the manor began to swell in her, too – the sensation as oddly physical as desire, and nearly as irresistible.

Now the long clock at the bottom of the stairs strikes the hour but still he doesn't come. Deep in the bowels of the house, she can hear activity. She imagines she can hear Ottoline's famously dulcet tones. She can't wrest her eyes from the baize door she's certain her lover's wife is about to walk through. Another flicker of fear tries to light inside her but gutters out.

Restless by ten past, she goes up to where the staircase splits into two elegant, curving halves. She chooses the left, sitting down when she's high enough that anyone passing along the hallway below won't easily spot her. When she peeps through the gaps in the banister, the pattern of the tiled floor below expands and contracts, like a camera lens trying to focus.

'Here you are,' he says, from the gallery above, some indefinable amount of time later. 'I've been waiting for you.'

She opens her mouth to contradict this: she can see the hatstand from where she is, and he hasn't been near it. But then she closes it again and goes up to join him. The pot is beginning to wear off now, numbness sharpening into edges again.

They start their strange tour on the top floor, where the ceilings are lower, and work their way down. Only one door remains closed on the first floor.

'What's in there?' she says, but even as she asks, she thinks she knows.

'My baby girl's room,' he says, looking down so that a lock of dark-gold hair covers his eyes. She assumes they'll move on, but then he pushes open the door.

She knows only a little about Caroline, who died so suddenly at the end of the previous year, horribly close to Christmas. She, Astrid, had only arrived at Tanglewood the week before. She'd already caught Karl's attention, but left soon after, taking her own girl with her, as though what Caroline had had might be catching.

It wasn't just her. Everyone left. But in the bleak days of the new year, grief reflected in the leafless trees and the gunmetal sky over them, he had hoped she would return. He wished for it, he later told her. Wrote a song about it, in fact, and then another and another – all of them variations on the theme of her coming back to the valley in time for spring. And when she did return, in late April, he said he knew that destiny was at work, both for her and for his folk-rock masterpiece.

Now, he goes to sit on the end of his daughter's four-poster bed and pats the eiderdown beside him. His face darkens as she hesitates, just a fraction, but enough to make her do it. It's usually easier to just do it, with men. With this man, for sure.

'I don't come in here much,' he says. 'O's kinda claimed it, you know? She and Caroline were close, maybe a little too close.'

'I can't imagine it,' she says, and though it's a phrase worn thin, it's also true. She literally can't imagine going on without her girl. If she tries, her brain seems to short-circuit. All she sees is dark empty space, way out beyond the furthest stars.

'It was her heart, wasn't it?' she says. She places her hand on his, squeezes gently.

'Can I tell you something?' he says. He glances at the door, which stands slightly ajar, then back at her. His expression is one of pleading and it's so unfamiliar, especially lately, that chilly apprehension whistles through the pot haze.

'It was her heart, but it wasn't some . . . birth defect.'

The word makes her flinch, but he doesn't notice.

'You gotta understand it was a total accident. She shouldn't even have been awake. She'd been put to bed and then got up again. She must have heard the music, the voices. Wanted to join in. And it was near Christmas, you know? Well, sure you know. You were there.

'She'd been counting down the days, the tree was up, and she was obsessed with that tree. O was doing the advent candles with her, too. They were both crazy about all those traditions.'

He stops, looks towards the door again. She hasn't heard anything, but he knows this house in a way she doesn't and never will, whatever he says to her sometimes, when he's inside her. She knows, in fact, that this doesn't just *feel* like Ottoline's house. Legally it's hers, too.

'Anyway, O had gone to bed, but plenty hadn't. Me and the guys were all still going: Jimmy, Jeff, McQuinn and Casper. All those cats. You know 'em. McQuinn had got this stuff from Amsterdam, I think it was. Got it through Customs somehow.'

It starts to dawn on her, what he's working up to saying. Without thinking, her hands go to her belly. There's nothing to feel yet. She hasn't even been nauseous. The only sign she's had, beyond a single missed period, is a deep stretching ache that wakes her in the night.

'She found this little box with pills inside. It was small, had jewels on, like something you'd buy in a bazaar. Her little magpie eyes must have seen it there and she always did love pretty things. I worked it out afterwards, because they were missing. She must have thought they were candy. They were different colours, you know. But they weren't candy. They were some kind of benzos. Mother's Little Helper. There were maybe a couple of Quaaludes, too.' He sighs. 'McQuinn had shoved this little baggie in the box to keep it away from prying eyes, waiting staff and some of the wives, O included, and then we all got crazily high, flying from acid, and taking these fucking peyote buttons someone had brought over from the States in the lining of his guitar case.' He turns to her, takes both of her hands, begins kneading them, a shade too hard.

'I didn't even see her. I didn't even see her there. Someone else did, took me aside after the undertaker drove her away and said they'd seen her there, in her white nightdress. Like a baby angel.'

He lowers himself to her lap and weeps. She wasn't up at the manor that night. She was burrowed into the warmth of her child in their tent. She heard about what had happened the next day, had felt guiltily grateful she hadn't been present for any part of that terrible night. Now, she wishes she could go back in time and steal that little jewelled box. Intercept Caroline as she crept down the stairs and lead her back up to this lovely bedroom. But it's impossible. She's gone.

Karl cries for a couple of minutes, then straightens. She reaches out to wipe his face with the cotton hem of her long skirt. She doesn't think she can tell him that what happened wasn't his fault. She doesn't really believe it wasn't, in some sense.

So she tells him instead what she'd decided she wouldn't, before the joint.

Even as she opens her mouth to speak, she's still questioning the wisdom of it. She loves Tanglewood, but the presentiment is muscling back in.

'I need to tell you something, too,' she says, a swooping feeling coming over her, as if she's chosen to step into nothing and can't remember why. Maybe it's simply down to the way he wept for his lost daughter. 'I'm going to have a baby,' she says. 'Your baby.'

Chapter Thirty-Five

Ottoline finishes her story, chest heaving from the unburdening of it.

'Caroline's death wasn't from natural causes?' I say. 'Oh, Ottoline.' Inside my head, another question forms: *Astrid was pregnant?*

I go to where she's sitting, on the little armchair where she used to embroider because it got the best light. When Ottoline was a girl, her own nanny used to darn her small stockings in the same chair. Another era. A happier one.

I kneel at her feet and take her hands in mine. 'I'm so sorry. I don't know how you survived it.'

She looks blankly at me, then smiles. 'I don't know that I did. At least, I don't think the old me did.' She gently squeezes my hand. 'Another person took over. Another Ottoline.'

The back of my neck goes cold. The feeling spreads down my spine, chilled fingers tracing a line to my waist, making me shudder, though I try to suppress it. She seems not to notice.

Outside, next to the scaffolding, something large and lumpen under tarpaulin has been unloaded onto the grass from a flatbed trailer. It looks like it might start moving at any moment, a huge animal stirring from a tranquillized sleep. When I look back at Ottoline, her gaze is fixed again on something other than me and, already spooked, I turn, half expecting a small, nightgowned Caroline to be shimmering from the corner, here and then gone again, like a radio frequency not quite tuned in.

But it's not her. It's the baby monitor. I hadn't noticed the green light in the bright room.

I go over and can just about make out Lennie in the darkened room, a small hump under the bedclothes, one pale arm flung loose and glowing out of the screen.

'Shall we see if Lennie wants to join us?' I say, as lightly as I can. 'She's probably feeling better now, after her sleep.'

Ottoline doesn't reply. There's an emptiness in her face I've never seen in all the years I've known her. She's gone far away from herself, and it frightens me more than Karl did in the carriage-house.

'It was simply unendurable,' she says, as though already engaged in a different conversation. 'I thought Caroline's death was unendurable, but then I suppose, at least in some sense, I did endure. But for him to replace my child with another woman's, as though Caroline had never existed? As if the two of them and their debauchery hadn't had a hand in her death? No.' She shakes her head.

'She hadn't long arrived. It was just before Christmas. She was one of a new batch of hangers-on, but I could see right away that she had caught Karl's eye. Her name wasn't really Astrid. She'd made that up. Her real name was something very ordinary.' She sits up straighter. 'My belief was that she needed my daughter to make way for the one she would have.' She nods with remembered conviction. 'That was the first part of her plan, though of course I had no idea at the time, stupid as I was. To me, she was simply another of Karl's moon-eyed girls.

'But then, by summer, when I heard the two of them scheming in Caroline's room, I understood immediately. Of course, it was much too late by then. Too late for my Caroline. Too late for me, I suppose. But, still, it couldn't stand. It would have been insupportable to let it stand. And Caroline agreed, didn't you, darling?' She nods towards the corner. 'She came to me, like she has today, and said so.'

I rub my arms, even as the honeyed sun streams in through the windows. 'Ottoline, what did you do?'

She smiles, not at me. 'So little, really. It took so little in the end to put a stop to it all.' She sits forward in her chair, eyes avid. 'You're so clear today, my sweet girl. Clearer than you've been in years.'

As she communes with her invisible long-lost child, I can only stand motionless, head full of a sound like rushing water. What has she just admitted to me? That she hurt Astrid? I brace myself to ask but then the baby monitor's green eye blinks and it focuses me again.

'Ottoline, I need you to give me the key to Caroline's bedroom.'

She blinks at me in confusion, almost annoyance. I've interrupted the two of them. 'A key, you say?'

Something like comprehension is dawning on her face when the bedroom door bangs open, so hard it bounces back off its own frame. I stumble into the bedpost with the shock of it. Ottoline, attention caught again by an invisible presence, barely reacts.

'What are you doing here, Rain?' Karl says. He looks wrong in Ottoline's room. I've never seen him here. Somehow, it's not a space for men. 'Everywhere I look you're meddling in matters that don't concern you.'

My knees start to tremble but I gesture towards the baby monitor. 'Why is Lennie locked up in the middle of the day?'

'I said to you before,' he raises his voice, 'that Lennie ain't none of your business. What am I not making clear here? I told you yesterday. Nothing is going to ruin this Gathering for me. I want you out of here.'

'Fine, I'm going.' I skirt around him and rush towards the door. I need to get away from him, this room, even Ottoline. I'll be back for Lennie but, right now, I need to go.

'No, you wait a minute.' He reaches out, as agile as a much younger man, and grabs me like he did before, squeezing my wrist bones so hard they grind together. 'When I say I want you out, I don't mean this room. I mean the estate. I want you off my land. Angie, too, if they let her out of jail.'

'But . . .'

'But what? You're here by my grace only. Run away back to London, Rain. You're good at that and I'm making it real easy for you because you ain't welcome here any more.'

I've never understood the phrase about sticks and stones – about words never hurting. They do hurt, and Karl's in that moment feel devastating and yet somehow unsurprising. It's almost as though I've been waiting to hear them my whole life.

I run down the hill to the cottage, half blinded by tears. Strangers who have already arrived for the Gathering stare at me. All I can hope is that Caleb will be there, but it's empty and silent when I go inside. The fridge has died again. Even the pigeons have gone. The place feels thoroughly deserted, as though Angie and I left for good some time ago.

I go upstairs to my room, to the window Astrid once stood at. I turn the window catch and push it wide, wondering if there's even a single cell left of hers on the painted metal where she touched it three decades ago.

It's too quiet. I feel like I can hear my blood pumping round my body too fast. In desperation, I try Harkin's number but it goes straight to answerphone. I wish I could ring Caleb but I doubt he even has a mobile, and I don't have the wherewithal to trek up to his camp right now. Hopefully, wherever he is, he's got hold of the videos, hidden them somewhere. I'm no longer convinced Harkin is going to show up. I consider phoning Dan but where would I begin? *I* can't make sense of it all.

If Ottoline hurt Astrid, *put a stop* to her and her unborn child, what about Willow? And what about Karl? I can't wrap my head around it.

Numb, frightened and at a loss for what else to do, I pack my small bag and straighten the bedclothes. I look around the room, as if coming to terms with never seeing it again. For someone who has avoided this place so assiduously in recent years, I feel totally bereft. Maybe it's an overreaction to believe I'll really be barred from Tanglewood, but I wouldn't put anything past Karl after what I've seen today. I've always known his will was iron, but I've never run into it until now. It feels like an immovable object.

Chapter Thirty-Six

I drive to the back way out. I can't handle being flagged down by Karl for another warning or display of strutting machismo when he sees I'm obeying orders. The Gathering is beginning to feel less like an attack of déjà vu and more like I've strayed to the wrong side of enemy lines – where I'm outnumbered and without allies.

When I get to the old gates, I can see without getting out of the car that there's a shiny new chain and padlock looped around the bars. Probably it's for keeping out gatecrashers, but it feels like a message just for me. A signal that I can't come and go as I please any more, not even via this special way I think of as mine, but which was never mine at all.

But maybe it's a signal that I shouldn't leave yet, that maybe I need to try to check on Lennie again. I can't face traipsing up the hill in the heat so I drive slowly up, crossing my fingers as I grip the wheel that Karl won't spot me. Even in the short span of time since I was out here, activity in the Great Meadow has ratcheted up. Cars are being parked in tight rows in a small field close to the road, and I can see flashes of fluorescent yellow moving in the woods, like wildfire sparks.

Another man in a hi-vis jacket is having a smoke next to a load of metal barriers.

I park and go over. 'What are they doing in there?' I point at the woods.

'That's where the stage is going to be,' he says. 'There's some massive tree up there or something. Talk about making life difficult.'

I can already hear the deep throb of bass: someone testing the sound system. All this for Karl's ego, more or less. It hits me again: that he would go ahead with this when Lennie's mother has only just died. It's astounding, even if he had nothing to do with it, which I still find difficult to believe, despite what Ottoline seemed to be saying.

I head towards the manor on foot, sticking to the drive, where there are other people and I'm less likely to be seen. My heart lifts when I see that Caroline's windows are open, the curtains drawn.

Until today, I have trusted Ottoline my whole life. To doubt her sanity is awful, but recalling again how she looked as she chattered on in an undertone to a child who died thirty years ago makes me shiver under the hot sun. Could she really have done something to Astrid in some deluded revenge for her child's death? I can't get my head round that concept. Not even slightly.

At that moment, movement on the terrace makes me stop. It's Ottoline, an arresting sight in a long cream dress I've never seen before, her hair released from its usual chignon and tied in a loose plait. From this distance, she could be any age. I watch, transfixed, as she holds out her hand towards the open French windows, and then – thank God – Lennie appears. Instead of her usual jeans and T-shirts, she's also in a dress, tied at the waist with a large bow that makes me think of Alice in Wonderland. They walk towards the white marquee, hand in hand, Lennie nodding to some question I'm much too far away to hear.

I'm so relieved I feel winded. She seems fine. I wonder if I've actually dreamt the whole day, but then my phone starts to vibrate in my pocket, making me jump. It's a withheld number.

'Is that Angela Valentine's daughter?' says a man with a thick country burr.

My whole body goes cold. 'What's happened?'

The signal cuts out briefly and he has to repeat himself. 'IT'S STROUD POLICE STATION,' he bellows. 'YOU CAN COME AND COLLECT HER. SHE'S FREE TO GO.'

It takes me a moment to absorb the news. Then, with a last look towards the marquee, which has swallowed Lennie, I run back to my car.

At the gates, I realize with a lurch that two security guards are setting up a post. I'm the only one leaving; I hope I can get back in.

Out on the road, I have to brake for a group of twenty-somethings, who move unhurriedly to the verges to let me pass. You would never mistake them for a group of wholesome walkers. They're dressed extravagantly and rather anachronistically, in long cheesecloth dresses and open shirts with bell sleeves. One is wearing a deer-head mask. Another has a guitar strapped across his chest, dark hair past his shoulders. For a heart-arresting moment, Caroline still fresh in my mind, I think they're ghosts, that time has glitched and I'm somehow back in 1970.

But then one of the girls holds a mobile phone aloft, shouting something to the others, and I realize they'll be the privileged grown-up kids of the bohemian set who came here the first time round, whose multi-million-pound houses in Notting Hill and Camden Town were squats before they bought them for a song.

Unlike last time, I take it slow on the roads to Stroud. The sun is hovering over the fields at an angle that lights up every smear and dust particle on the windscreen. I pull down the sun-visor but I still have to strain to see the road ahead.

Angie is sitting on the wall where Lennie sat less than a week ago. It seems like months. She's engaged in animated conversation with a man wearing a jester's hat, who's played his lute for change in the high street my whole life. His huge grizzled-grey lurcher is resting his head in Angie's lap.

I park and go over, and even though I'm weak with relief to see her looking so much like herself, I don't rush over to hug her. It's been so long since it's worked that way with us.

'Here's my girl,' she calls, like I've joined them at the pub. 'You remember Dex, don't you? Dex, this is my Rainbird, come to get me.'

I nod at Dex, whose name I've never known, and stroke the dog, which has ambled over to greet me.

Angie pushes herself off the wall. 'Right, we'd best be off. I'm totally whompered. I want a stiff drink and my own bed, in that order, or maybe together.'

'Good for you, Ange,' says Dex, before moving off. 'Don't let the bastards grind you down, eh?'

'You're surprisingly chirpy,' I say in the car, as I wrestle to fasten Angie's seatbelt for her. 'I've been worried.'

'I wasn't great, but then I had a vision I wouldn't be in for much longer. Dex was in it and everything. After that, I was all right. Just had to wait it out.'

I don't have the energy to query any of this. In the rear-view mirror, I look awful, but Angie doesn't appear to have noticed. She seems wired – some weird combination of demob-happy and determined.

Once we pull clear of the town, Angie leans out of the open window, breeze whipping the hair around her head. She looks like a Medusa whose roots need doing.

'That's better,' she cries. 'I couldn't breathe in that place.'

When we're about a mile from Tanglewood, I pull into a passing place, yank on the handbrake and turn off the engine.

She turns to me, cheeks pink, which clashes with the orange shot-silk sky behind her. 'What are you stopping for?'

'Five minutes won't make any difference. Look, a lot has happened since you've been gone,' I say, then laugh because it's such an understatement.

'Go on,' she says, wary now.

'Well, for starters, we might have trouble getting back through the gates,' I say, trying to prioritize the practical.

'What you on about?'

'Karl's angry with me. He told me to leave the estate.' I shoot her a glance. 'He said something about you, too.'

She frowns. 'What the hell did you do?'

'What about what *he* might have done?' I say. It comes out so sharply that she flinches.

We sit there in silence for a while. Beyond the windscreen, two butterflies dance against a sky that's turning fiery. Angie seems deep in thought, and I'm trying to work out what to tell her about first: Ottoline's awful story or

Karl's sinister filing cabinet. There's also Warner's tarot-card revelation, though I expect Angie is well aware of that one after her spell in custody.

'How come they let you go anyway?' I say eventually.

'I couldn't get a straight answer out of anyone just now,' she says, 'but I s'pose they just didn't have enough to charge me. Bloody hell, though, I thought I was done for in the first interview, when Harkin said she had another tarot card.' She stops. Of course, she doesn't realize I know about the card found on Astrid.

'Well, anyway, I'll explain all that when we're back at the cottage,' she says, in a rush. 'I think Harkin's been sent back to HQ in Gloucester. She wasn't there when they came to let me out. I wonder if she ruffled too many feathers over this way, but that's just my guess.'

'I rang her a few times while you were in,' I say. 'Told her she was looking in the wrong place. Karl lied about his alibi the night Willow died. It sounds like he was back on the estate much earlier than he said. So them letting you out might have something to do with that, too.'

Angie reaches over abruptly to grasp my hand. When I turn to her, surprised, her eyes are shiny with tears. 'I know I drive you round the bend, but you've come through for me with this. You're a good girl.'

I don't know what to say. I'm so tired under the adrenaline that I'm danger of crying too.

'Come on,' she says, saving me. 'I need to go home. You can tell me everything there. There're some things I need to tell you, too.'

Chapter Thirty-Seven

We round the last bend to find a line of cars queueing along the lane to get through the gates. No doubt there'll be many more tomorrow.

Bass reverberates through the steering wheel as we move forward, and the security guards come into sight. They appear to be waving everyone through except that, when we get to the front of the line, the rattier of the two puts up his hand and walks unhurriedly round to my side. His beefier colleague comes to stand in front of the bonnet with his arms folded.

'Like I haven't had enough of this posturing bullshit after forty-eight hours with the filth,' says Angie.

Ratty regards me through the window, consults a clipboard, then raises his chin. 'Can't let you in.'

'We live here,' I say. 'We're tenants on the estate.' I pull out my driving licence, point to the address. I've never changed it.

He pretends to read it. 'I've had my instructions. Turn around.' He steps away, deliberately not making eye contact, and does a circling motion with his hand. It makes me want to run him over.

'Told you,' I say to Angie, shoving the car into reverse. 'That bastard.'

'Hold your horses,' she says, putting her arm across me.

'Let me deal with these tosspots.' She gets out and slams her door. 'Oi!' she shouts. 'Not so fast.'

The men turn in unison. Angie approaches them, a broad-beamed ship in full sail, the sky ablaze behind her.

The bigger one steps towards her, but she points a finger at him. 'Don't even think about it,' she says. 'I've got Gypsy blood in me and I'll curse you soon as look at you if you cross me today. I'm not joking, big lad. I've been in a police cell for two days and my patience is worn to a ravelling.'

To my astonishment, he puts up his hands and backs off. I let out a shocked laugh and someone from a car behind us cheers.

She heaves herself back into the car. 'Right, let's go before the silly pricks change their minds. Don't bother with the seatbelt. As I keep saying, it's not my time. Not yet it isn't.'

Lights flicker and sweep around the valley as we drive past the impromptu car park and along the sweeping curve of the Dark Ride. The sunset is growing more spectacular by the minute, shards of pink and orange stretching out along the horizon like broken cathedral glass. Below them, the valley is fast fading to black.

As we pass the manor, Angie taps me on the arm. 'Quick, turn those bloody headlights off before Karl catches sight of us. If we run some drunken idiot over, that's their look-out.'

The cottage is in darkness. I can't imagine ever telling her, but it's a comfort having Angie beside me.

'I wouldn't put it past him to have changed the locks,'

I say, as we go up the garden path. 'There was a new padlock on the secret gates when I tried to get out that way.'

'You're being paranoid now,' says Angie, as she puts her key in and opens the door. 'He's got bigger fish to fry tonight, with everyone arriving for tomorrow. He's locked that gate so there's only one way in and out for everyone, not just for you. Look, Karl's not going to get rid of me, is he? He can't.'

I elect to say nothing to that.

We sit down opposite each other in the kitchen, a single candle burning between us on the table so that, to someone patrolling outside, the cottage still looks deserted, though Angie is probably right that Karl has other things on his mind right now. In just over twenty-four hours, he's due on stage – his first performance in a long time.

The music coming from the Great Meadow is much fainter in the cottage, thanks to the natural cleft it's built into and its thick limestone walls. You could almost pretend the Gathering isn't happening. Angie has poured herself a strong gin with some flat, room-temperature tonic, the fridge yet to resurrect itself for a second time. I feel oddly like I'm about to step out on-stage when I'd rather stay in the dark safety of the wings. I'd love a drink, but I'm sticking to water. *In case*, I think automatically.

'Right,' she says. 'You first.'

So I tell her, and it's cathartic to pour it all out, even though I suspect she knows quite a lot of it already.

'I didn't know about Caroline,' she says, her voice

heavy. 'I swear I didn't. I thought it was a heart condition, like everyone else.'

I shake my head. 'In the same minute Ottoline finds out her daughter died because Karl and his mates had left drugs lying around, she also finds out that, when she was sunk so far in grief that she couldn't get out of bed, Karl had knocked someone else up.'

'That must have felt like sacrilege,' Angie murmurs.

'What?'

'Sacrilege, that would have been – to Ottoline. To any woman. I'd have killed him if he'd done that to me.'

'You?' I turn to her, try to soften my voice. 'When have you ever gone against Karl?'

She smiles grimly. 'Oh, you'd be surprised. You don't think I've ever had Karl over a barrel?'

I open my hands. 'What does that mean?'

She takes a big gulp of gin. 'I didn't know about Caroline, but I did know about Astrid dying. I'm guessing you've worked that out. I'm sorry I acted like I didn't know who she was but I panicked.'

'How was she killed?'

'I didn't know that she was. I was told it was an overdose and that the few of us who knew had to keep it a secret or Karl would be in big trouble.'

'Did you start to think there might have been more to it after Willow died?

'I don't know, Rain,' she says. 'I can't imagine Ottoline doing anything to hurt anyone. But I don't want to believe that Karl would . . .'

'I know. I don't know what to think about Ottoline, but Karl's lied and lied. Not just about Willow but Astrid, too. He assured me that he hardly knew her, but they were on that film I found.' I gesture to the cottage around us. 'Here. In *our* cottage.'

She nods slowly, eyes faraway. 'He went behind my back on that. He'd said it would be mine months before. And then I saw her there, looking at it like she already had the keys. Turns out he'd said she could have it, just like that.' She clicks her fingers.

'Where were we living, if we weren't already in the cottage?' For the thousandth time, I wish I could just remember.

I look up to find Angie staring at me intently. So intently it makes me shift in my chair.

'I said I had Karl over a barrel back then, yes?'

I nod.

'Well, I did and I bloody used it. Used it for *you*.'

'That's about as clear as mud. For me how?'

She leans across the table, making the candle flicker. 'Remember that time I came and fetched you from the manor – went upstairs and took you out of bed?'

I nod again, cold creeping over me because I was only thinking about it earlier, with Caleb, when it hadn't entered my head for years and years.

'Ottoline wanted you, right?' says Angie. 'She said *she* could take the best care of you, up in that princess bedroom of Caroline's. I honestly think she believed she was entitled to you, like her kind think they're entitled to everything. Like you could be a replacement for her own lost girl.'

Like Lennie now, I think.

'Well, I said no. I said to Karl that you would live down

here with me and Lady O would just have to lump it. Because if she didn't, I would go to the police about Astrid dying and them hushing it up. I don't know if I would've, to be honest – you know I'm allergic to the law – but Karl never dared call my bluff.'

I'm baffled. 'Why on earth would Ottoline think she could have me, anyway? Oh, wait,' my heart plummets towards my feet, 'was it because you were using? Were you . . . not fit to look after me?'

Angie's hand tightens around her tumbler. 'It was nothing to do with any of that. I know I wouldn't have won any prizes as a mother later on, and God knows I'm sorry for that now, but back then? No, I was fine. And I wasn't about to let you go up there with Ottoline still off her head with grief and Karl's mates partying at all hours. Maybe I knew in my bones what had happened to Caroline.

'Anyway, I said to Karl, "You'll give me that cottage like you promised, and I'll bring up the little one there as if she were my own."' She stops, spreads her hands. '*That's* what I'm trying to tell you. It's coming out all muddled but that's the nub of it. Before you were mine, you were *hers*. Astrid's. And when she died and left you with no one, I took you on. And whatever you've thought of me at times, Rainy, I've never regretted it for a moment.'

The room jolts and shifts around me. Outside, the bass seems more audible now, to have gone up a couple of notches: a low-pitched heartbeat thudding deep inside me.

'But . . .' I stop. I can't think of a single coherent thing to say.

Chapter Thirty-Eight

Angie pours herself another inch of gin. I still haven't said anything.

'The thing is, I couldn't have kids,' she says. 'I mean, no doctor ever told me that but, back when you had to be married to get the pill, I took some risks and nothing ever came of it. I was always regular as clockwork, whatever I got up to. And then what happened to Astrid happened, and I realized I was supposed to be your mother instead.'

I stand on shaky legs, go over to the front door and pull it open. I need some air. It rolls in, warm and perfumed, with a base note of smoke – tobacco, weed and bonfire all mingling together. I try to absorb what I've just been told but my brain shies away, distracts itself instead by working out what song is playing uphill. Fleetwood Mac, maybe. Yes. It's 'The Chain'.

Still weak, I shift position to lean against the doorway and my foot makes contact with something. It falls over with a clink and, as it rolls, it catches the last of the dying light. A glass bottle with something pushed into its neck. It's a piece of paper. I snatch it up and unfurl it.

Just wanted to let you know that I've got the tapes and that Lennie's fine. I've been at the manor and she was having dinner with everyone else. Cx

Caleb. If he was here, I'd be in danger of kissing him.

'What's that?' says Angie, joining me at the doorway. She hands me a bottle of beer.

'Caleb,' I say, holding up the note.

She squints to read it and nods. 'Heart of gold, that lad. He's one of the good ones. God knows how, but he is.' She scrutinizes me. 'There could be something there, with you two, if you let there be.'

I give her a look and take a long drink of my beer. 'A few days ago, I was still wondering if Karl might be my father,' I say. 'Now I find out I didn't even know who my own mother was.' *I'm an orphan.* It's a hard thought.

I let my head rest against the cool limestone of the cottage. I feel boneless. Closing my eyes, I can still see Astrid smiling at my bedroom window, caught on film but lost in every other way. And then I think of the shadow that crossed the end of the garden when Angie and I were sitting on the stairs, just before she was arrested.

I look up. 'The Lady of the Valley,' I say. 'The one you see sometimes, at this time of year. It's her, isn't it? It's Astrid.'

And Angie nods. 'You look like her, you know. More and more.'

'I was always so busy trying to see if I was like Karl. I took it for granted I was like you.'

'Only in colouring. But I . . .' She stops. 'I hope some of me has rubbed off on you over all these years. It hasn't been easy but I'm not all bad.'

I reach out to touch her. 'I know that.'

Questions flutter in my head: where did she live before me, how did she get me a birth certificate, did she ever regret taking me on, have I got more family out there somewhere, and so many more. But there's only one I really need the answer to right now.

'Where is she?' I say, so softly I'm surprised she catches it.

'They buried her. I never knew exactly where, love, but she's still here, at Tanglewood, just as her soul is.' She cups her hand, holds it up. 'The land's held her all this time.'

1970

It's obvious when they're drawing close: Tanglewood's king and queen. The hum of the crowd rises in pitch, even as the shouts and laughter fall away. Even as the orange sun drops below the shadowed valley walls, like the lights going down before a performance.

People naturally part ahead of them, which means their presence is felt long before you actually see them. And though she'd never dare say it to Karl, they want to glimpse Ottoline as much as they want to see him. Or maybe that's just her.

She holds her hand up in front of her and watches it tremble. She had another joint before she changed into her diaphanous white dress, but it didn't do what she needed it to. It seemed to have the opposite effect, in fact, dialling up her paranoia and instinct for danger. She feels skinless.

To take her mind off herself, she tries to concentrate on Ottoline. There is the rarity factor at play with her, for sure. Karl is often seen around, usually wearing one of the shirts that perfectly match the blue of his eyes, which he would claim is accidental but isn't. He tucks them loosely into his baggy cotton trousers, and keeps them unbuttoned to the waist, his narrow chest brown and almost hairless, the skin as supple as a boy's. She still thinks he's beautiful. It's just that he's also the most self-centred person she's ever encountered. He frightens her.

Ottoline's a much rarer sighting. She keeps mainly to her rooms but has been known occasionally to appear at her upper-floor windows, like a medieval queen about to distribute alms to the peasants below.

Of course, Astrid understands Ottoline's remoteness much better since Karl made his disquieting confession on the bed of his dead daughter. She feels terrible for the way she, like everyone who comes to Tanglewood, has speculated about this grieving mother. Has made fun of her, even – laughing about the rumoured streak of madness in the Mortimer line; about poor, long-suffering Karl and his mad woman in the attic. It makes her feel sick. All of it makes her feel sick.

When she finally comes into view, Ottoline is so pale and ethereal next to Karl that she doesn't look entirely human. Like, if the light behind her was bright enough, you'd be able to see right through her. Her long dress, made from some kind of heavy silk, undulates around her legs like poured cream, and her ash-blonde hair is arranged in a low, complicated knot that looks Edwardian. She's even holding a parasol, white and lace-edged, ebony-handled. Next to her, everyone else looks vaguely soiled, like a baser species of creature altogether. You wouldn't be surprised if they dropped to their knees at the sight of her, an angel too dazzling and unearthly to behold.

Her inspection of Karl's wife is so intense that it takes her a while to notice that Ottoline is holding the hand of a child. And then, a huge jolt to her heart: holding the hand of *her* child, who is wearing something entirely different from what she was dressed in this morning when she went haring off towards the woods with the other children. The old hand-me-down T-shirt and shorts that she got for free are gone, replaced with an old-fashioned ruffled dress that looks starched and scratchy. Her little friend Caleb, Karl's boy – whose white-blond head she searches for like a beacon when she wants to find her dark-haired daughter – is nowhere to be seen.

She wants to march over and take her girl back, wrench her small hand out of Ottoline's soft white one. But she doesn't. She can't move, somehow, as though she's been there for so long that the grass has grown around her ankles. Green shackles, holding her in place. The cold pebble, huge in this moment, grates against her rib bones as it turns inside her.

Frozen, she watches them pass, towards the stage, the three of them smiling, even her daughter. The same daughter she teases for always being so solemn, her little face, caught in repose, so often serious well beyond her years. *An old head on young shoulders*, she says to her sometimes. *An old soul.* She says it lightly, but that takes effort because underneath she worries that it's her fault. That she is responsible for her child's strained look, for her big, worried eyes. Sometimes the new name that she chose for herself seems too apt.

'Are you sure?' she said, when her daughter announced it.

And Rain nodded. 'I dreamt it,' she said. 'It's what I'm supposed to be called.' Astrid added the 'bird' as a gentle joke, and to make it lighter – more like her fine-boned, feather-haired girl. *My little Rainbird.*

An older woman told her a story next to the fireside last night – told her quite casually before turning to the person on their other side, unaware that she'd entirely blown someone's mind. She said that every woman was born with all her eggs already inside her – that even while she was still a tiny baby herself, she was already a mother-to-be.

She hasn't just known her daughter her whole life. Her daughter has also, in some miraculous, minuscule way, known *her*, Astrid, from her own beginnings. And yet here she is, so young and yet already operating independently. Making her own decisions. Harbouring secrets. Holding the hand of another woman and wearing a dated, repressive dress Astrid would never choose.

She has never felt further from her child. It makes her sway, like there's an invisible barrier between them. No, worse. Like she's watching her daughter on-screen. Like if she stepped forward to take her back, she'd only hit glass.

Rain doesn't notice Astrid, but Karl does. His Judy Collins Blues seem to look right through her, but his body gives him away. She sees him register her presence with a tiny spasm. She wonders if Ottoline feels it through their clasped hands. Which, now that she's looking closely, she can see aren't entwined at all. Karl is holding Ottoline tightly by her wrist, her fingers dangling limply. Astrid presses her thumb into the bruises on the inside of her own wrist, from where Karl clamped it too tightly.

What would happen if she held it up to Ottoline

for inspection, pointed out the marks, matched them to her husband's fingers? What if she stepped out and announced that Karl's child is growing inside her? For a dizzying moment, she's tempted.

After she left her parents' house, she made a pact with herself to follow her own urges, to go against the prim little voice her mother had planted in her head, the one that always said a nice girl wouldn't do that. She decided she would always say yes, instead. Sometimes she regretted it. Mostly she didn't. What stops her now is her daughter, who is glowing like a tiny sun from all the attention, from feeling pretty in her fussy dress.

She adjusts the silver bangles that tinkle as she moves, so that they cover the bruises. There are more elsewhere on her body. Some are developing from just a few hours ago, when Karl pushed himself into her on the floor of Caroline's room. *No*, she'd said. *Not here. Please not here.* But he didn't seem to hear her.

She looks again at Ottoline and finds that Ottoline is looking back at her. Her face is as rigid as a mask but there's something in her pale eyes that makes Astrid step back. They pass by and climb the steps to the stage – Rain, too. Above them, above the spreading branches of the ash, the sky is fire.

'Welcome, everyone,' Karl says, into the microphone that's been placed centre-stage. He looks out, gives the crowd the smile that used to make her weak for him, and stands back, arms outstretched, to receive the applause, cheers and whistles that rise up like a huge wave.

Her body, sore and shaking, is by now screaming for her to leave, screaming that she's almost out of time. She doesn't move. She can't. On stage, Ottoline is standing behind Rain, hands gripping her daughter's narrow shoulders. *I've just got to get through tonight*, she says in her head, for courage. *Just tonight. Then we'll leave.*

She walks slowly towards the wings, where the flower crown is waiting for her.

Chapter Thirty-Nine

Saturday: the Gathering

For once, I sleep like the dead, waking just before nine. After my protracted battle with insomnia all these years, the only vaguely psychological explanation I can come up with is that uncovering the truth about myself has allowed my unconscious mind to stop trying to fill in the blanks.

I dreamt all night of girls and women wearing sheer white, weaving a path ahead of me through a sun-struck forest, golds and greens and silvery water twisting below us, long dark hair sending out sparks as it rippled and lifted. I ran all night, or so it feels, but I never once caught them up. My cheeks feel tight with dried tears.

I shake away the feeling of the dream, though it clings, sad and lovely. I need to piece together everything I've found out and tell Harkin. Lennie and what happened to her mother need to take priority. After all, it's her who's here, in the present. It's her who's living in the manor with Karl and Ottoline. The past is going to have to wait a bit longer.

I upend the rucksack I brought in from the car last night and throw on some clothes. I pause at Angie's door but she's snoring rhythmically. It's still quite early for her, especially after what she's been through with the police, and with me, and I leave her to sleep on.

I tiptoe down the stairs and out of the front door. There's no music on yet. All I can hear is birdsong. I decide to work through my thoughts in the hollow. I'll wake Angie at ten if she hasn't already surfaced.

I go over the words from Caleb's note again. Lennie was *having dinner with everyone else*. I'm not sure who 'everyone else' means and worry starts to sidle in again. Presumably it's Karl's special guests: his musician friends and their haphazard entourages. McQuinn and the rest of them. The thought of him in particular makes my stomach roil.

Ottoline's words from yesterday reverberate around my head, my imagination doing the rest – cutting and splicing what happened in 1970 with what's going on up there right now, transforming the manor into some sort of bacchanal, Lennie picking a path through the scattered drugs and pretty cocktails while everyone else has passed out. I push away the image. Lennie is ten, not four. I knew exactly what pills did well before my tenth birthday.

To stop my mind spiralling out of control, I watch my bedroom window. But Astrid doesn't come, and I can't sense any stardust afterburn of her either.

That she was my mother hasn't penetrated yet. Neither has the other side of that mind-blowing coin: that Angie *isn't*. I looked at my face in the mirror for a long time last night. So long that my exhausted eyes stopped seeing it as a face, reducing it instead to an alien arrangement of angles and shapes. That little girl I've been worrying about, when I haven't been worrying about Lennie – that little girl is *me*. That's going to take a while to sink in.

I remember what happened when I saw Karl the first day I got back: the way he stared at me so intently, and for too long. The way he said, *Look at you. Just like your mother standing there.* Of course: he hadn't meant Angie. He'd meant Astrid.

'Here you are, back in your old hidey-hole.'

I jump at the sound of her voice. Not Astrid, but Angie, standing over me, holding a steaming mug. 'And it's coffee, not tea, before you start moaning.'

I'm confused. 'How did you know I was here?'

She hands me the mug. 'Oh, I could always see the top of your head from upstairs, couldn't I?'

'Oh.'

'You grew up too fast in some ways, and I'm sorry for that.' She sits down heavily next to me. 'No wonder you had to come out here, get a bit of space. I understood it then, too. That's why I didn't let on I knew where you were.'

'It was hard for you, too,' I say. 'Karl told me you were using again yesterday. I didn't believe him.'

'That piece of shit.'

'What are you going to do?'

'What do you mean?'

'Where are you going to go?'

She stares at me, perplexed. 'I'm not going anywhere. This has been my home for thirty years.'

'But Karl . . .'

'Right. For one thing,' she holds up a finger, 'this is not Karl's land, it's Ottoline's. For another, we made a deal back then, and he'll keep to that, or I'll do a Graham Warner and go to the papers myself.'

'But you know we're going to have to speak to the police about Astrid, back up what Warner's been saying.'

'Oh, I've got plenty more dark secrets up my sleeve, believe you me. Lots of them about the people who used to come here, people who are probably up there right now, pretending they're still twenty-five. Some of them are very famous – one's in the bloody Lords. Anyway, I've got a signed bit of paper from the estate's trust saying this place is mine for life, and yours after.'

She raises an eyebrow. 'I know you've always thought I was an insult to the feminist cause but I'm not completely daft. I came here without a penny or qualifications, and no family I wanted to have anything to do with. Look at me now: a rent-free Cotswolds cottage with a view,' she gestures around, 'a clever daughter who lives in London, and no husband getting under my feet. I might not have money in the bank but I've never had to do some soulless nine-to-five, either.'

'When you put it like that . . .'

She reaches out to squeeze my shoulder. 'I should've told you about your real mum, I know. But it only got harder as the years went by. Besides, I'd promised, hadn't I? That was part of the deal with the cottage: that I wouldn't say anything about any of that, which of course was made much easier by you erasing everything from before she died.' She stops, looks at me for a long moment, and I think she's going to tell me something else but then she moves on. 'And, listen, I got chucked out of home when I was fifteen,' she says. 'When I made the decision to bring you up as my own, that was my priority: a roof over your head for as long as you needed it.'

'What do you think happened to her that night? Tell me honestly.'

Angie sighs, looks off across the valley. 'I swear I thought it was an accident, like it really was with Caroline. That night . . . Well, it was a mess. Chaotic. She seemed out of it on stage. Didn't even make it to the end of the song. Karl looked like thunder when she walked off.'

'Warner said something about her being scared on stage.'

'Did he?' Angie hangs her head. 'I hope I didn't have anything to do with that. I'd gone up to her earlier that day, had a bit of a go. I was only jealous and upset about the cottage but I regretted it after.' She stops, heaves in a shaky breath. 'That was how she had one of my cards on her when Warner found her. I didn't know she'd kept it, did I? I threw it at her before I stormed off, and she must have picked it up. Harkin thought she had me bang to rights after they found another card in Willow's hand, but it must just be a horrible, morbid coincidence, and they can't prove otherwise. I didn't hurt either of them.'

And then it clicks for the first time about Astrid's pregnancy. 'Oh,' I say.

Angie nods. 'Such a lot to take in. I didn't think you'd got there in your head last night, but I also didn't think you needed that to contend with on top of everything else.'

'I would have had a little brother or sister.'

She sighs. 'You and Lennie. So many similarities. It's uncanny.

'I promise I thought it was an accident when Astrid died. I still remember Karl's face when he told me. And then, later, I found out that you . . .' She puts her hand to her heart. 'Well, anyway, when the same thing happened to Willow, I had to wonder, didn't I?'

'But when I first came back you seemed totally sure. You said you could see it coming, that Willow was reckless.'

'I didn't want to face up to the possibility of it. If someone had hurt her, someone had likely also hurt Astrid. And that someone was going to be Karl, wasn't it? Who else? So where did that leave me? With a daughter whose birth mother had been murdered by the man I'd loved all these years. Who'd done it again, leaving another little girl without her mum. I felt like I just couldn't go down that path for my own sanity, so I pushed it away, as best I could. That was wrong. I know that now. I honestly think those hours in the cells were a hidden blessing for me.'

Pushed it away. It's exactly what I've been doing.

'I'm worried about Ottoline.' I say it in a rush. I've spent my life not mentioning Ottoline to Angie, and Angie to Ottoline, and it's hard to unlearn that.

'You were always worried about her,' says Angie, but surprisingly gently.

'But you didn't hear her yesterday when she was talking about overhearing Astrid tell Karl she was pregnant in Caroline's room. How it was *unendurable*. As though finding out those two things on top of each other – that Caroline's death had been preventable, and that a new baby would be coming along – tipped Ottoline over the edge into proper madness.'

'I think it would anyone,' says Angie.

At that moment, the music starts up, much louder than last night, or so it seems in the hollow. Above us, birds explode out of the trees. It's jarring, to think of all those strangers up there.

'I'm scared all *that*,' I gesture uphill, 'has made her mad again. Everything replaying like last time: same music, same stage in the woods. It's like Karl's determined to record over what happened before with this new version. Maybe he's mad, too.'

'The woods? What do you mean, in the woods?' Angie looks alarmed and it makes me straighten.

'They've built a stage inside the clearing, up by the big ash tree.'

She grimaces. 'Oh, Christ, why's he done that?' She struggles to her feet, and I have to steady her from below when she almost overbalances. 'Why does he think doing it all again would bring anything but bad luck?' I realize she's talking more to herself than to me.

I follow her back to the cottage. 'What were you going to say before?'

She turns.

'You stopped yourself. You said about Karl's face when he told you Astrid had died. And then you said, "I found out that you . . ." What did you find out? No more lies between us, okay?'

She swallows, presses her hand to her heart again. 'I don't know, love. There's plenty of time to unpick—'

'Please. It was my life, my life before, and I can't remember any of it . . .' I push the heels of my hands into my eyes to stop myself crying. I'm worried I won't stop if I start.

Angie takes hold of my wrists, pulls them down and cups my face in her hands. 'You were nowhere to be found after Warner . . . came upon Astrid at dawn. Someone went to your tent, but you'd gone. When you were found, in the woods, you wouldn't speak. You didn't speak for days. And then . . .' – she drops her hands, wipes her eyes – '. . . and then you started speaking again and it was like nothing had happened. We didn't know much about trauma and all that. I thought that if you'd forgotten, it would be like a clean slate for you. I'm sorry, Rain.'

I put out my hand to stroke hers. 'It's okay. It's not your fault. But . . .' – I glance behind me, towards the path snaking uphill – '. . . what if Lennie's forgotten something important, too?'

1970

The girl wakes to a scream of laughter, right by her head. The shock of it lifts her clear of the hard ground under her sleeping bag, or so it seems. Heavy footsteps stumble past, and another shriek of laughter rings out, but they're getting further away now. She lies there, wide-eyed in the dark, hand to the small cage of her ribs, where her heart is jumping around like it's trying to escape.

In the close darkness of the summer night, the tent smells even more strongly than usual: of damp night-breath and waxy canvas and trapped bonfire smoke. The music has stopped but a few people are still awake; she can hear singing and talking, though only faintly because their tent is pitched at the furthest edge of the Great Meadow, at the point where the woods begin.

She sits up and feels around in the dark for her mother, though she knows, really, that she's still alone, that she hasn't come back. Shuffling over to the mouth of the tent, she tugs the stiff zip open.

There are other tents nearby, but her mother put theirs up so the opening would face towards the trees. 'This way, we've got our privacy when we need it,' she said. 'When we want it to be just you and me.'

The woods are a void, much darker than the night, though there are no stars. Her mum is teaching her about the constellations. 'My dad taught me before he died,' she said. 'Your granddad.'

Now, the girl stands and faces the wood. She knows it's the same place she plays with Caleb all day. She knows she could walk the paths blindfolded if she had to. Still, the thought of going in there makes her heart trip.

It seems like days ago that she watched her mother on-stage in the clearing but it was probably only five or six hours. She watched her from the opposite side of the stage, Ottoline's hands heavy on her shoulders.

When her mother simply walked off before the end of the song, she went to follow but Ottoline held her fast. 'I'll go, darling,' she said. 'It'll be women's troubles. Women's sadness. You stay and listen to the rest of the music.'

She likes Ottoline a great deal. She's never cross and she always remembers things she's told her, even silly things. It's just that sometimes she feels like she has power over her that she doesn't want. She has the sense that she could hurt Ottoline very badly just by saying one wrong thing.

Earlier, when Ottoline was doing up the buttons that ran down the back of the special white dress, she caught sight of her, reflected in the wardrobe mirror. Her face was like a mask, mouth open, the lips pulled back to show her teeth. As though she was in agony but wasn't allowed to make any noise.

She chooses Silver Snake. It's not the shortest route to the clearing but it's the path she knows and likes best. The sound of the spring is louder in the dark, and it's a comfort. She has the idea of pretending Caleb is just behind her, like he usually is, because he's younger. 'Come on,' she says out loud, which makes her tremble with her own daring, 'my mum's waiting. We need to find her.'

The ash is huge in its clearing, the biggest she's ever seen it. It's strange how it changes. She told her mum about it and she said it happened to her, too.

'The thing with time is that it's happening all at once,' she said. They were walking hand in hand across the Great Meadow through the thickening dusk. 'The past and the future and all the moments in between. They're all going on, right now, even though we can't see them all, just like we can't feel the world spinning at a thousand miles an hour.'

She'd stopped, shaken her head. The idea was too big, too slippery.

'That's why it's special here,' her mother said, bending down to whisper in her ear. 'At Tanglewood, if you look closely enough, you can find the holes, the slippage.'

It's so much lighter in the clearing. Her eyes, which had adjusted to the woods' deep dark, can see everything now. She looks around and her gaze is caught by something pale lying next to the broad trunk of the ash.

'There she is!' she says, turning to Caleb, and remembers he isn't really there. She'd only pretended to herself that he was so that she didn't feel so afraid.

Her fear has gone now anyway. She's found her mother. She's been here, asleep, all along. Rain sets off towards the tree, towards the white glow of her dress. It's as bright as the moon.

Chapter Forty

Angie is uncharacteristically quiet as we climb the hill, much slower than if I was alone. The sun is a glaring white eye over us, the music a dull solar-plexus thump. When I glance back to check she's okay, her face is pale, even though she's out of breath, chest heaving.

'Are you feeling all right?'

She nods, and I suspect she can't talk. I take her arm and guide her over to a patch of shade. Above us, the manor has just come into view. For the first time in my life, the sight of it frightens me.

I turn back to Angie. 'Deep breaths. There's no rush.'

'There might be,' she says.

My skin prickles. 'What do you mean? Have you sensed something?'

But she only gestures towards the manor. 'Let's keep going,' she huffs. 'Don't worry about me.'

Now it's daylight, I can see how full the camping field is, how thickly the Great Meadow is teeming with people. Out towards the gates, rows of cars and campervans are just visible, glinting in the sun.

In the middle of everything there is an enormous effigy, twenty feet high. It must be what I saw arrive yesterday, hidden under tarpaulin, when I was with Ottoline. *Karl's surprise.*

It's a woman, sculpted out of some pale, pliable wood

that's been twisted into smooth curves and lines to create her flowing dress and her long, rippling hair. Atop her head is a crown of real flowers. She's beautiful but, still, the sight of her turns me rigid.

I turn to Angie and catch the moment she sees it, her eyes widening.

'He's a reckless, callous bastard,' she says.

'What do you mean?' I whisper, tears constricting my throat again.

She squeezes my hand, points with the other. There's a banner at her feet, the words in looping silver lettering: Lady of the Valley.

'He's had it made out of willow,' Angie says, in disgust. 'Of all things, when that poor woman is barely cold in her grave. But it's not even a tribute to her, it's Astrid. It's how she was posed in the photograph Karl had on the original album sleeve. The one he pulled when she died. He had to foot the bill for that – or, rather, Lady O did. The record company wouldn't pay. I've never wanted to face it, but Karl really loved Astrid, in his way. He never got over her. He says that to me sometimes, to be cruel.'

There's something seismic going on with Angie and her feelings for Karl. I have the sense of scales falling from her eyes, one after another.

The manor is quiet when we get there, the sound cutting off abruptly as soon as we step inside the open door. I'd expected houseguests to be wandering about, the smell of breakfast mingling with unfamiliar perfume, but it feels deserted. It makes Ottoline's strangeness yesterday feel even more prescient. I massage my jaw. I've been clenching it without realizing.

'I'll have to stop here a minute,' says Angie, sinking onto the seat of the enormous hatstand. 'Get my breath back.'

I don't want to leave her, but she waves me on towards the stairs. I run up them as silently as I can, heart stuttering. I don't know who I'm more afraid to see: Ottoline or Karl.

Upstairs, the door to Caroline's bedroom stands open. I rush in but it's empty, the bed covers flung back, the eiderdown fallen to the floor. At that moment, a low moaning sounds from across the hallway, rising to a wail as I stand there paralysed, blood booming in my ears. It's coming from Ottoline's rooms.

I go straight in before my nerve can fail me; the terrible keening so much louder inside. She's sitting in the little armchair where I left her yesterday, when Karl came bursting in, except that now she's rocking, her face a mask of distress.

I kneel at her feet, taking her hands in mine and rubbing them hard to bring her out of herself. 'Ottoline,' I say. 'It's me, Rain. What's happened? Where's Lennie?'

Her eyes are almost rolling; she doesn't seem to register me. It feels cruel but I grip her shoulders and shake. Her eyes begin to focus. 'Lennie,' I say loudly. 'Where is she?'

'Gone,' she pushes out, voice hoarse. 'Gone.'

'What do you mean, gone?'

'Taken her things and gone. Run away.'

My head drops. Not the worst kind of gone, then.

'I'm certain I locked the door last night,' she says,

voice rising to a sob. 'All the people that were here. Karl's people. I had to. But then, this morning, I went in and she'd gone.' She lifts her arm to gesture weakly, lets it fall again.

I grasp her hands, stroking them until her breathing slows and her eyelids droop. I lead her over to the bed and she lets me tuck the sheet around her, like a docile child. I can't bear to think about what she might have done in the past. Besides, Lennie needs to be found first.

Angie hasn't moved when I get back downstairs, and I don't like the look of her, either – skin grey, beads of sweat standing out on her forehead and upper lip.

'What the hell was that awful noise?' she says weakly. 'Where's Lennie?'

'She's run away. When Ottoline said she'd gone, I thought for a second . . .' I stop. 'You look terrible. Have you had a premonition or something?' I've been scathing about Angie's so-called powers for ever. Now I'm beginning to be afraid of them. 'Tell me.'

She waves her hand in the direction of the front door. 'Nothing specific. I'm just getting myself worked up about that bloody effigy out there, and them putting up that stage by the ash. You have to be careful with ash trees. You can't damage them or bad things happen.

'Karl's trying to turn back time, resurrect a night that should be left well alone, that turned out bad enough the first time. I could have told him nothing good would come of it and now look: Willow dead, Lennie missing and her . . .' – she lifts her chin towards the stairs – '. . . well, she's lost her last marble, hasn't she? It's not even nightfall.' She shudders again.

A shadow splays across the hall's tiles, making us jump. Someone is standing there in the sunlit doorway, reduced to a silhouette. For a second I think it's Karl. It makes me reach out for something to hold onto and I almost trip over my feet. But it's not Karl.

'Caleb,' Angie cries, 'just when we need you.'

'What's going on?' he says, coming to perch next to her. She pats his knee and blows out a long breath.

'Lennie's run off somewhere,' I say. 'Ottoline just told me.' I glance towards the stairs. 'She's not in a good way but I should've asked her more questions. We need to try to work out when Lennie left and where she might have gone.'

Caleb stands, runs his hands through his hair. 'Okay, let's think. Rain, why don't you go back up and try to get more out of my mother? I was just coming to check on her now Dad's out of the way, working the crowd with his *crew*.' His face hardens. 'But I reckon you've got the best chance with her. She clams up with me.'

'I want to look for Lennie.'

'Angie and I will make a start on that. I'll go and search the bus, and check my camp in case she came to find me. Angie can start in the Great Meadow, asking the Gatherers, the security blokes, that kind of thing.'

When I get back upstairs, Ottoline is lying exactly as I left her, covers pulled up to her chin. She's not asleep.

'Dear Rain,' she says, sounding more lucid.

'Caleb and . . .' I trail off. 'We're going to look for Lennie. We'll find her, too.' I hope I'm right.

My eye catches on the baby monitor. 'Wait, did you check Lennie on that last night?' I point at the little green screen.

Her eyes flick back and forth. 'I've been so anxious these past few days. All these people,' she gestures towards the windows, 'all these strangers on our land. I didn't think it would be so difficult. I didn't think it would take me back so powerfully. But I would've noticed if Caroline's door was unlocked. Wouldn't I?' She looks at me pleadingly.

'It's *Lennie* we need to find,' I say, because I'm not positive she isn't back in the past, Lennie now and Caroline then muddling and merging in her mind. 'Maybe you looked at the baby monitor instead, to check on her. Can you remember doing that in the night or this morning? If we know roughly when she went, it'll help us work out how far she might've got.'

She struggles into a sitting position. 'I *did* look. I remember. I like to do it every couple of hours, in case she needs me. I woke up and checked it and I remember there was light behind the curtains. Just faint. Just first light. But she was there. I could see her. She was breathing. I could see her chest moving.' Tears roll down her cheeks and I reach out to wipe them away.

'But that's really good, don't you see?' I say. 'It means she didn't leave in the night. It means she wasn't out there in the dark and that she can't have got too far.'

She nods uncertainly, reminding me again of a small child, desperate to be reassured.

'She's a good girl, Lennie,' she says, just as I'm wondering whether it's safe for me to leave her alone. 'She's such a good-hearted child. I said as much to her mother when she came to see me.' She shifts back down the bed, adjusts the covers with unsteady hands. Her eyelids flutter closed. For the first time, I notice a pill bottle on the bedside table. Tranquillizers, perhaps.

'Her mother?' I say. 'Willow was here, with you?'

Muses weren't welcome at the manor, just like Angie. That went without saying.

'Ottoline?' Her eyes are still closed. 'When was Willow here?'

'It was last week,' she says faintly, eyes opening again, but not quite focused. 'Friday, I think. Yes, it was. I know it was because I always change the flowers on Fridays. I took her to the Chinese room and offered her tea but she refused. She told me why she'd come. I tried to reason with her, particularly the part about going to the papers. I said she must think of her little girl, how it might feel for her to be embroiled in some . . . tabloid scandal.'

Her hands ripple over the sheets like water. I wait, breath held, but then she stills, chest rising and falling slowly. She's slipping into sleep.

'Ottoline,' I say, as calmly as I can manage. I stroke her cheek with the back of my finger. 'Ottoline, what did Willow say she was going to the papers about?'

She makes a visible effort to focus. 'Oh, she shook her head at me, smiling as though I was an imbecile. I'm sure she thought I was one. She said, "But it's Lennie I'm doing it for. Lennie and the baby."'

I absorb that: what it might mean, that Ottoline found out Willow was pregnant, just like she found out Astrid was.

'And what did you say?'

'I didn't say anything. You see, Karl came into the room at that very moment. He'd just returned from his rehearsal sessions.'

I have the sense of falling, though I don't move a muscle. So Ottoline wasn't mixed up before. He *did* come back before Willow died. 'And what happened then?' I say, barely more than a whisper.

'Oh, he was shocked at first. To see her there, with me. None of us said a word. It was quite peculiar, like we'd all been turned to stone. But then he broke the spell by smiling. He smiled at us both. He said that Willow should come to the carriage-house later. That he'd written a new song he wanted . . . he wanted her *take on*. That's what he said.'

I remember the way he forced his temper down with me, also in the carriage-house, the disquieting way his face went blank and smooth.

'And then?'

'I didn't see her again.' She turns her head to me, face pleading. 'But I think Lennie did.'

'What do you mean?'

'She's not been herself this last day or two, as you know. She's had a fever. I was sitting with her, to make sure she didn't . . . Well, she was half in dreams, whispering and mumbling about going to hear the song written for her mother . . .'

I can see she's fading. 'Ottoline? Was there anything else? It's important.'

'The carriage-house. I think Lennie went to the carriage-house after her mother.'

And then she's gone, deep into unconsciousness. Questions queue up in my mind. Did Karl overhear what Willow said to Ottoline, in a strange reversal of what she heard Astrid telling Karl, three decades earlier? Did

Ottoline finding out that Karl had made another woman pregnant set in motion the same series of events that happened then, too?

I just don't know. I can't equate Ottoline with violence. I can absolutely imagine it of Karl.

'Lennie,' I say softly to myself. What did she see or hear on the night her mother died? What happened to her at the carriage-house? I think of my own scene there yesterday, when Karl found me invading his privacy, digging up the parts of the past he doesn't want to unearth. What Willow did was much more drastic: not just breaking the unspoken law that Ottoline and the manor house were off-limits, but threatening to go public with her pregnancy ahead of his big anniversary Gathering.

I remember his cold blank fury and I know in my bones that he killed her.

Chapter Forty-One

The manor feels even more eerily deserted when I get downstairs, the contrast with the crowd's rising hum outside only accentuating it.

The shell-case is propping open the front door, as it has my whole remembered life. Sun spills through the doorway to light the tiles and I catch the end of a new old memory: Caleb with his childhood shock of blond hair, pulling me through the same door – only instead of day it's dark and cooling night, heady with sound and scent. I cling to his hand, the other clutched to my stomach, which is hurting because I haven't seen my mother all day, haven't been able to find her.

'Come on,' Caleb says, voice boyish-light. 'I know where she'll be.'

My mother. *Astrid.*

I know, without needing confirmation, that this fragment is from the last day. Her last night.

Lennie, I think. Concentrate on Lennie. There'll be time afterwards for what happened then. It's already been thirty years. Again, it's going to have to wait a little longer.

I half run towards the Great Meadow, weaving around Gatherers who look at me strangely. I touch my face, check my clothes, but it's probably just fear they're sensing. *Bad vibes.* I pull out my mobile to dial 999 and report Lennie missing, but I don't want to bring her to their attention when she might turn up at any minute. I don't have any bars anyway. Too many people for too weak a signal.

I'm just wondering if I should go back to the manor to use the landline, indecision holding me up again, but my eye is caught by a slight girl with a long, fair plait on the far side of the meadow, where the trees begin. She disappears into their deep, green shadows before I can get a better look.

I break into a proper sprint, drawing more strange looks. I scan faces as I go, hoping to see Caleb or Angie, but I don't know any of these people.

A dozen or so paths twine through the woods. I knew every one of them intimately, once. We children gave them names, this coming back to me so fast it feels like a slap. The Broad Track. Tumble Turn. High Pass. The girl I'm praying is Lennie must be on Silver Snake, which follows the course of a spring to the clearing where the ash is. Where Karl's stage is waiting for its big moment tonight.

There's no sign of her on the path as I jog along it, hot now, sweat making my clothes stick. The sunlight flickers and dapples, tricking me into seeing movement ahead, but each time I reach the spot, there's nothing.

As I approach the clearing, I feel less and less sure of what I saw. There's no sixth-sense prickle that anyone has passed by here for a while. Which is strange in itself, when there must be roadies, and Gatherers who know their Tanglewood history, who know where that last performance in 1970 was held and want to get a sneak preview before nightfall. Instead, I feel totally alone, as if I've wandered into a different time altogether, the thought turning me cold because it feels so much like the truth.

The sunlight is cast strangely in the clearing when I reach it: a wide yellow shaft that makes it empty but for the ash, which is much smaller than I remember. But then I take another few steps and everything shifts, the tree soaring and spreading, and the stage, an open shell raised up on cross-hatched metal, tucked neatly into the tree's lower limbs.

At the same moment, a siren breaks through the dull thud of music I can abruptly hear again. After the quiet, it's like a bright thread of pain. I'm a long way from any roads – it must be coming here, *already* here, at Tanglewood. *Harkin*, I think, mind already back to calculating what I could say to set in motion a search for Lennie, without condemning her to the care system.

I run back along the path, slightly downhill now, the going so much swifter for it. Bursting out onto the Great Meadow, I see it straight away, blue lights turning on the Dark Ride below the manor. But it's not a police car. It's an ambulance. And while I don't really believe I have any kind of second sight, I know it's nothing to do with Lennie. It's here for Angie.

I break into a sprint, but the Gatherers are thick, impenetrable clots that make me want to scream and shove. I finally get past the last group, only to slam into one of the metal barriers I saw being erected yesterday. I catch a glimpse of her inside – whey-faced, oxygen-masked, red-strapped to the gurney – before an ambulance-man bends over her to adjust something, obscuring my view.

'Angie,' I cry, but I'm out of breath and it's lost in the

noise of the crowd. 'Mum!' I try again, but it's no good. I try to climb over the barrier but my sweaty hands slip on the metal.

'Rain?'

I whip round and it's Caleb. I rush at him, hard, and he puts his arms around me, which makes me burst into tears.

'Oh, God, what's happened?' he says, mouth against my hair.

I pull back, point at the ambulance. 'Angie.'

He vaults the barrier in one easy movement, then helps me over. I race to the back of the ambulance.

'Mum!' I shout, and this time they hear me: the ambulanceman *and* Angie, who is at least conscious behind her oxygen mask.

'What's happened?' I say to him, as I clamber into the vehicle. 'I'm her daughter.'

'She's going to be just fine in a minute,' he says cheerfully, stepping aside so I can crouch next to her. I take her hand. It's cold.

'We've checked her heart,' he says, pointing at the monitor and tubes, 'and her other vitals. Oxygen was a bit lower than we'd like, hence the mask, but basically you've just overdone it, haven't you, Angie love?' He smiles at her.

I look between them, slow on the uptake.

'Heat exhaustion and a panic attack on top,' he supplies.

I exhale, my shoulders dropping. I catch sight of Caleb standing there, and give him a thumbs-up.

'I thought I was a goner for a minute there,' Angie croaks, lifting the mask.

'Back on, please,' says the ambulanceman. 'You can take it off when you've had the once-over in hospital.'

Angie struggles to sit up.

'She doesn't really do hospitals,' I say.

She pulls her mask down again, holds up her other hand. 'I need to be here. Little Lennie's missing.'

The ambulanceman needs some persuading but eventually a compromise is reached. Angie is driven down the hill and put to bed in her own room, with strict instructions that she needs to stay there for at least twenty-four hours.

'You go on,' she says to me, as soon as they've gone. Her colour improved as soon as she was back in the cottage. 'Go and join Caleb. I've got your mobile number.'

'It doesn't work properly round here. What if you feel ill again?'

'Then I'll ring nine-nine-nine and get those nice ambulancemen back, won't I? Look, there's nothing wrong with me. How many times do I have to tell you—'

'It's not your time,' I interrupt. 'You keep saying that, but if you're so sure, why did you have a panic attack?'

I watch as she chews on her lip. She still doesn't look herself. Then she scrabbles for my hand, squeezes it hard enough that her big rings dig in to me. 'Thank you,' she says.

'What for?'

'For caring, I suppose.'

'Of course I care.'

She smiles. 'Go and get me a cup of tea, then.'

I see it the instant I walk into the kitchen: a single sheet of paper held down by Angie's empty gin tumbler. I pick it up, take in the careful looping writing before any of the words, and know it's Lennie.

Dear Rain,

I wanted to say thank you for being my friend. I am sorry I did not say goodbye before I left. I wanted to see you but you were not here. I will be fine though so don't worry. I am really good at taking care of myself. My mum said I was old before my years and had more common sense than most grown-ups.

Please say sorry to Ottoleen for me. I know it will hurt her feelings that I have gone but I was scared when she talked to Caroline and when she said I was Caroline. Plus she locked my door and I don't think that is right.

Rain, I know you were trying hard to help me find out what happened to my mum. So I need to tell you something that I didn't know before. On that night I went to the carridge house to hear the song Karl wrote for my mum but there wasn't really a song. I was upstairs but then when they came up I hid in another little room. I could hear them through the door. He laughed at her but he was also really angry. They were shouting and fighting and then it was quiet. Then I heard his boots going downstairs and I just stayed there because I was am a coward.

I just remembered it and now I need to go.

I will always remember you and Tangelwood.

Love from,
Lennie

I missed her. She was here and I missed her. If Angie and I hadn't gone up to the manor when we did, Angie might not have collapsed, and we'd have been here and— I stop.

There's no point. It doesn't help Lennie. It doesn't help me now.

I picture that little room, those alphabetically arranged green folders. I was so busy checking for Angie's when I was in there that I didn't even think to look at the back for W. I hate the thought of Lennie in there, but it gives me an idea.

'Right, then,' I say aloud, as I fold the note carefully and tuck it into my back pocket. 'Make tea and then up to the carriage-house.'

And, like a vote of confidence, the fridge suddenly whirs and clunks into life, the light clicking on even though the door's closed.

Chapter Forty-Two

The cobbled courtyard is deserted when I get there. Karl and his buddies must be elsewhere, as I'd hoped. I have to steel myself to go back up that spiral staircase, my body protesting, tensed and ready to flee. When I feel as if my nerves are going to fail me, I picture Lennie's empty little cat purse.

She's not in the sterile room with the TV and filing cabinets but I'm pretty sure she was. On the floor is Willow's green folder, lying open, the photographs turned face down. My instincts were right. It's just that I'm too late again.

I sit cross-legged on the floor to think, and notice something I didn't last time: a square, box-framed black-and-white print hanging on the back of the door. When I get closer, I see it's a vinyl LP set behind glass. It's *the* album cover. I've never seen it before, only read a description.

I see now that Angie was right earlier: from the curving sculptural lines she creates as she twists away from the camera to the circlet of flowers in her hair, it's clear what inspired the willow effigy outside. I run my finger over her face. I can see it now: the likeness between us.

I pull Willow's folder of photographs towards me. I hate the thought of Lennie going through them, seeing her mother pose like this for a man who didn't deserve it – deserve her.

Then I come to a different set. Instead of the vaguely arty nudes in black-and-white, these are Polaroids showing

Willow posed exactly like the effigy. Exactly like Astrid on the cover. Some have crosses in marker-pen on them. There are also a couple of sketches in charcoal. Maybe Karl used her as a model, for whoever built the Lady of the Valley effigy for him.

All day I keep looking, a nagging worry that I'm missing something scratching away at my insides. Caleb does the same. We meet up periodically, hopes dashed each time we realize the other hasn't found Lennie. Whenever I get some signal, I ring Angie to give her a quick update. Each time she picks up the phone almost instantly.

'Nothing,' I say, and she sighs.

Caleb and I are exhausted. We must have covered miles criss-crossing the estate. We feel as though we've asked every single Gatherer if they've seen her. No one seems very concerned, including the police, whom Caleb rang when it got to mid-afternoon – not once he'd explained that, yes, Lennie knew the area, that it had been just a few hours, that there was a festival going on, full of interest and excitement for a kid, and with hundreds of people to get lost among.

I'm horribly aware of the earth's inexorable turn, the ink of night spreading towards us from the east. The thought of the approaching dark frightens me on multiple fronts. The day is speeding away from us, taking Lennie with it. I can't shake the awful feeling that I'm running out of time to find her.

And then, all too soon, night has fallen and Karl's big performance is about to start on the stage in front of the ash.

When I get back to the Great Meadow after checking the bus for the third time today, the crowd is already leaking into the woods like floodwater. I loop round to the entrance of High Pass, which is hard to find if you don't know the place as I once did. As I do again, apparently, my own dam opening, inch by inch.

I rush along the narrow path, eyes cast down to check for roots that might trip me. To the left is a sheer drop down to Broad Track, where most of the crowd has been directed. Even from where I am, high above them like a stalking animal, I can tell that a different kind of energy is pulsing among them now that the sun has almost gone: excitable, frenetic, verging on frantic. A woman's scream stops me dead until it bubbles down into a laugh. If they were children, you would warn them that it will *all end in tears*.

The clearing is filling fast. I've come out a long way from the stage and instinct tells me I need to be closer. It's heaving at the dark heart of the crowd and I have to shove my way through, trying not to hate people for being drunk and off their heads, for being oblivious to everything but their own pleasure.

And then, from the stage, the huge ash silhouetted against the dying light, the first minor chord of 'Lady of the Valley' sounds. The Gatherers roar as one. Karl is spotlit as he plays the opening chords I know so well and lighters start to come out, one by one, fireflies in the gloom. It looks like those vigils you see for dead girls on the news. The lights that aren't trained on Karl wheel around dizzyingly, turning the tree's branches into gnarled fingers that look as though they're about to reach out to rake through the oblivious crowd.

I keep moving, weaving and ducking under arms until I'm directly below the stage. Everyone is intent on Karl's performance apart from me. I scan faces instead, searching for Caleb and finding Graham Warner instead, conspicuous in his conservative clothes, everyone else either in jeans and T-shirts, or looking like they've stepped off the cover of *Rumours*.

Towards the end of the song, a woman – young, probably in her early twenties, significantly younger than the music she's come to hear, anyway – clambers onto the stage. There's no security that I can see, and cheers and wolf-whistles go up. I think she's going to rush Karl or one of the others, try to shout into the microphone, but she doesn't.

She goes to the far front corner of the stage, quite close to where Warner is, and starts to dance. It's a strange, swaying, liquid movement, totally unselfconscious. Her eyes are closed, her expression rapt. She's wearing a long, pale dress, which, under the fierce stage lights, is just sheer enough to reveal the outline of her legs.

A sensation like ants starts to crawl over my skin. I feel as if I might be sick. A buzzing sound inside my skull begins to edge out the music. I don't fall: I try to focus on the woman's long hair as it moves, the redness of it, like a new copper coin. The non-darkness of it. It's not 1970, I say to myself. It's not Astrid.

But apart from the colour, I have seen this before. I have stood here before.

The earth under my feet knows it. So do my blood and bones. My heart.

I tell myself that when 'Lady of the Valley' ends, I have

to get moving. But first I need to sit down, just for a little while. I'm swaying, sickness rising. I'll just rest for a second, I tell myself again.

I stumble into the dark void behind the stage, instinct taking over and leading me to the huge trunk of the ash. It's cooler here, and I suck in clean air, unpolluted by dry ice, cigarettes and sweat.

I tuck myself into a cleft between the roots, the ground mossy and soft, springy with moisture where the sun hasn't managed to penetrate. I put my hand flat to it, picture again the woman I've just seen in my mind's eye, dancing on stage. Not the woman with the copper hair. Astrid.

But it's not just the dancing I remember, the way she moved on her last night as I stood off to the side and watched her, like a stranger. It's what happened afterwards, too, conviction filling me until there's no more doubt: she's here. It ended for her here. She's in the ground, beneath the ash. She's been here all along.

I curl into a ball, fingers digging into the damp earth, shifting until I can feel the trunk, strong and comforting against my back.

Chapter Forty-Three

When I tune back in to the music – I know every note – the moon has risen above the tree canopy. Bar a couple of new songs, tonight's set-list is simply the album played in order, and it's nearing its end. Soon, the crowd will start making its way back to the Great Meadow for the rest of the night's entertainment.

I get up and brush myself off. The sickness has gone. There's something more I haven't quite grasped yet, but while I wait and hope for an answer to come to me, I need to find Caleb.

Warner has gone and I wonder if I imagined him, or if it was another glitch in time. But then, in almost exactly the same place Warner stood, on the edge of the crowd, I see Caleb. His hair gleams in the lights from the stage, much paler than in daylight. He looks just like the boy who was my friend.

As though he senses my eyes on him, he turns his head and looks right at me. I watch his face light up. I start making my way stealthily towards him. As unlikely as it is among so many people, I'm wary of Karl spotting me from the stage, though when I dare to glance up at him, his eyes are glazed – he's either locked in some ecstasy of the moment or high, or both.

'I've been looking for you,' Caleb says, when I get to him. He pulls me into a quick, fierce hug. 'I always swear

I'll never buy a mobile phone, but after today . . .' He suddenly focuses. 'Still no Lennie, presumably?'

I shake my head.

'I really thought we'd have found her by now,' he says, perfectly echoing my own thoughts.

'We still don't know what happened to her between leaving the note and now. Call it eleven this morning when she left the cottage. It can't have been before that because Angie and I were there until then. That's getting on for ten, eleven hours ago. How far can you get in that time?'

'A fair way,' says Caleb. 'Even for a little kid, and Lennie's bright. If she had money, she could have caught a bus to Stroud, got on a train there. She could be anywhere by now.'

I think of the cat purse again. 'She didn't have any money, though.' I cover my face with my hands and Caleb pulls me into him again.

'I feel like she's still here,' I say, voice muffled in his arms. 'I don't know that, obviously, but also, I do. I feel like she's close.'

'But if you're right, that's good, isn't it?'

It should be, but there are knots inside me and I'm unable to articulate why.

My phone vibrates in my pocket, making me jolt. It's the cottage number and my heart leaps in case Lennie has gone back there, then plummets at the thought of Angie being ill again.

'Rain?' she says, when I answer, as clear as if she was standing next to me and obviously fine. 'I've had one of my thoughts.'

I half run towards the trees to get further away from the noise, terrified the signal is about to drop out.

'Christ, I can hear the music,' she says, voice cracking slightly. 'Hold the phone up a minute, will you?'

Back on stage, a spotlit Karl is minutes into the extended guitar solo of 'Lay Her Down'. He might as well be the only person on stage, the rest of the band cast into darkness.

After about thirty seconds, I hear the crackle of Angie's voice. 'That's enough,' she's saying. 'I always thought that one went on too long.'

'We still can't find Lennie,' I say.

'I know that. That's why I'm ringing. She's still there, somewhere. On the estate. I know she is. You know it too, don't you? So, you've got to keep looking.'

I drop my voice, move away from Caleb, further into the trees. 'I've got this weird feeling. Like there's something I'm not quite getting. That if I did, then . . .'

'Then you'd find Lennie.'

'Yes.' I exhale.

'You've just got to clear the decks, girl. Empty your mind. Then it'll come. You can't force these things.'

I nod, though she can't see me.

'You remembered something, didn't you?' Her voice is gentle. 'About back then.'

'I think so.' Tears swell again and it's a relief to let them go. How many times has that happened since I've been back?

'Tell me,' says Angie.

I feel a hand on my back, between my shoulder blades. It's Caleb, and suddenly it doesn't matter if he hears.

'It was that night. The concert night. I was watching her dance.'

I hide my face in Caleb's shirt. Tentatively, as if he's scared I'll run, he begins to stroke my hair.

Time passes and I become aware that the music has stopped, the crowd's white noise gone. We've been standing here for a while. I disentangle myself gently from him. The clearing has emptied once more and the stage is in near darkness. Quietly, much quieter than the live music, the instrumental version of 'Lady of the Valley' is being played through the speakers. With everyone gone, it's ethereal, other-worldly.

I'm still clutching my phone. 'Mum?'

'Still here,' she says. 'You figured it out?'

'I don't know. You know when I went to the carriage-house, I saw the album cover – the original one, of Astrid, and it was just like the effigy. Or, rather, the effigy is just like her.'

'Yes. I knew I was right about that. I knew it was Astrid straight away.'

'Well, the photos of Willow that were out on the floor weren't just . . . arty ones. There were Polaroids too, with her posing in exactly the same way as the album cover. Some sketches.'

'Maybe for the wood sculptor to use,' she says.

'That's what I wondered. I'm pretty sure Lennie went there and that's why they were out.' And then, finally, it happens: a spark lighting up in my mind. 'You said earlier that Karl was doing everything the same as the last Gathering. Was there an effigy then, too?'

'Oh, yes. Terrifying, it was. When that *Wicker Man* film

came out a few years later, it brought it all back. It was this huge thing – not a woman but a man. I honestly think that's where they got the idea.'

'What happened to it?'

'It was set on fire, of course. Burned to cinders. You could see it for miles, apparently.'

I grab Caleb's hand, pull him after me, across the clearing towards the shortest path back to the Great Meadow.

'Where are we going?' he cries. 'Rain?'

I half turn. 'The Lady of the Valley,' I say. 'The effigy. I think Lennie saw those pictures of Willow posing for it. I think she's inside it.'

We run.

Chapter Forty-Four

She's about to be lit. The crowd, some of them brandishing flaming torches, look medieval. They've tipped into a new, darker mood, almost aggressive. Feedback shrieks from the sound equipment set up behind, slashing open the night and making people scream in shock. Drum and bass starts up, deep and low, the incongruity electric. I went through a D&B phase in my twenties, the beat busy enough to stop me thinking. I know this one, search my brain for the name. It lands: 'Valley Of The Shadows'.

'Come on.' I drag Caleb through the crowd. The air is already thick with smoke. As we get closer to the wooden figure, I realize it isn't just coming from the torches. The Lady of the Valley is already alight. I can hear the crackle and spit of the willow wood.

I pull my hand free of Caleb's and run straight towards it, ignoring him as he shouts after me. When I get right up to it, I can see the willow hasn't lit evenly. There's a gap near the bottom and, before someone can stop me, tackle me to the ground, I hurl myself towards it.

The noise inside it is immense and terrifying. It's roaring like a dying animal. I'm as low to the ground as I can be but it's a struggle to breathe already, to see anything through the smoke.

I keep moving, crawling towards the very heart of the effigy, and finally I see a shape that makes my heart leap.

She's curled herself into a tight ball and she's so still, even when I reach out to her, that I think she's already dead. Not burnt yet, but put to sleep by the smoke, small lungs already damaged beyond repair. But then she shifts, just slightly, and I use the last of the air in my lungs to pull her towards me and over my shoulder.

I stagger to my feet and rush at where I hope the gap is, no breath left and the heat searing, and then there are arms reaching through, Caleb and other people, and they wrench us clear.

A huge groan goes up from the effigy, so terrifyingly human that my heart nearly stops. I look up, just in time to see whole thing collapse in on itself with an almighty crash.

Chapter Forty-Five

Caleb carries Lennie back to the cottage. She clings to him, conscious and apparently unharmed, but trembling and entirely mute.

Upstairs, Angie clucking around her, we wash the worst of the soot off her face, then take her to my bed. She lets us tuck her in, propping her up against the pillows and, despite the heat of the day, covering her with the duvet. I fetch her my old teddy bear and she clasps it to her chest. Angie insists on going down to the kitchen to make her a special sweet tea. When she brings it back up, she sets it down on the side and says she'll leave us to it. 'She doesn't need us all crowding round her.'

Caleb sits on the end of the bed and I perch carefully next to Lennie. She sips her tea slowly, hollow-eyed and still ash-streaked. At least she's stopped shaking.

'I didn't leave,' she says. Caleb and I lean towards her because she's speaking so quietly. 'I meant to go. I was going to catch a bus and then . . . But I couldn't. I climbed over the wall because the back gate was locked but then it felt wrong to leave her. To leave without her.'

'You don't have to tell us anything now,' I say. 'You'll stay here tonight, with me and Angie. We can talk about it in the morning. We can sort it all out then.'

'No,' she says, small jaw tight. 'I need to say tonight.'

We wait. The shutters are closed against the night and

the roll of the hypnotic drumbeat is only discernible if you strain for it.

'When I got back to the Great Meadow, everyone had gone into the woods for Karl's concert,' she says finally. 'It was practically empty. Even the people on the stalls had gone to watch him. All that was left was *her*, standing on her own.'

'The Lady of the Valley,' I say. 'The wooden effigy.'

She nods, looks down. 'When I was in that little room in the carriage-house, on the night my mum . . . well, *that* night, I'd gone there to hear the new song he'd written for her. She'd come back to the bus to tell me about it after she went to see Ottoline and she was excited. She said everything was going to be all right.

'She dressed in the white costume she was going to wear at the Gathering and I helped put the flower crown on her head. We'd made it together earlier. I brushed her hair for her. She showed me the card with the Empress on it.'

She stops, seeing something in my face.

'The tarot card, you mean?' I try to smile encouragingly.

She nods. 'She folded it up, said it was good luck. She wanted to have a smoke then, and I wanted to hear the song, so I said I was going for a walk, but I didn't.' She glances at me, eyes huge. 'I went to the carriage-house. Karl was in there, at his desk, but I sneaked in and went upstairs so I could listen.

'But then they came upstairs so I hid in the little room. I didn't know what to do. After a while, they started arguing. I heard Karl say that the Lady of the Valley wasn't meant to be her. It wasn't *for* her.' She grips her mug with her small hands, knuckles white. 'He was being horrible.

He said it was of someone else, someone he loved much better.'

'Did you hear anything else?'

She nods. We wait quietly while she goes back to sipping her tea. Eventually, she takes a shuddering breath. 'Karl was angry because Mum had gone to see Ottoline. He kept saying horrible things, but sort of laughing at the same time, like he was making a fool of her.

'My mum lost her temper then, her voice went all high and weird. I knew she shouldn't do that because you could tell Karl was already angry, even when he was laughing. Angry but in a really cold way.

'Mum kept shouting and screaming, and I kept saying, *Stop, stop* in my head, but she didn't. I knew . . .' She sucks in another breath. 'I knew she was making it worse. She called him an old man who lived off his wife's money because he'd only ever made one record, a hundred years ago.

'I think she only said that because he'd been so mean to her before. But it was like she couldn't stop then. She said . . .' – Lennie stops, swallows – '. . . she said he was past it. She said, "You think you're God's gift to women but you're not. Why do you think I went to your son?"' Lennie gulps again, eyes darting towards Caleb, whose face instantly drains of colour.

'Oh, God,' he says, hunching over, hands over his face. 'Oh, no.'

Lennie brings her knees up to her face and begins to sob, her sooty hand still clutching the mug. I take it from her. I squeeze in next to her and she leans into me, lets me rock her, stroke her hair. Over her head, I mouth, 'Not your fault,' to Caleb.

'I'm a coward,' she says, so muffled I only just make it out. 'I should've done something. But I couldn't. It was like I was frozen.'

'It's okay,' I say, still looking at Caleb. 'You're a child. There's nothing you could have done.'

She sits up, rubs her eyes with the heels of her hands. 'There were bangs then. I think they were fighting. Then it went quiet but I still couldn't move. I didn't for ages. Maybe hours and hours. I was so scared Karl was still in the room next door, waiting. But when I did look, because I needed the toilet so badly, nobody was there. It looked the same except the lamp was knocked over.

'I took ages going down the stairs in case Karl was in the studio but he wasn't there either. Neither was my mum. Outside, it was so quiet, like the middle of the night, and for a minute I thought I'd fallen asleep and the whole thing was a bad dream.

'I ran back to our bus. I was crossing my fingers that it really was a dream and Mum would be there. But she wasn't.' Her head droops. 'I got into our bed and waited for her to come back but I must have fallen asleep then. When I woke up, it was morning and Ottoline was there. She took me away from the bus. To Caroline's room. And after that I didn't remember any of it properly. It was like it *was* a bad dream then, and when I tried to get it back, it just . . . I just couldn't keep hold of it. I couldn't remember it all properly until I saw the photos today.'

'What made you go back to the carriage-house?'

'It was you.' She looks up at me with her big grey eyes. 'I saw you coming out of there the other day. You looked strange, upset. You ran off. I think you were crying. I was going to come after you, but then Karl came out and stood there.' She stops, her lip trembling. 'His face.'

'He looked angry?' Caleb glances between Lennie and me.

She thinks. 'He looked like he sounded that night. Cold and . . . I don't know. Empty. After that, I started remembering things.'

She fades quickly after she's unburdened herself. Before I leave her to sleep, I whisper in her ear that she's safe now, but she's already under. The moon, riding high and free of cloud at the window, casts the room in a cool, beatific light. Lennie's face is clear, all her pinched misery gone, at least for now.

Caleb and Angie are waiting for me at the kitchen table when I get downstairs.

'You should be in bed,' I say to Angie.

She waves her hand. 'I'll go back in a minute. How's Lennie?'

'Fast asleep.'

'Good.' Angie nods. 'So what's the plan now? Ring Harkin?'

I gape at her.

'Oh, I know,' she says. 'So much for my principles. But we've got to get him, haven't we?'

I persuade her back up to bed. She's still too pale and drawn. 'I think you're right about the police,' I say. 'We'll ring them tomorrow morning, first thing.' Like Lennie, she's totally spent. She's already snoring softly by the time I get to the door.

In the cupboard under the stairs, I retrieve the bag

for the Hi-8 camera I took from the office when I left to come here on Monday. It feels like whole decades ago.

'What's all this?' says Caleb, when I get back to the kitchen, gesturing at the bag.

'I've had an idea.'

He frowns. 'I don't like the sound of that.'

'I asked Karl before if I could interview him. He'll think it's for the documentary.'

'What? You're thinking about that now? After everything that's happened.'

'You heard what Lennie said upstairs. And we already knew from Ottoline that his alibi was a lie. It was Karl who did this, at least to Willow. But there's no proof. Not really. Lennie didn't see anything. No one did. But if I can get him on camera saying something . . .'

'You're not going up there to try to *entrap* him or something? Rain, I'm not going to let you. It's too dangerous. He's already angry with you.'

'Flattery will help. You know better than most what an egotist he is. Look, I'm not going to do anything stupid.'

I sound convincing enough, but it's only so Caleb will let me go. Tricking Karl into incriminating himself on tape is exactly what I've got in mind. I don't think the police are going to do anything, otherwise.

'I'll just get him talking,' I say, 'see if he says anything revealing of his own volition. I'll be fine – there are hundreds of people up there. He'll be surrounded.'

Caleb gets to his feet. 'I'm coming with you.'

'You know that won't work, not the way you and your dad are. Besides, I need you to stay here, with Lennie and Angie.' I reach for his hand. 'I won't be long, I promise.'

'I don't like this. I really don't like it.'

'I know, but it's going to be all right. Promise.' I reach up to kiss his cheek.

Outside, the moon lights the path uphill for me. I hoist my camera bag onto my shoulder and set off. When I glance back to the cottage, Caleb is silhouetted in the doorway. He raises his hand.

Chapter Forty-Six

I stop to catch my breath where the road begins to flatten and broaden into the Dark Ride, just shy of the Great Meadow. The D&B is still tripping and pounding through the dark.

Back in the day, Karl might have been in the thick of the crowd, but not now. He'll be in the carriage-house with his chief acolytes. They'll be hailing him as a living legend.

A couple of security guys are pacing close to the carriage-house's entrance. Fortunately, it's not the pair from last night, although there's a good chance they wouldn't remember me anyway, not after Angie stole the show.

I push back my shoulders and walk confidently towards them, already gesturing towards my camera bag.

'I'm the documentary director,' I announce, as airily as I can muster. 'I'm doing a post-concert interview with Karl and the band. I need to set up.'

'Don't know nothing about that,' says one of them.

I roll my eyes. 'Look, everything's way behind schedule already, and I need to get the lighting right and the interviews done before they're all completely off their faces.' I pull out my mobile. 'It's all right, I'll give Karl a ring, get him to come out. *Obviously* he's going to hit the roof for being interrupted but . . .'

'Hang on, hang on,' says the bouncer, hands raised. 'I didn't say you couldn't go in, did I?' He stands back, and I stride past him before he can change his mind.

Inside the carriage-house, the door to the studio is closed, voices and music muffled behind it.

I count to fifty to slow my breathing, rap quickly on the door and go straight in before my nerve can fail me.

He spots me straight away. My eye goes immediately to him, too, right in the middle of them all, holding court like the king he believes he is. He glances around, but no one else has noticed me. There must be thirty people squeezed in there, all looking pretty out of it. Bottles and ashtrays are scattered everywhere, and there's white powder on Karl's desk.

He stands and comes slowly over, never taking his eyes off me.

'You're braver than I woulda given you credit for, Rainy,' he murmurs into my ear. He smells sharply of sweat, cologne and something sharper. 'I guess that's Angie's influence.' He gestures to a bucket full of melting ice. 'Wanna beer?'

'Sure,' I say.

He plucks out two and nods at the door. 'Come on. It's too crowded in here.'

My heart ratchets into a higher gear as he goes over to a bank of switches and the spiral stairs light up.

'After you,' he says, opening his arms, a beer in each hand. 'Heard Angie had a turn,' he says. 'How's she doing?'

'She's fine. It was just the heat.'

'Yeah? I'm glad to hear it. She's part of the furniture round here.' He smiles and bends down to turn on the floor lamp Lennie saw knocked over. I watch him go over to sit on the chrome-and-leather chair, my mind turning. I thought he'd be raging at worst, petulant at best. I wasn't expecting him to be friendly like this. Like the Karl I thought he mainly was until this week. It's as if the awful scene in Ottoline's room never happened at all.

But then he says, 'So, what do you want?' and I don't think I imagine the spark of cold fire in his eyes. It comes as a strange relief. It reminds me of why I'm here.

'I know we've all been stressed over the last few days, but this has been such a special night. I was in the crowd.' I pause, smile, as though I'm still not over the magic of it all. I hold up my camera-bag.

'I want to interview you for the documentary,' I say. 'Just as we discussed. I want an insight into the mind of Karl Lund, thirty years after the first performance of his iconic album, on the night when he's returned to the spotlight and taken everyone on the most amazing trip back in time.'

He gives me a long, considering look, eyes narrowed and head on one side. Then he looks at the camera, and I know in the instant before he smiles that I've got him, narcissism winning the day, just as I've been counting on.

'Okay,' he says. 'Let's do this.'

I set up my little tripod, press record and begin with the obvious questions. And, as I weave a spell of flattery around him, asking about his creative process, his unique sound, the early struggles that have since been carefully recast as his glory days, it occurs to me that he might not be drunk, but he's definitely high. And not on one of those chilled-out hippie staples, either. His body is taut, jaw muscles flickering if you look closely enough in the low lamplight. I think about the powder downstairs and wonder how much he's had. It strikes me then that Karl was never one of the peace-and-love brigade, not really. He was just drawn to their light, like a dark moth.

'And what about the women who've inspired you over the years?' I say softly. 'The muses.'

He finishes his beer as he considers. 'I'm inspired by so many things,' he says. 'Things I observe around me. Nature. How the systems of the planet work in synchronicity.'

You reckon you're so profound, I think. *And you're not. You're full of shit.*

'You wrote something cryptic about the Lady of the Valley in the sleeve notes for the album that made some fans believe she was real,' I say. 'Is that true?'

He looks at me, cocks his head. 'Where we going with this, Rainy?' He picks up his empty bottle, puts it down again.

I reach out to hand him mine and turn on a full-wattage smile. 'I'm just exploring the Karl Lund mythology a little more.'

'You could say she was real,' he says, in a low voice. 'She was . . . well, she was something else.'

He doesn't know, I remember, that I know Astrid was my mother. At least, I don't think he does. Wouldn't he say something now, if he did? I'm not sure he'd be able to resist. What I really need to do is bring him up to the present day, but I think he'll walk if I mention Willow.

'You heard about Lennie going missing, I guess?'

It's an awkward segue, the exhaustion beneath the

adrenaline beginning to show, but he seems not to notice. He's inspecting something under one of his fingernails. 'She'll turn up,' he says. 'Bright kid. I told O, you can't wrap 'em in cotton wool.'

Outrage rises inside me, like a dark wave. That he could say this to a woman who lost her child to drugs left lying around by him and his friends is unbelievable to me.

Harness it, I think. Use it.

'She's so lucky you and Ottoline have taken her in,' I say. 'You want to know something sad, maybe even pathetic?' I smile ruefully, watching him from under my lashes.

'What?' He's looking at me again now.

'When I was little, I used to wish I belonged to you two, that I lived with you in the manor. On my way back to the cottage, there was this little rhyme I'd chant. *My name is Rainbird Mortimer-Lund*, over and over.'

He grins, drinks some of my beer.

'I'm sorry about before,' I say. 'Nosing around in your things. I was looking for extra material for the documentary.'

'It's all forgotten, okay? I said some things I didn't mean, too. Heat of the moment, yeah?'

'You know something else?' I say. 'I always had this suspicion that you were my dad. Angie didn't confirm you weren't until the other day. All these years, I've been wondering, looking for similarities between us.'

I'm skirting dangerous ground again, not so much for Karl but for myself. I can feel my resolve weakening as sadness sidles in. But I can see it's doing the trick, and that keeps me going. Karl's guard is coming down, or the alcohol is kicking in, damping down the coke – or both.

'Hey, you meant to be recording still?' he says suddenly, and I wonder if I've underestimated him. 'It's got pretty personal.'

'Shall I stop recording?'

'No, but let's get back on track.' He checks his watch. 'My people will be missing me.'

'I just wanted to ask about tonight,' I say. 'How you felt it went. Not just the concert, which was obviously incredible, but afterwards. The effigy was breathtaking. It made me think of *The Wicker Man*. It had the same kind of weird energy. But I guess she was modelled on Willow Green. I thought that was a beautiful tribute.'

His face sharpens. 'No one said it was her. I wanted her to be a . . . What's the word? A composite. All women. All the women I've ever loved.' His eyes glitter. His pupils are huge.

'So, a bit of Astrid, a bit of Willow. Angie. Ottoline. I don't know them all.'

'What you driving at here, Rainy?'

'Do you think people might think it's in bad taste to burn an effigy of a woman who died here a week ago?'

'Okay, time's up. Turn that thing off.'

'You were here, at Tanglewood, when she was killed,' I say. We both hear the quaver in my voice.

Karl stands. 'I said, turn that thing off.'

When I don't move, he lunges, knocks over the tripod, the screw securing it to the camera snapping off, the whole lot going down with a crash.

I back away from Karl while he stares me down, fists clenched, jaw pulsing.

'I know you lied about your alibi. You killed her, didn't

you?' I say, my voice shaking now. 'The night you weren't even supposed to be here. The night the *guys* said you were with them. She said you were an old man, that you were past it, that she preferred sleeping with your son, and you lost it.'

He's breathing hard now. He rolls onto the balls of his feet like he's preparing to run at me.

'I think you killed Astrid too,' I plough on. 'I think she crossed you. I think she wanted to leave and you wouldn't let her go.'

He starts shaking his head. 'No, NO.' He bellows it. 'Not her, I didn't kill her. Willow was different, she was nothing. Some two-bit fake hippie who thought she could manipulate me. Who thought she had some power here.' He gestures around him. 'She came in here that night, all dressed up like Astrid with a white dress and flowers in her hair, thinking the willow dancer was in honour of her, and then when I told her it wasn't, that I just used her for the sculptor, she started shouting and screaming at me.

'She'd already gone to my wife, threatened her with the tabloids. She'd already got herself knocked up when she swore to me she was taking precautions. She just kept cryin' and screechin'. I had to make her stop. She wouldn't fuckin' *stop*.' He comes to a halt. He's breathing like an animal about to charge.

He tries visibly to calm down. 'But Astrid? No way, man. I never touched her. I would never . . .' His voice cracks. 'I don't know what happened to her. She left the stage, wandered into the woods. She must've taken something. I've always wondered if she did it on purpose. She looked so unhappy that night. I don't know what I did.' His voice rises in a wail, and then, too quickly for me to react, he's up on his toes, upper body going back in a swing, and punches the sloping eave. I hear the bones of his hand crunch but he doesn't feel it. Without another look in my direction, he turns for the stairs, feet lead-heavy on the metal treads.

When my heart has slowed to something like its normal speed, I kneel to check the camera. The red recording light is still on. And, in the distance, a siren rises, high and urgent over the bass of the music coming from downstairs. I know it'll be the police this time.

1970

She walks off stage because she's been fighting the urge to run for days and she's simply got no fight left. She doesn't look back. She doesn't want to see Karl's expression, his blue eyes boring into her.

The music fades surprisingly quickly once she's left the clearing and walked deeper into the woods. She doesn't know where she's going. Her thought processes feel pin-sharp and woozy at the same time. She shouldn't have taken so much stuff today, especially with the baby. She's had so little of anything lately that her tolerance is low. She tries to list them. Pot, champagne and whisky backstage, and whatever pill McQuinn insisted he put on her tongue himself. A Quaalude, maybe. She shudders at the memory.

Dizzy, her legs so boneless and rubbery that her feet keep catching on the roots, she stops to rest on a tree stump lit by a cool shaft of moonlight.

She hasn't been there long when a flicker of pale movement in the trees makes her struggle unsteadily to her feet, hand over her mouth to stifle a scream. But when it steps into the moonlight, it's not a ghost. It's Ottoline. She must have followed her.

She blinks and, when she opens her eyes again, Ottoline is right next to her, inches away, as if she has leapt across time and space. She backs away but Ottoline keeps coming. She reaches out and takes hold of Astrid's wrist, making her bangles hiss and jangle.

'You're not afraid of me, are you?' Her face looms in close.

She shakes her head. She can tell she's shaking it too much. Around her, the leaves whisper and shiver, though she can't feel any breeze.

'What have you taken?' says Ottoline. 'You shouldn't be doing that, not when you're expecting a child.'

Somehow, then, she's back on the edge of the clearing, except that everyone's gone now and she's lying on the ground, Ottoline kneeling over her.

'Take this,' she says, tipping a small bottle towards her lips. 'It'll make you feel so much better. All the fear will be gone.' She smiles, cadaverous and unearthly, but still beautiful in the cold light. 'I think about taking it myself, sometimes, when I need very badly to forget.'

The liquid smells of almonds. It slips down like bitter silk.

When she slides into something like consciousness again, the moon is high over her. She watches it wheel across the sky. She thinks of her father, of her little girl. The baby inside her. She's been so afraid, but she's not any more, even though it's the end. She knows, somehow, that it is the end. She didn't think she'd be so calm. The earth spins under her, and she lets it take her.

Chapter Forty-Seven

2001, the next spring

Lennie wakes me at nine with a cup of tea. 'Come on, get moving,' she says imperiously. 'Caleb will be here any minute and we said to Graham Warner we'd be there by ten. I'll go and get Angie up. She's snoring her head off as usual.' She skips out of the room.

I pull back the curtains and sunlight pours in. Outside, the cottage garden has gone wild. May has made the valley so green and lush that it's almost obscene.

In a few short weeks, it'll be a year since the Gathering. A year since the police came for Karl, initially so they could interview him about some *discrepancies in his statement*, but then, once I handed over my recording, and a child psychologist interviewed Lennie, for much more.

What we didn't know – what the police had kept to themselves – was that the pathologist who found the tarot card also noticed a faint line of bruising on the side of Willow's neck, just below her ear and hardly more than a shadow. A barely-there sign of strangulation, which they almost discounted because her hyoid bone was still intact.

Karl is now awaiting trial, not just for Willow's murder but Astrid's. I don't know for sure, but I don't think he killed my mother. I think he's taking the blame for Ottoline, as some kind of long-overdue penance for little lost Caroline.

He told police that Astrid was buried under the spreading branches of the old ash tree, just as I'd sensed during the night of the last Gathering. Just where I found her myself, as a child all those years ago. That's a memory that hasn't returned to me, and I'm grateful for it.

She was reinterred there, after the police had done what they needed to do. Willow lies next to her. There are two small plaques marking the spot, a star etched into the stone above my mother's adopted name.

Lennie and I often go there for picnics, and to take them both flowers. Sometimes, when the day is running out and the light is just right, a shadow moves across the clearing. 'It's the Lady of the Valley,' Lennie whispers. 'She's here.'

As for Ottoline, she never leaves her room, rarely leaves her bed. She said to me she's afraid that, if she does, Caroline won't come to her any more. Despite what I'm almost certain she did to my mother, I just can't commit her to prison. She's been a mother to me, just like Angie.

Caleb drives us slowly through the lanes to Warner's little almshouse. He's taken back his old boyhood bedroom at the manor, though he often stays at the cottage with me, these days, to Angie and Lennie's shared delight.

'What's this all about anyway?' says Angie now, as Caleb helps her out of the back seat.

'He wants us to see something he missed before,' I say.

We traipse up the stairs and squash into the workroom, all five of us. It's too small really, and I feel the prickle of claustrophobia that made me faint the first time I ever came here.

'You'll have to keep your eyes peeled, mind,' says Warner, as he fits the reel into its slot. 'I only caught it by accident.'

'Caught what?' I say.

He turns and smiles. 'You'll see what I mean. I didn't notice it before. Didn't even know she was in shot at the time. But once I spotted it . . .'

He pulls the curtain across, plunging the room into darkness. 1970 flickers back into life. Beside me, Angie sighs and Lennie's hand curls into mine.

It's the close-up I saw the first time, when I was trying to see who Astrid was smiling at, who she was reaching out for. To see if I could make out a reflection in the dark mirror of her pupils. It was at this exact point that Warner paused it before – to help me into the chair because I was so dizzy.

I glance at him now, confused, but he lets the film run on and, after a few frames of static, that lost Tanglewood comes back into focus. It's the Great Meadow again, but now at a new angle.

He's right: she's only just caught in shot, at the top of the screen. Still, I see her immediately, even though she's only a background figure; even though she has her back to the camera. It's as though my eye goes to her automatically, like some strange telepathy across time.

Then I notice who she's standing between: two children, whose hands she's holding. One has a long dark tangle of hair, the other's is a shock of white-blond.

'Do you see them?' Warner says, and I nod. Caleb

finds my free hand and we stand there together in the dark, watching as the three of them walk away into the unknown future, arms swinging, until they slip out of focus into a sun-spangled blur.

Acknowledgements

One of the things I loved most about writing this book was the setting's proximity to my own tucked-away Cotswolds cottage. When I needed an extra hit of inspiration, I simply set out on foot towards the more secluded end of the valley where I've spent the last decade. On one of those days, when I'd nearly finished the second draft, I decided to go right past the private house on which I based Tanglewood's manor. I'd done that many times and never seen (or heard) a soul. But on that hot July afternoon, one of the big upstairs sash windows had been pushed right up and someone inside was singing their heart out. It felt like a good omen for a story in which music is so important.

Of course, after the inspirational walks comes the hard work of shaping, reshaping and packaging a story, and I couldn't have done it without my excellent editor Grace Long and the top-notch team behind her, particularly Maxine Hitchcock and Joel Richardson, as well as Emma Plater, Lily Evans and Ellie Morley. On the production side, extra thanks are due to my sharp-eyed copy-editor Hazel Orme and proofreader Alex Newby, and the endlessly patient and cheerful Katya Browne. I feel in such safe hands with all of you.

Huge thanks also to my wonderful cohort of writer friends in Stroud, Cheltenham, London, Bristol, Bath and beyond, who just *get it*, and who are such generous early readers. I always say this, but what would I do without you? Extra special thanks to Claire McGlasson, Emylia Hall and Alice Kuipers for always being so kind when I'm struggling to get out of my own way and just write the bloody thing. A big shout-out to my Novelry family, too. I couldn't love coaching our writers all over the world more, and what stellar colleagues to do it alongside!

All the love to my family and the rest of my friends for being such brilliant champions and supporters: most especially my parents and siblings, but also assorted Reardons, Parkers, Williamses, Towners, Muirs, Strachans, Owens and Hockenhulls. Particular gratitude to Jeremy, Jade, Darren, Bruna, the Cornish contingent, the neighbour gang especially Steve and Sharon, and my lovely Exeter lot (thirty years!). Extra special thanks to beloved dogs Morris, Jen and Lucky.